the wait

a novel by

FRANK TURNER HOLLON

the wait

a novel by

FRANK TURNER HOLLON

MacAdam/Cage
155 Sansome Street, Suite 550
San Francisco, CA 94104
www.macadamcage.com

Library of Congress Cataloging-in-Publication Data

Hollon, Frank Turner, 1963-
 The wait : a novel / by Frank Turner Hollon.
   p. cm.
 ISBN 978-1-59692-291-4
 1. Life—Fiction. I. Title.
PS3608.O494W35 2008
813'.6—dc22

                          2007050807

Paperback edition: May 2008
ISBN 978-1-59692-293-8

Manufactured in the United States of America

10 9 8 7 6 5 4 3 2 1

Book design by Dorothy Carico Smith.

Between the wish and the thing, life lies waiting.

—*Unknown*

PART I

in the beginning

My father almost never got drunk. When he did, it was usually a happy, goofy drunk. But one night when I was nine years old, after a Christmas party, for reasons still unknown, he told me the story of my conception. This is how I remember it.

Bobby Winters stared out the motel window. From behind he could hear his little brother in the bathroom. It was a day like any other day, except Bobby knew something bad would happen soon. He could always tell when his brother was about to do something stupid. It was just a matter of trying to keep the damage to a minimum.

Mark came out from the bathroom completely naked with a pistol in his left hand.

"We're gonna rob this motel," is what he said.

Bobby just kept staring out the window. He knew better than to argue. Everything had already been said before.

Mark continued, "We ain't got no money left. After it gets dark, I'll go into the lobby alone when it's clear. You keep the car runnin'. We'll haul ass outta here. Maybe go to Texas or somewhere."

Even though they were only nineteen and twenty years old, it seemed to Bobby he'd been keeping Mark alive for centuries.

Bobby turned around and said slowly, careful to control his voice, "Don't hurt anybody, Mark."

Mark smiled. "You worry too fuckin' much. Like somebody's grandmother or somethin'."

When the sun was gone and the lobby empty, Mark pushed open the glass door and walked quickly to the man behind the counter. The man was standing alone, bent at the waist, reading a magazine open on the counter. Before he could raise his face from the page, Mark placed the barrel of the pistol against the crown of the man's head and pulled the trigger.

Bobby heard the shot. "Jesus," he whispered, and then began to count out loud quietly for no particular purpose. "One. Two. Three. Four. Five. Six. Seven. Eight. Nine. Ten. Eleven. Twelve. Thirteen. Fourteen. Fifteen. Sixteen."

The car door slammed. Bobby spun the tires on the gravel and yanked the steering wheel to the right. Mark counted the cash. Twenties in one pile, tens in another. The odd bills were stacked to the side.

"Two hundred forty dollars. Shit, that's pretty good. It'll get us to Texas. That's for damn sure."

The siren ended the sentence. Bobby saw the police car in the rearview mirror.

"Where'd that son-of-a-bitch come from?" Mark asked, like he couldn't believe it. Like he couldn't believe a police car might actually be there.

Bobby ran through a yellow light and tapped the gas. His chest pounded.

"What did you do back there, Mark?" he asked, looking in the rearview mirror.

"It don't matter," Mark answered.

"I need to know," Bobby said.

Mark turned around to see another police car joining the chase.

"It don't matter," Mark repeated.

Bobby raised his voice, "I need to know what I'm runnin' from, Goddamnit."

Both men were aware, on different levels, and for different reasons, who held the pistol and who didn't. Mark felt himself squeeze the handle.

"Put it this way, they ain't takin' me. I ain't goin', so you better haul ass."

Bobby took a slow, deep breath. A promise was a promise, he thought. Blood is blood, and you can't turn your back. Whatever happens, that's just the way it is. You gotta ride it out.

So he pushed down on the gas and the car topped one hundred miles an hour. In the darkness, down the country road, the bushes and trees passed so fast they were only shadows. The blue lights of the police car spun around, reminding Bobby of a toy he had as a little boy. It would shine with colors in the sunlight, and for a moment he wondered where it had gone.

Bobby passed a truck on the two-lane road and then another truck. He could see houses and lights up ahead in the distance. The two police cars got stuck behind the second truck, unable to pass because oncoming cars couldn't pull over in a construction area. Space grew between the chaser and the chased.

Bobby pushed the accelerator against the floorboard. He looked in the rearview mirror. Sweat eased slowly down the skin underneath his arms to the waistband of his underwear. His heart still pounded.

"Those stupid motherfuckers," Mark said, looking back over the seat, laughing like a crazy man.

The hill came so fast. The road was flat, and suddenly there was a hill. No time to slow down. No time to know until the car was in the air, the road curving to the left, and the car flew into the field, landing hard, flipping over and over, slinging mud and grass and bits of plastic until it slammed sideways into a cow and finally twisted to a hissing stop, quiet on the downslope of the hill, outside of sight from the road.

The police cars barreled past, slowing down for the hill the drivers knew would come and then turning left around the curve, the drivers looking ahead into the distance for red taillights.

Bobby's first thought was nothing. Then he knew something bad had happened, like he was sure it would.

"Mark," he said.

It was dark in the field. One of the headlights of the

car shined out away from the road and Bobby could see a cow on its side.

"Mark."

Bobby crawled out the busted window. He could feel burning on the side of his face, and his right arm hung limp. Bobby walked around to the far side of the car, and in the darkness, like a mannequin in the grass, he saw his brother's body. The shirt was yanked up over his face and his pants pulled to his knees. Dirt and grass covered a portion of his underwear and stuck to the blood from the peeled back flesh.

In the distance, Bobby could hear the sirens.

"Mark," he said, bending over his little brother.

But Mark was dead, and the promise had been broken, no matter who was to blame. It was over, just like he knew it would end, sooner or later.

Bobby felt a strange relief. A heaviness lifted from his body. Something he could not define or admit, a lonely freedom.

Bobby Winters stood and looked out across the field. He could see lights through the woods, far off, flickering as the tree limbs moved gently in the evening breeze. He began to walk toward the lights and away from the car, and his brother, and the cows. As he walked he didn't think of much, only walking. Beyond the lights he didn't wonder where he might go, or what would happen, because it didn't matter. He was alive, and Mark wasn't, and there was a reason, whether he understood it or not.

At the edge of the field, Bobby turned back for one last look. He could see the blue lights circling down the long road. He could see the one headlight from the upside-down car, and the cows, and a bump on the ground he knew was his brother. He turned and walked into the woods and kept walking until he reached a house. It was a small house, with a front porch and rocking chairs. Bobby saw a light in a back window and followed the light. He looked inside and saw a woman lying naked on a bed. Before he could decide what to think of her, a man, wearing only socks, the lady's husband, came to the bed. He stood looking down at his wife in a way Bobby had never seen before.

The man touched his wife on her leg with the back of his hand and then ran his hand slowly up to the edge of her hip. And she let him touch her, but not in a way Bobby had ever had a woman let him touch her before, but instead, in a way he couldn't possibly describe.

He knew it was wrong to watch, but it wasn't a choice. The man leaned down and they kissed. His hand slid to his wife's breast, and he squeezed gently and released, leaving his hand resting on the breast. Bobby could see her breathe. The air pulled in, the chest expanded, and the air pushed out. The man opened his wife's legs and positioned himself in between, rising above her like he was floating, careful not to touch until she guided him inside.

Bobby watched as they moved, the man floating above, the husband and wife only touching where he entered her, slowly back and forth, where she accepted him, the two looking only at each other like there was nothing else in the world worth seeing. And rising, and building, deeper, and a tiny bit deeper, until the man closed his eyes and pushed one last time while Bobby Winters watched at the window and witnessed the acts leading to the conception of James Early Winwood.

There was a sound behind him, but he didn't turn around. He didn't stop watching until the gunshot opened the night, and the bullet tore through the neck of Bobby Winters, shattering the skin and slicing through the cord, bringing Bobby to his knees, his cheek skidding down the brick wall until he was in the dirt, face down under the window. And his heart stopped.

The gunshot spewed blood all over the window. The man inside dismounted like he had taken the bullet himself and fell to the carpet in complete nakedness, leaving his spread-eagled wife afraid to move a muscle until she saw the outline of the police officer's head at the window. She jumped upright, covering her nipples with the palms of her sweaty hands.

My father told the story like he was the man at the window, knowing things he couldn't possibly know. My mind has filled so many gaps through the years it's not possible to reconstruct what my father actually told me that night after the Christmas party. We never spoke of it again.

Perhaps the single most important moment in each of our lives is the moment of conception. Thank God most of us are spared the nasty little sexual details of our parents churning away on one another. Although I'm fascinated by my father's story, I wish he'd never told me. I already had some vague feeling of oddness surrounding my creation before I knew about the Winters brothers, but now the oddness has taken form. I'm left with a trap door of anarchy shaped unfairly by events beyond my control. The fact it happened before my birth makes it no more or less unfair.

Certain cultures believe the soul of the person who dies travels to the nearest new life and takes up residence. It's a curious belief, perhaps predicated by our desire to continue, or at least exist day-to-day with the hope of unlimited life. But let's be honest, how much of Bobby Winters do you think drifted through the cracks around the window, floated invisibly into my mother's vaginal canal, and affixed to the embryo, invading like a bad smell caught in the fabric of a boy's underwear? Probably not much, but the way my dad told the story, who the hell could say what's not possible.

When I was in high school, a group of us drove to the beach for a party one Saturday night. There was this girl there, the younger sister of a friend. I'd seen her before, but she was two years younger, and two years is a lot when you're eighteen. I tried not to look at her, but there was something beyond my control happening. I was attracted to her like a mayfly pulled to a yellow dock light.

I went outside just to break away from the tension. She came outside behind me, took my hand in the shadows, and led me away without a word between us. She started to run, pulling me behind, and my heart beat like a bank robber's. We veered between two houses and ended up in the backyard next to a pool. It was so dark I couldn't see her face.

"The Prestons are in Mexico on vacation," she whispered.

I heard the snap of her blue jeans, and the sounds of undress. I tried to equalize my breathing so she couldn't possibly hear the wheeze of my asthma, so she couldn't possibly tell I was on the verge of hyperventilating, maybe fainting, and cracking my stupid head on the patio cement.

She giggled. "Take off your clothes."

My eyes began to adjust to the moonlight and there she stood, as naked and pure as anybody had ever stood, anywhere, in the history of mankind. And I felt this feeling I'd never felt before, maybe like my father felt about my mother on the night Bobby Winters watched. I don't know.

I took off all my clothes, and we walked down the steps into the coolness of the black water. I kissed her, and touched her body like a starving man. We held on to each other, and then she stopped me from doing what we had no business doing, what I couldn't stop myself from doing, and it was the last time I ever saw the girl. Even now, this many years later, when I'm alone in my bed I can think about her and touch the feeling again. Like I'm there, in the dark waters of the Prestons' pool, in the summer moonlight.

People are born with ranges of potential. One man may be born with athletic potential and, if left unfulfilled due to worldly circumstances or laziness, it may be wasted. On the other hand, the man may reach levels unreached before, taking advantage of the possibilities. I cannot hit a baseball out of Yankee Stadium. I cannot get my bat around on a ninety-five-mile-per-hour fastball. My individual potential lies in awareness. As a young child I remember sitting in new surroundings, watching. There is so much to notice if you know what to look for. So much to be aware of around you.

My mother said when she took me to a new place I wouldn't speak for at least an hour. Just looking around at movements, listening for inflection, establishing the walls of the fish tank. I wonder if my range of potential awareness has anything to do with the strange circumstances of my conception? I wonder if the feeling caused by my friend's sister was a result of the blinding darkness of the night, the quickness of the situation, or the finality of our contact? I don't know, but I'd love to see her naked in the darkness again, if only for a minute.

The first moment which I am aware of being alive is the flash of a memory. I am looking up from the confines of a crib at the face of a man with a black mustache. I can see him clearly, but I don't know who he is. The man is wearing a white button-down shirt. His hair is medium-length black. He's neither smiling nor frowning, just leaning over me like a stranger.

I've never figured out who the man could be, but surely there must be a reason the moment remains my first memory, as opposed to the moment before, or the moment after. We are forged by a handful of events from conception to death. These events, together, form the sound that life makes.

And so I was born nine and a half months from the date Bobby Winters was shot to death watching my parents on the other side of the window. Born unto this world, another soul amongst many. A tiny, cold, wet-skinned child, filled with the fear of this life and the outcry of potential. But I can't remember anything until the mustached man appeared over my crib rail. I imagine my father was both amazed and overwhelmed at the miracle of my birth. I imagine my mother was absolutely sure she would never have another child, for any reason, ever, and I was blessed at such an early age with the inability of being aware of anything whatsoever. Instead, my lungs concentrated on drawing the next breath, the simplest possible act of living, and in this simple act, set in motion the rest of my life.

two

It would be best if we could tell the intelligence of a person instantly by the size of their heads. A big-headed man has more brains and therefore more intelligence. A little-headed guy is obviously stupid and will be treated accordingly.

My mother called me Early. My father apparently tried to stick with James, but it became obvious fairly soon that James didn't fit. Oddly, neither did Early, but my mother won the battle anyway. She had a secret weapon in such battles. The weapon of indifference. Impossible to counter. Virtually invisible, but nonetheless lethal, like a small daily dose of poison. It'll wear you down until quitting seems right.

My mother was unnatural, removed, artistic, and dramatic. We looked at her a lot and sometimes she looked back, usually extraordinarily busy with some project or another. She would paint entire rooms and then paint them again, a different color, the next day.

My father would come home from work and ask, "Christine, wasn't the dining room blue yesterday?"

Usually, my mother wouldn't answer such questions. I think she believed she was truly a special person born in the wrong time and place. I called her Christine because she said it was her name, and it only seemed weird when I turned four or five years old and none of the other kids called their mothers by their first name. Around other people I would say "Mom" in a very low voice at the beginning of my sentences.

"Mom, can I have a popsicle?"

"What?"

"Mom, can I have a popsicle?"

Outside I would say, "My mom likes to give me popsicles," emphasizing "mom."

My father was the opposite. I remember him as warmth, a smile. He was very human, but of course, in retrospect, I know my father's memory enjoys the benefits of death. He died in a car accident when I was eleven years old, leaving me and my mother alone like two strangers connected and disconnected from my father.

It changed me, as you can imagine, forever. One day he was there before I left for school, and then he never came back to us. I couldn't possibly forgive him. I understand it wasn't his fault. I understand he didn't drive away and live somewhere in California.

My father was hit by a train. One of those cross-cutting

events. We watch TV while somebody down the block miscarries. We eat a piece of pie while a man dies across town in a pool of his own blood. But sometimes, the events cut across our lives like the time the train killed my father while he sat in his car listening to the radio, drumming his hands on the steering wheel, with a big black train bearing down.

If he did it on purpose, it was an inefficient way to die, but brilliant. It leaves everybody thinking, would a man kill himself with a train when he could take a handful of pills, or blow a hole through his head? If he wanted it to look like an accident, he might.

I can barely read my own handwriting. After my Dad died I wrote down imaginary conversations we probably never had.

Dad: When you're having a bad dream, Early, just remind yourself it's only a dream.

Me: I don't know how.

Dad: You're smart. Just say, 'Hey, it's only a dream. I can do whatever I want because I know I'll wake up in the morning.' And then punch the monster in the nose, or light the bad man's hair on fire, or stand on the train tracks and watch the engine run right through you.

Me: Somebody told me, if you die in your dream, you die in real life.

Dad: And how do you suppose the person who told you that could know? They couldn't ask anybody who ever did it, right? Because they're all dead. You're a smart boy. Be in charge of your own dreams, real and unreal.

The story of the Winters brothers is another example

of one of those cross-cutting events. The boy could have gone to another house, another window, but he didn't. He could have died at the wreck scene, or shown up two minutes later, but he didn't. His life-ending event coincided, collided, with my life-beginning event, and nobody planned it that way.

My mother made a big deal out of Thanksgiving. It was really weird. Birthdays were uneventful. Christmas, Fourth of July, Easter, just another reason to be out of school. Most of the time she was too busy to pay any attention to us at all, but when Thanksgiving rolled around, it was a different story. We had to have all the excess, the biggest turkey in town, three kinds of cranberry sauce, mincemeat pies. It was some sort of trade-off I never really understood and still don't. But who says I'm supposed to understand everything anyway? And who says I need to figure it all out?

If I breathe deeply, eyes closed, for three full minutes, it suddenly doesn't seem so important anymore. Nothing can endear one person to another like allowing oneself to be saved. Or demanding it. Or requiring it. Vulnerable, spread-eagle emotionally, like my mother, I've remained detached and efficient the majority of my life. And like my father, I've allowed the world at times to be too much with me and prayed for the train to come. This balance, or imbalance, is the essence of my person.

Eddie Miller was my best friend from ages five to seven. He was one year younger and soft, like a chubby marshmallow. Eddie would do anything I said, follow me anywhere I went. He was getting hurt all the time, once falling off his bike in the road carrying a Coke bottle. The bottle busted and Eddie ripped a gash in his chin. Of course, he was getting the Coke for me. I was three blocks away in a tree fort, waiting impatiently for my cold Coke that never arrived.

Mrs. Miller asked me to step outside one day.

"Why did you tell Eddie there's no such thing as Santa Claus?"

I played dumb.

"Answer me," she said, louder.

I said, unapologetically, "I thought he should know it's a big lie."

The scowl on Mrs. Miller's face left a deep impression.

"Well, Mr. Know-it-all, we've got one or two good Christmases left. If you ruin it, I'll whip your bottom red. I don't care who your parents are."

At the time, I didn't pay much attention to the last sentence. I immediately went back to Eddie in his room.

"Eddie, that stuff I said about Santa Claus wasn't true. He's alive, and he'll probably come see you for two more Christmases. After that, you're on your own."

Eddie didn't listen. He just stood up and peed in his toy box like he always did. He told me I could pee in the toy box, too, if I wanted, but it never seemed right so I didn't do it.

My other best friend was Jake Crane. He was a year older and the complete opposite of Eddie Miller. Jake's mom was wild as hell and good-looking. I knew she was good-looking even before I knew the difference, mostly by the way my dad acted around her.

Miss Crane was black-headed and wore tight pants with high-heeled shoes. She laughed and smacked her red lips. There were rumors she took a shower with Andy Bradshaw's brother who was in college, but who knows if that was true.

Jake's grandmother lived in his house. She was the meanest woman I've ever known. The first time she back-handed Jake's little brother I froze in fear. The kid was lifted from the floor and rolled across the room, his nose bleeding, like a boxer. And for nothing. Just changing the television station. That's how they lived, in between the sexual energy of their mother and the violence of an old woman.

Jake stole cigarettes from his mom. He taught me how to cup the cherry so nobody could see it at night. One time we were in the dark outside his mom's bedroom window smoking one of those long, skinny cigarettes when she came into the bedroom. Neither of us said anything to each other as she took off her shirt, reached around to unhook her bra, and stood before us naked from the waist up. I had never seen such a thing, and truthfully it scared the shit out of me, but I didn't turn away. Thank God she went in the bathroom to take off the rest of her clothes or I might have passed out in front of Jake Crane.

People wanted to be near Jake in elementary school. There was a power about him. A loose energy field. But it was the best he'd ever be. At sixteen, all of his good days were mostly behind him, his loose energy dissipated into the air of the world. It's like an airplane. It has to reach a certain speed to lift from the ground and take flight. That was the reason no one before the Wright Brothers could invent the airplane. Such speeds weren't possible. Once they were possible, gliding in the sky was a given. For Jake Crane, he never quite reached the speed of lift.

three

At around age four, I started having dreams of a scary circle on the floor. I know it sounds ridiculous, but I'd awake from those dreams in terror. The circle was black and a few feet across. In the middle of a perfectly good dream, the circle would appear on the floor. I never knew if it was a hole or what. I only knew the monster was the fear itself.

Other people running around in the dream couldn't see the circle. I'd yell. I'd warn them. One time I pulled a kid away from the hole. Nobody ever stepped inside. Besides being weird, there were no signs the circle was evil or dangerous, but I knew what it meant. I knew what the black circle held.

My grandfather was a very patient man. He was from a time before the world became too busy to enjoy, and we went fishing sometimes in a pond out in the country. I was maybe five or six. Paw-Paw would spend hours gathering together two cane fishing poles, red-and-white plastic corks, crickets, cheese sandwiches, and a little cooler with two grape sodas. The ritual was part of the event, as satisfying to him as the fishing itself, and I would watch him thread the thin, clear fishing line through the tiny hole in the hook, the knot just right, imagining the tug of the fish swallowing the kicking cricket.

The pond had lots of turtles. Paw-Paw let me push the boat away from the pier and the little motor would take us to parts of the pond my grandfather was sure the fish would bite. I learned catching a fish wasn't really important. For Paw-Paw, the importance seemed to lie in the silence. Watching a turtle sunning on the bank. Staring at the red-and-white plastic cork floating on top of the coffee-colored water. The beauty, for my grandfather, was in the wait. For me, the wait was agonizing. It would always be. It was hard to understand anything except the joy of seeing the cork bob, and the line pull tight, and the unfortunate little fish dangling from the hook through his lip.

It must be frightening for the bream. His wet google-eye scanning for something familiar, but instead seeing big round faces, and grape soda cans, and the hand that wraps around the body and holds tight while the other hand unhooks the hook from the lip.

My grandmother was very different from Paw-Paw. Nanny was small and quick. She laughed hard and found certain things funny I didn't find funny at all. She cooked and sang little songs in the kitchen, laughing sometimes at herself, and finding a rhythm in the work. Paw-Paw took her fishing with him once, and afterwards they both agreed never to do it again. Apparently, she talked incessantly about turtles, and ripples in the water, and all the other things in which my grandfather found such solace. However, there was no solace to be found in the discussion of these things, only in the things themselves, and besides, Nanny told me, "One stick of dynamite in that stupid pond, and we could eat fish for a year. What's the point in trying to trick the silly things into biting a cricket on a hook?"

My grandfather heard her make that particular statement as we sat at the kitchen table eating biscuits and honey for breakfast. The old man rolled his eyes at me and sipped his coffee from the saucer. After his cup was empty, he had a habit of lifting the saucer to his mouth and drinking all the coffee he'd spilled from the cup. The low slurping sound sticks in my memory and makes me wish I could see my grandfather one more time.

When I was seven years old, I had my worst asthma attack. I was with my grandfather just after we pulled the boat from the pond. It was springtime, and all the weeds were in bloom. For some reason I decided to run around the other side of the pond to see a bullfrog I'd seen from the boat. I couldn't find the bullfrog, but when I arrived, there was a wheezing in my chest. It wasn't until I ran back to my grandfather that the tightness began. It was like the devil had wrapped his big red hand around my heart and started to squeeze, and squeeze, until there was no room for the air to go inside.

My grandfather saw the look on my face. He dropped the cane poles where he stood and carried me to the car to get my inhaler. The car was parked under a shade tree, and he put me on the backseat. I'd had asthma attacks before, but the one at the pond was the worst. I was afraid I'd die, and as my grandfather got down on one knee next to me at the car door, he started to pray.

"God, hear me pray now. Today we need you to put your hand on Early in the backseat of this car here. And loosen the grip on his lungs so he can breathe your air freely. And if you feel the need, take me with you in return, but I'll stay here if you want, and I promise to never sneak another sip of scotch whiskey."

He spoke the words so slowly it was like the world had fallen into slow motion. I watched the leaves on the trees up above swaying gently in the breeze, and I started to feel the panic subside, and with the panic gone I felt my chest loosen. I could breathe again.

On the ride home, Paw-Paw kept looking at me in the rearview mirror, afraid to take his eyes away from either me or the road for too long. It was probably the day I began to struggle with the idea of God. Had He truly put his hands upon me, as my grandfather prayed, and loosened the grip, or instead, was my grandfather's prayer itself soothing and calming, allowing me to escape the panic and provide time for my body to return to normal? And what kind of God would care to trade my life for my grandfather's secret whiskey sips? It just seemed enormously confusing, and my abilities of perception—usually so helpful in crawling inside the minds of other people—actually seemed to complicate the idea of God.

Nothing in my young life really compared to the day my father died. Up until then, things were moving along fairly well. Besides Eddie's mom yelling at me about Santa Claus, the occasional asthma attack, and the lingering questions concerning my conception, life was pretty good. By age ten, I'd already made a conscious decision to be average. It seemed much easier than the alternative. The truly gifted, original, unique people in society must be prepared to suffer and fail as miserably as the ungifted, lazy, and idiotic. We like to pretend our culture embraces originality, but in truth we embrace repetition, familiarity. We only appreciate originality in hindsight, when it's no longer original.

It's much easier to decide to be average. The expectation level is mild. Disappointments are infrequent. I imagine the suffering of unacceptance is highly overrated. How easy can it be for a person to know they're better, but endure ridicule from a lesser man, a lesser man defending lesser men? Don't get me wrong. I'm not some self-suppressed genius. I'm probably average anyway. I just cut short the discovery process. I was unable to figure out how God could take my father away and leave me with my mother. It didn't make any sense at all, from any direction, so I figured hiding amongst the average was the safest place to be. I wish I could say I had a cold shiver up my eleven-year-old spine the moment the train killed my dad. I was at school, probably chasing somebody around in the dusty schoolyard during P.E. class, or picking my nose in the back of Mrs. Eubanks' room, or thinking about something stupid when it happened.

When the principal came to the door of the classroom I thought I was in trouble for pushing Missy Jesup earlier during a softball game. It wasn't much of a push, but I was afraid she'd told on me and the principal, Mr. Walker, might be at the door on Missy's behalf. I was afraid I was in trouble. Instead, my father was dead.

My mom stood beside me in the principal's office with her hand stiff on my shoulder.

Mr. Walker said, "Early, I need to tell you something."

The door was closed and the window shades were shut.

"Missy Jesup exaggerates," I said.

Mr. Walker got down on one knee. He was a tall man, and on his knee we nearly looked eye to eye. I remember he wore a white button-down shirt. The sleeves were rolled up, and his tie was loosened a little at the neck. The skin around the collar was red and bumpy, like chicken skin.

I don't know why my mother didn't tell me. I don't know why she just stood there and made Mr. Walker say the words.

"It's not about Missy Jesup, Early. It's about your father."

That's when I felt the world turn a little bit.

We looked at each other hard for a few seconds, and I could see the redness in his eyes.

"No," I said, "it's not about my father. It's about Missy Jesup. I pushed her."

Mr. Walker looked up at my mother. The hand on my

shoulder didn't twitch. It was like a deadweight, a sock full of brown sand.

"There's been an accident, Early. Your father passed away."

I remember thinking, "Passed away? What a strange way to put it. Like he vanished into thin air."

I managed to say, "I don't understand."

I didn't look up at my mother when she said directly, "Your father died today. He got hit by a train."

Mr. Walker and I were still face to face. Like some sort of interpreter, he nodded his head and said softly, "It's true."

My father was dead. I'd seen him that morning before I went to school. And the next time I saw him he was dead in a coffin, propped up like he'd fallen asleep watching baseball on television. I wanted to touch his shoulder, wake him up, remind him it was time to throw the football in the yard. But he didn't wake up, and they buried him in the ground.

A few days after the funeral I went into my mother's room. She was sitting up in bed reading a book. We looked at each other for a long few seconds.

I finally said, in a flat voice, "I just don't understand. Why would God, the same God who made us, kill Daddy with a train?"

My mother didn't answer. She just looked at me.

I said, "When I get older, will I understand it better?"

My mother continued to hold her book open on her lap like she hoped the conversation would be short. "Probably not," she said.

The words seemed to pass slowly from my mother's mouth to my ears and then inside me. They were very final, but I couldn't leave it.

"So when kids grow up, they don't figure all this out, about God and dying and that kind of stuff?"

"No, Early, they don't. I guess we just become more comfortable with the mystery."

My eyes wandered down to the floor. My father's shoes were next to the bed. Mom leaned over to look down at the shoes herself. There was a space between us. It had always been there, but before, when my father was there, he and I shared the space my mother required. It didn't seem so big back then.

"I wish that day never happened," I said.

Mom said, in a slightly different voice, "Save your wishes, Early. You'll need 'em later. Life is for doing, not undoing, and wishes are for the future, not the past. Your father loved you."

Did you ever see a kid drawing a picture? And it looked so easy? The face of a clown, or maybe the wings of a bird, and you thought, "I can do that. It's like riding a bike, or eating. Anybody can do it."

And then you tried. The wings didn't look like wings at all, but more like brown walls. The clown looked like nobody.

And then it occurred to you. That kid can do something I can't. That kid can draw.

four

After the death of my father, I fell into a moral tail-spin, grasping at right and wrong, ultimately choosing the rebellion of invisibility. But before I settled on invisible and average, I managed to break a few laws.

We used to take our bicycles to school. Eddie's mother wouldn't allow him to ride to school with Jake, and Jake considered Eddie to be just this side of retarded. So I alternated between the two. Eddie and I stopped at the drugstore most mornings. I stole candy.

I didn't just steal the candy haphazard and random. I spent entire days drawing diagrams of the store. Locating mirrors, cameras, the viewpoint of the pharmacist in the back and the fat lady at the front on the register. I made Eddie repeat the plan over and over.

"I stand by the candy bars and keep my eyes on the

door."

"And how long do you stand in that spot?"

Eddie squeezed up his face.

"I forget."

"Five, Eddie, five. Count slowly. Five Mississippis. By then I've got the property in my pocket. If you stand there too long staring into space they'll get suspicious."

Eddie said, "Why don't we just pay for the candy bar? I've got a dollar."

I would say, very condescendingly, "You just don't get it, do you? It's the plan, Eddie. It's the point. Remember? We agreed. Everything should belong to everybody."

Eddie thought a moment. "Does that mean somebody could just take our bikes outside and ride away?"

I didn't have an answer for his question.

The next day, at the drugstore, we put the plan into action. It had already worked twice before, but on this particular day I decided we'd go for the mother lode, two Snickers bars.

We walked around the store very awkward and stiff. Looking at mirrors, pretending to size up hairbrushes or some other such thing. The adrenaline rushed through my veins like a raging river. The only thing that kept me from vomiting was the requirement to look composed in front of Eddie. He picked up a tube of shampoo, and his hands shook wildly.

Eddie whispered, "I don't really want a Snickers."

"Don't back out on me now. We've come this far."

I took Eddie by the elbow and led him toward the candy. The janitor, a black man older than my mother, was mopping something off the floor near the front door. He glanced in our direction and went back to mopping.

I positioned Eddie according to the diagram. One by one I checked each point of interest. With my eyes directly on the eyes of the fat lady stocking the shelf behind the counter, my hand reached out and fumbled for the candy bars. I shoved them quickly into my pocket. It felt like my heart would explode.

From behind, seemingly out of nowhere, I heard the black man whisper, "It ain't worth it."

I turned and saw the janitor mopping the floor only a few feet behind me and Eddie. His eyes were looking downward. I couldn't speak. I thought of running but my legs wouldn't move me, so I just stood there. Eddie's mouth was actually open. He was white as cotton.

With his eyes still looking downward, the man whispered, "Put 'em back."

I'd never been so afraid in all my life. All he had to do was raise his voice, or look up at the fat lady, and we'd be caught. Maybe go to jail in a police car. Who knows?

I slowly slipped the candy bars out of my pocket. Keeping my eyes on the black man, I put the candy back on the shelf and waited to see what would happen next.

The janitor pushed the mop a few extra times across the linoleum floor and turned away. He left us standing there. Eddie was the first to move and I followed him outside, never to return to that drugstore again in my life.

I've often thought about that day. If my plan had been successful again, and maybe again after that, would I have lost the fear of being caught? Would I have slipped over the edge and learned to steal for a living? Probably not, but who really knows? The small daily twists and turns through the maps of our lives are sometimes just as important as the big dramatic forks in the road.

Years later I read in the newspaper about kids making elaborate plans to kill people at school. They drew up diagrams, considered evacuation routes, and planned it all down to the detail. One kid was the leader, and one kid was the follower. They couldn't have been more nervous than me that morning standing by the candy with Eddie Miller, but at the end of their day those boys murdered twelve kids and then stuck guns in their own mouths. Somewhere along the way they must have gotten extremely lost.

The first completely naked woman I saw was in a magazine. Jake Crane stole two dirty magazines from Mr. Henderson's garage. We'd been in the garage a few days before to help the old man move a worktable. In the corner was a stack of *Playboy*s and *Penthouse*s. After my encounter at the drugstore I was hesitant to plan a theft, but this was different. They were just stacked up in the garage. It's not like they were worth much on the open market, but to two twelve year olds, the value was high. Curiosity and hormones drove the scheme, and Jake took the wheel.

The old man didn't leave home much. We staked out the place after school for three days in a row. Documented his comings and goings. Finally, on the third day, the old man drove away and left the garage door wide open. Jake waited for the car to turn the corner and took off like a shot. There was nothing subtle or sly. Snatch and grab, run like hell to the spot in the woods, and stare at vaginas.

We both acted like we knew a lot about the damn things. This many years later, from experience, I don't think anybody knows a lot about the damn things. Not even women. And yet our mothers have 'em, and babies come from 'em, and God knows what else goes on in there. But that day in the woods, turning the pages of Mr. Henderson's dirty magazines, I was transfixed, and so was Jake.

It didn't make a lot of sense, but I knew we had to see a real one. The opportunity presented itself when Jake's cousins came to visit. Two sisters, Mona and Janine, seventeen and eighteen years old.

It was nighttime. The cousins, their mom, and Jake's mom were all talking in the living room. We waited until the right moment and slipped outside. Jake and I climbed on his roof and positioned ourselves directly above the bathroom window. The window was small but strategically located above the shower.

Mona was the first to enter the bathroom. We laid our bodies at a downward angle, faces peeking over the roof edge, just a few feet from the small rectangular window. We counted on the darkness outside, and the bright light in the bathroom, to make us virtually invisible.

Mona messed with her hair and looked in the mirror very intently at a bump on her chin. She pulled off her t-shirt and dropped it to the floor at her bare feet. In an instant the white bra was on the floor next to the shirt. I could feel a slow rise in my jeans and a dryness in my mouth. No words passed between me and Jake.

Mona walked from the mirror to the tub, her small-ish, taut breasts barely moving as she walked. She turned the shower on and looked upward at the window, but did-n't flinch. We held our positions, the edge of the black shingle shoved up against the bridge of my nose.

And then she dropped her pants to the floor. And before we could wish for more, the cream-colored panties were down. The brown patch was there to be seen for an instant, and then Mona stepped into the shower.

We watched her wash herself and I remember being amazed at how little time she spent touching the good parts. It almost seemed she didn't understand their importance, or certainly there would have been more attention to the details. The part where she dried herself with the white towel, as I recall, was the best. Mona squatted down a bit to reach far places and ran the towel through the crack of her ass. The pressure in my pants reached new levels, like an unscratchable itch deep below the surface in some primal region of my loins. I closed my eyes for a few seconds and hoped Jake didn't notice.

I'm not sure of the exact moment, but at some point I became uncomfortable watching the girl. She went back to the mirror and spent more time examining the bump on her chin. She stepped away and looked at her body in the mirror, clearly unhappy with her hips. It became apparent that Mona wasn't just perky tits and a patch of brown. She was a person. A person in the bathroom, believing she was alone, looking at herself in a time of privacy, and I wondered if anyone had ever spied on me in such a time.

Mona left the bathroom. The window had fogged up slightly, so we moved our heads to find clear spots and waited for the next girl. Jake's mother came through the bathroom door. There was no protocol for such a situation. I waited for Jake to speak, and secretly wished he wouldn't. Since seeing Miss Crane topless that fateful day, my imagination had painted vivid pictures in my mind.

Miss Crane flipped off her shoes. She unsnapped the button on her pants. Jake lifted himself up, and I immediately followed suit. We sat that way for a while.

"Let's steal a beer from the cooler."

"Okay," I said.

And we did. A Budweiser. I tried not to let my face show the nasty taste, swallowing the cold liquid quickly and handing the beer back to Jake. After just a few sips my head felt light. We brushed our teeth with our fingers to get rid of the smell and sat down in the living room with the women. I couldn't look at Mona. She wore a yellow t-shirt with no bra underneath, and a pair of shorts. Just minutes earlier I'd watched while she washed and dried herself. Knowing she was so close, with no window between us, no contrast in darkness to hide my face, I felt an odd mix of dirty and good. Unable to look at Mona, but at the same time surrounded by her presence.

Twenty years later, in the grocery store, I ran into Mona in the cereal aisle. She was fingering a box of Captain Crunch. I barely recognized her. She was at least a hundred pounds heavier, and those perfect little breasts, three children later, hung like dog teats from her chest.

I continued to smoke cigarettes off and on, separate from any physical addiction, but learning to like the idea of smoking alone. I'm sure my mother knew, just like I'm sure she knew about the beer, and the dirty magazines hidden in my closet, and sneaking out my window at night to terrorize the neighborhood, ringing doorbells and lighting things on fire. But she never said a word. She never started the first conversation about any of it. At the time it seemed purposeful, cold, like she'd be damned before she paid me the least ounce of attention. It wasn't until many years later I figured out she simply wasn't capable.

I entered high school in this state of misidentification. I didn't fit any of the standard categories, and I wasn't strong enough to start my own. It seemed everybody else had a better idea of the world than I did, and on the first day, the very first day of high school, I was tested. After weaving through the lunch line in the unfamiliar cafeteria, I found an empty table. A goofy-looking freshman named Peter Jankins sat next to me. Although I secretly longed to belong to a group, Pete Jankins wasn't exactly what I had in mind. He was even goofier than me, acne between his eyes, big shoes.

A few minutes into our delicious meal, two guys sat down across from us. Seniors. Big sons-of-bitches. One of them wore a football letter jacket. The other just smiled at us, reminding me of the time I watched the neighbor's cat push around a lizard until the lizard gave up all hope.

After a few minutes of me feeling like the lizard, the guy with the smile on his face turned up his chocolate milkshake and filled his mouth. He rose slowly from the chair, leaned over my tray of lunch, opened his mouth, and spit a stream of milkshake down upon my Salisbury steak and brown gravy.

The guy leaned back and sat down in his chair, content to watch the lizard. I looked at Pete, his mouth agape, and then looked at the guy across the table. If I did nothing, just let it happen, it would continue to happen my whole life, in one form or another.

Time seemed to slow down, but there was really no time to think. I just shoved my tray as hard as possible across the table, stood, turned my back, and walked away at a crisp pace. As I walked away, I expected to feel a large hand on my shoulder. Maybe a fist against the back of my head. But I didn't look back. I just walked outside, turned the corner, and wore a baseball cap to school the rest of the year, hoping I'd never see the smiling guy again, and if I did he wouldn't recognize me. I stayed out of the cafeteria, and on at least two occasions had the opportunity to hear Pete Jankins tell the story like I was David and the milkshake guy was Goliath and I killed the giant, when really all I did was push away my lunch tray as a minimal display of defiance and flee the scene.

Although I was pleased to have taken such action on my own behalf, spending the rest of the year in hiding helped contribute to my desire to become invisible and my decision to remain average. I started to seek people to save, because in retrospect, after the death of my father, I was never really able to build strong friendships, and everybody knows, if you're unsteady, become a savior.

five

Who am I?

The universal question, for the high school student in particular. Repeated like a mantra in the teenage subconscious, a low hum below the surface, everpresent, annoying yet elusive. I loved baseball, but I wasn't good enough to play in high school, so I didn't fit with the baseball players. My grades were average (fittingly), and therefore the National Honor Society skipped me. For a while I tried to pass as a drughead, or whatever the hell they call themselves, but I didn't care much for drugs. I remember actually putting pepper in my eyes one morning before school so I'd look stoned.

Monica Houston said, "What's wrong with your eyes?"

I smiled stupidly and mumbled, "What do you think?"

She squinted to see. "It looks like bits of black pepper."

I panicked and defended myself too lucidly. "It's not pepper. That's stupid. I smoked a big joint on the way to school."

"With who?" She asked.

I hesitated an amazingly long time. "Nobody."

Monica Houston said, "Let me make sure I understand. You smoked a big joint on the way to school by yourself and somehow ended up with black pepper in your eyes."

It was too much work to be a drughead, especially since I didn't like drugs, so I fell into a sort of no man's land. The high school abyss. But all that changed the day I met Kate. She became my focus. At first from a distance, and then later with no distance between us at all.

There was a graveyard down Dugger Road, tucked away under big oak trees with Spanish moss hanging from the limbs like long gray beards. During the day the sunlight would cut through in sharp spears to the ground below, succeeding only briefly, allowing the earth to stay moist and the gravestones to turn a dark shade of green. But at night it was the scariest and darkest place in all the world.

Who knows where or when the legend of Onionhead began? He was described as a large man, some sort of caretaker of the cemetery, with a bald head and huge black boots. Some said he was grotesquely deformed, one eye lower than the other, with six fingers on his right hand. The image and description was formed through years of eyewitness accounts and outright lies, but if you were sixteen years old and taking your first midnight ride down the long twisting road to the cemetery, almost anything was believable.

I'd heard about Onionhead since grammar school. He didn't become real until we were able to drive. Going out to the cemetery on a Saturday night with a carload of teenagers was one of the things to do. At the time we had no idea why we did it. It was an early challenge of manhood, I suppose. Facing fear to impress each other, or more importantly, to impress a girl. I can remember my first visit to that cemetery like it was yesterday.

Jake somehow got permission to use his parents' van. At the time, I was working as a stock boy at a local grocery store. My shift ended at nine o'clock on Friday nights, when the store closed. I saw the gold van sitting out in the parking lot. There was no plan to go look for Onionhead. The plan was to drink peppermint schnapps and smoke cigars. Beer had long since lost its luster for us. We'd moved to a level of importance in the world worthy of peppermint schnapps and Swisher Sweets. The van smelled like a barroom.

Joey Shannon sat in the passenger's seat. His nickname was Bluto. He was round and unshaven, with a unique ability to shotgun a fourteen-ounce Old Milwaukee like it was nothing. He was the arm wrestling champion of the western world and often took on challengers at strange times.

The other guy in the gold van was Toad. I never knew his real name. His nickname was such a perfect fit it never crossed my mind he might have another name. He was the guy who always sat in the corner. One night he rode home in the trunk of a girl's car because there wasn't enough room inside. Toad didn't seem to mind.

We all drank from the same bottle and tried not to make a face when the warm schnapps burned our throats. We inhaled cigar smoke and blew smoke rings when the van wasn't moving. As lost as I was in the world, it felt good to be young. There is a beauty in youth that exists all alone. A freedom that can never be recaptured.

And then Bluto said, "Let's go out to Onionhead."

The suggestion may have lingered and died, covered up by a new idea, but Jake immediately followed with, "Hell yeah, let's go out to Onionhead."

We made a U-turn on Front Street and headed toward Dugger Road.

"I've seen that big bastard," Jake said. He was the best cusser amongst us. Jake's cuss words seemed to fit in his sentences like they belonged. He took a drag from his cigar and held his arm out the window for the ash to blow away.

We went further and further out of town. There were no streetlights and the houses were set back from the road, offering just a twinkle of light through the woods as we sped past. Jake turned down the radio when we pulled off on the dirt road. The van moved slowly and then we turned down another skinny dirt road. Jake switched off the head-lights. I couldn't see anything except the cherry ends of the cigars, like little Christmas lights inside the van.

And then we stopped. I wondered if anyone else could hear my heartbeat. There was total silence. Bluto opened the passenger door and the dome light covered us in a dull yellow. We piled out of the van and closed the doors gently. My eyes adjusted to the darkness enough to see we were standing in a circle in front of the vehicle. We were only a few yards from the entrance gate to the graveyard.

Jake whispered, "Follow me. And be quiet. Don't talk until we get where we're going."

Toad asked, "Where we going?"

"You'll know when we get there," Jake said.

In a line we walked through the gate. I could see the shapes and shadows of gravestones. There were no lights in any direction, just the moon. I was third in line, behind Bluto, who was behind Jake. I followed the big white t-shirt in front maybe fifty yards, until Bluto stopped. Toad bumped into me from the back.

I heard Bluto whisper, "Jake? Jake?"

He turned to me and said, "Where the hell's Jake?"

Nobody wanted to be the first to run.

"Listen," Toad said.

We listened. There was a distant rustling of leaves. And then silence again. I was more afraid than the time in the drugstore, but not so afraid to be the first to run. The first person to run would hear about it the rest of their lives. They'd hear the story told over and over in class, at the football game, forever, about the time they ran.

The silence was broken. The horn on the van blasted. I felt Bluto brush past me as he took off. I ran. There was the sound of footsteps all around. The horn continued to blare in the night. I expected to feel a hand grab my shoulder, a six-fingered hand, and pull me back to the cemetery. I expected to die.

I passed Bluto and arrived at the van ahead of the others. The first thing I saw was Jake standing at the driver's door, his arm inside the van on the horn, holding the bottle of schnapps with his other hand, laughing. I stopped and then felt the force of Toad's body hit me from behind, knocking me to the ground face-first. He fell over the top of me, and the dome light in the van came on, shining a yellow light on Jake's laughing face.

It was quiet again.

"Y'all are a bunch of titty-babies," Jake said. "There ain't no Onionhead. It's all made up. My cousin made it up."

"How do you know?" Toad asked from the ground beside me.

"There ain't no tooth fairy either, Toad, or Santy Claus," Jake explained.

I stood up. Jake handed me the bottle of schnapps, and I took a swig. It was the first time I noticed I no longer held my cigar. I looked back the way we'd come to see if I could see the little red dot of light on the ground. There was nothing to see.

We laughed. Knowing there was no Onionhead was almost disappointing. Bluto opened the other bottle of schnapps, and we lit up a new round of cigars.

Overcoming the myth, rising above Onionhead, made me feel a little more like a man. It was a separation from all those kids at school who still talked about it like it was real. Those kids who lied about ever going to the cemetery in the first place.

"I've got an idea," Jake said.

Even though I felt more like a man, and even though I was glad to shatter the Onionhead myth, I was ready to leave that place and go back to town.

Jake continued, "Let's go back and get Lori and her

two friends. One of us will stay out here and hide. We'll get the girls to walk out to the middle of the graveyard, and the guy can jump out of his hiding place and scare the holy crap outta the girls. It'll be classic."

Jake liked Lori. I'd never met her two friends before. Jake said, "One of the girls is a year older, seventeen. She's good lookin'. I don't know about the other one. I think she's a Fatty O'Patty."

Bluto asked the question, "Who's gonna stay?"

Jake answered, "I'd stay, but I've gotta drive the van. The rest of you can draw straws."

It was hard to argue with drawing straws. We each had a sixty-six percent chance of not having to stay. The odds were good I'd be sitting in the comfortable van for the ride back to town. Jake picked up little sticks and turned his back to measure two sticks the same size and one smaller. When he turned back around he held in his hand the tops of three sticks. "Who goes first?"

Bluto grabbed one and held it up. "You're safe," Jake said.

There was just me and Toad. It seemed right that Toad should be the one to stay. He was the runt of the litter.

"You pick," Toad said to me.

I took a deep breath. It appeared fate would be on my side. Toad seemed destined to lose and stay in the graveyard.

I pulled the stick on the right and held it up. It was short. Too short.

Jake held up the third stick. He looked at me and said, "You're short, big boy."

He handed me a bottle of schnapps and said, "Follow the same path y'all walked before. About twenty yards ahead of that spot, where you stopped last time, you'll find a big headstone. It's the biggest one out there. You can't miss it. Sit behind it. We'll be back in thirty minutes. When you see my lights flash, you'll know we're comin'. Wait until we get the girls all the way there before you jump out. And then scream."

Toad said, "This'll be great. I bet Lori pees her pants."

I was slightly in shock. Somehow I'd forgotten Onionhead didn't exist. I'd forgotten my newfound manhood. I just stood there while they piled in the van. The headlights kicked on and illuminated the cemetery. Far in the back I caught a glimpse of a big headstone. The van backed out, turned around, and left me alone in a graveyard. I stood still and listened to the van until I couldn't hear the engine. I began to walk slowly in the direction of the big headstone, quiet with my steps, holding the bottle by the neck to use as a weapon if necessary. Every ten yards or so I'd stop and listen. I tried to imagine where the van might be. How close to town? How many more minutes until the headlights would be back at the gate?

My heart pounded. I took deep breaths and held my eyes as open as they would go. I listened for any sound. Finally I could see the big headstone. It was as tall as my chest. Instead of getting behind it, I decided to sit down in front. I figured I'd have time to hide when the lights showed up down the dirt road.

I squatted with my back against the stone. I could feel the coolness through my shirt. I set the bottle down next to me and wondered again where the van might be in the journey. What if they couldn't find the girls? Maybe it was a joke. Maybe they weren't coming back. My mind shot in quick circles, trying to decide what to do if they didn't come back. Where to go? I sat there for what felt like a long time.

And then I heard a sound. It was just sound. A noise where there had been none before. It could have been a bird on the ground, or a rabbit in the leaves. And then I heard it again. It was louder the second time. A footstep, and then another, off to my left. There was nothing to see. I looked down at my shirt and thanked God it was dark blue and not white, like Bluto's t-shirt. The sound stopped. It stopped long enough for me to believe I had never really heard it in the first place. And then I heard it again. A step, and then another step. Someone else was in the graveyard. Someone was walking in my direction.

My hand reached out and took hold of the neck of the bottle. I could run, I thought, but where would I run to? And what if I fell? I might run right into a gravestone, or a tree, or the fence.

There was another step, and then another. To my left, moving closer, maybe thirty yards away, three first downs on a football field. I looked toward the front gate. How long had it been? My hand tightened on the neck of the bottle, still half-full. I lowered my head so my white face wouldn't show in the darkness, my chin against my chest, eyes cutting hard to the left.

Slowly, a figure appeared. At first it was nothing but a movement in the black dark. And then it was an outline.

Ten yards to my left I saw a person appear. A very large person. Dark clothing with a white head. A large, bald, white head. He was looking toward the back of the grave-yard, his profile etched in the black background. It was Onionhead. It was no myth. It was no concoction of teenage lies. It was a very large man with a very large head. A head like a big onion.

To this day I can see the figure, the arms down at his sides, the milky-white hands at the ends of the sleeves, the enormous head resting like a glow-in-the dark ball on his broad shoulders.

His head began to turn very slowly toward me. He seemed to be scanning the cemetery for anything out of place, anything disturbed. As he turned further, I could see something wasn't right with him. Something was off-center, distorted. I was sure he could hear me breathing, or smell the cigar on my clothes or the peppermint from the bottle. If his face made a full turn, if his eyes met mine, I decided I would run. I would run toward the gates. Whatever happened would be better than feeling the hands of Onionhead upon my clothes. If he took one more step in my direction, I would go.

The lights. Through the woods I saw the headlights of the van. Onionhead turned to the lights, and then turned to me. It was only two seconds, maybe three, that we looked at each other, but God knows it felt like eternity. I ran. I left the bottle and ran toward the gate like an arrow shot from a bow. I didn't look back.

The van turned the corner of the dirt road and stopped at the gate, the headlights like spotlights shining

THE WAIT

and showing the way. I didn't care if anyone laughed. I didn't care if the girls whispered at school about my blind run through the cemetery. I had seen Onionhead. I had come face-to-face with the legend of Onionhead and lived to remember it all. At least that's how I felt as I ran in the direction of the gold van. But as I got closer I saw Jake, and Toad, and Bluto, and three girls climb out and stand next to the van. And the next thing I knew I was there with them. I recognized Lori, and the fat girl, but the other one, the seventeen-year-old, she was something else. She was different.

And that's how Kate first saw me. Running like a wild man out of the blackness of a midnight cemetery with my face contorted in pure fear. I turned around. There was nothing behind me. No gigantic white-headed man. No murderous Onionhead.

"What the hell, man?" Jake said. "You were supposed to wait until we got 'em back there. Are you stupid?"

To this day I can recall the feeling of not being able to take my eyes from Kate's face. I just stared at her. There was something besides beauty. Something you had to look for. It took me years to figure it out. A brokenness underneath.

Λnd so began the era of Kate Shepherd. I couldn't stop myself from thinking about her. With every lull, every blank space between normal thoughts, my mind clicked back to Kate like a mechanism. It was my first taste of love. Blind, convoluted, complicated, teenage love, from a safe distance, and yet it didn't seem safe at all.

I located her locker in fourth hall, inventing reasons to wander past and then running like hell back to first hall so I wouldn't be late to class. I wrote notes, anonymous notes, written left-handed, or backward, so no one could identify the penmanship, but eventually threw them all into the trash instead of hurriedly shoving the papers through the vent-cracks of her metal locker door.

I followed her home from school one day. She got a ride to a fast food restaurant, waited around a few minutes, and walked three or four blocks. I kept my car far behind until she turned down a driveway. I couldn't see the house as I drove by. It was set back far in the woods. The dirt driveway and the section of town made me think it wasn't the fanciest house. An old, short-haired dog stood guard at the entrance of the property near the end of the road. One of his ears was chewed clean off and the other stuck up to the sky.

My sophomore year ended, and I spent the summer working construction. The alarm clock woke me up every morning at four-thirty. I had to be at Huey's house by five. He was the foreman. I rode in the back of his brown pickup truck almost an hour to the job site. I'd lie with my back against the truckbed and watch the sky turn from black to gold. It was my first construction job. No place for the hardworking. Most guys exerted themselves as little as possible trying to maintain the appearance of working. I never really figured it out, I guess. I busted my ass in the summer sun from the moment I arrived until I climbed in the back of Huey's truck at the end of the day. Even Huey told me once to slow down before I killed myself, but like I said, I never really figured it out. It seemed to me there wasn't much point in working if you weren't working hard. And it didn't matter what anybody thought, including Huey. I didn't compare myself to the other men. How hard I worked had nothing to do with them at all. Mostly they watched me and talked about how fast their cars would go or the size of their dicks.

I worked construction off and on for years after that summer. I learned two things. I learned I worked harder than most people, and I sure as hell didn't want to spend my life listening to some lazy hungover bastard talk about his pecker, or his car, or both. Huey and the boys did more to motivate me to go to college than anything else.

It was harder to find opportunities to see Kate during the summer. On weekends I'd ride around in Jake's van, inspired by the possibility of seeing her outside McDonald's or in the car next to us at a red light. As the months passed, time began to lift Kate onto a pedestal, approaching mythical status, without a flaw. I'd see her, and she'd smile, and I'd wonder if she knew we'd end up together. And then I'd wonder if such a thing was possible. She seemed so far above me, but at the same time she seemed so vulnerable, and the vulnerability slowly took on the appearance of something else. Something romantic, exciting, even sexual.

At the end of the summer, just a few weeks before school was set to start, I got my chance. A kid had a party. His parents were out of town. Jake knew the guy, sort of, and we showed up on Saturday night after a bottle of cinnamon schnapps and a pack of Jake's mom's cigarettes. We got there late, and the place was already out of control. Jake's girlfriend, Lori, was there, and I hoped Kate had come with her.

Lori was sitting on the swing. After a few minutes of conversation, I casually asked, "Is Kate here?"

Lori smiled a drunken smile. "You like Kate, dontcha?" she asked.

I took a swig of the warm schnapps and tried to think of an answer. Nothing came to me, so I just sat there like no question had been asked.

Lori kissed Jake on his sweaty neck. She smiled again.

"Kate's in the car. She drank too much and got sick. We put her in the backseat."

I'd noticed Lori's car parked out by the road. Now it was just a matter of separating without being noticed, slipping away and walking alone down the long driveway.

A few minutes passed.

I said convincingly, "I left the cigarettes in the damn van."

"You don't even smoke," Lori said.

"I smoke when I feel like it, and I don't smoke when I don't feel like it. It's not the cigarette's decision."

Nobody said anything.

"I'll be back in a minute," and I moved off slowly like a cow from the herd, easing down the path.

The driveway was dark. I slowly passed Lori's car, trying to see if Kate was sitting up in the backseat. From behind the car I lined up the back window with the front window and the lights in the house to catch a silhouette of her head. There was no silhouette, so I put my face to the window and tried to see. The outline of the shape of Kate's body resting on the backseat slowly formed. I tapped lightly on the window, a bold move for me, but clouded in the warmth of the schnapps and Kate's state of intoxication.

There was no response. I tried the driver's door and it was unlocked. The dome light came on, revealing Kate lying on the backseat, face up, eyes closed, asleep. Or at least she looked asleep. She very well could have been dead. Her hand rested on her stomach. Her fingers were small, with the nails chewed to the quick. I'd never noticed before. It struck me as strange. What would a person like Kate worry about?

She was wearing shorts. The way one leg was lifted and the other was down on the floorboard, I could see the edge of her panties between her legs, white in the light from inside the car. I'd never looked at a girl so closely in all my life. The lines on her face. The tiny hairs where a mustache would be. The rise of her breasts beneath the thin red shirt, and the smooth skin of her belly between the edge of the bottom of the shirt and the top of the short pants.

It was a glorious experience, and in the glory of the moment it occurred to me we were alone, and drunk, and she was so near. I closed the car door gently and caused the darkness.

I waited a long time until my eyes readjusted. From my place in the front seat I looked down upon this girl who occupied nearly every minute of my mind. My hand was so close to her body. Just a move away from touching skin, or resting on the fabric of her shirt, or God knows, sliding my finger through the space left open to the warm panties underneath.

I took a big breath. The air inside the car was hot and stagnant. For some reason I thought of the morning I stood next to Eddie in the drugstore, stolen candy bars in my pocket, waiting. Kate's breathing was deep and consistent. I closed my eyes and tried to smell her. The clean, perfumed smell of a girl, even in a hot car, passed out drunk, rising above all else.

"Kate," I whispered, hoping she would answer, but there was nothing.

I looked back toward the house in the distance. There was no movement along the driveway. The sounds of laughter were far off, nowhere near the car, or me, or Kate, or my hand reaching between the front seat and the back and descending so slowly downward until the fingertips touched the softness of the skin, and moved gently, and it is wrong, and I know it's wrong, and I cannot pull my hand away, and there's a sound outside the car, and I jerk my body around to face forward, and close my eyes like I'm asleep, and when the car door flies open I act confused, blinded by the light.

"Get your asses up," Jake said, and a few minutes later, when no one was looking, I put my hand to my face and it smelled like Kate, and I wondered again how anyone like her could chew her fingernails to the quick.

With Lori's help, Kate woke up and lifted herself to a seated position. I climbed in the backseat beside her for the ride to take her home.

"My head hurts," she said.

Jake turned up the radio, and I wished he'd turn it down again.

"Turn off the radio, please," Kate said, and I looked at her. She saw me looking. "I look like shit," she said.

"No, you don't."

She was seventeen. I was sixteen. She would be a senior in a few weeks, and I'd be a junior. Jake slowed down and then gunned it through a stop sign. We were almost to Kate's street. I waited for Lori and Jake to start a conversation in the front seat between themselves.

"Why do you bite your fingernails?" I asked quietly.

She looked at me, straight into my eyes, the street-lights passing outside. It was a look I hadn't seen from her before. Like I'd gotten a glimpse at something I wasn't supposed to see. Like she was surprised I'd noticed anything about her fingers. But there was no answer. Just a stare, and then Kate noticed where we were.

"Stop here," she said.

"What?" Lori asked.

Kate raised her voice, "Stop here."

"Stop," Lori told Jake. "She wants to get out here."

Jake slowed down. "But her house is up the—"

Lori pushed Jake on the shoulder like he was being inconsiderate.

"What?" he asked, not catching on to the signals of a woman.

Lori raised her eyebrows. "Stop here, please."

The car rolled to a stop. Kate got out with no words and closed the car door.

"Go," Lori said.

Jake asked, "You want me to leave her on the side of the road?"

Lori whispered, "Just go, Jake. I'll tell you why."

And the car rolled away, leaving Kate Shepherd on the side of the road. I looked back through the rear window. She stood, bent over slightly, looking at the ground near her feet. She was under a streetlight, and the shadow thrown by her body spread out on the pavement like a tall ghost. When we were far enough away, Kate started to walk.

Lori explained, "She doesn't like people to go to her house."

"Why not?" I asked.

"She just doesn't. I don't know why. I always pick her up at different places. I think something's the matter with her father. Robin says he's crazy or something, and the house is like a shack, all rotten, with dogs everywhere."

I looked back through the rear window, but we'd already turned down another street.

"What about her mother?" I asked.

Lori stuck her head in the backseat. "You do like her, dontcha?"

I was weak. The night had taken its toll. "Maybe," I said.

"What about her mother?"

"She never talks about her mother. I don't know."

"Does she have any sisters or brothers?"

"I don't think so. I think she moved here from Oklahoma."

After that night my focus became even stronger. Kate filled all the empty places in me. She rounded the rough edges and gave me purpose. She didn't know it yet, but Kate was my girlfriend, and I had plans. Detailed, elaborate plans, considering every possibility. I could save her from all that was bad and protect her from the world. And who I was, who I would become, would have a starting point, a structure, a method of measurement. The difference between me and Kate would narrow into nothing.

seven

People who make bad grades in school sometimes like to say they're bored, or it wasn't challenging. The implication is clear. They made poor grades because they were smarter than everyone else, including the teachers.

I don't know how my smartness compared with other people, but I know my grades weren't too good. Of course, I spent a large percentage of my junior year in high school creating vivid sexual fantasies and searching for shortcuts. I'm not sure why there was such a contrast in my drive to work hard on a construction site and my quest for shortcuts in the classroom, but the contrast existed and I didn't do anything to figure it out, despite the motivation for a college education caused by moronic co-workers.

Mr. Lee taught Biology. He was a small Asian man.

Back then we thought all small Asian men were Chinese. We called him China Lee. I think he was from Vietnam, or Korea maybe, I'm not sure. His accent was strong and his fingers were thin like pencils, holding up things in front of his special safety goggles.

"Okay, cass. Weed pwoblem numbar fwee."

It took Jody Gardner two weeks to understand Mr. Lee well enough to respond to his name at roll call. He was marked absent every day.

The first two tests didn't go well. I needed to make a B on the semester exam to pass the class, so I decided to cheat. On a piece of paper about the size of a business card, I wrote, in super-tiny letters, the answers to every question in the damn book. I messed up once and had to do it again, but finally, in super-tiny writing, I had everything I needed to know.

I taped the piece of paper lightly to the backside of my thigh, just above the hem of my khaki shorts. The idea was to position the paper under my leg in the chair so I could simply move my leg to the side an inch and see the cheat sheet as needed during the exam.

Mr. Lee was like a prison guard. He roamed around the room watching with those beady eyes. Every time I looked up he was watching me, waiting, somehow knowing my plan, like he'd gotten inside my house and watched me write the tiny cheat sheet, twice.

Out of sheer frustration I started reading the questions on the test. To my amazement I knew almost all the answers. Answers I surely hadn't learned in class in between sexual gymnastics and inappropriate thoughts.

But there they were, coming out of my pen all over the page. Fill-in-the-blank. Multiple choice. Bing, bing, bing.

In my plan to cheat I'd learned I didn't need to. Finding the answers in the book, identifying them as somehow important, and writing them down in such a focused and concentrated fashion burned the answers in my mind. They were there to stay, and more importantly, I learned a study method that served me well throughout my higher education. Prepare to cheat, and then don't.

I was left with a peculiar dilemma. Beneath my leg was proof of my immoral intentions, but I never looked down. Under Mr. Lee's burning eyes, how was I to get up and walk away? I'd managed, by fidgeting and sweating, to disconnect the cheat sheet from my leg. The tape was folded over and the evidence was left between my bare leg and the wooden seat.

People began to stand and walk to the front of the class, but Mr. Lee's eyes stayed on me. I'd finished the test. There were only two questions I couldn't answer. I'd never looked down, but who would believe me? Who would believe I could make an A on the final exam after making F's on the other tests without cheating? I'd created a sticky quandary.

Everyone was gone but me.

"Meester Weenwood, au yuu feeneshed?"

We looked at each other. I wondered what was running around in that crafty mind of his. Had he seen me sneak my hand down to adjust the paper under the leg? Had he noticed the glistening of sweat on my upper lip in anticipation of the misdeed? The room seemed overly warm. I felt a touch of asthma and moved my hand to feel the bulge of the inhaler in my front pocket.

I held the exam in my hand and reached it out in the direction of Mr. Lee, who stood to my right, twenty feet away. I held it there, waiting for him to move, or not move, or whatever came next. I half-expected police officers to arrive and take me into custody, but instead, Mr. Lee walked over to my desk and took the exam from my hand.

He studied the papers, looking occasionally at me over the top of the page. When he finished, Mr. Lee lowered the exam from his face. I held his stare.

"I didn't cheat," I said.

Mr. Lee's mouth tightened. His chin seemed to rise slightly. There was not the tiniest hint of a smile.

"I know," he said.

We were only a few feet apart. There was no way to snatch the cheat sheet and shove it in my pocket, or eat it, or anything else. I was left in the shaky hands of fate, with my eyes still locked upon the eyes of China Lee. I stood slowly from my chair, prepared for a small piece of paper to fall at my feet, taking the eyes of Mr. Lee with it to the floor.

But there was no such feeling. And his eyes stayed with mine. And I turned and walked, hands in pockets, out the door into the crowded hallway. Around the corner I reached my hand and felt the back of my leg. And there, hidden beneath the edge of my shorts, stuck to my sweaty leg, was the cheat sheet. When I'd sat down, the pants leg edge had pulled naturally further up the thigh. And when I'd stood, the edge naturally hung down lower, covering the evidence of my evil scheme. Fate had rewarded me and I made a D+ in biology. Maybe I was just bored.

I had a job as a waiter that year in a nice restaurant downtown. I found it difficult. Instead of being able to lower my head and work my ass off like I'd done in previous construction jobs, suddenly I had to talk to people. What's more, I had to pretend like they were interesting and important, and I cared whether they wanted regular or low-fat ranch dressing on their stupid little salads.

The balance was difficult. It kept my mind off Kate, but not for long. She looked tired sometimes. I'd watch her across the baseball field sitting in the aluminum bleachers doing her homework. She'd look out across the green field at nothing for long stretches. Sometimes she'd shut her eyes and take a deep breath.

Everything she did was very mysterious. I'd never been around women much, except my mother, and I don't think my mother was typical of women in general. I wasn't comfortable asking my mother questions about anything at all, much less sex, or menstrual cycles, or the hopes and fears of teenage girls.

Instead I mostly watched Kate and tried to learn things. I practiced conversations with myself. I tried to imagine situations we might find ourselves in. I took notes on small pieces of paper, like my cheat sheet, in case I ever got up the nerve to call her on the telephone. Notes of things to say to fill the ungodly dead spots in a hypothetical conversation. As the year drug on, my obsession with Kate became familiar, like a favorite shirt. It wore well and aged one day at a time.

I continued, along with everybody else, to struggle with identity. I embraced the role of savior but slowly came to recognize a savior must have someone to save, or you're really just a stalker. It's hard to tell what Kate knew or didn't know of my obsession. The sight of a certain face, Kate's face, made me feel physically different. I didn't need to actually see her. I could think about her and the chemicals would squirt out and leave me drunk. It was hard to understand why it didn't happen to everybody else who saw Kate. People seemed to pass all around, even speak with her in the hallway, or sit next to her in the classroom, and then walk away unfazed.

In the middle of my junior year there was a school dance. I generally stayed away from any school-related functions, social clubs, or any other organized activity for that matter. I might have been average, but there's a big difference between being average and being a conformist. A conformist is an average guy sitting around the room with a bunch of other average guys. I was average alone.

I went to the dance because I knew Kate would be there. She was on a date with a guy named Jeff Temple. I'd seen him around her before. Jeff was a senior, played on the baseball team, and had no appreciation whatsoever of the value of Kate Shepherd. I could tell by the way he walked with her, and the way he smiled at all the right times. He just didn't know.

I wasn't really mad at him. How could I be? I was more frustrated than anything else. Frustrated that neither one of them could recognize the obvious when they walked into the dance together. I sat over in the corner with Jake and Lori, hidden in the dark recesses of the high school fringe. Kate seemed to be having fun, but I knew she wasn't. She acted like she liked Jeff Temple, but I knew better. It wasn't possible at the time to understand the woman I believed I knew so well didn't really exist. I'd created my own person. Built, like the bride of Frankenstein, to be exactly who I wanted her to be. That's the problem with love. The chemicals make you drunk. People in love shouldn't be allowed to operate heavy machinery.

He left her alone for awhile to stand next to his buddies. I wanted her to see me. I stood and walked out of the dark corner into a patch of light.

"You don't belong here," I wanted to tell her. "Let's leave. You and me. Go drive around. Go sit together at night in the aluminum baseball bleachers and talk about nothing. Just hold hands in the dark, and you can tell me what I already know," I wanted to say.

But we never say things like that in the real world, only in the movies. And in the real world, the boyfriend comes back before Kate sees me, and they walk off together, and I go home and masturbate.

It all came down to one night. The night of Kate's graduation. I'd squandered the entire year, never gathering the nerve to ask her on a single date, or call her on the telephone. The fear had extended beyond the natural boy/girl fear into a category of being afraid the real Kate Shepherd couldn't measure up to the Kate Shepherd inside my mind, the one that caused the release of all those chemicals. But I'd decided I couldn't just do nothing. I couldn't let her graduate, and maybe slide out of my life without something. Anything. I wasn't even sure what it would be.

It ended up being one of those nights we remember our entire lives. There was a party at David Ansley's house after the graduation ceremony. Kate was laughing and drinking. I'd heard stories of her drinking too much and worse.

From the other side of this party I watched Kate go from happy and laughing to alone and stoic, and eventually to drunk and angry. It was the talk of the party. She cussed out Jeff Temple by the pool and he broke up with her in front of the world.

For everyone else, it was high school drama at its best. For me, it was painful. Through the past year I'd melted into Kate Shepherd, and as I said before, the difference between me and Kate narrowed to nothing. I could see the brokenness. It wasn't just a random act. It was the night of her graduation. It was everything coming together. It was Jeff going to college when she wasn't. It was being dropped off a block from her home. It was the knowing and not knowing.

I followed her out to the road in front of David Ansley's big house, but lost her in the darkness. I called out her name but didn't get an answer, and wondered if she recognized my voice, or if she was passed out in the woods somewhere.

Back at the party Jeff Temple didn't seem to have a care in the world. He drank a cold beer and laughed with his buddies. I watched him grab a girl on the ass with a cigar hanging from his mouth.

I wanted to beat the shit out of him. I wanted to make him stand before the crowd, blood trickling from his nose, tears in his blue eyes, and say, "I'm sorry, Kate. I was wrong. You're too good for me."

But of course I didn't do it. Of course I just watched him from across the party as long as I could stand it, and then left alone to find Kate. There was still no answer on the street. I figured she might have gotten a ride home. One of her friends must have cared enough to get her safely to her bed.

I drove across town in the direction of Kate's house. It was midnight, and I had no real plan. Of all the situations I'd envisioned, this wasn't one.

I parked out by the road, near the mailbox. The dirt driveway snaked through the center of the wooded lot. Far back in the lot I could see a single yellow light. There were a few houses on the street, but everything was quiet. I got out of my car and closed the door gently. This was it. The moment I'd waited for. She needed me. I could tell her why. Everything would come together for both of us. She needed saving, and I could explain the reasons, and then I could proceed with the plan.

I put my hands in my blue jean pockets and started down the driveway. I could barely see the road at my feet as I twisted around one curve and then another. The yellow light came from the porch of a small wooden house. It hadn't been painted in twenty years. A scruffy white dog crawled from beneath the porch. Her teats were engorged and hung below a fat belly. I could hear the whimpering of puppies. I stopped to wait for the dog's decision to bark or not to bark. She wagged her tail and smelled my shoe.

I stepped up on the porch. The boards creaked under my feet. There was a dull glow from the single yellow bulb. It wasn't until I reached the door that I realized it was only a screen door. Inside was dark like a cave. I pressed my face against the screen and tried to see anything at all. The outline of a piece of furniture, a couch, anything.

In a low voice, almost to myself, I said, "Kate?"

There was no answer. No sound of any kind inside. I put my hand on the handle of the screen door and pulled gently to test whether it was locked. The door opened a few inches, the hinges making a rusty squeaking sound.

In the silence my ears were raw for sound, listening for any noise. From below, on the other side of the door, came a deep gutteral groan, low and long. I froze with my hand on the handle of the door.

The noise stopped and I waited. It came again, the prelude to something violent.

From inside the room I heard a man's voice, "He won't bite."

I couldn't see anything in the direction the voice had come. With the light outside, I knew the man and the beast at my feet could see me clearly, the outline of a stranger testing the door at midnight.

A lamp flicked on inside. In an instant I could see what I could only imagine the second before. At the base of the screen door, sitting on a dirty welcome mat, was a stout, red-faced pit bull with a brown leather collar. In a reclining chair in the corner of the room sat a man with one leg elevated. He wore a short-sleeved gray shirt and a pair of old dark pants, unbuttoned at the waist. We looked at each other.

The man repeated, "He won't bite," but the tone of the statement was neither friendly nor unfriendly. The words were tired, spoken out of habit.

"Is Kate here?" I asked, my hand still holding the door between me and the world inside the room.

The man's foot was swollen and black. I could see crust on the top of the foot, the big toe white against the darker colors. The man's other foot rested on the floor next to a bottle of clear liquid. It looked like a liquor bottle without a label.

The smell from inside was hard. Old cigarette smoke, dog hair, and sour milk, maybe. There was no ceiling fan or air conditioner running. The wall of hot air started where my nose touched the screen. The man looked to be maybe fifty years old. He'd been sitting in the dark waiting for God knows what. I couldn't imagine Kate in such a place. I just couldn't see her walking through that room, passing the man in the chair, stopping to open the screen door, stepping around the pit bull, smelling the smell.

The man kept his stare on me. "Kate ain't here. She left," he said, in the same flat voice as before.

"Where'd she go?" I asked, and noticed his eyes drift slowly away to a place on the wall, just an empty place on the wall, no framed picture or even a stain to look at.

"Where does anybody go?" he said.

The man moved slightly in the chair and winced in pain. I looked down at the dog at my feet and when our eyes connected he made his favorite sound again. A deep, slow growl from a place inside his thick chest.

The man took both hands, placed them on either side of his knee, and lifted up the foot high enough to move it a few inches. He settled back in the old chair.

I asked him, "What happened to your foot?"

"I shot a hole in it," is what he said.

His answer begged more questions, but suddenly I didn't care. I came for Kate. The old man, whoever he was, didn't matter. If he wanted to die in that chair in the dark it was his business, not mine, and not Kate's anymore either.

"When's she comin' back?" I asked.

The man reached for the bottle next to his chair. He lifted it to his lips and took a swig. There was no reaction to the clear liquid rolling down his throat, and just by the way he swallowed I knew the man had taken so many swigs like that in his lifetime he couldn't tell you anymore if it burned or not. He was a dead man, kept alive by inertia and the gravitational pull of millions of years of evolution. He was less alive than dead.

"She ain't comin' back, boy. Not this time. She's gone for good." From his voice I could tell he believed it was true.

"How do you know?" I asked.

The man smiled, or at least it looked like a smile, mostly on one side of his face, and he said, "You must not know Kate too good, do ya?"

If the dog hadn't been there I'd've flung the screen door open and stood above that old man. I'd've told him he didn't know what I knew, and he never would, and whatever he thought he knew about Kate was bullshit, and he'd never see her again because she'd be with me, and I wouldn't allow it. But there was a pit bull at the door, and a wall of hot air, and the feeling that if I ever went inside that room I wouldn't be able to leave. I'd be like the old man in the chair, staring at a place on the wall and hoping to die before the sun came up.

eight

Nobody saw her all summer. I drove past the house late at night, but eventually even the yellow porch light through the trees burned out. Lori heard Kate moved back to her mom's house in Oklahoma. Jeff Temple told people she always talked about going to California. He also told people Kate gave him a blow job behind the concession stand between innings of the high school baseball playoffs. After I heard him say it, the picture in my mind was like a snapshot. Jeff in his baseball uniform behind the brick wall encircling the air-conditioning unit. He's peeking over the edge of the wall with his hat backwards and baseball pants to his knees. Kate's bent over at the waist, her mouth around him, a buzz in her head from the two mixed drinks she had earlier in the car. I have to remind myself I wasn't there.

I've got very little recollection of my entire senior year of high school. Blurred images of classrooms, waiting tables in the evening, skinny dipping with the wonderful sixteen-year-old girl that night on the coast and feeling guilty about it the next day like I'd cheated on Kate, even though Kate had gone away.

I stayed to myself, mostly. My mother and I passed each other in the house. I wondered why she didn't date. Christine wasn't the type of person to mourn her husband's untimely death by remaining a widow, but outwardly she seemed to have no interest in men, or anyone else for that matter. She was a complicated person. Creative and driven, yet off to the side, lonely for a particular unseen reason.

I thought about my father often. Right after he died I found a photograph of him in a bottom drawer. As my memory of my father slowly eroded, the photograph took the place of real memories. It was the way I'd remember him my entire life. Smiling, his head turned a bit to the side like he was considering something mischievous, wearing a t-shirt, extremely alive. When I thought of him, I thought of him this way, and it always made me feel good.

"What happened to that girl?" my mother asked. I was sitting at the kitchen table in my underwear, eating a bowl of cereal. It was the first time my mother ever asked about Kate or any other girl.

"What girl?" I asked, looking down into the bowl.

"Wasn't her name Kate?" Christine asked.

I turned and looked at my mother where she stood by the refrigerator. It was the first time I'd looked at her, really looked at her, in an awfully long time. She seemed older.

"You wouldn't like her," I said.

My mother answered, "It doesn't matter whether I'd like her. It only matters whether you like her. That's kinda the point, isn't it?"

It seemed like a very profound thing to say. I was a week away from driving off to college and my mother decided to say something profound in the kitchen.

"Aren't you worried I'll fail out of college?" I asked.

"No," she said.

Between words, the kitchen was quiet. There were no bellowing televisions or radios in the house. No sounds of traffic in the neighborhood.

"Aren't you worried I'll piss away my money on beer and road trips?"

"No," my mother said.

"I mean, I'm eighteen years old. I'm driving away to college in a few days. Into the den of temptation. Aren't you worried I'll do something stupid?"

"Not really," Christine said. "Why would you start now? You've always worked hard. You're a smart kid, good with your money, you'll find your way around."

She was standing, leaning against the refrigerator, her arms crossed over a long faded blue night shirt, no bra.

"Do you ever think of Dad?" I asked.

She seemed to study me, and then smiled just a little bit. It was almost like she didn't want to do it. Didn't want the smile to get the best of her, and when it did she waited for it to come and go, her mouth slowly melting back to the way it was until there was no smile left.

"Sometimes," she said, and I knew it was true. I knew he slipped around the corners of her mind like he did with me, and I wondered what he looked like to her. What pictures she held in her memory of my father.

"Dad told me a story once," I said. "A story about two brothers robbing a motel, and one of them gets shot outside our bedroom window."

Christine didn't answer. I could see her mind had drifted free to someplace I couldn't go, a place only she and my father were allowed to go, and now it was her place alone.

I interrupted, "What are you gonna do here by yourself when I leave?"

"Same things I do now," she said.

A week later I loaded up the car to go to college. Christine left earlier that morning for some important appointment, probably scheduled just to avoid saying goodbye, and so I sat in the car in the driveway alone. I backed out, looking at the house where I grew up. Looking at my bedroom window.

In just a few minutes the car was on the highway. I rolled down the windows, turned up the radio, and started to get a certain feeling. It was the entrance into my time of selfishness, a time of free flight, between the dependence of childhood and the responsibility of age. At the moment, I didn't have the understanding to describe the feeling in words. Like so many things in this life, freedom can't be appreciated until later, after it's gone.

I found a niche in college. The stupid high school categories didn't exist. There were people from all over the world, and they seemed self-contained, more interested in standing out than fitting in. The lines between independence, fear of the future, and loneliness faded slowly, until I began to see myself in the mix.

My grades improved. In the evenings I worked at a barbeque restaurant. My clothes smelled like hickory smoke and sauce. I had a roommate who failed out after the first semester, and then another roommate who just disappeared one morning. He was there in the bed when I went to class, but when I got back he was gone. He left behind a can of Pork N Beans and one sky-blue sock. I never saw the guy again. I threw the sock in the trash and waited two weeks to eat the beans, in case he came back. His name was Barrett, Barrett Kinard I think, or something like that. I remember he wore a pair of strange rubber booties in the shower and over explained a toe fungus problem he'd had since childhood.

After the first few weeks of newness, I felt like I belonged in college. The library was vast and quiet. Between the circle of buildings, long sidewalks cut through patches of bright green grass, girls sat cross-legged on wooden benches, and towering oak trees spread shade. It was really a beautiful place to be, and I stayed there my freshman summer and into my sophomore year.

When I went home, Christine seemed happy to see me, but after a day it usually wore away and then it was like I'd never left. My room was exactly the same, which seemed strange to me. I'd changed, but my room, the place I'd fallen asleep so many nights, had the same posters on the walls, the same baseball pillowcases, and the same smell. I wondered if my mom ever sat on the edge of my bed and thought about me. Probably so, but we couldn't talk about it, and who'd want to anyway.

Eddie Miller was a year younger. At the beginning of my sophomore year, Eddie became my new roommate. He was lazy and funny and mostly unfocused. When I went to work, he went to sleep. When I went to the library, he went to the bar down the street.

"You're gonna fail, Eddie."

"Naw," he said, and smiled, lying on the couch in the middle of the day watching a soap opera. He wore shorts and a pair of white socks.

"Hey, remember that girl you used to like in high school?" he said, out of nowhere.

I still carried her with me. I hadn't seen Kate for almost two years, since the night of the party. I hadn't heard her voice. Sometimes, when I walked across campus, I'd see a girl up ahead and I'd think it was Kate Shepherd, and I'd follow her and it wouldn't be. It would be another girl instead, a girl who didn't even really look like Kate, but it would get me thinking about her and wondering where she might be.

I pretended not to remember who he was talking about. "Who?"

"That girl, Kate, the one who got drunk at David Ansley's party and disappeared."

Sitting at the old, beat-up dining room table, I flicked a piece of french fry across the wooden tabletop. It spun to the far edge and came to a stop hanging on the cliff, half-on, half-off.

"What about her?" I asked.

"I saw her last night," Eddie said, his mouth covered by the brown square couch pillow.

"What?" I asked.

"I saw her last night at the bar next door to Nicky's, up the street. She was fucked up. Could barely walk. Whatever happened to her anyway?"

I teetered on the edge. To ask another question would pull me into the reality of finding Kate Shepherd, maybe saving Kate Shepherd. Or I could just let it go. Go to work. Spend a few hours at the library. Get up tomorrow and make it to class on time as always.

"I think she had a black eye," Eddie said, watching TV as he spoke.

I had always wanted to touch her face. To hold it in my hands.

"A black eye," I repeated.

"Yeah. She looked pretty bad. Whatever happened to her anyway?" he asked again, not really expecting an answer.

I thought about it for a little while. "I don't know," I said. "I don't know what happened to her."

Eddie's eyes slowly shut like cat's eyes, and then opened up again as he floated between sleep. The show he was watching had something to do with rich people living in a very exclusive town, and a serial killer who stalked only women with red dresses.

"How can you watch that stupid shit?" I asked.

Eddie mumbled something I couldn't understand.

Somewhere in the world, in a foxhole, a soldier was glad
Eddie Miller wasn't watching his back. He was a good-
hearted guy, but fourteen hours of sleep a day is just too
much for anyone.

It was dark outside. I threw the book bag over my
shoulder and headed in the direction of the library. I
knew I wouldn't stop there. I walked past the library steps,
turned left down the side street, and ended up at the front
door of the bar next to Nicky's. It was just a hole-in-the-
wall. A long wooden bar with fifteen or twenty stools.
There were two pool tables in the back and a side area
with tables and chairs. The smoke from a million cigarettes soaked into the walls. Beer and urine, perfume and
onion rings. It was a college bar, the early crowd already in
their seats. I found a small table in the far corner and sat
with my back against the wall.

At the bar sat a guy and his girlfriend. They talked
about people they knew and drank beer out of big, cold
mugs. He didn't look at her as she spoke, but she almost
always looked at him, like he might get away if she didn't
pay enough attention. As she drank down the beer in
front of her and ordered another, the girl's voice got pro-
gressively louder and louder and the guy joined the
conversation less and less. He stared off into the distance.

Two big white guys and one skinny black man shot
pool to my left. The black man was older, maybe fifty, and
leaned over the table to line up his shot, a cigarette hanging from the side of his mouth. The smoke caused his eyes
to narrow until it looked like he was closing his eyes on

purpose to shoot a blind shot. He wasn't as good as the white guys thought he was, but I sat in my chair and watched him win game after game anyway. Money changed hands.

I recognized a few people in the bar. Just enough to nod my head. Whenever a figure would appear at the door, my head would swing around to look. But Kate wasn't there. Maybe Eddie was wrong. Maybe it was somebody who looked like Kate. What would she be doing there anyway?

It was dark outside. I'd had all I could stand of the drunk girl at the bar telling a story about the day she almost drowned at the beach. By the end of the story I wished she had drowned. Maybe her boyfriend could find some peace. I grabbed up my book bag off the table and left the barroom.

Outside the door, to my right, were a few restaurants and other bars. It was fairly well lit, with people roaming around outside. To the left, the street headed into a more residential area. I went left and planned to cut across the railroad tracks back to campus and then to my apartment on the other side.

A police car passed and the red-headed officer eyed me. I walked down the sidewalk, cracked and broken with roots pushing up from underneath, and thought about the old saying, "Step on a crack, break your mama's back." What a terrible thing to tell a child.

Up ahead I saw the dark figure of a person sitting on the curb of the street. She was huddled over, her arms wrapped around her bent knees, her face turned to the side, resting cheek-down on the top of one knee.

It was a girl, or a woman, with dark hair and some kind of dark, flowing dress. As I got closer I could hear her humming, more like a lyric mumble, and she rocked her body forward and back slowly.

I got behind her, only a few yards away, and stopped. Was it Kate? It looked like her from the back. But I couldn't see her face and I couldn't make out the words she hummed. Next to her was a small bottle, and next to the bottle, in the light from a passing car, I saw a glass pipe.

She said in a low voice, "It's the only color I know."

Was it Kate's voice? It sounded like it. I moved closer and leaned my body over hers. A car passed, and I could see part of her cheek and the edge of her chin. The rest was covered by brown hair hanging down.

There was a part of me that wanted badly to walk away and not know. The part that never missed a class, and showed up early at work, and knew Eddie would fail. The part that balanced my checkbook, and looked forward to my time in the library, and secretly liked the way my boyhood room never changed. But Kate had been with me all along, and I couldn't make myself walk away without knowing.

She said, "He held it in his hand. I saw it." And it sounded less like Kate because she said it drawn-out and slurred. I wasn't sure how to feel about wishing it was Kate, or wishing it wasn't, or hoping it was someone else lost in this big world. And I wasn't sure if I was still a savior, but I remembered the man in Kate's house that night, sitting in the darkness, his foot propped up and rotten, waiting for something to happen. He was probably dead by now.

"Kate?" I whispered, the same as I had the time she was passed out in the back of Lori's car.

"Is that you?" I said.

She didn't respond, just kept rocking. Kept humming.

So I reached my hand down to pull back the brown hair. I touched it, and pushed it back off her face. I held it that way until another car passed, and in the few seconds of light from the headlights I saw it was Kate Shepherd, the girl I'd thought about for so long. Alone, her eye black, sitting on a street curb talking to no one, a crack pipe by her side.

There wasn't much thinking to do. I'd been through it a million times in my mind. I knelt down, put my arm under her knees, the other arm on her back, and lifted the girl off the ground, my book bag on my back. She didn't flinch. She just put her face into my shoulder, and I could feel the low hum against my skin under the fabric of my shirt.

nine

It's the nature of this round world, spinning around and around in circles, eventually everything comes back to you if you only wait. Kate came back to me, and I carried her across the campus that night. Her bones were light, but even so, by the time I reached my apartment the muscles in my arms were burning.

I put her down on my bed. Eddie was out for the night and his bedroom was dark. I sat down in the chair across the room from her and stretched out my arms on each side, feeling the burn slowly dissipate. It was dark in the room, and quiet, with the only light coming from the kitchen. Kate's breathing was low and the mumbling had stopped. She was asleep like a child, completely, with no cares and no idea where she slept and who watched.

In my mind, like I said before, I'd rehearsed a million

times the moment like the one on the street when I picked up Kate and took her away, but after that moment of gallantry I hadn't really considered what would happen next. Now she was here, in my bed. The moment of gallantry was over. My arms didn't burn anymore. This girl, a girl I really barely knew, would wake up in my room. She might not even remember my name. Should I take off her dress and put on a t-shirt and a pair of my shorts? Where should I be sitting when she opens her eyes?

I sat in the chair and just let my mind spin like the world. It was done. She was still pretty, thinner than I remembered, but with the same gentle face and presence. It didn't matter where she'd gone the night of David Ansley's party until I saw her sitting on the curb. We were together like I knew we'd be.

I heard the front door open and close around two-thirty in the morning. Eddie was home. I hadn't slept all night. No part of me wanted to sleep. I saw him walk past my bedroom door on the way to the bathroom. He sounded like a racehorse pissing on a cookie sheet. It went on and on until I couldn't believe any man's bladder could hold so much beer. On the way back down the hall Eddie stopped at my open door. He craned his neck inside to see me sitting in the chair. He turned his head a click to see Kate in my bed. I could smell the burnt smell of cigarettes and spilled beer from ten feet away.

Eddie entered the room quietly. We still hadn't spoken. He stood by the bed between me and Kate, looking down at her. I rose from the chair and stood next to him.

"She's beautiful," I whispered.

Eddie didn't say anything. He looked at me, and I could see in his face he didn't agree. I could tell he was confused about the situation, the girl in my bed, and the fact I'd gone and found Kate at the bar next to Nicky's. He didn't see her the way I did. Maybe nobody would. But for the first time, the very first time, it was clear to me I saw Kate Shepherd physically different than other people saw her.

Eddie went to his room and closed his door too hard, the way drunk people sometimes do. I sat back down in the chair. When I woke up and opened my eyes, Kate was looking at me from her place on the pillow. The morning light from the window was a deep yellow. Her eyes were brown like I remembered. A rich brown, the darkness of chocolate. We looked at each other for a few seconds, and then a few seconds longer. It lasted so long I wondered if one of us might be dead, but I was afraid to move. Afraid of what she might say, the first words that might come from her mouth. Finally, finally, she smiled. It wasn't much, just a tiny upturn of the mouth, but it was a smile. No doubt about it.

And then she said in a voice I could barely hear, "Early Winwood."

She remembered my name. To hear her speak it was the best possibility. It allowed the moment to float forward, the potential to remain unlimited. Maybe it was better than I'd imagined. Maybe she came looking for me. Maybe it was no natural coincidence her world crossed mine outside a bar on that certain night.

"What are you doing here?" she whispered, childlike.

"You're in my apartment. You're in my bed. I carried you here."

The expression on her face didn't change, and we were staring at each other again for impossible periods of time. But as the minutes passed, the discomfort of the silence left the room, steadily, until there was no discomfort at all. We just looked at each other, and I stopped trying to figure out what she was thinking, or what she might say next.

"Where are your parents?" she asked.

"My mom's at home. My father is a writer in New York City," I said.

For the life of me I don't know why I lied. I'd never said such a thing to anyone before. As soon as it left my mouth I wished it was never said, but there didn't seem to be a way to take it back or explain it. The lie hung between us. It occurred to me she thought we were at my house back home. She didn't even know what town she was in.

"Where do you live now?" I asked.

Kate's face on the pillow didn't move. Her words were certain.

"Here," she said.

More time passed. Maybe five minutes. Maybe more. I can't be sure.

"Where's your stuff?"

"I don't know," she said.

I reminded Kate where I'd found her the night before. Her eyes drifted from me to the window and then back to me like she was searching for a memory, found it, and brought the memory to her lips to speak it.

"There's a house down the block from there, a yellow house. My suitcase is upstairs."

I stood from the chair and left the room. The yellow house was where she said it would be. A girl from my business class passed me on the sidewalk. It would be the first class I'd missed all semester.

I knocked on the front door. There was no answer. I knocked again. Still nothing.

I tried the doorknob. It was unlocked. The house was a wreck inside. A rolled up carpet rested upright against the far wall. Ratty clothes, towels, and trash were strewn across the floor. It wasn't the remnants of a party the night before. It was old trash, the smell of neglect and decay. A house uncared for.

I didn't call out. I turned up the stairs and walked slowly, listening for any sound. I stopped at the top of the staircase. Still no noise inside the house. The air was musty and stale, like an attic. I moved slowly into the first bedroom to the left. In the corner, on a thin, stained mattress, was a body. The body of a man asleep on his back, bare chested. He was unshaven, one sock on and one sock off. Next to the mattress was a bent aluminum can with the tell-tale black residue on top and a pack of open restaurant matches.

The room stunk of human odor. Clothes were scattered on the floor. There was a hole the size of a fist through the sheetrock near the man's head and a splattered stain on the ceiling. I was disgusted at the idea of Kate inside a place such as that. Anywhere in the house. Anywhere near the man asleep on the piss-stained mattress.

"Where's Kate's stuff?" I said.

He didn't move. He didn't even twitch. He didn't jump up, startled the way a normal person would be startled by a stranger standing in their bedroom. The man's mouth was open, and I could hear his body sucking air inside him, despite everything.

I raised my voice, surprised by the angry edge, "Where's Kate's stuff?"

The man began to open his eyes, struggling against the glare from the window. He lifted his hand to his face to shield the light and finally focused on me standing near the doorway.

All he said was, "Fuck you." That's all he had to say. That's all that came out of his mouth, and it's all it took for me to lose control of myself like I'd never done in my entire life.

The reaction was instant. There was no internal discussion. No weighing the options. The anger was overwhelming. I was over him, the first kick landing squarely in his rib cage. My fist came down against the side of his face with a force I'd never felt, bones crushed underneath. The second punch, and then the third, and I could feel spit flying against my face, his and mine. And I swear to God I wanted to kill the man. There was blood on the wall around the hole in the sheetrock, blood on my hands. It was violence I'd never imagined could come from me. Extreme and beyond control, with my fist down again against his teeth, caving inside, and I wanted to bite him, rip a piece of his flesh away in my mouth before I fell backwards from the force of my own rage and stood again over the man I'd brutally beaten in his bed, his face in his hands, curled into a fetal position, soundless and wet.

I said, "Where's Kate's stuff?"

One of his hands left his face, slowly and then upwards until the index finger separated from the ball of blood and pointed down the hall.

I left the man and went to the next room. There was a big blue suitcase open on the floor with clothes out and around. In the corner of the room was a pile of burnt things, looked like a newspaper and a child's doll, with black streaks and soot up the wall nearly to the ceiling. I put the loose clothes in the suitcase, zipped the sides, and carried it down the stairs like it was a normal day in a normal house, a normal man carrying a suitcase, with blood beginning to dry on my right hand, beginning to feel stiff over the skin.

When I got back to the apartment Eddie was sitting at the old wooden dining room table, eating a bowl of cereal. He watched me carry the suitcase into my bedroom. Kate wasn't in the bed, and I thought she'd gone. I thought he'd let her walk out the door. But then there was a sound from the bathroom. The sound of vomiting retching.

I opened the bathroom door. Kate was on the floor, her head resting on the toilet seat. I wiped her mouth with a towel. Her eyes still closed, and I wondered if she knew it was me, or maybe thought it was the man in the yellow house. But when she opened her eyes there was no look of surprise.

"I got your things from the house," I said.

She looked up at me, and again I was struck by the

way she stared. I thought of Jeff Temple's story of the time behind the concession stand during the baseball game, and I knew it couldn't be true. I imagined the man on the mattress in the yellow house was Jeff Temple, his baseball cap on backwards, pants down to his knees, a smile on his bloody face.

"I'm pregnant," she said.

In hindsight, these many years later, it was the moment I could have let myself off the hook. It was the fork in the road. I probably should have been rattling off questions like, who's the father? How can you get drunk and use drugs with a baby inside you? Did you plan to bring your child home to the room in the yellow house with the burnt doll and rancid smell and the man sleeping on a piss-stained mattress?

But those questions never entered my mind. Instead, I could see her clothes hanging in my closet, making room for her underwear in the chest of drawers, asking my boss for a few days off of work to get Kate settled, finding a doctor, being with her during the first days her body craved the drug, wiping the vomit from the side of her mouth.

And then, with the same uncharacteristic lack of thought I displayed in the violent attack earlier, I said out loud, "We can get married."

For a moment I wasn't actually sure I said the words loud enough to be heard. Kate's face was unchanged. There was no reaction at all, and for some reason I thought of my father, and his hand in mine when we walked together one morning on a beach a long time ago, when I was maybe four or five years old.

"What do you want to be when you grow up?" he asked.

And I said, "I want to be with you."

He squeezed my hand a little tighter and looked down at me as we walked. When he looked back up across the water there was a smile on his face not meant for anyone but him. A pride in me, his son, he never found anywhere else. And I wondered what he would think of me as I lowered the towel and wiped the glistening saliva from Kate's chin where it rested on the toilet seat.

ten

We talked all day. I fixed Kate a sandwich for lunch. She told me about leaving the party that night, and getting a ride home, packing a bag and leaving her father sitting in the living room where I found him later.

"I went to Oklahoma to stay with my mother and her boyfriend, but she just had a new baby. It didn't work out."

"Where'd you go from there?"

Kate answered my questions with a tired indifference. She was worn out, surviving for the sake of survival when there was nothing else better to do.

"A boy in the trailer park, his name was Darren, offered me a ride to California. I had a friend who lived in Sacramento. We mostly slept in the car…"

Her eyes drifted past me again, and she seemed to remember something she'd forgotten.

"Let's talk about something else," she said. "Let's talk about you."

I told her about my job, and taking business classes. I told her about Eddie, and the time we got caught stealing. And then I told her about going to her house that night and talking to her father.

"He was sitting in the dark. There was a dog at the door. When's the last time you talked to him?" I asked.

"That night."

"You haven't talked to your father since then?"

She didn't answer right away. She didn't even seem to hear my question. I waited.

Kate said, "Why did you go to my house that night?"

It was the question I knew would come eventually. The dilemma I expected to face. Should I tell her about my infatuation? Would she consider my dedication honorable or creepy?

Through the years, in anticipation of such a conversation, I'd changed my mind back and forth. Eventually, I'd settled on a middle ground, waiting to size up Kate's reaction, waiting to actually get to know her before gauging her possibilities.

"I was just worried about you."

I thought about Jeff Temple, the cigar in one hand and beer in the other, standing by the pool, laughing. I thought about the man on the mattress in the yellow house.

"Do you have a boyfriend?" I asked.

She smiled, and even though I'd seen her smile earlier, I'd forgotten what it did to me.

"No," she said, like she'd never been asked before.

I called in sick to work. Kate took a shower and we ordered pizza. My mind was a whirlwind of ideas and plans. In the mirror, accidentally, I caught a glimpse of Kate in her bra and panties. It was only a glimpse, maybe lasted one second, and I turned away, but it was a remarkable one second. I can still see her closely in my mind, wet hair, bent over slightly looking for something in the drawer, white panties, freckles on her back. She seemed not to recognize the value of her body, just moving around like nothing at all.

It was nighttime again. The whole day had passed and we'd never left the apartment, barely stepping foot outside my room. We sat down on the bed together. Kate smelled clean. I held a notepad and pen in my lap.

"Do you want to make your life better?" I asked sincerely.

Kate smiled. "Yeah," she said.

"I mean really? Do you seriously want to make your life better? Because we can do it. We can sit here and list out every part of your life, and under each part list out how to solve the problems, how to make each part better."

She seemed not to understand, so I moved forward.

"See, on this first page we'll break down the sections of your life: education, employment, finances."

I wrote as I spoke, making sure to pick the most general categories first.

She was hesitant. "Okay," she finally said, and then asked, "What else?"

"Well, family relationships. Maybe substance abuse issues. The baby."

Kate touched her hand to her belly, reminding herself it was real. My categories had become more specific. She could see I'd thought about what I was saying. She seemed to be impressed I'd taken the time to break her life into identifiable pieces, something she'd never considered.

"What else?" she asked curiously.

"Maybe, spirituality. I don't know. And long-term goals, like marriage, maybe."

We both looked down at the list I'd made, top to bottom, in a column like a grocery list. Like we could go to the store and pick out each of the items and mark them off one by one.

"Now what?" she asked.

"Well, we turn over to the next page, and we write the first thing on the list at the top of the next page in big letters. Education. And then, underneath, we write down what kind of education you want and how to make it happen. Do you want to enroll in college here? What kind of classes do you want to take? Would you rather go to nursing school, or one of those places they teach you to be a court reporter, or what? What do you want to be when you grow up?"

We both laughed at the idea we weren't already grown up.

After a moment, Kate said, "I don't have any money."

"Don't worry about that part yet. Let's just talk about what you want. Then we'll talk about how to get it."

I could tell she'd never even asked herself the question. Probably her mother and father had never asked her the question, because it wasn't a possibility. It wasn't something possible, and so there was no point. It wasn't a subject avoided. It was no subject at all. The same as they probably never discussed how many light years it takes to reach the furthest star, or why our blood comes out red. I thought again about the man in the chair, beaten down by the day, a bullet hole through the top of his foot, in the dark.

I said the words again, "What do you want?"

She looked like a child. "I think I'd like to take some history classes. I always liked history."

I was surprised by her answer, and excited for her. She'd probably never told anybody before, and then a wave of unforseen anger came over me. She'd spread herself naked for men, maybe sucked the dick of Jeff Temple like he said, given herself away in so many ways, and none of those people cared a shit about what she wanted, and maybe I was too late. She was pregnant with another man's baby. Who knew what they'd done to her, all of them, and now I was charting how to fix it. How to fix everything, right down to the details.

I wrote, "History classes, enroll for next semester," and closed my eyes halfway through, the words tailing off down and away.

We stayed up for hours, talking and writing down pages of notes underneath capitalized titles. She had credit card debts. Her brother lived in New Mexico. She believed in God, but thought he'd given up on us and wasn't really paying attention anymore to what was going on.

We circled employment opportunities in the Classified section of the newspaper, weighing the advantages and disadvantages of each type of job. I balanced a hypothetical budget based on what the two of us could make, plus Eddie's share of the rent, and took into consideration a monthly payment toward Kate's credit card debt. The interest accrued at a rate higher than we could pay down, an endless cycle of wasted resources.

She didn't want to see her father again, and didn't like to talk much about her mother in Oklahoma.

"Do you know if you're having a girl or a boy?"

"I don't know. It feels like a girl."

"Do you have any names picked out?"

"No."

"Why not?"

"I'm just now gettin' used to the idea there's somethin' living inside me. I haven't gotten around to naming it yet."

On the pad of paper, I wrote down, Baby Names.

We both stared at the page.

Finally Kate said, "I like the name Gretchen."

I wrote it slowly on the paper. Gretchen. Kate said it out loud again. It was old-fashioned, original. I hadn't heard the name in a long time.

"I like it," I said. No one spoke for awhile as we stared at the word on the page. Seeing the written name made it more real.

"You can't do any more drugs, Kate. And you can't drink. Not just for yourself. For the baby."

"I know," she said.

"Do you need help, or can you do it yourself?"

"I can do it myself. It's just a diversion. I don't need it."

We were sitting very close together, our heads nearly

touching as we leaned over the pad, backs against a mound
of pillows stacked at the headboard of my small bed.

She smelled glorious, a clean soapy smell mixed with
a soft, feminine scent. I glanced down and could see the
top of her breasts, light brown and smooth, leading to the
border of the white bra just north of the nipple line. I felt
a stir in my shorts. Just a stir at first, but as my imagination slid slowly across Kate's body the stir became a full
erection, hidden behind the yellow pad of paper in my
lap. I felt my breathing deepen and wondered if she knew.

Her face rolled to my face and I felt Kate's lips brush
my cheek and stop. She kissed me. I'd been through it a
thousand times in my head. In cars, hotel rooms, open
fields. There was almost a familiarity, an expectation, but
in reality it was new ground.

I turned my face until our lips touched and closed my
eyes. There was a moment, a tiny fleeting moment, when
I wondered if it was real or just another vivid, detailed
daydream. And I moved against her, and we kissed. And I
moved again until I was above, and she was below, and I
could feel her breasts pushed against my chest, and our
hips together with the pressure in between.

My left hand found its way and cupped Kate's breast,
firm, but not too firm, a light squeeze, and the desire to have
it in my mouth. I pushed downward, my lips on her neck,
and then slowly to the skin of the chest and then up against
the place I wished to bury myself, the softness and the smell
like nothing my imagination had been able to capture.

I slid back up and kissed her again on the mouth,
harder, and felt Kate's legs wrap around my waist. It was

actually happening, and I tried not to think about it. I tried just to do the next thing, think the next thought, apart from the whole. And with our clothes still on, Kate started a slow rhythm, our bodies moving together into each other, and God help me it was more than I could control, and the instant came upon me like a wave of water and I raised up with involuntary sounds from my mouth, and Kate must have known because she pulled me to her and held me hard, wrapped up in arms and legs until the shuddering stopped and the embarrassment came quietly down upon me like a dark blanket. It was the sign of things to come.

"I'm sorry." I whispered. "It's never happened before."

When I said it, I was actually thinking it had never happened before in all those vivid daydreams. Those dreams of red panties and short skirts always ended well, the timing perfect.

I rolled off her and we lay side by side, looking up at the dotted ceiling. I felt the yellow pad under me and didn't bother to move. I was afraid to look at Kate, but when her breathing began to come and go in a rhythmic flow I finally looked over to see her eyes closed. I worried about what had happened and felt the wetness in my underwear, but our arms were locked together so I didn't try to get up, and lying next to Kate Shepherd, her breathing slowly put me to sleep.

I woke up alone to the sound of the front door gently closing. The clock showed 1:13 A.M. Kate was gone. I bolted up from the bed and changed clothes quickly. I ran outside and headed in the direction of campus, watching for figures of people moving in the dark shadows or under the lamp lights.

I traveled in the direction of the yellow house, hoping I would be wrong. Hoping there would be a simple explanation, until I found myself on the street of restaurants and bars, looking left and looking right, and there she was, with her back to me, walking in the direction of the yellow house, and the man on the floor, and the burnt doll in the corner of the room.

I followed at a safe distance. Maybe she forgot something? Maybe I'd left behind a dress or a shoe when I zipped up her bag? She turned up the walkway to the yellow house, its windows dark. I stepped into a bar off the street and found a place to stand where I could see Kate and the house. She went inside without knocking. Just walked into the dark house.

Somebody behind me said, "You want anything, buddy?"

It was the bartender. A big guy with curly blonde hair and a t-shirt with no sleeves.

"Yeah," I said, "a cigarette."

He didn't hesitate. The big man pulled a pack of cigarettes from his top pocket and with one hand shook out a single cigarette. He held the pack out to me and I took it.

I never really understood the idea of addiction to cigarettes. I'd smoked off and on but never felt the physical demand. It was just a cigarette, and with a pack of matches from the top of the bar I lit the end and stood next to the open swinging doors, my eyes fixed on the yellow house halfway down the short block.

Ten minutes passed. I glanced back and forth at the big clock behind the bar. How long would I wait? Was Kate in some type of trouble? I picked a number, twenty minutes, and decided I'd go get her if she didn't come out by that point.

I thought about what happened earlier. How awkward it became so quickly, and how she'd fallen asleep without so much as a word about it. Maybe she didn't consider it a problem? Maybe she considered it a compliment? I would, if I could cause a girl to shudder in pleasure with a simple kiss and the mere touch of a breast.

Fifteen minutes passed. I noticed the bartender watching me, suspicious, or maybe just curious about my presence and the importance of something down the street and the passing minutes on the clock.

I decided at seventeen minutes I'd start walking down the block. I estimated, at the twenty minute mark, I'd be standing at the door of the yellow house ready to do whatever I needed to do.

I stepped out of the bar onto the sidewalk as the second hand crossed the twelve. At that exact moment, Kate came out the front door of the yellow house. I took a backwards step through the open door into the bar, feeling the bartender's eyes on me. Kate held nothing in her hands and walked back the way she'd come, eventually passing me in the bar as I moved in a step behind a large plant between us. I couldn't read anything on her face. Her hands were in her jean pockets. I ran out of the bar in the opposite direction, jumped a chain-link fence, and ran in the dark over the railroad tracks around the Arts & Sciences Building back to my apartment. I got inside, took off my shoes, and struggled to catch my breath.

Should I lie down and pretend I was still asleep, or should I confront Kate with what I'd seen? Was it a one-time thing, or would I always wake in the night alone, wondering?

I sat down in the chair in the bedroom. The front door opened, and closed, gently. Kate came around the corner through my bedroom door. She looked at me, and I couldn't tell anything from the look.

"Hey," she said.

"Hey," I said back. I waited, but only a few seconds, and then said, "Where'd you go?"

"For a walk. I couldn't sleep."

Maybe it was true. Maybe she couldn't sleep. Maybe she just had one last loose end to tie up before she changed her life. I wanted very much to believe.

Kate came slowly across the room, bent at her waist, and kissed me on the lips, casual, comfortable, like she'd done it a thousand times before and planned to do it a thousand times more. It was all I needed.

eleven

Eddie never asked me anything about the girl living in our apartment, which was odd, but I suppose not so odd as my going out into the night and bringing the lost girl home in the first place.

In a short time I crossed over some sexual barrier into a place I never knew existed. A place of experimentation, comfort, physical pleasure, and it left me dumb and hypnotized, like an opium addict. We wouldn't leave the room for days, choosing the flesh over reason, another position over food. I had no idea it could be like that, and Kate seemed happy to be locked away and safe. I spent hours exploring every portion of her skin, every fold, especially the parts I didn't have myself.

"I feel like I'm at the doctor's office," she said once, and I felt stupid, so I turned off the flashlight.

Sometimes, when Kate slept, I'd go through the written plan, adding things and marking things off. Kate got a job as a hostess at a restaurant. She enrolled in only two history classes, deciding to take it slow in the beginning until the baby was born.

Eddie failed out, as I knew he would. He packed his things and left on a Wednesday evening without much fanfare. We had more space, but it certainly didn't help in the rent department. I put Kate in charge of the utility bills so she could handle her own money and gain a little confidence. Sometimes, right after we accomplished a particular goal, I'd make a big deal out of pulling the yellow pad from under the bed, turning to a certain page, and marking a dark line though the word on the list. I didn't notice until much later how little Kate really cared about my list, and marking things off, and any of the rest of it.

For a month and a half we were like a happy little married couple, wrapped up in each other in my small bed, taking turns cooking inexpensive meals, even studying together. I felt like it could be that way forever if I could only lock the door, nail boards over the windows, keep out the world and everybody in it. We could be like two humans kidnapped from Earth, taken by aliens to another planet to be observed naked in a homelike setting, except for no telephones or televisions, and nobody else to talk to, self-contained and happy, fornicating and eating ice cream all day. But we couldn't live that way for long, and eventually the world outside would seep under the door and we'd have to pay bills or file taxes or clean out the wad of hair from the sink drain.

Kate's little belly swelled. I could rest my head on top and listen deep inside. It was hard to imagine a baby in there, floating quietly in a sack of warm liquid. And if my head happened to be resting in a particular direction, guilt would mix with lust to form a separate uncomfortable feeling, until the lust would eventually win out.

"I know it's not my baby inside you, but it feels like my baby."

Kate didn't say anything.

"If we get married, she'll have my last name. They'll put me on the birth certificate."

I thought I felt something move next to my cheek underneath Kate's skin. I stayed still and waited to feel it again. Waited for the confirmation.

"Should we tell her?" I asked.

Kate didn't say anything. She had her hand on the top of my head, rubbing lightly through the hair. Maybe she wasn't listening at all.

Sometimes I imagine waking up in the morning to see a giant eye on the horizon. The Earth held up between a huge index finger and a thumb, being examined, the way we might examine a child's marble. And seeing the giant eye, and knowing the Earth is just a single grain of sand on the beach of some planet far away, I am relieved of worry and responsibility for everything and anything.

What a wonderful burden Jesus carried, all of mankind on his shoulders, when I'm allowed to save only two, Kate and the baby. But at the same time, what a relief it must have been to be tortured to death on the cross by those Romans, set free of worry and responsibility, at least for a little while. Some things were only meant to be carried for short distances.

"Let's go up to the courthouse and get married," I said.

Kate's hand stopped rubbing my head, and then started again.

"When?" she asked.

"Now," I said.

I couldn't see her face and didn't want to. Hesitation was unwelcome. Inane questions were unwelcome. There was just me, and her, and whoever was inside of her, and the giant eye on the horizon. There was just Jesus, and the Romans, and the wonderful burden.

"Okay," she said, matter-of-factly. Not overjoyed, not sad, but without much hesitation, and naked, with my head resting on her warm belly, pointed in the wrong direction on purpose.

I rose and started to get dressed, very conscious of each muscle, each movement, listening behind me for sounds of Kate rising from the bed, getting dressed for our marriage.

I hadn't told my mother. I hadn't even told her Kate was living in my apartment, or Eddie had failed out, or I was on the verge of changing every single thing about my old life. But as I got dressed I imagined sitting at the kitchen table telling my mother all about it, and having Christine, braless and distant, listen to everything I had to say. And then the phone would ring, and she'd hurry out of the house, leaving me at the kitchen table, mid-sentence, with both of us knowing it was her way of showing me how much she really cared.

Kate brushed her hair. She wore a blue sundress, light blue, loose around her waist so no one could see the bulge. I wanted to ask her if she'd always dreamed of a big wedding, with a white dress and bridesmaids, maybe a band at the reception and shrimp cocktail. But I didn't ask her, because I didn't want to know. I hated the possibility she was disappointed, it wasn't the way she'd dreamed it would be. So we kept getting dressed, brushing our teeth in silence except for a few short sentences.

"Have you seen my other shoe?"

"No."

And then a few minutes later, "Is this your other shoe?"

"Yes."

I'd saved every extra penny for the past weeks. In the car, on the way to the courthouse I said, "Afterwards, we could go out to eat."

"That would be good," she said, but I couldn't tell much from the way she said it. My usual sharp instincts of perception had become dull and self-centered like the opium addict.

I let my left hand sneak down from the steering wheel to my left pocket. The bump in the pocket was my grandmother's ring. She gave it to me when my father died. We were alone in her kitchen after the funeral. She didn't make a big production of it.

"One day," she said, "you'll meet a special girl." And she placed the ring in the palm of my hand and bent my fingers inward into a fist around the ring. Now it was in my pocket, all clean and old-fashioned.

The lady at the marriage license desk asked us questions. She liked to guess to herself which couples were pregnant. I could tell by the way she glanced at Kate's belly from time to time, unsure. I wondered if some of the questions she asked were really necessary or if maybe she just enjoyed knowing things about other people. People getting married. Pregnant people.

We walked upstairs and sat in a judge's office. The secretary was too busy to ask us anything and simply said the judge would be with us shortly.

My stomach felt like I'd swallowed a pinecone. One of those hard green pinecones, and after it sat awhile in the juices of my stomach, the pine cone must have expanded. Kate looked down at her hands. We both thought about the baby inside her. We both had all those natural and unnatural doubts. I thought maybe if the judge didn't come out soon one of us might get up and leave, not in a hurry, but just get up and go outside and heave up a green pinecone.

"The judge will see you now."

We went in the office where he stood in a black robe. The secretary sat down against the wall. She was the witness. There's always a witness.

We shook hands with the judge and made small talk. He looked over the marriage license and then opened a small notebook.

My knees were weak, and I tried to think about the yellow pad under the bed, and the lists, and how good it was to rest my head on her soft belly and listen inside, and my grandmother, and my father's hand holding mine.

Mostly his voice when he told me things I needed to know.

"Marriage is an institution of divine appointment and commended as honorable among all people. It is the most important step in life, and therefore should not be entered into unadvisedly or lightly, but discreetly and soberly," the judge said.

It was like a train beginning to move and slowly picking up speed. Once it started, it would be damn near impossible to stop, and I was glad.

"Into this estate these two persons come now to be joined. If any person can show just cause why they may not be lawfully joined together, let them speak or else hereafter forever hold their peace."

I turned around and looked at the secretary. She was staring blankly at the floor. She'd probably stood quietly by as thousands of ill-suited idiots married each other, only to eventually end up back in the courthouse fighting over kitchen tables and visitation rights.

"Wilt thou, James Early Winwood, have this woman to be thy wedded wife, to live together after God's Ordinance in the estate of matrimony? Wilt thou love her, comfort her, honor and keep her in sickness and in health; and forsaking all others, keep thee only unto her, so long as ye both shall live?"

"I will," I said.

"Wilt thou, Katherine Anne Shepherd, have this man to be thy wedded husband, to live together after God's Ordinance in the holy estate of matrimony? Wilt thou love him, comfort him, honor and keep him in sickness and in health; and forsaking all others, keep thee only unto him so long as ye both shall live?"

I looked at the side of Kate's face. She was crying just a little bit. I wanted to hold her right there, and tell them to leave us alone. Let us lock the door and cover the windows and stay in my room forever with the aliens watching us through the glass.

"I will," she said.

"Please join your right hands."

My hand was wet, and her hand was wet, and we held hands because the judge told us to.

"Repeat after me, please," he said, and I did as he directed.

"I, James Early Winwood, take thee, Katharine Anne Shepherd, to be my wedded wife, to have and to hold from this day forward, for better, for worse, for richer or poorer, in sickness and in health, to love and to cherish till death us do part, according to God's holy Ordinance."

I stopped repeating at the tail end, thinking for a moment he said, "God's holy orifice." I looked at Kate, and I think she thought the same thing because we smiled at each other like no one else could see us, like the judge was a robot.

The judge looked at Kate and said, "Repeat after me." And she did.

"I, Katherine Anne Shepherd, take thee, James Early Winwood, to be my wedded husband, to have and to hold from this day forward, for better, for worse, for richer or poorer, in sickness and in health, to love and to cherish till death us do part, according to God's holy Ordinance."

And right when he said the last part Kate and I looked

at each other again, and she started laughing, and God help me, I'd forgotten what her laugh could do to me. It was a medicine.

The judge said politely, "The ring?"

I reached my left hand deep into the pocket and pulled out my grandmother's diamond ring. Kate held up her left hand with a look of surprise on her face, and I slipped the ring onto her finger.

That was that, I thought. That was the hardest part.

The judge said, "Inasmuch as this man and this woman have in the presence of God and these witnesses, consented to be joined together in the bonds of matrimony, I do now pronounce them husband and wife.

"Ephesians: Husbands love your wives, even as Christ also loved the church and gave himself for it…He that loveth his wife loveth himself.

"May the Lord bless and keep you, may he make his face to shine upon you, may the Lord lift up his countenance upon you, and give you his peace now and evermore. Amen."

And when he was finished saying what he had to say, I kissed Kate Shepherd long and hard in the judge's office, and she kissed me back in front of the witness. It was almost like the act of marriage was the proof we needed that Kate loved me, and I loved her, for all the right reasons, and it wasn't as crazy as it seemed.

There was a sound like a gunshot. And then silence. Through a window we saw men in uniforms running. Heavy footsteps down the hallway.

I looked to the judge, but he looked afraid, and he looked at the secretary who had broken free of her trance. A large deputy sheriff came through the office door.

"Judge, there's been a shooting downstairs. I'm gonna take all four of you through the back entrance, evacuate the building."

The judge asked, "Has anyone been hurt?"

"Yes," he said.

No one wanted to move. It seemed pointless, and the next day, in the newspaper, sitting in my fucked up little room, I read about what happened in the courthouse on our wedding day.

ON TUESDAY AFTERNOON at 2:15, shots rang out in the County Courthouse. Investigators believe Clay Namen (age 28), and his estranged wife, Jamie (age 26), were embroiled in a custody battle over their six year old daughter, Deanna. The case was scheduled for a trial in the Courtroom of Judge Francis, and according to authorities the Court broke for lunch after the wife concluded her testimony.

Apparently, by yet unknown means, Clay Namen was able to smuggle a gun past the security checkpoint and into the Courthouse. A spokesman for the Sheriff's department refused to speculate and stated only, "This has never happened before."According to sources, after lunch Mr. Namen testified in the hearing, acknowledging he had made mistakes during the couple's marriage, but begging the judge for the opportunity to see his daughter regularly. Witnesses report that before the judge issued a ruling, and during another break in the trial, Clay Namen fired a single shot in the hallway in the direction of his wife. The bullet missed Jamie Namen and apparently ricocheted off the wall, striking the six-year-old child in her face.

The child was pronounced dead upon arrival at St. Martin Hospital.

PART II

somewhere in between

It was just a regular day. The doctor's appointment was scheduled in the afternoon. It was the day we expected to see the sonogram and learn if it was a boy or a girl inside. I knew there was a part of me resentful of this baby, but I suppressed the resentment and tried not to think back to Kate's time away from me, and the yellow house and all the other possibilities, but instead to the plan mapped out on the pad of paper under the bed.

We sat in the waiting room with the other pregnant women, some with men next to them. I wondered if they were the fathers, or just men waiting for something in the waiting room. Anything. A place to wait quietly, apart from all the hustle and bustle outside.

"Are you nervous?" I asked Kate.

"Yes, I've got to pee."

We were called to the back, and I sat on a stool in the corner of the room. The doctor placed the stethoscope on Kate's belly, moving the silver circle from one spot to another.

"Excuse me just a moment," he said, and left the room.

Kate lifted herself up on her elbows. "Do you think anything's the matter?" she said.

"No, nothing's the matter. He probably just forgot something in the other room. Don't worry."

But she looked worried, and somehow the silence and the disinfected environment didn't help like it should have.

The doctor came back in the room with a nurse. This time the nurse moved the silver circle around on Kate's belly, listening.

The doctor said, "I couldn't pick up the baby's heartbeat. It's not unusual. Sometimes Shelley is better at it than me."

The room fell silent again. Any second I expected Shelley to say, "There it is. I hear it," but she didn't, and the moment expanded slowly like a balloon filled with warm air until there was a pressure all around us.

The nurse said, "Let me try the other one."

She left, and the doctor followed, leaving us alone again.

"Oh, God," Kate said. "Something's the matter."

"No, it's not. Nothing's the matter. You heard the doctor, it's not unusual."

I believed what I said. I'd imagined the birth of the baby, our lives together, even crazy things like one day encountering the natural father, but my mind had never imagined no heartbeat. It wasn't on the list. It wasn't part of the plan.

But it happened anyway. The baby died inside Kate, never reaching the outside. She cried with a sadness I'd never seen. I tried to hold her, but she was limp in my arms like she was dead, too.

We crawled along through the next days and nights at home and then at the hospital. I tried to imagine what it was like for a doctor to scrape the dead baby off the side of the womb and feel nothing at all, like it was a blister. To ball it all up together in one of those little metal bowls and then throw it away, hearing the thud in the trash can.

We didn't talk much during those days. There was nothing to say. Once, when I was sitting at the kitchen table alone, I felt Kate looking at me. I lifted my eyes, she kept looking, and we just stayed that way, me trying to figure out what she was thinking, and Kate wondering if I'd wished for it. Wished another man's baby to die inside of her, like I had a secret list somewhere, hidden, with such things written on the page. Such things as "I hope the baby dies…"

Looking back, the death of the baby inside Kate seemed to start in her an unstoppable process of decay. Who knows, maybe it was already unstoppable and all I did was slow it down awhile, but nothing was ever the same again. For my part, I was driven to deposit my seed, to put another baby where the last one had been, right the wrong, fix the problem, put everything back the way it had been. But it wasn't so simple. The lightness was gone. She pulled back from my hands, and looked at me like I was a cripple, turning me slowly from a savior to a beggar, leaving me to make ridiculous rational arguments, sometimes out loud.

"For everything I provide to you, the roof over your head, an education, and you can't let me touch you? You can't give yourself to me for just a few minutes? Once every two weeks just isn't enough for me."

And another one. "It's funny, I'm supposed to be strong all the time, like a statue, like a tree, always solving the problems. I can't be weak for a minute, not even weak for you, physically. Even that weakness is unattractive to you."

The arguments always sounded better alone. When I tried them out loud, the whole structure caved in upon itself until I was a blithering idiot and the words had no meaning, only a cutting anger and frustration. Success was rare.

One day I called Kate's restaurant.

"May I speak to Kate, please."

Pause.

"Hello?" I said.

"She doesn't work here anymore."

Pause.

"What do you mean?" I said.

"She's no longer employed here."

We had a gigantic fight that night over the definition of being fired. I never could figure out exactly what happened, and in the middle of the fight the electricity went out. The man on the phone said we hadn't paid our bill, but Kate swore she sent the check.

I could barely function. I found a bottle of vodka

behind a box of tampons. The bank called to say Kate had bounced three checks at the grocery store. The phone started ringing at night, and Kate would go outside and whisper. I'd press my ear to the window and pick up pieces of words, inflection in Kate's whisper, a soft laugh.

And then, one day while I was in economics class, my wife packed her bags and went away. I couldn't concentrate. Everything had unraveled. In just three or four months it had gone from my head resting on Kate's belly to complete and utter chaos. I couldn't focus on schoolwork. I'd slept on the floor, on the couch, or sometimes next to the corpse in my bed. I'd argued with myself, and Kate, and swung from one end to the other, until the day I came home to the empty apartment. Everything had happened so quickly, at least that's the way I remember it now. Life just wouldn't slow down.

The door was unlocked. I thought it might be another one of those nights I'd end up staying awake listening for the sound of her getting home late. But it was different. This time, even her ghost was gone, and the apartment felt like it used to feel when Eddie laid around in his socks watching daytime television.

Sitting on my bed, I closed my eyes and let myself believe for a minute it was all a dream. One of those crazy nonsense dreams you wake up from and you're glad it's over but wish you could get back in the middle of it a few more minutes. But it wasn't a dream. I was married and had no idea where my wife had gone. She didn't leave a note or anything else. Even the tampons and vodka were gone, leaving in their absence a recurring visual analogy of a person drowning in a pool, calling out for help until someone jumps in the pool and pulls them to the side. And then, a few minutes later, when nobody's looking, the person paddles back out to the middle of the deep end and starts to drown again, calling for help, until they're saved again, and so on and so on until finally nobody comes when they call and so the person either drowns or struggles to the side, and by then maybe nobody cares anymore, no matter how beautiful they are or how worthy they may be, because maybe God made some people unsavable on purpose.

I remember one time on the couch, after the baby died. Kate had fallen asleep. I climbed over and crawled in beside her, my front against her back, and smelled her hair. With my top hand I ran my index finger along the skin on her upper arm and slowly let my arm relax downward until I cupped her breast. We were still for a moment, the rain outside falling sideways against the window, and then, with her eyes still closed, Kate said, "You'll be feeling me up on my deathbed."

I remember thinking, as loud inside of myself as possible without anyone else being able to hear, "No, I won't." And knowing what I already knew, saying to myself, "You're not who I wanted you to be. I can't save you. I can't even save myself."

I left the empty apartment and got in the car to drive home. It seemed like the only place to go. I drove past the street with the restaurants and turned the wheel. I could see the yellow house up ahead. It was a cloudy day, thin gray clouds covered the world like a blanket. The front

door of the house was wide open, but I couldn't see anybody. I drove past slowly to the end of the street, turned
around in a driveway and went by again. Standing in the
doorway I saw the man I'd beaten on the floor before, and
he saw me. We watched each other and I thought of him
on top of Kate, kissing her mouth, her open legs around
his waist, the burnt doll in the corner watching, fixated,
and then I felt my lungs seize up, and the last free breath
leave my body, and the burning panic like I'd felt before.

I didn't stop driving. I opened the windows and got
on the highway heading home. It was the middle of the
week. I had classes the next morning. I was in the thick-
ness of an asthma attack. My wife was gone, everything
had come apart. I had no detailed plan for such a day, so
I drove, and wheezed, and tried to make each breath just
a bit easier than the one before. I thought about my father
on the train tracks, and how until I found Kate he was the
person I felt closest to, and he was dead. And now the person I'd brought closest to me didn't want to be close to me
anymore, but my father didn't have a choice.

I pulled into the driveway of my mother's house after
hours of driving and driving. It was raining, big drops
pounding against the metal roof of the car. I thought
about opening the car door, but didn't. I thought about it
again, but my hand didn't move, and I wondered if maybe
my body had decided not to listen to my mind anymore.
Maybe the rebellion had reached my own arms and legs,
a complete rejection of any plan I'd made, or would ever
make in the future. Maybe my hand would decide if and
when it would open the car door, and my legs would

decide if and when to go inside the house, and my mind would just have to wait.

I sat for awhile, just listening to the rain, feeling sorry for myself. I saw my mother come to the front window of the house. We looked at each other, and I wondered if she knew instinctively somehow that something was wrong, or if she was devoid of any such instincts and saw only a car in the rain in her driveway in the middle of the week.

We stayed that way for minutes, me and my mother, in a silent conversation, but I needed more from her. My hand opened the door and my legs took me in the house, wet and shivering, and after an awkward continuation of our silent conversation, my mother actually hugged me. She held on long enough for me to know the sacrifice.

"I got married."

She didn't react. I might as well have told her it was Wednesday.

"How about a cup of coffee?" she said.

We sat down at the white kitchen table. My mother's house was always extremely clean. In fact, it reminded me of one of those model homes where no one actually lives. Just a house, with furniture, and books on the shelves not meant for reading.

"I got married to that girl from high school, Kate Shepherd. We went to the courthouse. It was the day the man shot his little girl in the hallway outside the courtroom. We were there that day, upstairs, getting married, me and Kate."

My mother took a sip of her coffee. "I'm not sure what to ask. Why did you wait until now to tell me?"

I felt myself wanting to cry. I hadn't cried but I felt the feeling in my throat and then up into my face and eyes.

"I screwed up," I said, trying to force back the emotion.

My mother said, "Everybody screws up, Early. Everybody."

"She left. I don't know where she went."

I started to cry, and when I started I couldn't stop. My mother stood and leaned over me, her hands on my shoulders, her face resting on the back of my neck, and I cried so damn hard I thought the asthma might come back, my body shaking, eyes squeezed shut in my hands.

My mother didn't offer any advice, and I'm glad she didn't. Whatever she said would have cheapened how I felt, and it wasn't the reason I drove to see her anyway. I drove there because it was still my home, good or bad. It was the place where my father used to walk in the front door from work every day, and I'd hear the door open and run like hell to see him, until that last day when he didn't come home at all and the world changed colors.

The agony slowed and I was able to speak. "'I've got to go back to school, Mom. I've got classes in the morning."

She didn't try to make me stay the night. She didn't tell me it was crazy to drive all day to get there in the rain just to turn around and drive all the way back. She didn't tell me everything would be okay, because it wasn't, and we both knew it, and what would be the point of patting each other on the backs and saying, "Everything will be all right?" No point.

Back at the apartment I tried to focus on the next thing only, the next class, the next day at work. I counted on the routine to pull me slowly from the mire, but it was too slow to notice, like the movement of the minute hand on the clock. You know it's moving, you just can't see it, and so you can't really be absolutely sure it's moving at all.

Weeks passed, and then months. Kate didn't come back. She didn't call. One night I found the pad of paper under the bed. Pages of words, all in my handwriting, outlining a life other than my own. No wonder it failed, but as time passed some of the bad things about Kate diluted and some of the good things rose slowly to the top. Maybe she was in a horrible situation? Maybe she needed me? I drove around town, past the bars, past the yellow house, past the bank, the restaurant where she used to work. No one had seen her. She hadn't gone to her classes. Maybe she went back to Oklahoma. Maybe back to Jeff Temple.

On a cold morning I opened my front door and stepped outside. There was a man.

"Are you James Winwood?"

I was startled. My breath came out white in the freezing air.

"Yes."

And he handed me some papers. Divorce papers. Katherine Shepherd Winwood, plaintiff, vs. James Early Winwood, defendant. The papers said Kate was pregnant, and I was the father, and she wanted custody, and me to pay child support, and she planned to marry a man, an older man named Russell Enslow, with a good job, financial stability, who would help her provide a fine home for the baby. And the papers said I had "tendencies of violence," having beaten a man in his home, and I was controlling, "stalking the plaintiff since high school," basically "imprisoning the plaintiff in my apartment," and more and more and more.

I expected to read, "He tried to feel me up on my deathbed." It was like we were in two different relationships, in two different places, with me and my Kate on the faraway distant planet, enclosed in glass, observed by aliens as we ate ice cream and fornicated happily all day, while the other Kate and the other me were locked in a musty apartment strung out on control issues and implied threats of violence waiting for something bad to happen. We didn't have to wait long.

two

My lawyer looked like an idiot, tall, gaunt, with big ears, one sticking out farther than the other. I guess I shouldn't complain. My mother paid his bill.

Kate's lawyer was sharp-dressed and angry. He pranced around the courtroom pointing his finger and raising his voice. Kate's new boyfriend, the rich old guy, Russell, paid his bill.

The judge said, "I'm not entertaining the issues of paternity or custody until the child is born. After the child is born and the DNA tests are completed, we'll deal with all of this, gentlemen. In the meantime, the mother can move to California as long as she comes back after the birth of the child and consents to jurisdiction here."

I tried to stare straight ahead. I tried to look at the judge, the bailiff, a black speck on the top of the table where I sat. I didn't want to look at her. I didn't want to see her. I suppose the man who shot his wife in the court-house hall on my wedding day must have felt such things. The anger of losing something. The fear of falling to your knees and begging to get it back. The prospect of a life-time alone.

The falling apart happened so fast. The healing seemed not to move at all. I surrounded myself with the fortress of daily routine. Class and work, brush my teeth, remember to eat, go to the library, don't think. The worst parts were those minutes between the tasks. Forced to acknowledge there would be a baby in the world soon, and I would be kept from her, by a judge, by distance, by a sharp-dressed angry lawyer, by my own stupid decisions and mistakes. And it was all outside my control, happening to me when somebody else decided it would happen.

I started smoking cigarettes again to fill the empty spaces in the routine, but I found myself creating more spaces than the ones I filled.

"What if I'm not the father?"

But the question went unanswered, sitting in the dark on the ground with my back against the wall next to the barbecue grill, smoking another cigarette. Sleeping sometimes wasn't possible. It's when all the loneliness settled in the room until I couldn't breathe. Everything she'd touched, I threw away. The sheets, the shampoo. Everything that smelled like Kate I carried out to the dumpster in the rain. It was impossible to separate her from what was happening to me, from the self-pity, the futility, the embarrassment, the longing. But the options were limited, and I got up again, and did it all one more time, and waited for the healing to begin.

Gretchen Anne Winwood was born in Sacramento, California on April 22. My lawyer called to give me the news. The divorce and custody trial would be scheduled in the summer. I hung up the phone and then sat for a very long time, thinking about my father, and how, if he hadn't been killed that day, things might be different. Trying to go year by year in my mind, from age eleven to the present moment, imagining my father still alive, and how his simply being alive could have changed me. And it made me think about the baby girl so far away born into this world without me being the first to hold her. Some other man being there instead, and how she could get confused by everything and think I didn't love her, which wasn't true.

The DNA test was positive. It was my mindless sperm responsible for locating and penetrating the ripe egg despite Kate's disdain, her limp legs wide open, our relationship smoldering like a bombed-out city. You would think an entity as capable of creating the miracle of life could take a few minutes to grasp the circumstances of the surroundings before deciding to plow ahead and make a baby inside a madwoman. But no. Nature hasn't quite caught up to the complexities of a modern overpopulated world. The crazy sperm blindly twisting and swimming at all costs for the opportunity to further complicate the universe.

My mother walked over to Kate and Russell where they sat in the hallway with baby Gretchen. The same hallway where Clay Namen had accidentally killed his daughter. My eyes scanned the walls for bullet holes, but I couldn't find any. There were sections with slightly newer paint, and I imagined a man on a ladder filling the holes with plaster and painting over the spots.

"May I hold my granddaughter?" Christine said.

I stayed at the other end of the hall, sitting in my suit, listening. She said the words without begging, without sympathy.

My mother sat down next to me, holding the baby. She was pink and quiet, with a nose you could see up inside, and eyes like Kate's. She looked at me like I was just another person in the world. Like it was perfectly normal to meet your father for the first time in the hallway outside of a courtroom. I wanted to say, "Don't you understand what's happening here? Don't you see what's going on?"

The lawyer told me we should reach an agreement. He said I was in no position, working and going to school full-time, to take care of a baby. He said if I agreed to let Kate have custody out in California, which he said the judge would undoubtedly do anyway, they'd agree for me not to pay child support until after I graduated college and could afford it. He said I could visit Gretchen, and talk to her on the phone, and later, if I wanted, I could come back and try to get more visitation, or even go for custody if Kate slipped.

His ears stuck out from the sides of his head like they were pulled by invisible fishing line. I felt myself wanting to reach up and cut my hand through the air along the sides of his head to reveal the clear string, pulling the line tighter with the pressure of my hand, forcing the ears outward even further.

My mother told me it was the right thing to do for the time being. We couldn't prove Kate's drug problem. She'd never been arrested and she tested negative on the urine test. She would impress the judge holding the baby in her arms as she testified. Russell's money had bought good legal representation, a nice place to live in Sacramento, California, and I couldn't match their financial stability. What judge would order the baby removed from her mother's arms to be handed over to a part-time barbeque restaurant cook who could barely pay the electric bill?

I couldn't stop thinking about Clay Namen, having the only thing he loved in God's world taken from him, his daughter. Walking past his wife and her smiling family on his way to the bathroom and knowing they would win and he would lose because everybody knows a father can't be a mother.

I graduated from college in finance and took a job as an investment broker in a national firm. There were three of us in the office and three secretaries. I sent a child support check every month to a central collection office. Sometimes when I'd call to talk to Gretchen they'd answer the phone. More often it would ring and ring and ring and I'd slam the fuckin' phone against the nearest wall. I'd send cards and never know if they were received. Father's Day passed with nothing.

I buried myself in my work for ten years. I remember very little about the efficiency. I bought a small house,

with a room set up for Gretchen. The first time she came
to visit we sat on her bed like strangers. She was six.

"You've got your own bed here. And look at the sheets.
Pink, your favorite color."

She held her little bag in her lap like she might stand
up and walk out the door any minute. Like a small replica
of her mother.

"There aren't any toys here," she said.

She was right. It was like a picture of a child's room in
a magazine. Perfect color coordination. Perfect alignment
of the furniture, but no toys, or stains on the carpet, or
half-eaten Pop Tarts.

"We'll go get toys," I said. "We'll go buy as many toys
as you want and fill up the room."

She didn't move. I expected a fine reaction, a big
smile, a hug.

"You don't have any books to read, or movies."

"We'll go to the bookstore. We'll go to the movie
store, too. I promise."

We sat silent on the bed. My tie was too tight around
my neck.

"Just give me a chance, Gretchen. Please. Just give me
a chance. I'm your dad, and I know it's all weird, but we've
got to get a chance to know each other."

And I started telling her more than I planned. "My
dad died when I was eleven. For a long time I was really
mad. Mad at my dad, mad at God. When I got older,
instead of being mad about all those years I didn't get to
spend with him, I started being happy about the first ten
years we had together."

On Gretchen's visits I used my vacation time from work. It always took us days to get familiar again. Every time I heard her call Russell "Daddy" it was like a cold icepick shoved in my ribs. I took her to the zoo, the theater, the park, trying to cram a year into a week, a lifetime into a few days. Each time I saw her she seemed like a different child, older, taller. I stayed away from the subject of Kate but secretly looked forward to fragments of information, stored later inside my mind in a certain place, all together.

"Why don't you have a wife?" Gretchen asked one day.

I hadn't dated much. I'd overheard one of the secretaries at work tell another secretary she thought I was gay. I couldn't even muster the energy to tell her any different. Nearly every woman I met scared the shit outta me. What was behind them? What poison lay just under the skin? What secrets did they hide until it couldn't be hidden any longer, until it was too late? If I'd been so wrong before, I could be so wrong again, and it just wasn't possible to survive another round. Goals at work could be reached. Bonuses earned. On some channel, somewhere, a baseball game, or a boxing match, was happening, pure. I started running. Long distance running. It allowed me to organize my thoughts, discipline my mind to a degree. I looked forward to it, hated it after a few minutes, and then loved it again standing in the shower.

Kate and the old man had gotten married. They'd had another child, a girl. It's all I really needed to know, but I knew a lot more. Through bits and pieces from Gretchen the picture had come together. Russell was the father figure I couldn't be. The father figure Kate always needed. She felt safe, secure, and it didn't matter if she loved him, or if he loved her. She was a long way from the house in the woods down the dirt driveway. A long way from the old man sitting in the darkness. But both of us knew, both me and Kate, she was never too far away from where I found her.

Gretchen asked, "Why does your house smell funny?"

If it smelled funny, I didn't know it. Ten years of living alone does strange things. Empty refrigerator, hair on the soap bar, too much fast food, too much sausage. Nobody to point out all the obnoxious habits until they build on top of one another and sooner or later you're not fit to be around people, unable to smell your own smells. Some people might say those ten years were wasted time. They weren't wasted. They were lonely, necessary, but not wasted. There was a time I thought I'd never heal.

And then one day I was in the grocery store. There was this woman, about my age, up ahead of me in the cereal aisle. I don't know what it was about her that made me stare. There was no ring on her left finger. She was buying food kids would eat. I liked the way she moved. Quietly and gently, like she was quiet and gentle inside. Her hair was clean and short, sandy blond. She dressed casually, but carefully.

There was a rhythm to her existence. It's hard to explain. A simplicity.

I passed her and took a deep breath through my nose, trying to smell her. Not too much perfume. I lagged behind at the oatmeal until she passed me by again. I hadn't felt such a way since Kate, light like a boy. Like anything was possible.

"Hello," she said.

"Hello," I said back, too quickly. Premature response.

She smiled. A good smile. An inviting smile. A new light at the end of a long tunnel.

three

I went to the same grocery store every day at the same time for a week. I saw her again. There she was next to the milk. I'd planned the moment. She needed to see me first. I'd be able to tell everything from her immediate reaction, before she had time to be polite. Would she be glad to see me? Would she be pleasantly surprised? Or would she not even recognize my face, turning away to check the expiration date on the milk?

I stood in front of the cheese ten feet away. So many different kinds. White and yellow, shredded and block, Mexican, mozzarella. Out of the corner of my eye I watched her put a small carton of half-and-half in the buggy. She stared at something level with her eyes, and then glanced at me to her left. My timing was perfect. I turned a split second after her glance and we were looking at each other.

She smiled again, like before, except this time with recognition. She remembered me and was glad I was only ten feet away next to the cheese.

I forgot my line, betrayed by the exhilaration, and instead said, "There's lots of cheese."

"Yes, there is," she said.

"My name is Early Winwood," I said, and stuck out my hand like I was meeting a guy at the lumber yard. She stuck out her hand and we shook, awkward but nice just the same.

Her hand was very soft and well-manicured. She was smaller than I remembered, relaxed with herself, and me.

I abandoned the master plan altogether. The coy little conversation I'd rehearsed in front of the mirror. She liked me. There was no need to beat around the burning bush. I was over thirty years old, not seventeen. We were grown-ups, in the grocery store, liking each other.

"Would you go to dinner with me tonight?"

She didn't flinch one way or the other. Just stood there, smiling. I tried to put myself in her place. I could be a murderer, a rapist, a con man. She not only had herself to protect, but probably children. The children at school, looking forward to drinking milk when they got home.

So I said, "I'm thirty years old. I'm an investment broker. I've never been arrested. I've got a ten-year-old daughter, Gretchen, who lives in California. I'd like to be more coy and mysterious, but we wouldn't be able to have dinner tonight, and it would be at least another week until we ran into each other again. And then I'd probably say something stupid like, 'There's lots of cheese,' so I was wondering, would you like to go out to dinner with me tonight?"

She listened to all my goofy crap with the same pleasant smile. Her eyes were good and blue. A deep blue. Almost gray, and her skin looked extra-soft. I was struck by the desire to reach out my hand and touch her on the face, but I didn't, thank God, and instead waited patiently for her answer.

"Yes, Early Winwood, I would like to go to dinner with you tonight."

I went home in a new mood, feeling things I hadn't felt in a very long time. I called Gretchen on the phone, not to tell her about my date, but just to talk to her, connect my good things with each other.

"Is it a beautiful day out there in California?" I asked.

I didn't expect her to question my upbeat mood, or even notice it. Gretchen sometimes struggled with the obvious. I had, however, detected in her some perceptive ability. She was shy in new surroundings. Watching. Noticing. And picked up on things about people.

"I can't wait until Thanksgiving," I said. It was Gretchen's next planned visit. Christine and Gretchen had a bond. It was subterranean and strong. They seemed to have an understanding, sometimes looking at me like I was the weak link in the chain. I was jealous of the bond at the beginning. It seemed I'd never be as close to either one of them as they were to each other. But the jealousy went away, and it was healthy, appropriate, and provided me a glimpse into my mother I couldn't get otherwise.

"I've got a date tonight," I blurted out to Gretchen on the phone.

I hate to think I said it hoping the news would get to Kate, my ex-wife of ten years, the wife of Russell Enslow, the woman who packed up and left me while I was sitting in economics class. But who knows why I said it. Maybe the motivation was pure. Maybe I just wanted to share it with my girl.

"Daddy's got a date," she said out loud to someone in the room with her. I couldn't hear what the other person may have said.

"Where are you taking her?" Gretchen asked.

"You got any ideas?"

"You're the Plan Man," she said, and laughed like the other person in the room with her shared the thought.

"Maybe not anymore. Maybe it's time to stop planning anything at all, just wake up and go through the day. Whatever happens, happens. Carefree. You can call me Mr. Carefree. Who knows? Maybe I'll buy a horse and become one of those people who rides the horse real fast around barrels."

"That would be fun," she said. "I think you should get a horse."

I should have kept Kate locked away in my mind. I shouldn't have ruined her with all that impossible reality. Some things need to be left alone. The memory, the memory of her before that night outside the bar on the street curb could have been a great thing to visit. A place to go when I needed her, in between parts of my life, anytime I wanted.

I stood at Samantha's door, as nervous as a bird. The house was huge, in a fancy neighborhood. My modest car looked pitiful in the driveway next to the white Mercedes. Samantha Kilborn was rich, or at least somebody was.

I knocked on the door. A boy, maybe ten years old, Gretchen's age, opened the door. He was dressed neatly, and we looked at each other for a moment.

"Is Samantha Kilborn here?" I asked.

The boy turned and walked away, leaving the door open. I heard him call out, "Mom." There was whispering, and then Samantha and the boy came to the door together.

"Early Winwood, this is my son Allen, Allen Jr.," she said. "Allen, this is Early Winwood."

"Hi," I said, again too eager, like a big, over-friendly dog.

We all stood there. Allen Jr. said, "Early? That's a weird name."

Samantha scolded him. "That's not a nice thing to say."

I tried to be funny. "Better Early than late."

It was brutal. Nobody laughed. We stood there like three well-dressed mannequins in a window. I ended the brutality with a simple, "Okay, are we ready to go?"

Samantha and the boy retreated inside. More whispers. I caught a glimpse of a third person, a babysitter maybe. And finally we were outside in my modest car going to a restaurant. I wanted to know everything about her. I could feel myself begin to surface from the disconnection. Someone new. The excitement. The sexual undercurrents.

We laughed a lot at dinner, which is good. She remained relaxed, gentle, and told me she was divorced from Allen

Kilborn. Allen Sr., she called him. They'd been divorced for three years and she really hadn't dated much. She didn't work outside the home because Allen Sr. wanted her to raise their only child, Allen Jr., who was eleven years old and struggled with his parents' divorce.

I told her about me, leaving out most of the weird parts. I dwelled on simplicity and Gretchen, skipping all the stuff about Kate, and the oddness of my conception, and my father's death, and my vow to be average and invisible. As I edited my responses I wondered how much Samantha edited what she told. I looked for signs of mental instability, pent up anger, propensity toward misery. I analyzed and over-analyzed everything she said, but at the same time tried with all my might to keep it light and fresh.

At one point, when she had a piece of chocolate cake on her top lip, I wanted to kiss her. I wanted it more than anything I'd wanted in a long time. And my mind took off on its own with a quick sequence of imagined sexual events, starting with the kiss in the restaurant, and my hand sliding underneath her shirt, and me falling to my knees with my head under her skirt, and finally the two of us up against the far wall next to the painting of the Italian landscape, knocking the painting off the wall.

"Where does your ex-wife live?" Samantha asked.

"She lives in California. Sacramento."

"Do you get along with her?"

I thought about the question. "We don't really talk. Gretchen's old enough to talk for herself, so we don't need to. What about you? Where does Allen Sr. live?"

"He lives outside of town."

Her face revealed the slightest sign of tension when she spoke of her husband. Just enough to show.

"Do you get along?" I asked.

"Yes, I suppose," she said, and wanted to say more, but didn't.

After dinner we parked downtown and walked around looking in the windows of the shops. Maybe it was the wine, maybe the cool evening, but there was no discomfort between us. No sense of wanting to get away from each other to assess the situation and organize thoughts. We were walking along and came to a crosswalk. Samantha took my hand as we hurried across ahead of the cars. When we arrived on the other side of the street, she left her hand in mine, and it felt really good. I kept my mind on the moment. Tried not to let it slip into the fear that I'd misjudged again, and it might be good for awhile, but then confusing, and eventually unbearably painful, and I'd be rolled up in a ball again on my living room floor crying until I coughed.

Driving home I wrestled with the idea of the goodnight kiss. Should I try in the car? Should I wait until we're at the door? But I didn't want to freak out the kid. He already seemed freaked out enough by his mom going out on a date. Maybe skip the kiss. Ask her on a second date. Plan the kiss. Location. Circumstances. Eliminate the possible complications.

I walked Samantha to the door. She reached for the knob and the door swung open. Standing in front of us was a large man. Maybe six foot three, two hundred thirty pounds. His face was hard, and that's the way he seemed to like it. I felt the potential immediately. The posture of the confrontation. I knew it was Samantha's ex-husband. The man she wanted to tell me more about, but didn't.

Samantha wasn't prepared.

"I didn't see your car," she said to the man.

"I guess you didn't," he said back, in a voice matching the body. A crushing tone over the words as he looked down at us.

"Did you leave Allen with a babysitter again?"

Samantha's demeanor had changed. She was more childlike, apologetic, like she'd been caught sneaking a cookie.

I stuck out my hand. "My name is Early Winwood."

He looked down at my hand and left me standing there.

"Early Winwood?" he repeated, like he was making a mental note of the spelling. Like he'd be checking me out and needed to remember the name.

My hand was still out. I decided to leave it there.

"Do you see this house?" he asked me.

I looked across the door frame. "Yes," I said.

"I bought this house. Just like I bought that car in the driveway. Just like I bought everything inside the house. I don't know who you are, and I don't really care."

He'd been a bully all his life. I could tell. And all his life it worked. People did what he told them to do. He'd raised intimidation to an art, believing himself superior in size and intellect. It must have scared away so many competitors. So many potential problems. Like one of those big black gorillas in the rainforest pounding a fist against the dark flesh of his chest and howling.

If I shrunk away, Samantha and I would never see each other again except perhaps with uncomfortable sideways glances in the grocery store from time to time. It was terribly early in our relationship for such a test, but there it was before me, and I decided to leave my hand extended in front of him, without moving. There was no way to pull it away with dignity. I was back at the cafeteria table so many years ago with the senior leaning over, emptying a mouthful of chocolate milkshake on my lunch tray.

"My name is Early Winwood," I repeated.

The big man looked over my head to the street. I turned to see a car pulling up in front of the house under the streetlight. He walked past me, past my outstretched open hand, toward the car.

I stared at the back of his head and had a clear vision of the future. Something bad would happen, and it would be me, and not him, to make it happen. I heard the first click of the machine in my head, the first microscopic movement toward a plan. A detailed, mapped-out, absolute plan. The man walking across the green lawn would ultimately affect my life, perhaps more profoundly than any other single person.

Samantha and I watched him. Allen Kilborn looked back at me over the top of the car before he climbed inside and went away. My hand was still outstretched.

"I'm sorry," Samantha said. "I should have told you."

"Can I kiss you?" I asked. It came out quickly, before I could think about it.

She seemed surprised by the question. She seemed surprised I hadn't run away like one of those smaller gorillas in the jungle, looking over my shoulder.

"Yes," she said, "you can kiss me."

And so I did.

W̶e went out again, and then again. My expectation
level was high, but despite my expectations, I found myself
liking Samantha more and more. She was the polar opposite of Kate, soft, gentle, patient. Her smile was genuine,
no hidden agendas or unwritten rules. We seemed to fit
together.

The more I learned about Samantha, the more I learned
about Allen Kilborn and the dynamics of his relationship
with Samantha and their son. He was everpresent, exerting
control over every facet of their lives. To an outsider like
myself, it was hard to imagine allowing such a presence, but
to Samantha and Allen Jr., it was hard for them to imagine
anything else.

He seemed to come and go from the house as he
wished, even entering when no one was there. By keeping

Samantha at home and out of the workplace, he not only limited her contact with the outside world, he also kept her financially dependent. He paid the bills. He paid the house mortgage. He doled out money with so many strings attached they hung in the air like kite tails.

The control didn't stop with money. The man used his child, and the threat of taking his child, as the trump card. The kid worshipped his fucked-up father like a god, believing the suffocating control was a powerful version of love. The power and manipulation was sometimes subtle, sometimes not, and my hatred of Allen Kilborn Sr. grew with each day.

The most obvious area of control was physical. He was a large man with a constant edge of volatility. Samantha would never tell me if he put his hands on her, but it didn't really matter. With every movement he instilled the belief the next moment may hold a fist up against the side of a head or a hand wrapped around a soft throat. He seemed to show up at odd places at odd times. Samantha told me he cheated on her more than once. He was obsessed by the idea another man might notice his wife, and yet felt entitled to break his vows. And like everything else, Allen Kilborn ultimately took control of the entire divorce process, setting his own terms, his own rules, despite being the one to violate the sanctity of the marriage. It made me wonder what part of him was broken in order to need such control. What had happened to make him feel so inadequate? But those questions could never be answered. The man had buried any vulnerability underneath a lifetime of debris. Besides, what could possibly justify twisting your child in a knot to serve your own purposes? What could possibly justify treating a woman like Samantha as if she was a possession?

The idea of Samantha underneath him sickened me. Underneath him physically, thrusting himself into her, and underneath him mentally, afraid she might wake up in the night with the man standing above her in the darkness. Worried her son might be taken away, or the house sold, or the electricity turned off. I felt a jealousy, wrapped around anger, and the old secret desire to protect, fix, and save, began to mix together with the jealousy and anger to form a new emotion.

After three or four months of seeing each other, I was at Samantha's house on a Saturday. Allen Jr. kept me at a distance. Our conversations were always short and meaningless. I'd never walked the line of stepparent, or potential stepparent, and therefore decided to walk slowly, particularly under the circumstances. Where did I fit between mother and father, between the role of big brother or no role at all?

Little Allen, as he was sometimes called, stood in the kitchen. Samantha was somewhere in the back room. Without provocation, Little Allen said, "I don't have to listen to you."

It caught me unprepared, obviously something his father had told him. I said, "Well, I suppose nobody has to listen to what anybody says."

He looked at me. Eleven years old, but already beginning to look like a version of his father, staring with purpose, head tilted back just enough to notice.

"I'm just saying, legally I don't have to do what you say. That's the law."

I thought about it. "What if I married your mother? What if we all lived in a house together? Don't you think you'd want to listen to me then?"

I didn't intend it as a threat. It was just a direction for the conversation. A hypothetical situation. Allen Jr. looked at me until his face hardened, and he left the room in a hurry. I knew he'd call his father. After that, I wasn't sure what would happen.

Ten minutes later my uncertainty was answered. I was in the front yard trying to start the lawnmower. Samantha and the boy were inside the house. The large white truck pulled up to the curb and stopped with a jolt. Allen Kilborn slammed the truck door and headed in my direction. I stood my ground and waited on the far side of the lawnmower. It was the space I might need if the man took a swing.

He was dressed well, like he'd just left a business meeting. He stopped on the side of the mower, and we stood there looking at each other.

"You think you're the first guy to hang around here?"

Samantha told me she hadn't dated much.

"I don't know," I said.

"You're not," he said. His voice wasn't loud, but the words had the same crushing tone as before. Like everything he said was more important than anything anyone else could say. It was my turn to speak.

"Okay," I said.

He leaned his heavy frame over the lawnmower and

merely whispered, "You'll stay around here as long as I let you stay around here. Understand?"

I considered my options, having run through this scenario many times in my mind. If I told him I'd stay around as long as Samantha let me, it would only push the pressure back on her, and eventually she would fold under the weight, unable to stand against him, unable to choose me over the alternative. It would be easier, even if she loved me, not to face the threat of losing her only child, or the house she loved, or going back into the workforce, or being afraid every day, every time a white truck passed her office or the phone rang in the middle of the night.

I looked at the man and felt the second click of the machine in my mind, the second microscopic movement toward a plan. It was justified. He'd justified it himself by his actions every day. By choosing himself over his marriage, his wife, his child. Choosing bad over good, evil over cleanliness, the deadly sins over God's choice. Allen Kilborn would never stop. He would eventually force the end of Samantha for me. Force me back inside the hole where I'd spent the last ten years. Force his son to hate me, and to hate his mother, and eventually the entire world, until the boy got married himself, and had his own boy, and felt entitled, and followed the endless circle back around. Allen Kilborn would never end the cycle on his own volition, and therefore, someone else had to do it.

All those thoughts, and more, passed through my mind in the few seconds we stood looking at one another. How much he knew of my thoughts I wasn't sure, but he seemed like a man too busy with his own intentions to figure out other men. I knew much more about him than he knew about me. It was only one of my advantages. He would underestimate me, and I would let him.

Allen Kilborn walked away and got in his big truck. I turned to the house to see Samantha and Allen Jr. standing at the window of the living room. It reminded me of the time I sat in the car in my mother's driveway in the pouring rain and looked at her for a long time. Samantha could probably no longer even contemplate what was best for her. And the boy, God knows the boy understood nothing. He probably thought his father looked tough walking across the front yard back to the big white truck.

On a Friday evening when I knew Allen Kilborn was at a local football game with Allen Jr., I drove to his house. The road off the highway was long and newly paved. There was one streetlight at the beginning of the road, a mile from the house, and one in front of the driveway leading to the house. The driveway was also paved, which made things easy. No tire tracks could be left behind in the dirt.

I drove past the house and turned around. The closest neighbor was a quarter mile away. I saw an older man working in a flower bed. He didn't see me. The name on the mailbox was Welty. No dogs barked. The trees between the houses were thick. I doubted the Weltys liked Allen Kilborn much.

On the way back past Allen's house, I slowed to a stop. Again, no dogs barked. I took out my notepad and drew a crude draft of the house and surrounding area. From the driveway to the front door there were walking stones, which made things easy. No shoe prints left behind.

I sat in the car and smoked a cigarette, glancing every few seconds in the rearview mirror to make sure Mr. Welty wasn't going out for a drive. The house was two stories. Ostentatious, like the man who lived inside. I made a note to shoot out the streetlight above a few days before I'd come back. I could use Little Allen's pellet gun.

The second part of the plan was to gather certain information from Allen Jr. through questions hidden in the flow of a conversation. I read a newspaper article once about how the vast majority of murders in America are heat-of-passion. Domestic violence. Alcohol-related. Bad drug deals. Late night fights in barrooms. The defendant gets convicted by eyewitness testimony, or the statement of an accomplice, or leaving behind evidence like DNA, or fingerprints, or a murder weapon. It seemed to me, with proper planning, ninety percent of those problems were easily eliminated. Wear gloves, don't have an accomplice, never talk about your plan or what you've done. Use a weapon that can't be connected, have an explanation for anything you might leave behind, be thorough, prepared, completely destroy everything afterwards that could possibly become a link back. Such as shoes, clothes, gloves. Just be smart, and patient, remove the emotion from the equation. Consider it a mathematical formula.

"Your dad's not home, Allen," I said, one afternoon in the yard. "Unless you've got a key, we can't take you over there."

"I've got a key," he said. "Dad gave me one."

"What about the house alarm?" I asked.

"He doesn't use it. Dad says it's stupid. He says the .357 magnum is a better house alarm anyway."

The boy was mimicking his father's words. I could detect a change in tone, a puffing up.

"Your dad's got a gun?" I asked. "I bet you've never shot it."

"I have so. We went to the pistol range. He lets me shoot it anytime I want."

I considered the next question carefully.

"I bet he didn't give you a key to the safe where he keeps the gun."

"Now that's stupid," the boy said, again mimicking his father's tone. "What good would a gun be locked up in a safe if somebody busted into your home? He keeps it in the kitchen drawer next to the refrigerator. It's a special place made just for the gun."

I have to admit, when I first drove out to the man's house, and even much later, it was just an idea. A crazy idea that rested in the back of the mind like a tiny seed. Something to think about alone in bed at night. Something to occupy the dead minutes of the day, to mollify the anger. I just toyed with the idea, kinda pushed it around to see if it would move on its own. I kept notes in the notepad. One thing led to another. Before too long, it was possible. More than possible, it became truly necessary. Necessary to me and Samantha having a life together. Necessary to Samantha getting out from under, becoming herself again. Necessary for the kid to have a chance in this screwed-up world. And there was something even bigger than all that. Some necessity to prove the angels right. Bad people should never prosper, and until I got involved, Allen Kilborn prospered like a king.

In another conversation, clearing off the dinner table, with Samantha in the bath, I said, "You need to go to bed early tonight."

"Why?" he asked.

"Your mom said you and your dad stayed up late last night talking on the computer. You've got school tomorrow."

"Dad stays up sometimes all night on his computer. That's how he gets his work done. He just fixed up the little room at the top of the stairs as the computer room. He's gonna give me my own new desk and new computer next to his. A lot nicer than the one here, that's for sure."

I wanted to say, "Of course it's a lot nicer, you idiot. He makes sure your mother can't ever win. The game is rigged, and you fall for it every time."

But with this last tidbit of information, everything fell into place. I'd long since passed the point of questioning the morality. It was now just a question of precision. With proper precision, the legal consequences didn't seem relevant. I never considered anything else. How it might change a man's life when he kills another man. Any man. Even a bad one.

I looked forward to seeing Samantha. She spent the night at my place whenever Allen Jr. was staying with his father and Gretchen wasn't in town. It was our time, alone, without distraction, free from ex-husbands and ex-wives, free from the complications of children and potential stepchildren. It was always the time I knew for sure I wanted to marry her, and live together, and not be on my own anymore.

She was funny. And in the bedroom Samantha didn't just wait around for things to happen. I'd forgotten how wonderful it could be with the doors locked, a few glasses of wine, a mischievous look in her eye as the panties come off.

But even at my own home, with the doors locked tight, I found myself peering out windows expecting to see Allen Sr. sitting in the big white truck outside my house. I knew he wasn't the kind of man who would ever allow another man living in the same house with his son, taking his place as a father figure, taking his place as the husband he could never be to the woman now outside his control, no longer dependent upon his money.

My plan was slow and patient. I took a business trip to Chicago. It was a seminar on new investment opportunities. On a Tuesday afternoon I skipped a class on alternative fuel source investments and rode a taxi to the far side of the city. At a Salvation Army store I got a pair of brown cotton gloves, khaki work pants, a button-down flannel shirt, a pair of thick dark socks, and a pair of cheap boots. I made sure none fit me well.

Next door, at a hardware store, I had a key made. The morning before leaving home I had taken Little Allen's key to his father's house and slipped it in my pocket. While the man in the hardware store cut the key, I made small talk.

"I've never really figured out how that machine works," I said.

"It's easy," the man said. "You just stick it in here."

I didn't pay attention.

"Can you tell where a key was made?" I asked. "I mean, if I found a key on the street, would there be any way to tell what machine, in what state, at what store, cut the duplicate key?"

"Naw," he said, "there's not a secret number on it. It's just a key."

When I arrived at the airport, I put the shoes, pants, shirt, socks, and gloves in the trunk underneath the spare tire in the wheel well of my car. That evening, over at Samantha's house, I waited for Allen Jr. to go outside and then replaced the key to his father's house back where I'd found it, later hiding the spare in my own house.

While in Chicago I toyed with the idea of buying bullets for a .357, but I couldn't get them home on the airplane and didn't want to risk sending a package through the mail. Surely Allen would keep his gun loaded. He was the kind of man to have a loaded pistol in his house, or at least bullets nearby in the special drawer in the kitchen.

I hadn't seen Eddie Miller in years. He still lived in town and worked for a rental car agency, but we never seemed to be in the same place at the same time until we ran into each other at a doughnut shop one morning.

It was good to see him again. He'd gained weight, probably from hanging out too often in the doughnut shop. We talked about being kids and the stupid stuff we did. We talked some of college days, but not a lot, and I told him all about Kate. He already knew most of it, but shook his head and listened anyway. He seemed happy for me finding Samantha.

We left the doughnut shop promising to go drink a beer together soon. We exchanged phone numbers and shook hands. His smile was the same as it always had been. Wide but reluctant, like he wasn't sure it was appropriate to laugh at certain things. Like maybe the world wasn't supposed to be a funny place, even if he found it funny sometimes.

The days kept passing and the plan kept moving forward by itself. On Samantha's calendar hanging on the refrigerator, a date was marked in red. I pointed with my finger and said, "What's happening here?"

Samantha leaned over to see. "Oh, Allen's father is taking him deep-sea fishing. They leave at five A.M. and get back around seven at night."

It was three weeks away. Suddenly my plan had a date, a day on the calendar marked in red. It became more real. Part of me hoped something would happen to change the course of events. The other part of me knew there were no alternatives. The next night, perhaps purely by coincidence, I was reminded of this fact.

Samantha and I were having one of our nights alone at my house. We had candles around the bathtub, and a bottle of wine, and the blinds closed tight. She bent over for me in front of the big bathroom mirror, and I was grateful for the chance to see us that way. A few minutes later, after midnight, while Samantha stretched out in the bathtub, I snuck out my back door to the secret porch in total darkness to smoke a cigarette. I was naked, and it felt good to be naked in the cool evening, the backyard surrounded by a privacy fence.

I kept a pack of cigarettes and a book of matches hidden in a crack between two boards above the door. Samantha didn't know I smoked a cigarette every few days. I'm sure she wouldn't have cared, but it wasn't how I wanted her to see me. I never smoked in front of anyone else, and sometimes went months between buying a new pack.

I reached up, fished out a cigarette, and lit it quickly. I held the menthol smoke inside my lungs, breathing out slowly, thinking about the woman in my bathtub, surrounded by candles. Thinking about the look on her face in the mirror, bent over with me inside her. I closed my eyes and let the smoke roll freely from my nose.

In the quiet, from the darkness twenty feet away at the far end of the screen porch, the voice said, "That's some sweet pussy, wouldn't you say?"

The shock of not being alone, the instantaneous outright fear, shot like electricity up my legs and into the core of my naked chest. I spun around, lost my balance, dropped the cigarette on the floor and fell against the door leading back into the house. It wasn't until I got through the door I recognized who it was, the voice.

I ran to the hall closet and grabbed a baseball bat. From the bathroom Samantha said, "What's going on?"

"Nothing," I answered quickly, and then pulled on a pair of shorts, the fear hardening into a brick of anger. How long had the son-of-a-bitch been there? Did he watch us through the tiniest crack in the blinds at the bathroom window? He had seen me smoking, naked, on the back porch, eyes closed?

I flicked on the kitchen light and swung open the back door to the porch, now lit from the lights through the windows. He was gone. My cigarette still lay on the tile floor, smoke rising slowly up and circling.

I heard Samantha coming up from behind. Before she could see, I picked up the cigarette and shoved the butt into the dirt of the big houseplant by the screen door.

She was wearing only a towel and carrying a glass of white wine.

"What's going on?" she repeated.

I decided not to say.

"It smells like somebody's been smoking out here," she said.

"I know. I thought I heard somebody. Probably just kids." I turned my head away so she couldn't get a whiff of my breath.

She stretched her neck to look around the doorframe.

"You've got a bat," she said.

I wondered whether Allen Kilborn was somewhere out in the darkness watching us, maybe even close enough to hear our conversation. The moment solidified my resolve. He deserved to die. He earned it. Sitting on my back porch in the middle of the night. I wasn't Samantha. He wouldn't intimidate me with his bullshit. And I remembered Allen Jr. was staying at his house that night. The man had left his eleven-year-old son alone in the house. What if the kid woke up? What if he had a bad dream and went to his father's bedroom for comfort? His father wouldn't have been there. Instead, he would have been on my back porch talking nasty about the mother of his son. Scaring the holy shit out of me.

Two days before the date marked in red on the calendar, I drove in the very early morning hours to two designated spots. I put on the Salvation Army boots and walked approximately fifty yards to each place into the woods. I took a small gardening shovel I'd found a few weeks earlier at the local dump. With the shovel I dug two holes, one at each location, about two feet deep, in the soft soil. I piled up the dirt around the backside of the holes, careful not to leave any mud or dirt around the front of the holes, and careful to remove any dirt from the bottom of the over-sized boots before the boots were placed back in the wheel well. No cars passed on the secluded back-roads while I dug the holes.

Later that day I burned all my written notes and plans, along with the diagram of Allen Kilborn's house, and the maps of the backroads. I lit them on fire inside a ceramic pot, and after each piece was burned, I poured water into the pot, stirred it around into a black mess, and poured it on the flowers in the backyard. I burned the entire notepad in case anything I'd written or drawn had traced onto a bottom page. The diagrams reminded me of the drawings I'd made so long ago of the drugstore—locations of mirrors, the pharmacist, the candy bars, Eddie's lookout point. I'd forgotten the janitor, and learned from my mistake.

The day arrived. I didn't sleep well the night before. Looking over at the red numbers on the clock by the bed. Thinking, and rethinking, every part of the plan. Allowing myself to overthink and find flaws where no flaws existed. It was almost like the plan stood alone, out-side of me.

I knew the boy would be picked up by his father around five in the morning. At five-thirty I drove over to Samantha's house and let myself in the back door. She'd gone back to sleep like I knew she would and the house was quiet. I went to Little Allen's room and got his pellet gun. I drove to Allen Sr.'s house and pulled up at a spot on the road with a clear shot at the streetlight. I took aim at the light, pulled the trigger, and missed. The gun wasn't very loud, but I felt stupid missing the entire streetlight. I shot again. And then again. On my fifth shot the light busted and glass crashed to the ground. I drove away in a hurry, checking the rearview mirror for any cars coming from the direction of the Weltys' house down the road.

Back at Samantha's, I replaced the pellet gun in Little Allen's room, wiping my fingerprints away while she slept.

I took Samantha to breakfast and we spent the morning shopping at the mall. I tried to focus on little things, bacon, a kid sitting on a wood bench, swinging his legs, waiting for his mother to try on another pair of ridiculous shoes, a dog outside lifting his leg on the back tire of a new car, and then the front tire a few seconds later. I tried not to think about how the plan would ultimately end, only the next step. The next thing to do on the list in my mind.

I called Eddie Miller and set up a time in the afternoon to drink a beer together. He picked me up around three o'clock. Down the road on the way across town to the sports bar to watch the Saturday game, I said, "Do you mind swinging by Samantha's ex-husband's house? It's on the way. I'm supposed to see if the kid's back from fishing."

"Yeah, okay," Eddie said. He didn't care anything about the game.

As we pulled up near the front of Allen Kilborn's house, I pretended to notice the broken glass for the first time.

Eddie said, "Looks like somebody busted the streetlight."

I told Eddie to stop at a spot on the street where he couldn't see the front door. His windows were up and the radio was playing. Eddie was the kind of man who enjoys air-conditioning and music.

I walked on the pavement and then across the steps to the door, glanced back to make sure Eddie's car was out of sight, knocked on the door three hard times, and then opened the front door with the key cut in Chicago. I hurried to the kitchen and opened the drawer using the tail of my shirt between my fingers on the knob. Inside was a .357 pistol, just as Allen Jr. said, in a special wooden rest. It was loaded.

I went to the foot of the stairs and walked up slowly, stepping near the middle of each step. The seventh step squeaked in the middle. The right-hand side made no sound. At the top of the steps, straight across the hall, was the computer room. The back of the chair faced the stairs, with the computer in front of the chair, and a big window to the left. I went back down the stairs, again slowly, and avoided the middle of the seventh step. I ran to the refrigerator, grabbed two beers, stepped outside, locked the door, and walked across the stones and the pavement to Eddie's car, careful not to step near any broken glass.

"The door was unlocked," I said. "They're not back yet. I don't think he'll miss a few beers."

Eddie drank down nearly half the beer like he was

thirsty. In only a few minutes I'd accomplished a good chunk of the plan. I tested the key, verified the location of the gun, made sure it was loaded, and got the layout of the house. I checked out the stairs, saw the design of the computer room, made Eddie a witness to my visit to the house of Allen Kilborn, as well as the unlocked door and the busted light. Most importantly, I now had an explanation for any hair, fingerprint, glass shards in the shoe sole, stray eyelash, or anything else I could leave behind or take with me from the crime scene. I simply stopped by to check on the boy. He wasn't back yet. The door was unlocked, so I called inside, walked up the steps to see if they might be upstairs, grabbed a few beers, and left. And who could say the door wasn't unlocked? Allen Kilborn? He'd be dead in ten hours, according to the plan.

At around seven o'clock in the evening, according to schedule, Allen Sr. dropped off his son at Samantha's house. The boy was exhausted. He told us all about the day. He went to his room after a shower and talked with his father on the computer. By ten o'clock, Allen Jr. was sound asleep.

By eleven o'clock, Samantha was on her fourth glass of her favorite Chablis. I brought over two bottles, and every time I poured a glass for myself I'd fill it half with water. We watched a movie, and around twelve o'clock, midway through her fifth glass, Samantha fell asleep. I carried her to the bedroom and she was snoring like a sailor in just a few minutes.

I entered the boy's room quietly. He was hard asleep.

The computer in his room was turned off. I closed his door and then sat down alone in the living room. I could have laid down on the couch and just fallen asleep. I could have let the Saturday marked in red on the calendar pass by. Sometimes I wish I had.

I got the clothes from under the wheel well and changed in the front seat of my car. I drove the posted speed limit to the road leading to Allen Kilborn's house. The light was on upstairs in the computer room. The Weltys' house was dark except for a light on the front porch.

I parked away from the broken glass on the dark street. I could have driven away. I could have gone home and stood on the back porch smoking a cigarette. But I didn't. I closed the car door quietly, walked over the pavement and across the stones to the door. No matter how much you plan, no matter how precise and careful, luck demands a role. Allen Kilborn could've been standing in the kitchen in his underwear drinking milk out of the carton when I opened the door. He could have been at the top of the stairs looking down on me. But he wasn't. He was sitting, just as I envisioned, at his computer, with his back to the stairs, when I arrived behind him, holding the man's loaded pistol in my gloved hand. He didn't hear the squeak from the middle of the seventh step, because I didn't step in the middle. He didn't hear anything at all.

I was behind him. I could've gone back down the stairs. I could've avoided the squeak on the way down, replaced the pistol in the special drawer, locked the door on the way out, and climbed in bed with beautiful, drunk Samantha. But I didn't. I held up the gun and thought of

her on her knees with her mouth on him, with him looking down on her, and her eyes looking up at him. It
disgusted me, and I felt my chest tightening inside. Suddenly, I couldn't draw the next breath, just like the day at
the pond with my grandfather. My lungs seized. I felt the
panic rise through my body.

Allen Kilborn's fingers stopped on the computer keyboard, like he sensed someone behind him. Like he knew
I'd gotten the best of him. And according to plan, even in
the middle of a full-blown asthma attack, just as I knew I
would, I pulled the trigger, exploding the back of Allen
Kilborn's head like a ripe melon across the room.

I bent over at the waist and tried to concentrate. The
air sucked in, and I stood, arms outstretched, praying I
wouldn't collapse on the floor in the dead man's room.
Listening for my grandfather's words of comfort. Trying
to rationalize the irrational, and in time, the air came
more freely. I didn't look back at him. I kept the gun, ran
down the stairs, rubbed both doorknobs with my gloved
hand, and left the door unlocked on my way out. I stayed
on the stones, and then the pavement, and avoided the
shards of glass. I drove carefully, my hands shaking on the
wheel like a man with Parkinson's, my breath still short
and forced, to the first designated location on the back-
roads. I turned the car so the headlights would shine in
the woods, walked in my Salvation Army clothes to the
hole I'd dug, and dropped the gun into the hole. With the
shovel I'd left near the hole, I pushed dirt and mud inside
until it was full and covered the top with dry leaves. I
walked back, careful not to step in any mud, and removed

my boots before entering the car. I changed clothes in the front seat. At the second designated location, after parking the car again with the headlights shining my path, I walked in sock feet to the second hole. I dropped the shirt, pants, gloves, and boots into the hole, filled the hole, and again covered it with leaves.

Before entering the car, I removed the heavy dark socks and put my regular socks and shoes on my feet. A mile down the road I threw one sock out the window. A mile further, the second sock followed. And a mile later, the little shovel ended up in a gully and the spare key flew through the air and landed in a farmer's field.

I parked outside Samantha's house and opened the back door quietly. Again, Samantha, or even worse, Allen Jr., could have been standing in the kitchen getting a glass of water. But they weren't. Allen was still sleeping hard after a day fishing in the hot sun. Samantha still snored like a sailor. It was done. It was over. I stood in the shower and felt the hot water down the back of my neck, felt the shaking in my hands slow to a pulse, took long steady, deep breaths, in and out again.

I climbed in bed in my underwear and waited until my body warmed beneath the blankets. I touched Samantha and woke her with a kiss. If she only knew what I'd done for her and her boy. If I only knew how it would occupy my mind for the rest of my life.

She smiled. "You're staying the night?" she asked softly.

"Yes," I said. "I'm staying the night."

six

That night I dreamed again of the scary black circle on the floor. I hadn't had the dream in years, but it came back just as before, except this time in the dream I was an old man. I was alone in a bedroom, sitting in a wheelchair, watching television. I was very tired. The circle appeared slowly on the hardwood floor by the closed door. I watched it form, beginning as just a slight discoloration, and then taking shape until it was the same circle from my childhood dreams.

The black circle began to move toward my wheelchair. The movement was steady and slow, getting closer and closer to me. I couldn't move my arms. I was too tired to move my arms to roll away from the circle, and it got closer and closer until the edge reached the outer wheel of the chair, and the chair began to tip into the hole, and I woke up covered in sweat.

Believe me, my various motivations for what I'd done to Allen Kilborn did not completely escape me. I'd built a fortress of justification, but it was impossible to ignore my savior complex rearing its ugly head. The jealousy and anger held deep roots, and regardless of whether the world, and Samantha, and Allen Jr., were better off, I would forever struggle with untangling the necessities.

I lay in bed, thinking of the circle and waiting for Samantha to open her eyes and see me in her bed, see the clock, and know I'd slept with her throughout the night. I backtracked through my mind, making sure I hadn't forgotten anything. The explosion of the man's head was difficult to believe. How quickly he went from alive to dead. How suddenly I was alone in the house, his brains and blood across the computer and the wall. The next morning, it was hard to believe I'd done such a thing.

"Good morning," she said. The clock showed 8:07 A.M.

"Good morning. How do you feel?" I asked.

"Like my head got stepped on by a giant."

She went to the bathroom, and I put on my pants. While she took a shower and tended to her headache, I banged around in the kitchen until Allen Jr. wandered in for breakfast.

"What are you doing here?" he asked.

"I fell asleep," I answered.

The boy made a face of disgust. He went back to his room, and I knew he would send a message to his father telling him I'd spent the night. Tangible confirmation of my alibi. See, even the boy knows I spent the night in the house. I was there the next morning, in the kitchen, with no shirt.

Allen Jr. and Samantha arrived back in the kitchen at the same moment. She avoided eye contact with the boy, recognizing the anticipated repercussions from her ex-husband for allowing a man to spend the night in his home with his son in the other room.

Allen Jr. said, "Dad's not answering on his computer."

"Maybe he's still asleep," Samantha said.

The boy picked up the phone and dialed a number. I poured a cup of coffee and imagined the phone ringing in an empty house, the dead man upstairs in a cake of his dried blood, stuck to the floor. My stomach felt weak. The smell of the coffee was suddenly sickening.

"There's no answer," he said.

"Well, maybe he had to go out for something," Samantha offered. "We're gonna go to church this morning. We missed last week."

"Can I go?" I asked. I'd never been with them before.

Samantha seemed pleasantly surprised. "Yes, you can," she said.

I drove home, washed my clothes in the washing machine with hot water, took another long, thorough shower, washing my hair twice. On the way to meet Samantha and Little Allen at church, I stopped at a self-service car wash and vacuumed the car, including the trunk and under the spare tire. I sprayed down the car, concentrating on the tires and underneath.

The church was big and white. We sat near the front, and I was glad. The multi-colored, stained glass window of Jesus on the cross glowed in the morning sunlight, high above.

The Episcopal priest stood to deliver the sermon. He was a small man, thin, with not much hair left on his head. He spoke of our limitations, and how we shouldn't be disappointed in our inability to always behave like God would want us to. He said that's the very reason we need a God, to forgive us, to teach us, to help us find our way. What would be the role of God in a world full of God-like humans? None. Just like the Devil would have nothing to do in a world of sinners who fail to recognize their sins, or fail to repent. I tried very hard not to fidget or look around too much.

Afterwards, on the way out, I shook hands with several people I recognized, and knew they'd remember seeing me for the first time in their church. I shook the priest's hand at the door, but didn't overdo it or bring attention to myself. He hugged Samantha, and told her he was praying for her. I wondered how he had enough hours in the day to pray for everyone he knew, or even everyone he knew who needed praying for.

On Sunday night, alone on my back porch, I sat in the dark smoking a cigarette. All day I'd waited for the phone to ring, the news of Allen Kilborn's death, the suspicion cast on the ex-wife and her boyfriend. The coming down of everything upon the discovery of the dead man. I hoped it wouldn't be Samantha or the boy to see him first.

The phone rang. It was Samantha. "Allen wants me to take him over to his father's," she said.

"It's a school night," I said. "His father's probably not

home because he's stalking one of us again. Maybe he's hiding in my bushes right now, or putting sugar in my gas tank."

She laughed a little, but not really. It was more a nervous giggle, kinda like it was risky to say such things over the phone. Like there was nothing Allen Kilborn couldn't hear, or tape-record, or find out about.

It was impossible to sleep. I kept hearing the priest's words in my head. I kept going over and back over every detail of the plan, every unforseen mistake, and the black circle waited for me. Waited for my eyes to close, the cover of darkness, peaceful sleep, to sneak back into my room and maybe swallow me completely, sucking me down. But eventually I must have fallen asleep, because at 6:48 in the morning the phone rang, loud like a fire alarm.

"Hello," I said.

"Oh my God," the woman's voice said.

"Hello," I repeated.

"Allen's dead," Samantha stuttered. "Somebody killed him."

"Jesus," I said. "Little Allen?" I asked.

"No, no. Not Little Allen. Big Allen. They found him shot in his house. His business partner was supposed to meet him there at six-thirty this morning. He just called me. The police are there."

"Oh my God," I said convincingly. I knew the phone records would show Samantha called me immediately after hearing the news. I knew the investigators would jump to the conclusion we killed him together, and Samantha was calling me to tell me the body had been found.

"You need to go over there," I said. I figured her emotions would be genuine in front of the investigators. She had nothing to fake, because she knew nothing, and never would. The first impression she would leave with the investigators could be invaluable.

I needed to be seen at work, composed, yet concerned about Samantha. I ended the conversation telling her to go to Allen's house so she could give the police any information about the fishing trip, and her son's return Saturday night, and Allen Sr. not answering his boy's calls all day Sunday. I didn't want to be there with her, following the old pattern of the murderer returning to the scene of the crime.

I shared with the people in my office what had happened, appearing amazed and shocked. Later that morning, about lunchtime, Samantha called from the police station. She asked if I'd come down. The investigator wanted to ask me a few questions. I didn't hesitate or hurry, arriving at the police station and asking to see Samantha Kilborn.

A man introduced himself to me.

"I'm Frank Rush, the investigator on the Allen Kilborn homicide."

"I'm Early Winwood. Is Samantha here?"

"She's in the back talking to my partner. Would you mind stepping in my office? I was hoping you could answer a few quick questions."

"Absolutely," I said.

He was mid-fifties, slightly overweight, with a mustache and a patient way about him. I sat down across his desk. Behind him there was a picture of a woman with three grown kids, maybe college-age. The youngest looked very much like his father sitting in front of me, except without a mustache. The woman was remarkably unattractive, her face reminding me of a rodent.

"How long have you and Samantha been going out?"

"It's been months. She called me and told me what happened right after the business partner called her this morning. Has anybody told the boy yet?"

Frank Rush studied me for a moment. All of his thirty years of instincts were focused on my eyes, the inflection in my voice, the movement of my hands in my lap, my breathing. What if I had another asthma attack? An involuntary shut-down of my lungs in the office of the homicide investigator?

"The boy's in a safe place," he said. "You mind if I tape-record our conversation? It just helps me later when I have to put all the information in a report."

"No, I don't mind."

He pressed the button on a hand-held recorder, whispered the date and time and my name, and asked me, "Mr. Winwood, you know anybody who might want to kill Allen Kilborn?"

"Well," I hesitated, "no." I intentionally left a space between the words to invite the next question.

"You seemed to hesitate with your answer."

"Well, I don't know how much you know about Allen Kilborn, and I don't want to speak ill of the dead, but he was the kind of man someone might want to kill."

I could almost see his mind reeling inside. "How so?" he asked.

"He was…abrasive."

"Abrasive?" he repeated.

"He was a bully. I guess that's the best way to put it."

Frank Rush sat perfectly still, arms crossed on the desk in front of him. "Did you ever want to kill Allen Kilborn?" he asked.

"No," I said. "I never wanted to kill him. I would have liked to kick his ass a few times, but I wouldn't want to kill anybody."

"Do you have a key to his house?" he asked.

"No. I don't even think Samantha has a key."

"Have you ever been inside Allen Kilborn's house?"

I pretended to think. "As a matter of fact, yes. This past weekend. Saturday afternoon around three o'clock or three-thirty. I stopped by to see if they were back from deep-sea fishing. I knocked, nobody answered, the door was unlocked, so I went inside and called out for the boy. They weren't back yet, so we left."

"Who is 'we'?" he asked.

"My friend, Eddie Miller, was driving. We were on the way to watch a football game at a sports bar."

Frank Rush leaned back in his squeaky leather chair. "Is it just a coincidence, Mr. Winwood, that the first and only time you've been in Allen Kilborn's house was the same day he was murdered?"

I paused. "I guess so, but he wasn't home. They weren't back from the fishing trip. I'm sure you can verify that with the charter boat."

The man stared at me. I waited the required period of time. "You act like I had something to do with this," I said.

"Did you?" he asked.

"No, I didn't."

"Whoever it was who went to see Allen Kilborn this weekend went there to kill him. It wasn't a robbery. It was an execution. Do you own a gun?"

"No, I don't have a gun. I've never had a gun." I showed a touch of anger at the implied accusation.

Frank Rush said, "You wouldn't mind if we searched your house, or your car, would you? I mean, you have the right to say no, but if you don't have anything to hide…"

He shrugged his shoulders. It was a test.

"I don't have anything to hide. You can search all you want."

My car was taken behind the police station to a garage. I rode with Investigator Rush to my house. Two other officers met us there. I sat down on the couch as they combed through my house. Shirt, pants, socks, and shoes, all touched and replaced in drawers and on hangers. One guy crawled around in my attic with a flashlight and another sifted through the garbage in my garage. There was nothing to find.

My car had an odd smell, a chemical smell, when I got it back. After I left the police station I drove to see Samantha. Allen Jr. was with his grandparents. They'd searched Samantha's house, specifically asking about Allen Jr.'s key to his father's door. They took the boy's computer.

I tried to ease Samantha's concerns.

"This is routine, Sam. When somebody gets killed, the first place they look is the ex-wife or ex-husband, and whoever they're dating. Don't worry, we didn't do anything wrong. They've probably already figured out we're not involved. You know as well as I do the son-of-a-bitch probably had a dozen enemies who'd blow his head off if they had a chance."

She said, "They asked me if you spent the night Saturday night. I was embarrassed, but I told them the truth. They looked through my car. They took Little Allen's key and his computer. The man with the mustache said he was killed around midnight Saturday night. He said the only thing stolen was the gun. They think he was shot with his own gun. And they said the door was unlocked."

I went home that night. The highly trained police officers had failed to find my hidden cigarettes. I could've had the gloves hidden there, or the spare key, or a snapshot of the dead man sprawled across the floor, and they'd have missed it. As I smoked my cigarette in the dark, I wondered if Frank Rush was sitting in the bushes in my backyard watching. Maybe sitting in the same place Allen Kilborn sat weeks earlier after scaring the holy shit out of me.

On Tuesday afternoon Investigator Rush stopped by my office unannounced. I didn't act rattled, expecting to hear from him soon. This time, we sat across from each other at my desk instead of his.

"I just had a few more questions I wanted to ask you. You mind if I tape-record the conversation again, just to help my memory? I wouldn't want to get anything wrong."

"Okay," I said, and looked him directly in the eye.

"Where were you Saturday and Saturday night?"

"Allen Jr. went fishing with his father. I went to

Samantha's in the morning and took her to breakfast. We went shopping at the mall. After that, Eddie picked me up around three. We stopped by Allen Kilborn's house, like I said, looking for the boy. He wasn't there. We went to the bar and watched the game. I drank maybe two beers. I got back to Samantha's around six-thirty. Allen Jr. got dropped off by his father at seven.

"After that, Allen fell asleep somewhere around ten. Me and Samantha stayed up, watched a movie, went to sleep around eleven. I usually don't stay overnight when the boy is there, but I fell asleep and woke up the next morning around eight. I fixed coffee. I saw Little Allen in the kitchen before I went home to get dressed for church. And we went to church later that morning."

For the first time in my dealing with Frank Rush, I saw some doubt in his eyes. Doubt that I was involved in the death of Allen Kilborn. Doubt that solving this case would be so easy. Or maybe I imagined it.

"Did you notice anything odd, or out of place, at Kilborn's house that afternoon?"

"Yeah, as a matter of fact, the streetlight outside the house was busted. There was glass by the driveway."

"Anything else?"

"Only that I thought it was strange for the door to be unlocked in the middle of the day with nobody home. But then again, he lived out in the country. Maybe he didn't lock his doors. I don't know."

The investigator looked down at his notes. "There was a calendar on Samantha's refrigerator. Had Saturday marked in red."

"I think Little Allen did that. He was looking forward to the fishing trip."

"How long you and Eddie Miller been friends?"

"All our lives. We grew up together."

"When's the last time you and Eddie went to watch a game together, or drink a beer?"

"Before Saturday?"

"Yeah, before Saturday."

"Probably ten years ago. College."

He watched me closely again. "Is it just a coincidence, again, that the first time, the only time in ten years, you go have a beer and watch a game with your lifelong friend, Eddie, happens to be the same day, and the only day, you ever go inside Allen Kilborn's house, which happens to be the same day Allen Kilborn gets his head blown off in that same house?"

Conscious of the tape recorder spinning round and round on the desk between us, I said, "I guess so, Mr. Rush, but I'm not a killer, and neither is Samantha."

Frank Rush leaned over and turned off the tape recorder. "Would you mind, Mr. Winwood, providing me a written statement of your whereabouts on Saturday and Sunday? Just for the file."

"No, I wouldn't mind," I said.

"Oh, by the way," he said, "Eddie told us about your ex-wife. We pulled the divorce file, and called Kate to verify a few things. Did you ever get charged criminally with assaulting the man you assaulted in that house off-campus?"

For the first time in our conversations, I was caught off guard.

"No," I said, "and it didn't happen the way she said it did. People will say anything in a custody battle. Did she mention she was strung out on crack?"

It was near the end of our conversation. He accomplished his goal of shaking me up, but it wouldn't make any difference. He stood to walk out the door, and then stopped in the doorway. "Oh, one last question. How many times have you been to church with Samantha and her son?"

We looked at each other. "Once. Sunday was the first time."

He reached his hand up and scratched the back of his neck. Frank Rush said, "Another coincidence?"

But he didn't want an answer, and didn't wait for one.

The funeral was on Wednesday morning at the Episcopal church. Allen Jr. was the same age I had been when my father died. Watching him cry made me feel the way I'd felt twenty years earlier as I stood in front of my father's casket and wanted to wake him. Just wanted to touch his arm and remind him it was time to go throw the ball in the front yard. Watching Allen's body shake in front of his father's closed casket made me doubt what I had done. Maybe it wasn't for me to decide. Maybe the bad would outweigh the good, for all of us.

I looked up at the stained glass window above, Jesus on the cross, multi-colored and all-knowing, glowing in the sunlight of a Wednesday morning, and I began to wonder about who I was, and what I had done, and whether anything would ever make sense again.

seven

Two days after the funeral I had my first experience of leaving myself. It sounds crazy, I know, but the way it sounds is nothing compared to the way it felt.

I was driving down the four-lane interstate alone in the afternoon. Traffic was light, and up ahead in my lane, two or three hundred yards in front, I saw an old pickup truck. The bed of the truck was piled high with picked corn, still in the husk, and on top of the pile of corn sat a Mexican boy, maybe fifteen or sixteen years old. I found myself, within the drone of the radio, fixated on the truck ahead, and the corn, and the boy with the faded red t-shirt and black hair. I got closer and drifted into the left-hand lane to pass the old blue truck. I couldn't seem to remove my eyes from the face of the boy. It was like I was hypnotized or something. And he looked back at me, no expression, with dark eyes against smooth brown skin, the color of wood.

We were nearly side by side, my car and the truck, me and the Mexican boy, and then I saw myself. I saw me, driving my car, from the eyes of the Mexican boy sitting atop the pile of picked corn in the back of the pickup truck. I saw me staring, my hands on the wheel of the car. I looked down at the brown hand resting on the ear of corn next to blue jeans, and looked up again to see myself for just a split-second longer behind the wheel of the car. Just a split-second, and then I was back inside myself again, seeing the Mexican boy, and him seeing me, and passing the truck, trying to figure out what had happened. Looking in the rearview mirror to see if the boy would turn his head around to the front, recognition that something had happened to him also. It wasn't just me. But he didn't turn around, and I kept going, speeding up to get away from the blue pickup truck.

It happened maybe five more times after that through the years, after that day, but never so profoundly, never with such stark images and clarity of perspective. To see the world through someone else's eyes, if only for a second, and then return to yourself, moving away, never to see that person again. I've often wondered what happened to the boy. Where his life took him.

The fallout from Allen Kilborn's murder was immediate. There were possibilities I'd failed to consider. A week before Gretchen's next scheduled visit, I bought tickets for a play and made dinner reservations. I fixed up her room, wondering if I'd picked the right colors. Knowing I was only guessing what girls her age liked, or didn't like, or thought was stupid. I'd missed so much. I'd missed waking her up in the morning, holding her hand on the way to school, the bond that can only come from the repetition of one goodnight kiss after another.

She didn't come. The day before she was supposed to arrive, a deputy from the Sheriff's Department knocked on my door. I sat on Gretchen's bed, on the new quilt and clean sheets, and opened the envelope. My visitation was suspended. Kate's lawyer called me "the subject of a murder investigation," and said I was "cohabitating with a member of the opposite sex not related by blood or marriage." Overnight visitation with my child should be suspended temporarily, they said. There was an affidavit from Investigator Frank Rush cleverly worded to call me a suspect, and at the same time call everyone in the world a suspect.

I called Kate's house. No answer. I hung up before the machine picked up. I called again, and again. I wondered if Gretchen knew it was me, and didn't pick up because she didn't want to talk to me. Because she thought I was a murderer, and a cohabitator, and some strange man she didn't really know, or even want to know, who lived a million miles away and sat in a room that wasn't really hers, on a bed she didn't really want to sleep in.

What judge would order a child to fly across the country to sleep in the home of a man suspected of blowing a man's head off sitting at his computer, in his own home? Not me. What's more, I did it. I wasn't just a suspect. I was a murderer. A man capable of such a thing, even if I was the only one who knew.

I loved Gretchen. I wanted everything I'd missed. I would have been a good father. Better than good. If the judge had given her to me so many years ago, I would have fixed her breakfast every morning. Gotten her dressed. Taken her to daycare or pre-school and made sure no one was mean to her. We would have played in the backyard, and had things together. Like words we both laughed about, or stupid little songs only the two of us could sing, because we'd made up the songs. They were ours.

But she didn't come home with me. She went to California with her mother and her rich stepfather and now they wanted to cut the string of what was left. Maybe it was all a part of the investigator's strategy. Put pressure on me. Take away my little girl. Watch it eat me up inside until I told the truth, all of it, for a chance to see my girl again, or a pack of cigarettes, or a promise of redemption and everlasting forgiveness.

Eddie called and wanted to meet me for a beer at the same place we met before.

When I arrived, he was already perched at a stool, a cold frosty mug of draft beer in his hand. I sat down next to him. He didn't waste time with small talk. "This guy Rush has come to see me three times, Early."

He held up three fingers and repeated, "Three times."

"I know," I said. "He's been to see me, too."

Eddie took a sip of his beer. He said in a low voice, "He's asking me about you, and shit from college, and Kate, and the day we stopped by the dead guy's house."

He looked straight ahead while he talked. It occurred to me he might be wearing a wire. Frank Rush might be sitting in the back room of the bar, listening. He sent Eddie to see me. He squeezed Eddie with threats of arrest, co-conspirator accusations, and now, here we sat, me and my childhood friend Eddie Miller, not so far removed from the drugstore.

"He's asking me the same questions, Eddie. I guess they can't figure out who killed the man, so they just keep asking us the same things over and over. Since we didn't do anything wrong, we don't have anything to worry about. That's the way I look at it."

Eddie looked over at me and took a little sip of his beer. We were quiet for awhile. I glanced around the room looking for anything out of the ordinary. Maybe somebody watching me, a tiny camera lens. Maybe I was paranoid, I thought. Maybe I'd be glancing around rooms for the rest of my life wondering who was wearing a wire or why somebody was looking at me.

Eddie said, "When I was a little kid, why did you tell me there was no such thing as Santa Claus?"

I thought about it. "I don't remember, Eddie."

"That was a shitty thing to do, Early. Shitty. We only have so much time to believe in things like Santa Claus, and after that, it's bullshit and bills to pay, sittin' around knowin' we're gonna die at the end anyway. You shouldn't have told me that."

He was sincere. I began to doubt Frank Rush was hiding in the back room with earphones. The bartender walked over to us.

"I'll have what he's having," I said. "And bring him another one, too."

Eddie looked down at his glass.

"I'm sorry," I said.

Somebody slapped my shoulder from behind. It was Jake Crane, my other childhood friend, the polar opposite of Eddie Miller. The guy who laid on the roof next to me watching his cousins take showers. I hadn't seen Jake Crane in at least ten years. He was bloated, puffy in the face. I imagined ten years of cigarettes and whiskey, pool halls and local jails.

"It's like a reunion," Jake yelled. "Bring me one of those beers," he called out to the bartender.

In my paranoid state, I immediately wondered if it was a coincidence. Maybe Jake was in over his head with some drug charge. Maybe he was willing to wear a wire, accidentally run into his buddies, try to start a conversation about Allen Kilborn. Maybe Frank Rush had decided Eddie was involved in the murder, and me and Eddie did it together. My mind spun in circles and eventually came to rest on the puffy face of Jake Crane. He pulled up a stool between us.

I asked him, "Where you been the past decade?"

"Well, let's see," Jake said. "I been married twice, fixin' to be three. I spent a little time upstate after my fourth DUI. I got me a damn good job now, and I gained fifty pounds. That's about it."

I lied and told Eddie and Jake I had to be somewhere. The fallout continued in directions I hadn't envisioned. My two best childhood friends, and I couldn't trust either one of them to have a simple beer and a simple conversation at a bar. I left them sitting next to each other, and I knew when I walked away I'd never meet with either one of them on purpose again. I walked out and got in the car. I sat there thinking about the Mexican kid and the idea of fate. The idea that, if I left the parking lot ten seconds later, or ten seconds earlier, I might find myself in the path of a dump truck running a red light, or find myself not in the path of a dump truck running a red light, and how do I know when to start the car, and when to pull into traffic, and how fast to drive to avoid the dump truck that may not exist, or may very well crush me in my car on the way home?

Reasonable doubt. The very foundation of the American judicial system. A standard a jury must utilize to determine guilt or innocence. If you have reasonable doubt, a doubt for which you have a reason, then you cannot, according to the American judicial system, declare someone guilty. The standard, of course, exists to protect the innocent, but also harbors the well-organized, the well-prepared, the man willing to sacrifice. Maybe one of those sacrifices would be Eddie Miller and Jake Crane. Maybe the sacrifices would never end. Gretchen, then eventually Samantha, and finally, myself. Maybe fate would take it off my shoulders.

I wanted to marry Samantha immediately. I wanted her next to me every night, but it couldn't be done. A wedding so soon after Allen Kilborn's death would brighten the spotlight on me and Samantha. Her focus since the funeral had been on Allen Jr., which is where it belonged, but it left me utterly alone night after night on my porch smoking cigarettes in the dark.

I was finally allowed to talk to Gretchen on the phone. Her voice sounded like she was in the bottom of a deep hole. At one point in the conversation she called me "Early." I knew she'd been calling the old man "Dad," but she rarely slipped anymore. The worst part is, when she slipped on the phone, she didn't even catch it. It went right on by, the low voice from deep in the hole mumbling something about feeling sick, or not being able to miss cheerleading practice. After she called me "Early" it didn't matter anymore.

My mother called. "Why isn't Gretchen coming to visit?"

I couldn't tell her. I couldn't say it.

"She's sick. She can't miss cheerleading practice," I lied.

"That's a lie, Early. What's going on?"

I hesitated. "They filed something with the Court to suspend my visitation."

"For God's sake, why?"

"It's Kate, fuckin' with me. Taking advantage of the situation. They told the judge I was a suspect in the murder of Allen Kilborn."

"Are you?" she asked.

"No," I nearly yelled. "No."

There was silence on both ends of the phone. I could hear her breathing.

"What about me, Early?" Christine asked.

"What?"

"What about me, Goddamnit? Me and Gretchen? Our relationship? Forget about you for a minute. Why do I suffer because you end up in screwed-up situations? I miss the girl. Every day. She's my best friend."

More fallout. More unintended consequences. It didn't seem to make any difference if I got caught by Frank Rush or not. Even my mother would end up hating me. My father would know what to do. If he was still alive, things would be different. I would have married a nice, pear-shaped, stable girl from a stable family and lived securely in a well-built house. No savior complex. No drug addicts or courthouse marriages. No rich stepfather or abrasive ex-husbands. Smooth sailing, it would have been, if only my father had left the parking lot ten seconds earlier, or ten seconds later, crossing the tracks ahead of the train. It was just a matter of moments, like it's always been, and like it will always be.

Strangely, as the weeks passed, and then months, I felt a change in Allen Jr. Before it was always them against us. Little Allen and Big Allen against me and Samantha. The lines were clear. Now, he was just a boy. A boy without a dad. His dad died and left him alone with his mother, and me. The man who hangs around his mother.

"Are you gonna play baseball this year?" I asked.

We were sitting in the living room. Me in the chair and Little Allen on the couch. Since his father died, the boy was quiet most of the time, just like I'd been.

"Maybe," he said.

It was getting late. Samantha was in the bathtub. Every night, before Allen went to sleep, I said goodnight and went back to my house. He had enough to deal with in his world without seeing me walking around the house in my underwear or imagining me and his mother doing it in the bedroom.

"I think you should play. If you want, we'll go look for a new glove. You need a new glove."

He looked at me as I spoke, like he was seeing me for the first time. He didn't respond to the comment about the baseball glove. We sat quietly for a minute. I raised up in the chair to leave.

Allen said, his eyes staring at his hands, "You don't have to go home every night. You could stay here some nights."

It made me smile. It was justification, small, but justification nonetheless. Before, he would never have considered such a thing. I was the enemy. Not anymore. Now I was just a guy. A guy who liked baseball, and anybody who loves baseball can't be all bad. No matter what they've done.

eight

On the third ring, I said out loud into the phone, "Pick up the fuckin' phone." Before I'd finished the sentence, somebody picked it up. There was silence, and then Kate said, "What if Gretchen had answered?"

"Sorry," I said, and I was actually sorry. The frustration was maddening. To have no control over something so important, so simple as having somebody pick up the phone on the other end of the line.

"Nobody answers over there, Kate. I've called ten days in a row. I can't talk to your machine anymore."

Kate said, "We've got caller ID, Early. Gretchen can tell who's calling."

There it was. What I didn't need to hear. "Don't say that. Even if it's true. What pleasure could you possibly gain in saying that? You should see what it's like to be on this side. Why don't you send Gretchen down here? You can have three visits a year and maybe we'll pick up the phone, maybe not, and I'll be sure to rub it up in your face whenever I get the chance."

There was silence again.

"Don't hang up," I said.

I wasn't sure she was still on the line.

"I'm getting married," I said.

There was nothing do but wait for her to answer.

"To who?" she asked.

"Samantha."

"The dead man's ex-wife?"

"Yes. But it doesn't have anything to do with Allen Kilborn. She's a good mother. She's got a boy Gretchen's age."

It was strange, but Kate's voice still held me. There was something pleasant inside of it. I wondered if it was the voice itself, or some memory attached to it. If I'd never met her before, would the voice make me feel anything beyond the words?

"Will it be a big wedding?" she asked, revealing more curiosity than I expected, and maybe more than she expected.

"It didn't start out that way. At first we just had a list of about twenty people. A month later, it was two hundred. Now we've got two cakes, a band, shrimp."

She laughed. "A little different than the first time."

"Yeah," I said. "A little different. I think that's why Samantha wants the whole show. She did it like ours the first time."

It was the most normal conversation I'd had with

Kate since the day she lost her baby. Our baby. The baby inside her that died and made her hate me.

"I want Gretchen to be in the wedding," I said.

"I've got a court order."

"I know what you've got. I haven't seen her for eight months, Kate. I'm gettin' married. She's my daughter. I can't wait until she turns nineteen and then hope she sends me a Christmas card every year. Hope I can undo nineteen years of unanswered phone calls."

I tried to keep the tone of my voice level. Frustration seeped out between the sentences. I took a deep breath, soundless, so she couldn't hear my desperation.

She said, "Did you kill that man, or what?"

"What do you think, Kate?"

She didn't answer, and I imagined her standing in her high school home next to the man in the chair with the hole in his foot, a dim light and a dog at the screen door. A bottle of vodka by the chair. I could see it plain as day. She was wearing a dirty white apron.

"Is your dad still alive?" I asked.

I'm not sure what I meant by the question. Maybe I meant to remind her she had no relationship with her father, and maybe that was part of the reason she'd been so screwed up. And how could she want the same thing for Gretchen?

She finally said, "If Gretchen's going down there, I'm going with her, and we're staying in a motel. I'm gonna be there with her at the wedding, too."

It was unsettling on a number of different levels. Ex-wife at the new wife's wedding. Mostly it was unsettling to me personally. If her voice still held me, how would I feel about her in the same room? At my wedding? But I was in very little position to challenge. Another court battle could take months, and money set aside for other things. Just another conciliation in the great compromise. Wishing I'd left her on that damn street so many years ago didn't help, because there'd be no Gretchen, and then I'd have no idea at all what I'd lost.

"Okay," I said, and we ended the conversation.

People gathered in the church. I stood in a back room at the mirror with Allen Jr., tightening our tuxedo ties. I couldn't stay still.

"Are you nervous?" he asked.

I wanted to be the strong, silent type. I'm sure his father never looked nervous a day in his life. "Yeah, I'm a little nervous," I confessed.

Allen said, "I would think the nervous part would be asking a girl to marry you. That's when you really make the promise."

He was right. The hard parts were over. Minutes later we stood together at the altar waiting to watch Allen's mother walk down the aisle with her father on her arm. My eyes scanned the faces in the crowd. People from work. Not really friends, just people who work in the same place. Allen's grandmother on his father's side. Her face hard like her son's face had been. My mother, Christine, her eyes on Gretchen across the aisle from me. And Frank Rush, the investigator, his face near the back, uninvited. We looked at each other, and I moved along to the next face, and the next, but I felt my chest tighten, the breath stopping at a shallow point in the top of the lungs, refusing to go down deep.

I glanced at Little Allen, and he smiled up at me. He seemed genuinely happy about the marriage. His smile gave me comfort, and I realized that his was the only face in the crowd to bring the feeling. In the far side of my field of vision I saw Kate. For the past two days I'd managed to avoid the moment, but now there was nowhere to go. I didn't have the endurance to look away. She was beautiful. A woman now, not just a lost skinny girl with no home. Her presence made me weak in my legs. A moment longer, even one more moment of looking at her, and something bad would have happened. Instead, the music started, and my new wife turned down the aisle as pretty as any bride could be, her elderly father smiling wide just like the boy next to me, while the stained-glass Jesus looked down upon all of us.

And it happened again. Only for a few seconds, but it definitely happened again. I saw myself from Allen Jr's eyes. It was just a blink, the side of my head, the wedding song, and I could feel what he felt. An excitement. Not nearly as clear as with the Mexican boy, but real just the same, and I was grateful for the interruption this time. Not as shocked as before.

At the reception I focused on Samantha. All the other distractions had no place in the day. When I slipped away to the bathroom I thought I'd found a minute to smoke a cigarette and clear out my head. I was wrong. Before I could get the single cigarette out of my inside jacket pocket,

Frank Rush came through the door. If it wasn't an accident, he sure made it seem like one.

"Congratulations," he said.

I washed my hands. "Thanks."

It was like he was the gym teacher, and I was the kid
who smoked cigarettes in the bathroom, and he almost
caught me.

He stood at the sink, washing his big hands.

"I just wanted to see it for myself," he said.

I played along. "See what?"

"See if you could go through with it. Standing up there
next to that boy. Knowing how much he loved his daddy."

We looked at each other in the mirror. I decided not
to say anything.

Frank Rush dried his hands on a brown paper towel.
He never took his eyes away from me.

"I know you killed the man, Early. I know it down in
my bones. We can't prove it yet, but we will. Sooner or
later you'll tell somebody, or the gun'll turn up, or your
wife and Little Allen will figure it all out, and I'll get a call,
like I always do. And when that day comes, I think you'll
be glad to get it over with. You don't seem like a bad man
to me. Hell, maybe we're all better off without that abrasive son-of-a-bitch around anyhow."

The bathroom door swung open. Eddie Miller walked
in. He stopped dead still. There was a minute when we all
looked at each other. I almost laughed. Don't ask me why,
because I don't know why. It just seemed so ludicrous, the
three of us standing in the bathroom together.

"Hey," Eddie said.

"Hey," I answered. I turned and left.

Maybe, like I said before, it was fate. Leaving the parking lot ten seconds too early, or ten seconds too late, and getting pulverized by a train, except in my case, it was extreme violence so close in time and location to my conception. Maybe somehow the sound waves of the violence, the gunshot and the blood spatter against the wall, traveled through the small space of air from the window to my mother's womb, wobbled the egg sac somehow. Maybe I would kill again, and again, and no one would be safe around me, including Samantha or Little Allen or Kate or Eddie Miller. Or maybe I was right in what I did. And there's a place for violence, controlled violence, in a civilized world.

I drank too much champagne at the reception. Everywhere I turned there was stilted conversation with the mother of the man I murdered, or Frank Rush eating a piece of chocolate cake, or Kate's red dress on the other side of the room. So I drank another glass of champagne, and another, and for some godforsaken reason I decided it would be funny to snap a picture with somebody's disposable camera up the skirt of a stiff, middle-aged woman with black hair and a tight bun on the back of her head, until she turned around at exactly the wrong moment. And her husband saw me do it. And then somehow somebody apologized to somebody else and Samantha and I were whisked away to our honeymoon to have sex, anytime, in almost any way I wanted, for four days and four glorious nights. That's the way I remember it.

PART III
middle-aged anarchy

Our lives are not defined by the wide radical swings, but instead, by times in between, the leveling off. After the death of Allen Kilborn and my wedding, I tried very hard to smooth out my life into normalcy, the daily routine of living. After all, that's why I did what I did, so Allen Jr. and Samantha could level off. So our lives would not be wide radical swings every day.

The first step was committing myself to my career like never before. I was in my late thirties, a time in a man's life when he should hit his stride. Working for a national investment company had it advantages, I suppose. There were plaques on my office wall. Corporate trips to San Francisco and New Orleans. If I jumped through the right hoops I got a bonus, or a new title, or a call from some big shot in Seattle who told me I was "the lifeblood of the organization. The personification of the values that set the company apart from competitors."

I remember sitting at my desk staring at the back of the closed door for God knows how long. I remember feeling I was on the verge of slipping into some sort of cataleptic state, able to hear and see the world around me, but unable to make the decision to move a muscle.

The voice from the phone said, "You're the kind of man who moves this business forward, Early, and I don't just mean the business of our company. I mean the stock market itself, the free enterprise system, America. You're innovative, energetic, willing to work outside the lines, and you'll be rewarded in the short run, and of course, in the long run."

The words were like morphine. A dead warmth spread through my body. I remember saying, "Do you mean Heaven?"

The voice hesitated. "Heaven?" it repeated.

"Yeah, the long run. Do you mean all my innovation and hard work will get me into Heaven? Eternity with God and all the other people who earned a spot?"

The voice hesitated again and said, "Well, I was thinking more along the lines of district manager, but I suppose God likes hard work. It certainly can't hurt."

The back of the office door was off-white, the color of margarine. It looked good enough to lick, shiny. I began to imagine, in my cataleptic state, with the voice purring in the background though the phone, what it would be like to become part of the door, virtually melt into the off-white black hole of another object, until the voice said in a slightly louder volume, "Congratulations, Early Winwood."

"Congratulations to you," I said, which of course made no sense at all.

My relationship with Allen grew in direct proportion to the deterioration of my relationship with Gretchen. He looked forward to seeing me in the afternoons. We talked about sports. I taught him the secrets of baseball. Gretchen wouldn't return my calls. On one rare occasion when she answered the phone she told me she hated the idea of me sleeping in the same bed as Samantha.

"She's my wife," I said.

"I know. I was at the wedding. Remember?"

"Your mother sleeps in the same bed with her husband."

"No, she doesn't," Gretchen said.

"What do you mean?" I asked.

"They've got separate rooms. Anyway, it's not your business anymore. You didn't want to be married to Mom, so now you've got a new wife…"

I stopped her in the middle of the sentence. "What do you mean I didn't want to be married to your mother?" I said.

She hung up the phone. It was an odd revelation, Kate and her husband in separate rooms. I didn't know what to do with the information. Maybe I wasn't supposed to do anything with it at all. Maybe I was just supposed to not think about it one way or the other. Maybe I was supposed to be satisfied with my life, my job, my wife, and not reserve a corner of my mind for Kate Shepherd. The same corner she'd always occupied, maybe smaller now, but pretty much the same general location of the brain. The back left corner. Next to the part that thinks about food and oxygen.

Of course, there wasn't enough room in my mind for Kate Shepherd, or anything else for that matter, since Allen Kilborn Sr. crawled around inside every hour of my day. It got so bad I created a mechanism inside myself to cope with the problem. An automatic switch. When I'd catch myself thinking about the man, or what I did to the man, I'd switch to something else immediately. I started with Samantha, and then Little Allen, but it didn't work well. My thoughts would circle back. I tried unrelated subjects, like the batting averages of third basemen, or listing the presidents of the United States in chronological order, but the relief was temporary. The only subject I found successfully distracted my attention was sex. The images inside my mind were vivid enough to start a chain reaction throughout my body, and the natural instinct seemed to take over.

This caused new problems in the house. Since about a year after we got married, the sexual opportunities with my wife began a slow, steady decrease. There were plenty of excuses, and I began to obsess on the subject. It seemed like such a small sacrifice for her to make. I worked very hard. I provided. I was loyal and dependable. How could she let weeks pass without providing for me? I walked the line between beggar and brooder, and not very well I might add. A line I'd walked before, and just as poorly.

"Samantha, it's important to our relationship. I don't understand."

Sometimes, when she would give in, I'd find myself on top of a dead body, warm and supple like a new corpse before the onset of rigor, with her head craned way to the side, probably thinking about grocery shopping, like an animal pretending to be dead until the predator moves along. As much as the situation disgusted me, I wouldn't stop until I was finished, and satisfied, if only for a few hours. Sometimes, while we were doing it, I'd think about him on top of her and wonder if it was the same. Wonder if maybe with him she writhed and bucked and moaned.

The value of sex for a man in a marriage far outweighs the five-second orgasm. It's the ultimate reassurance. The ultimate display of complete trust, loyalty, and respect, to allow someone to enter you, literally, to physically enter your body. It's an act of appreciation that can keep a man getting up in the morning and going to a job he doesn't like, at least for a while.

I found myself creating a new mechanism. An automatic switch away from sex and nasty fantasies of my wife doing things she'd never let me do. I started thinking about nothing. Started visualizing a blackboard at school. On the blackboard were words like Allen Kilborn, Kato, district manager, Gretchen, cigarettes, step #7, and Frank Rush.

I would lie perfectly still on my back, eyes closed in the dark room, and start with ten deep breaths. Then I'd visualize the blackboard with the words written haphazardly from top to bottom. One by one the words would be erased, and with each disappearing word, my body would relax. Finally, all the words would be gone and I'd be left thinking of absolutely nothing. Dark, black, nothing, surrounded by thick metal walls to keep everything else away from the nothingness.

The front page of the paper said: SUSPECT ARRESTED IN MURDER OF KILBORN. The picture of Eddie's face these years later made him look blank and hollow. It was a booking photograph from the jail. His eyes seemed to look directly at me and no one else.

The article didn't give many details. I can still recall my first clear thought after reading the headline. It had to be a trick. A ploy to get me to come forward. There couldn't be any evidence against Eddie. He was innocent. All he did was drive me to the house earlier in the day. He couldn't confess to something he didn't do. He couldn't lead them to the murder weapon, or the clothes, or the key.

I sat at the kitchen table staring down at Eddie's picture. Samantha must have been looking over my shoulder.

"Oh my God. Isn't that your friend?"

I didn't react.

"We were friends in grade school. I haven't seen him but a few times since we grew up."

"He was at the wedding!" she yelled.

Allen Jr. ended up in the unhealthy conversation.

"He killed my father? Your friend killed my father? Why?" he asked me.

"It must be a mistake, Allen. I've only seen Eddie a few times since college. He always seemed like a good man. It must just be a mistake."

Samantha read the article. "I hope they execute the bastard."

Little Allen started crying. All the emotions came upward from wherever he'd locked them down below.

"It's just got to be a mistake," I said again. It was the only explanation I could offer. My mind started spinning around back to that day.

Frank Rush must have convinced himself that Eddie was involved. Out of desperation, he must have finally decided to make a move, try to shake things loose. Rush probably figured if Eddie was involved, certainly now, sitting in jail with no bond, and facing execution or spending the rest of his life in jail, he would tell what he knew. What if he made things up? What if he told more than he knew, or could know, just to give Frank Rush what he wanted, which was me?

The police car could pull up to my office any day, or maybe come to the house in the middle of the night, and they'd pull me off my limp wife and drag my sorry ass to jail. It could be me next week on the front page of the paper, with a washed-out photograph, and other people sitting at their kitchen tables saying what a nice guy I always seemed to be.

There was nothing for me to do but wait. It was ironic, if that's the right word. I would depend on the same judicial system for Eddie, an innocent man, as I depended upon for myself, not innocent, but prepared. If the system provided protection for a guilty man, even a well-planned guilty man with good intentions, then certainly it would protect Eddie Miller. If it didn't, what would I do? And was it possible Eddie was in on the trick?

That night, on the way home from work, I took a longer route through town. Nobody seemed to be following me. I drove south and then looped to the backroads where I'd dug the holes out in the woods. It was hard to tell exactly where they were. The area was being built up, new subdivisions, box houses one next to the other. I didn't turn my head to look into the woods as I passed. I just aimed straight ahead in case Frank Rush stood behind the line of trees waiting for me to pass. Waiting for me to coincidentally be on the wrong road, looking into the woods at the wrong spot, on the day after the wrong man was arrested.

I stopped at a convenience store and bought a pack of cigarettes. My first pack in over a year. At home, after Samantha fell asleep in the middle of a conversation, I checked on Allen. His light was off down the hall. On the screened back porch, in the dark, I lit a cigarette with matches hidden by the grill. I could feel the thick smoke fill my lungs and then disappear invisibly into the night. I let the silence come down on me, and I listened for any sound. A dog barked down the street. An airplane roared way above in the sky, taking people I didn't know to see other people I didn't know, and I imagined each of them thought of things like me, but different from me, and they didn't even know I was down below smoking a cigarette in the dark.

The back door swung open. My head spun around to see the silhouette of Little Allen, not so little anymore as a teenager, standing in the doorway. I dropped the cigarette to the brick floor and stood on top of it with my bare foot, twisting as I turned to Allen.

"Is everything okay?" he said.

"Yeah, yeah. I thought I heard something. It was just a dog."

He was in shorts and an oversized t-shirt. He was a good boy. Honest, with a full heart. It was the people around him who were crazy and disjointed.

"A dog? What kind of dog?" he asked curiously.

"I didn't see it. I just heard it."

"Is there something burning?" he asked.

It should be the other way around. It should have been me catching a teenage boy sneaking a smoke on the back porch at night. It should have been me at the door in my boxers asking the questions. Instead, I felt a burning on the bottom of my foot. The pain built to a point I nearly cried out, then slowly lessened until there was a sound in the bushes to the left of where we stood. We both turned to look.

"What was that?" Allen whispered.

"Probably the dog again," I said calmly, but we both knew it was a lie. It didn't seem like the sound a dog would make. It seemed more like the sound a man would make in the bushes. A man who watched me when I didn't know it.

two

I was in my office, daydreaming about nothing, when the speakerphone on the corner of my desk said, "Mr. Winwood, there's a Frank Rush here to see you."

The daydream ended abruptly. My secretary must have thought she was talking to an empty room.

"Are you there?" she asked softly.

"Yes. I'm sorry. I was in the middle of something. Send him in."

The door opened a few seconds later and Investigator Rush stood in the doorway. He was a bit larger than the last time I'd seen him, but the face was the same. Heavy.

He sat down, and as was the custom between us, I waited. A brown briefcase rested in his lap.

He said, looking around the room, "You've done pretty good for yourself."

The panorama of framed certificates seemed impressive, but it was all bullshit. Seminars where I sat in the back not listening to the boring guy stomping around the stage. Training sessions I didn't actually attend.

"Did you see Eddie in the newspaper?" he asked, focusing on a gold-leaf diploma to my left on the wall.

"Yeah," I answered.

I felt a line of sweat sneak from my left armpit down my ribs beneath the blue button-down shirt. Mr. Rush watched me, and I watched him, the usual dance. I'm not sure what he expected from me. I'm not sure what anybody expected from me.

In the silence between us I heard someone laugh in the outer lobby. It was the laugh of a woman, unrestrained, tickled by something, with no time to muffle the response. It was genuine, and I wished I was sitting next to her, whoever she was, instead of sitting across from the man with the briefcase in his lap, a thin line of cool sweat inching downward to my hip.

Frank Rush opened the briefcase and casually placed a large pistol on the desk between us. He closed the case. It was Allen Kilborn's pistol, or one that looked like Allen Kilborn's, only older, weathered, dug up from its grave.

"You recognize that?" the man asked. He pointed at the gun but started directly at my face. I leaned up a bit in my chair to see the pistol, and then leaned back again.

"No," I said.

The investigator leaned up in his chair also and looked at the gun like it was the first time he'd ever seen the thing.

"We found it at a construction site off Highway 33. It's a pretty remote area back there, but over the last few years neighborhoods have popped up. They were puttin' in the foundation for a house. It was buried about a foot and a half."

I glanced from his eyes back down to the gun.

"It's cleaned up now," he said. "It was in pretty bad shape. At first, I figured there was no chance a fingerprint could survive, but we sent it off to that fancy lab up in Virginia, the FBI lab."

In my mind, I watched myself put the gloves on my hands. I saw the gloved hand open the drawer and remove the gun from the special wooden rest. I saw the hole I dug, about eighteen inches deep. Two feet at the most.

"They found a fingerprint. One fingerprint."

I didn't flinch. I didn't swallow. I just looked him in the eye.

"Guess whose fingerprint?" he said.

The woman in the lobby laughed again. Almost identical to the first laugh, but longer. She let it linger at the end, trailing away.

Frank Rush said, "Eddie Miller's."

It was a lie. I knew it was a lie, and he knew it was a lie. Eddie never touched the gun. It wasn't possible. But I was the only person to really know for sure, and the investigator across from me looked so hard into my face for anything at all, anything, I began to feel physical pressure along the top of my eyes and down to my cheekbones, like his big hand was touching my face, holding my face like a soccer ball.

"I don't believe it," I said.

He studied my answer. "Why not?"

"Because Eddie Miller doesn't strike me as the kind of man who would kill somebody. And why would he kill Allen Kilborn? I don't think he even knew Allen."

Frank Rush said, "You can't always tell a killer by how he looks, Mr. Winwood. I believe we all have it inside us. The ability to kill, I mean. A man who wouldn't kill to protect his child, or his family, is a coward. We all have a reason, a reason worth killing over, most of us just never get to that point. I guess Eddie Miller got to the point, for whatever reason, and now he has to face the consequences."

I said, "I don't know much about you, Mr. Rush. When I was younger, I could see people a lot better. I don't see 'em so good anymore, but you don't appear to be the type of person willing to send an innocent man to prison just so you can close an old file."

The gun was directly between us and I tried very hard not to look at it again.

"What makes you so sure Eddie Miller is an innocent man?" he asked sincerely.

I turned my chair slightly to look at the gold leaf diploma displayed so proudly.

"Because when we were kids, maybe twelve years old, we planned an elaborate heist from the drugstore. A candy bar heist. Eddie's job was just to be the lookout."

I glanced back from the framed diploma to Frank Rush where he sat.

"He couldn't do it," I said. "He couldn't even be the

lookout for a candy bar theft. He started shaking all over and looking for excuses. He wouldn't be a very good murderer."

Frank Rush seemed to consume the story I told, and as it digested he shook his head up and down like he understood.

He said, "What exactly was your role in the candy bar heist?"

I thought of the countless diagrams I'd drawn. Diagrams with locations of mirrors, and employees, with an X marking the spot where the candy bars were displayed. Frank Rush stared so hard at the side of my face I felt he could steal the thoughts right out of my head.

My secretary's voice blared out from the speakerphone, startling the hell out of me, and in turn startling Frank Rush.

"Mr. Winwood, I'm sorry to disturb you, but Gretchen's mother is on the line. She says it's an emergency."

It was Kate. Something about a seizure. Something about Gretchen in the television section of a big store, she had a seizure, fell into a TV, she was at the hospital. Kate was crying. The doctors weren't sure what caused the problem. There were tests to do.

I hung up the phone.

"I have to go to California, Mr. Rush. My daughter's in the hospital. I need to be there. I hope I'm right. I hope you're not the type of person willing to keep an innocent man in jail, for whatever reason."

I stood and walked out of the room, leaving him in the chair, brown briefcase in his lap and the pistol resting on my desk. I walked past my secretary and the lady laughing in the lobby. She weighed at least three hundred pounds. Her blue dress was like a bed sheet draped across her massive body. She smiled at me and I smiled back.

Samantha helped me pack my bag. She wanted to know details, but I didn't have any details. She wanted to know exactly what Kate said, but I couldn't remember the exact words, and it seemed like a strange time to be thinking about herself. I looked at Samantha across the room, my eyes red from crying at the thought of Gretchen dying in a hospital in California, and it occurred to me Samantha wasn't capable of giving me comfort. She loved me when I was strong and dependable, because that's what she loved about me. There was no place for me to be needy. When I needed comfort, affection, sexual reassurance, I was no longer strong and dependable, I was weak, and she didn't love weak, so why would she want to have sex with a weak man, or put her arms around me and tell me she loved me?

I wanted to tell her right then and there that I killed Allen. Right in our bedroom, me standing by the closet, her standing by the bed, my suitcase open, my eyes full. I wanted to tell her what I'd done for her, Allen Jr., and all of us. Ironically, one of the primary purposes of killing the man was to remove all impediments in the relationship between myself and Samantha, but the guilt and suspicions, the underground doubts, had built a wall even larger, an emotional barrier we couldn't seem to cross. I created unreasonable expectations.

I turned away, but she knew something had clicked

inside me. She watched as I packed my bag. The picture of my father was in my sock drawer, down at the bottom, and until I saw it, I'd forgotten where it was hidden. I'd forgotten again exactly how he looked, smiling, his head turned a bit to the side. The white t-shirt had a dark stain near the belly like he wiped his hands across his shirt. Maybe working on his car. Maybe working in the yard.

Samantha watched me put the photograph in the suitcase. She let me walk out the door to fly to California to see my daughter in the hospital, without a kiss good-bye. Without putting her arms around me and telling me everything would be all right. Even if it wasn't going to be all right. Even if it was going to be bad.

I stepped inside one door of the waiting room just as the doctor stepped in the other. Kate and her old husband, Russell Enslow, stood. There was no one else in the small room. The doctor explained he believed it was pancreatitis. Rare in young people. The pancreas becomes inflamed, shuts down, wreaks havoc on the body. There would be more tests. It was a very serious situation. Gretchen was asking for her mother. The doctor took Kate with him, leaving me and Russell Enslow alone in the small waiting area.

I'd spent the last eight hours in airports and taxicabs. I could smell myself. The smell of self-pity and body odor. I hadn't spoken a word, just walked up in time to hear the explanation from the doctor. I sat down across from Russell Enslow. We'd never had a conversation. Not one. We'd passed each other in the hallway of the courthouse seventeen years earlier. He answered the phone sometimes and handed it off to Gretchen. But no conversation. I knew nothing about the man, and all he knew about me was the venom he'd heard spewed from Kate's mouth. He probably thought I smelled bad all the time.

We nodded to each other. There was no real anticipated relief. Kate's return might ease his anxiety, but not mine. I took a deep breath and closed my eyes. It was hard to believe earlier in the day I was sitting in my office with Frank Rush, a gun between us, and now I sat in a hospital waiting across from Russell Enslow, nothing between us except a coffee table covered in old magazines.

I was exhausted. All of it, Eddie in jail, the gun, the fat lady in the lobby, Samantha's indifference, pancreatitis, all of it on the same day. Just another seemingly random day empty on the calendar where circumstances converge and take the wheel of your life out of your hands, the feeling of falling, free-falling into the future.

I let my head go back on the chair. I let my eyes close. The sound of pages of a magazine turned by Mr. Russell Enslow created the only sound I could hear, until he spoke.

"My wife is in love with you," is what he said.

I thought I must have dreamed it. Could he have said anything less expected? Maybe, "Do you mind if I take a dump on the carpet?" or, "My left ear is on fire."

I swear to God I thought I dreamed it, maybe I'd dozed off, and without actually seeing Mr. Enslow in my dream, heard him speak. But when I opened my eyes, the man was looking at me, and I knew it wasn't a dream. He was angry, not because he said what he said out loud, but because it was true, and looking at me half-asleep on the other side of the coffee table, he just couldn't figure it out.

"What did you say?" I asked, just in case.

He spoke succinctly, "My wife, Kate, is in love with you."

We were in full-disconnect. I began to wonder if I was having one of my episodes, but even weirder than ususal, seeing a world that didn't exist instead of just seeing the real world though another set of eyes.

"I don't understand," I said.

"Believe me, neither do I, but our lack of understanding doesn't change the fact."

He appeared resigned to the situation, like years had passed since he found it out and surrendered to the knowledge.

"I'm married," I said.

"No shit," he said. "Me too."

It was no place to laugh. There was a strange comraderie. We were in it together, destined to share equally in the misery, both free-falling through the experience, no more in control than a butterfly in a storm.

We looked at each other for a long time. Me at him, and him at me. Russell Enslow was in his fifties, well-dressed, not overly handsome, but not ugly either. He had a slight paunch under his shirt and a sureness I never had, not even in my best moments.

"What are we supposed to do now?" I said.

"I don't have the slightest idea. I thought you'd know. I'm not unhappy. I love Gretchen. I'm excited about her going off to college in a few months. Kate respects me. She appreciates what I provide, financially and as a father.

You'd think it would be horrible to share your home with a woman who is in love with someone else, but it isn't so bad. I'd rather be me than you."

I wanted to stand up and punch him in his little head, but maybe he was right. Our first conversation hadn't really helped me in any way. There was a youthful excitement to it all, but I had a wife, and a young man at home who needed me, maybe more than anyone else in the world. Eddie Miller was in jail for a murder I committed, and I had an office covered in framed certificates and fancy plaques. Even if Russell Enslow was correct, and I couldn't imagine why he'd lie about such a thing, what would it mean in real life? It was all some crazy crap the world conspired to place on my doorstep at exactly the wrong moment, as if there would ever be a right moment.

Kate came to the door. Russell and I stood.

From across the room Kate said, "They think she's going to be okay."

"Thank God," Russell said.

Kate seemed to be looking at a spot between me and her husband, some comfortable middle ground with no eye contact. Maybe the fictional place she envisioned we should all come together in our concern over Gretchen.

"She wants to see you," she said.

I turned my body toward the door.

"No," Kate said, still looking at no one, "She asked for Russell."

He looked at me, but I saw no spite or satisfaction in his face. It just was what it was, no matter who was at fault. Right and wrong, good and bad, have no place in the present. They exist in the past and in the future, to be pre-dicted and judged. Different-colored highways on a map leading to some seemingly random day on the calendar, like the day where I stood in the place where I stood waiting like the butterfly waits for the storm to blow itself out.

Later, when I was alone in the room, I rooted my hand around through the clothes in my bag until I found my father's picture. I could see Gretchen in his face. Very clearly I could see her outline superimposed upon my father, two people a generation apart. Never allowed to be in the same room together, connected only by me.

three

I've always had a real need for permanency. A fundamental clinging demand for believing the idea that some things are forever, set in timeless stone, dependable certainties. Maybe it's a human characteristic, or maybe it's only a characteristic of me. The difference is difficult to distinguish sometimes.

It might derive from the shake-up of my father's death and the blunt-force realization at age eleven of the eventual loss of all things. It's a complicated concept, and even more complicated to overcome. The constant need to rotate around something permanent. Another person, a job, the vows of marriage, even the certainty of the arrival of the Sunday morning paper.

It wasn't until I was able to break through the idea of permanency, set it aside and see the world as it is, every

minute changing, evolving, temporary, unable to make or
keep a promise for tomorrow, that I set myself free.
Unfortunately, the cost of this freedom became a prepos-
session with suicide. The idea of it. The balance. The
reasons for and against. The manner of the deed. Not for
attention, nor for the purpose of some grand statement to
the world, but to be dead, at ease.

Maybe suicide, and the idea of it, was my mind's
attempt at replacing the concept of permanency. When all
else seemed beyond anyone's control, maybe my mind clung
to the idea that at least I could control how long I remained.

They say thoughts of suicide are supposedly symp-
toms of mental illness, but I didn't feel mentally ill. I
doubt seriously I suddenly suffered a rapid chemical
imbalance. It wasn't a knee-jerk reaction, an impulse to
run outside and hang myself from the nearest tree.
Instead, it came as a coldness, a vague narrowing of reason, and the idea, like a billowing white cloud, slowly took
shape, and then began to flow from day-to-day virtually
the rest of my entire life.

My mother was out of town and asked me to stop by
her house and water the plants. It was a good chance to
climb up in her attic and look for those baseball cards I'd
been telling Allen about. I found a box in a wooden chest,
and opening the box of baseball cards was the closest
thing to actually going back in time. The smell. Bent corners I remembered. Batting averages I'd memorized, with
the numbers so ingrained in my memory they came back
instantly, like addresses or phone numbers of childhood
homes.

I took the box and started to close the top of the wooden chest, but something made me stop. There was a small bundle of paper. Letters and envelopes, yellowed and held together with a rubber band, in the corner of the chest. I sat down under the hanging attic lightbulb and began to read.

They were letters from my mother to another man, and from the man back to my mother. His name was Bruce. The postmarks on the envelopes told me they were sent and received before my parents were married, before the night Bobby Winters was shot in the head outside the window of my conception.

He loved her, and he told her so in the words of the handwritten letters. And she told him how she thought about him all the time and wondered what her life would be like with him. There was a photograph of them standing together in front of a house I didn't recognize. He was a big man, much bigger than my father. His arm was around my mother's shoulder and she was looking up at him with a smile I'd never seen on her before.

I started to read another letter, a long one, and stopped. We never really know our parents, the events that shaped them before we were born. The first kiss. The first person they ever loved who didn't love them back. The choices they regret, and can't change, because time has pushed them beyond the chance to go back.

And so it goes that Gretchen and Allen will never really know me. They will know what they see of me, those parts shown, but not the rest. Because I couldn't tell them about the night that I sat staring at Kate passed out in the backseat of the car, or how good it felt to beat the man on the mattress into a bloody mess, or my fear of becoming my mother, or the idea I had yesterday morning of swimming out into the ocean, putting a gun in my mouth, and floating slowly away. And they wouldn't want to know those things anyway, just like I didn't want to know about Bruce, or the letters my mother kept, or the smile in the picture.

I was becoming more like my mother, and it was hard to decide how I felt about it, mostly because it appeared her detachment was based on fear instead of strength. And learning this fact removed yet another delusion of permanence. My mother was getting older. Her mortality was becoming clearer to us both, and it didn't seem to sit well with either one of us, for different reasons of course. She would never remarry, and we both knew that. Not Bruce or anyone else. She would hold bitterness for me, choosing to lay the blame on me for Gretchen being so far away. And I would accept the blame, the guilt so thick between us it sometimes seemed visible, like a fogbank.

Gretchen's illness got better, and my relationship with Allen continued to grow. We spent an entire week together looking for a car for him. He was genuinely a good kid, growing up, ready to become a man. He fought with his mother on occasion, and she expected me to be the disciplinarian. I walked the line between best friend and stepfather, and I must say I walked it well. We avoided using the "step" word whenever possible. I introduced him as my boy, and he was truly my boy, with the hint of something unseen nearby. I couldn't describe it, but Allen

Kilborn Sr. still occupied a place inside our home, our lives. We never spoke of him, Samantha and Allen Jr. avoiding the subject in my presence. I imagine they spoke of the man when I wasn't around.

My relationship with Samantha reached a routine oddness. We seemed almost uncomfortable around each other, but so dependent the oddness was endurable, inevitable. It was a constant struggle of miscommunication and unfulfilled expectations mixed with reliability, trust, and commitment. It occurred to me I might be entering a phase in a long-term relationship I'd never entered before. The leveling off I've spoken of. An apparent profound compromise, but without effect. Expectations settled like an old dog going round and round, coming to rest on the same comfortable pillow. There would be no more nights of unashamed passion. There would be no more flutter in the chest at the sight of her in the backyard planting flowers. But so what? I thought. Until the letter arrived.

It came to the office. The stack of mail was left on my desk. Maybe a dozen envelopes. There was one different than the others. Handwritten. I recognized the handwriting before I saw the name on the left-hand corner. Kate Enslow.

She hadn't written me a letter since the day she left. Not so much as a note. I held the envelope in my hands. If there was something the matter with Gretchen, Kate would have called like before. I remembered Russell Enslow saying the things he said in the waiting room at the hospital. I remembered Gretchen telling me they slept

in separate rooms. I turned the envelope around and held
it to my nose. There was no smell. No words written on
the back. There was nothing to do except open it.

>Early,
>
>>How are you?
>>
>>I know it must have been strange to see this
>>letter mixed with your business mail. I'm not very
>>good at explaining myself. I just felt like writing
>>you a letter.
>>
>>Last night I found a shoebox on the top shelf
>>in the storage closet with pictures of you and me. I
>>knew it was in the house somewhere, but I hadn't
>>been able to find it for the longest time. Getting
>>older is different than I thought it would be.
>>Watching Gretchen leave for college was harder
>>than I imagined. But I didn't cry, which is hard to
>>believe. I cry now at the drop of a hat. I sat down
>>in the closet and looked at the pictures. I could
>>hear you and feel your touch, but then it was time
>>to put you back in the box. I left a little crack in
>>the top.
>>
>>>>>>>Kate

I read the letter. Then I read it again. And again. I'm
not sure what I thought I'd see different each time, but
there was so much to see. So much to think about. All
those many years had passed, but one letter, written by her
hand, could still tie me up in knots.

I hid the letter in my file cabinet, in a file I knew no

one would look for. The next day I pulled it out to read again. It took a lot for her to do it. As much or more as it would have taken for me to sit down with pen and paper. Write the words. Fold the letter. Address and stamp the envelope. Put the letter in the envelope. And finally, drop it in the mail. Each part of the process as difficult to finish as the one before. More than enough time between each level to throw it in the trash. Reconsider. But she didn't. She finished every step, and now she knew I held the short letter in my hands. And undoubtedly she understood what it did to me.

She'd been looking for the pictures of us in her house. The feelings were strong enough to hear my voice and feel my touch, or at least to say she did in writing, which was equally amazing. And the part about the crack left in the top of the box. Just a little space for the possibilities to breathe. But I told myself, "She's going through a down time. Getting close to forty years old. Mid-life crisis. Her only child leaving the nest. A lull in her marriage, discontent."

It's easy to remember only the good things. It's easy to toy with the idea the grass is greener, and maybe life would have been different. Just like my mother, and Bruce, and the letters she kept in the chest in her attic.

Days passed. I felt guilty around Samantha for something I hadn't even done. At the baseball game, watching Allen, I knew I'd never leave him, no matter what. It wouldn't make any difference if Kate showed up at the front door and delivered the letter herself.

I agonized over what to do. Write back? Don't write

back? Pretend I never got the letter? But I ultimately couldn't do it to her. I imagined Kate going out to the mailbox each day. Worried she'd done the wrong thing. Full of regret one minute and the next minute wishing for my response to arrive.

> Dear Kate,
>
> I got your letter. It was a surprise, but a good surprise.
>
> Seeing your name in the corner of the envelope on my desk made me smile. Like we used to smile a long time ago. I wish you'd send me copies of those pictures. Somehow I didn't end up with any. It would be nice to remember, and have my own box, with a crack left in the top.
>
> You're right. Getting older is different than I thought.
>
> Early

I sent it four days after I received hers. Not too eager, but also not purposefully cruel.

My letter made no promises, but at the same time, invited a response. A chance to see another one of her letters, handwritten, in my stack of boring business mail on the desk. A chance to let my imagination run wild on Kate Shepherd, and be back in my apartment in college, and see all those imagined moments in high school, but still remain totally under control. Letters were one thing. Calls or meetings were altogether something else. I would control the situation this time. I would decide the rules. The next day I threw her letter away, and wished to God I'd never sent my own. What if Russell Enslow got the mail? What if Kate called the house and told Samantha she loved me, and that I loved her, and we were gonna be like those crazy-ass people who leave their husbands and wives for each other out in Hollywood ?

It was upheaval, but pleasant upheaval. I would keep her inside my mind where she belonged. At least that's what I told myself.

four

I read somewhere that not a single cell in our bodies is the same as the cells contained inside us at birth. Our bodies are constantly regenerating and replacing old cells, and so, technically, we are completely different people than the day we were born. If this is true, and I believe it is, who are we? Are we strangers to ourselves? Is it just our invisible souls holding us on a certain track of identity until we die?

The call came from the hospital. "Mr. Winwood, this is Sherilyn McNally. I'm a nurse. It might be a good time for you to come down and see your mother. She's asking for you."

"I don't understand," I said. "My mother's at home."

There was silence on the end of the line.

"Hello?" I asked.

"I'm still here," she said. "Mr. Winwood, your mother's very sick. She's not home, she's here in the hospital."

On the drive it occurred to me that I hadn't seen my mother in months. I worked. I concentrated on Little Allen. I paid bills. I walked in and out doors all day long, watching the stock market, worrying about Gretchen, agonizing over letters. My mother had her own life. It's the way she wanted it to be.

I was absolutely amazed at how different she looked in the hospital bed. She was in her sixties and looked like an eighty-year-old woman I'd never met before. My mother's face was gaunt. Her hands on the outside of the white sheets were hands I didn't recognize, bony and wrinkled, the skin dry, her fingernails longer than I'd ever seen them.

"Jesus, Mother. What is happening?" I whispered, like it was a secret. Like no one else could see what I could see.

"I'm dying," she said calmly.

"No, you're not," I answered.

She waited a moment, probably to allow the ridiculousness of my answer to resonate in the room.

"Yes, I am, Early. I'm dying."

It made me angry. While I'd been paying bills and smoking cigarettes on the back porch in the dark, something was happening to my mother, the last remaining vestige of my permanence on this Earth. And now she looked like a dead body resting in an open coffin, except her eyes were open, and she was speaking.

"Four months ago the doctor told me I had pancreatic

cancer, in an advanced stage. I decided against chemother-apy. I'm ready, Early. I've been ready for a long time now. Don't be afraid."

I heard myself say, "What if I'm not ready? Did you think of that? Did you? What if I'm not ready for you to die?"

At the moment, where I stood in the cold hospital room, it seemed impossible. All of it. Like a crazy dream where you tell yourself it's only a crazy dream. And then you wake up, and you're glad it wasn't real.

I left the hospital room and drove around for hours and hours. I thought of every memory of my mother. Every single detail I could recall about her, and me, and my father, and I cried like I didn't know I was capable of crying. Wiping my face at stoplights, ashamed, clear juices running from my nose down over the top of my lips, hyperventilating at times to the point of dizziness. I ended up in a full-blown asthma attack in my grandfather's backseat again. I pulled over to the side of the road and tried my trick of the blackboard full of words, each one slowly erased in my mind, until there is nothing to think about and the air began to flow freely again. The man on the radio said to expect lots of sunshine. He said tomor-row would be beautiful.

I had never taken the time to imagine my mother dying. After all, she was strong, removed, artistic, and detached. She wasn't like me or my father, weak to the world around us. My mother was immortal, almost unnatural.

It must have been nearly two o'clock in the morning when I pulled back into the hospital parking lot, all cried out. My soul was dry. There was nothing left to remember. Sherilyn, the same nurse who'd called me earlier, let me back in my mother's room. She was asleep. I sat in a chair by her bedside and looked around the room. This idea came to me. This idea of taking flying lessons, and renting a small plane on a clear spring morning, and taking off into the rising sun, turning south toward the Gulf of Mexico. In a bag on the seat next to me would be a bottle of good whiskey, a few books, and a large bottle of pills. As I cleared the coast, the white sands like snow on the beach below, I would start taking pills, swallowing each down with the hot whiskey, and reading passages from the books, my headphones off, the sound of the engine of the small plane drowning out everything. Not everyone is meant to live seventy or eighty years. Not with a soul as dry as mine.

"I thought you might come back," she said.

Her eyes were opened in thin slits. The liquid dripped down the tubes into the place in her arm. Tape covered the needle to keep it secure in her dry skin.

"I just don't understand, that's all. Why wouldn't you tell me?"

"You have enough going on, Early. And what would you have done anyway? It's better this way."

I felt the anger rise. "Says who? Who says it's better this way, Mother?"

She smiled a little bit, something I hadn't seen in a long time.

"I do, Early. It's my life, not yours. I get to decide."

The nurse entered the room and changed the bag of

school and resort to voluntary organizations, of which the old Hampstead Historic Society in which the Fabian leaders educated themselves for their democratic work is a classic example.

THE CONQUEST OF THE SECONDARY SCHOOL
BY THE SECONDARY SCHOOLBOY

Here, however, we must note a strange thing that happened to secondary education during the last half of the nineteenth century. This was nothing less than the conquest of the select public schools by the schoolboys. They drove scholarship out of the curriculum, and replaced it by cricket and football. They drove the classical masters out and replaced them by athletes. They abolished the old liberty of play and made games compulsory; so that at this moment, at preparatory schools for youths destined for schools of the Eton type, children too young to play games are forced to stand and watch older boys play them: a tyranny unthinkable fifty years ago. School is a paradise to the champion cricketer and footballer, though he may be the most disgraceful of dunces and cribbers. And as all the traditions of sport, from William the Conqueror's preservation of the New Forest downwards, are country house traditions, whereas the traditions of scholarship can never be quite divested of at least a Platonic Republicanism, this conquest of the secondary schools by the schoolboys of the privileged classes has, from the Labor point of view, changed their atmosphere for the worse.

THE MASSACRE OF THE INNOCENTS

Let us now glance at some of the results. In Germany at the beginning of the XIXth century, Goethe, Schiller and Kant had extricated themselves, and apparently rescued their country, from the ideas of the Prussian Junkers, and had made German culture illustrious by a humanitarian idealism which found its last expression in the Parsifal of Richard Wagner. But the schools took no notice of Goethe and Kant. The country houses took no notice of them. The army took no notice of them. The court took no notice of them. The notice they took of Wagner was to exile him when he escaped their attempt to shoot him. The views that were taught to the rising generation were the views of the Kaiser and General Von Bernhardi; and by this time Goethe and Kant might as well never have lived for all the influence they have in German politics.

In England Bentham and the Mills created the Utilitarian movement, the last words of which were uttered by Herbert Spencer. Then came the Free Trade movement of which Cobden and Bright were the apostles. Then came Socialist internationalism with Karl Marx as its prophet. Then came the reduction of Socialism to practical politics by the Fabians. Then came the Labor Party. Not one of these movements has been assimilated by the English people, or shown any power of surviving its first exponents and their disciples. The Utilitarian movement was essentially a struggle for individual liberty; yet when Sidney Webb and I, saturated with its traditions, began to preach Socialism on the assumption that the battle for individual liberty had been won and that there was no danger of its being sacrificed by the Socialists, we found that young England was as innocent of such traditions as if Bentham and Mill had been drowned like kittens the day they were born. All England at that time accepted Free Trade as a political matter of course; and all Liberals and Radicals were supposed to have the theory of it at their fingers' ends; yet when the Tariff Reform League was sprung on the country by the manufacturers of the Midlands, all the Midland politicians, headed by an ex-republican mayor of Birmingham, declared as one man that every window sash or door frame we imported from Belgium or Norway was a loss of money to the country and of a job to English labor; and the politicians from the coast, representing the shippers who carried the sashes, did not know how to answer them, though they were quite determined not to have the tariff. The Fabians, by dint of their propaganda of municipal socialism, captured the first generation of London County

Councillors and established the Progressive Party; but when that too brief generation passed, the Council relapsed into a condition of ancient vestrydom which would have scandalized the old Metropolitan Board of works, though it still retained the word Progressive. The Fabians had confuted and extinguished Anarchism before they founded Progressivism; yet when Anarchism revived as Syndicalism it caught on with Socialists, including many Fabians, to an extent which shewed that the economics and philosophy of Fabian Essays had dropped like stones into the sea.

Meanwhile, our attempts at religious development shared the same fate. Evolution came in 1790 as an epoch making discovery; but by 1830 Europe was back again in the garden of Eden. In 1859 Darwin demonstrated the method of evolution by external pressure which he called Natural Selection; and the controversy which ensued shook European thought to its foundations. Yet today Mr Belloc and the Salvation Army are as safe in the arms of Moses as if Darwin had never lived. In 1889 the great Norwegian playwright Ibsen reached us with an overwhelming exposure of the wickedness and disastrousness of the inhuman ideals which are the real tyrants of our society, and which mask themselves as romance and sentiment. The effect he produced was so great that for a time the old romantic and sentimental plays and books seemed obsolete and ridiculous. Today his name is never mentioned; the stage is more inhumanly sentimental and romantic than ever; and men are being slaughtered by millions on the altars of the idols he threw down. Not even Ibsen could keep them down when all the Governments in Europe were busy setting them up in the souls of little children day in and day out.

THE SUPREMACY OF QUEEN VICTORIA

As to parliament, these waves of thought never reached it except in the form of popular agitations for specific measures. When popular pressure became too intense to be resisted, the

Government yielded as far as Queen Victoria would let it, and no farther. Queen Victoria was the real ruler of the country, because her ideas, her prejudices, her moral code, her attitude towards labor, capital, and feudal privilege, were taught in every public school in the kingdom, from Eton down to the Church schools in the villages, and in the private schools also. Let me give a typical example of the result. When Mr Asquith, at the beginning of his political career, condescended to deliver a lecture at the Working Men's College, he paid out, in his lucid way, as the newest political economy, all the exploded Manchester School stuff that Lord Liverpool would have paid out sixty years before; and when the Socialists present, eager for the sport of wiping the floor with him, asked him to debate it, he turned on them with a haughty stare of genuine amazement at their audacity, and left the room, missing thereby his one chance of being educated in the modern sense. He spoke and acted as he had been taught to speak and act; he sincerely regarded Keir Hardie as an ignoramus because Keir Hardie was a century ahead of him in political science; and he spent many years at the head of the Government without ever discovering that political economy does not forbid statesmen to fix a minimum wage for miners or for anyone else. Mr Balfour, at the Industrial Conference of 1885, had made a precisely similar exhibition of himself; and today we have the Dean of St Paul's wasting a keen intellect and a sincere interest in public affairs on a gloomy fatalistic Malthusianism that was dead before he was born. But the fact that Mr Asquith and Mr Balfour and Dean Inge are stuffed with a Wages Fund *cum* Diminishing Return theory that is as completely superseded as Phlogiston or the Ptolemic astronomy did not prevent the first two from becoming Prime Ministers or the third from becoming the ecclesiastical chief of London's cathedral.

Worst of all, the Press, though largely staffed by miserably underpaid men and women, some of whom must be presumed to dictate their articles instead of writing them, as it seems incredible that they should ever have received either elementary or secondary education, remains apparently incorrigible and irreclaimable, and regards Mr Asquith and the Dean as leaders of modern thought cutting out a breakneck pace for Mr Balfour.

WHY BLAME HUMAN NATURE
FOR ARTIFICIAL BACKWARDNESS?

It is not surprising, in the face of all this, that self-educated men should either despair of the political capacity of the nation, or else write articles in The New Statesman urging the necessity for continual repetition of Socialist and Labor doctrines. You must not, they say, be content with telling the public the truth once, however lucidly and convincingly you may tell it. You must tell it seventy times seven, and then tell it seven times more. Now all this is great nonsense. It implies that the nation has been told all about Socialism and Labor, but has not been told often enough. The truth is, it has not been told at all. What it has been told is that Socialism is Anarchism, that Anarchism is plunder and murder, that Labor agitators are seditious setters of class against class and that their proposals are condemned by the laws of political economy no less than by respectable opinion and the laws of God, that the French Revolution was a sanguinary and hideous calamity which ended in the despotism of Napoleon, that Voltaire and Rousseau were atheists who died shrieking at the prospect of spending eternity in burning sulphur, that patriotism means standing up when the band plays God Save the King, that the squire and his relations are beings of a superior order by divine right as well as by having had more money spent on them, that Church people are more respectable than Baptists and Congregationalists, that the book of Genesis contains an exact account of the origin of the world and of the human race, and that anyone who questions these propositions is a doubtful character who should not be associated with, and will probably come to a bad end.

THE GROWING RISK OF PERSECUTION

Our self-educated men, if they are to be of any use to the Labor Party, must give up imagining that they have carried the world, and refusing to face the fact that our rising generations are still being taught exactly what Louis XIV would teach them if he were sent back to earth and condemned to earn his living as a schoolmaster. They walk about a garden in which millions of gardeners are busily sowing thistles under their noses; and then they wonder why the result is not a crop of rare flowers and delicious fruits. The real wonder is that they have not all been hanged long ago, as they certainly would have been if they were numerous enough to alarm the majority, or if the majority had been taught enough to understand what they are driving at. As it is, there is not a Labor agitator or a teacher of modern science or philosophy in the country who could not be prosecuted for seditious or blasphemous libel and punished like a criminal, although the most extreme Calvinist or Methodist, making children's lives miserable with threats of eternal fire, and destroying all sense of moral responsibility in adults by assuring them on the authority of God that salvation is independent of conduct, or a fanatical Royalist or Churchman preaching that the highest duty of man is to die for his Kaiser's ambition and that better and worse are equally sacred in marriage, cannot be touched by any law; nor will the press venture to say a word against him, any more than it will dare to say a word in favor of the poor Secularist lecturer who is pounced on by some ignorantly pious constable for ridiculing the Virgin Birth, and solemnly sentenced to imprisonment by a judge who knows perfectly well that if the victim had expressed a belief in the occurrence of a sporadic case of human parthenogenesis before a learned society, he would ruin all his chances of ever obtaining any sort of appointment or professorial chair as a teacher of science.

Meanwhile we keep telling one another that the blasphemy laws are obsolete; that the Crown has now no power and is a mere social convenience; that democracy has come to stay; and that we are all Socialists now. The truth is that these comforting assurances are survivals from the period of Victorian Liberalism, when both political parties set up a general theory of freedom because it gave countenance to their freedom to exploit the propertyless classes without mercy and without conscience. But in 1867 Disraeli gave the working class the vote in order to set up their ignorance and helplessness as a bulwark against his political opponents, who, three years later, set to work to educate the working class: that is, to inculcate in them all the beliefs and prejudices that were in danger from their freedom during childhood.

PIONEERING NOW A DANGEROUS TRADE

Since that time it has been growing more and more dangerous for men of modern culture to be honest in politics, religion, or science. It was not enough that, as all the recent political biographies prove, Queen Victoria had been, even in the heyday of Liberalism, as much more powerful than Queen Elizabeth as William the Fourth, popularly called Silly Billy, had been more powerful than Macaulay's hero William III. Mere demagogues soon began to do things that Queen Victoria would not have dared to do. By the time every proletarian interested in politics had been taught to read a half-penny paper, and provided with one to keep him away from such comparatively revolutionary works as the Bible and Catechism, the Treasury bench was open to the crudest demagogue-dictators and their nominees; and men who had made money by producing newspapers reactionary enough to have the largest circulations in the country threw baronies back in the face of the king and insisted on being made viscounts.

Our old Macaulayish Whig habit of assuming that the world must be progressing from ignorance to enlightenment and from servitude to freedom is still so inveterate that when I state that life is becoming more and more dangerous for men of modern culture I shall carry no conviction unless I point out not only the scores of instances that lie under our noses, but the general reason that underlies them. Before the enforcement of general elementary education in 1871 the governing classes always assumed that the man of advanced ideas had behind him the revolutionary spirit of the inarticulate millions of workers, and were correspondingly afraid of him. A fortnight ago on this platform Mr Henderson quoted the expressions of alarm with which they received the proposal to arm these supposed revolutionists with the weapon of education. Shelley and Byron, Landor and Swinburne, seemed men not lightly to be molested; for they spoke in the name of the mighty multitudes of the oppressed in the spirit that had struck off the heads of two kings. Karl Marx was able to keep out of prison as president of the Red International, though it was a European bogey to the governing classes in the eighteen-sixties. This toleration was not freedom broadening from precedent to precedent, nor England being the land where still a man may say the thing he will: it was the delusion that the International was a vast and formidable working class organization instead of a handful of lonely pioneers who never had twenty pounds in hand and often had not twenty pence. But nobody could discover the truth, because the workers could not read newspapers, and there was no other way of ascertaining what they really thought and felt, and whom they really liked and admired. The pioneers marched, like Moses and Aaron, with a pillar of fire by night, and a pillar of cloud by day, concealing their real strength from their pursuers, with the important difference that Moses really had a host hidden in his cloud, whereas Marx's cloud concealed the fact that he had nobody with him.

WHAT EDUCATION HAS REVEALED

The Education Act blew the cloud away, and revealed the pioneer as a lonely man in a strange land amid a hostile people. Today Mr Bertrand Russell, by profession a philosopher and by social position the brother of an earl of an old and famous Whig family, is in jail for referring in a casual sentence to the ironic fact that the soldier who enlists to restore liberty in another country may find himself employed to suppress it in his own. In the sixties, when the very Christmas Annuals were outrageous lampoons on the royal family, this platitude would have earned for its author a sarcastic recommendation from Henry Labouchere to go and write tracts. The headmaster of Eton has been mobbed from his post for remarking that our position in Gibraltar is part of the same problem as the position of the Germans in Kiel. Far from popular education having emancipated us, it has lost us even the freedom of the privileged classes and the academic Utopians. The Sermon on the Mount and the American Declaration of Independence are treasonable documents, like Tom Paine's Age of Reason a century ago. The word Toleration, common in my youth, has not been uttered once during the present century. We talk of the tyranny of the Northcliffes and the Rockefellers; but what is their tyranny but that of the mass of workers who would be Northcliffes or Rockefellers if they could, and whose opinions and prejudices and aspirations Lord Northcliffe has made his fortune by voicing? Thus the education and enfranchisement of the proletariat have transferred to the Chambers of Commerce and the country houses the weapon with which we formerly held them in awe. They thought we could at any moment set the mob on them. They now know that they can at any moment set the mob on us; and they are doing it so vigorously that there are as many honest men as rogues in the jails.[1]

THE WAR TEST

The full extent of the reaction was not apparent until the war put a severe testing strain on the traditions of Liberalism. Instantly the representatives of the people divested themselves of their liberty like prisoners throwing off their chains or drowning

1. The typescript contains the following canceled sentence: "This is not an accident of war: it is a discovery which the war has confirmed; and it will not be forgotten when the war is over."—ED.

swimmers trying to throw off their clothes. Not content with
falling abjectly at the feet of their old masters, they rushed to
every fool who was conceited enough to think that he could
save the country, and offered him, on their knees, such despotic
control of the people's persons, their food, their lives, their
property, and everything of which they stood possessed, as
neither king nor peer nor bishop would have dreamt of claiming in the middle ages. The men from the universities were
worse than the men from the elementary schools. To students
of modern political science the failure of this frenzied resort to
dictators, censors, military authorities, and all kinds of human
idols to produce any of the results hoped for from them was as
certain as the rise of the sun in the morning. But neither in
parliament nor in the street was there any sign that political
science had ever been heard of in England. As a matter of fact
it had not been heard of except by a handful of self-educated
people. One *deus ex machina* after another was tried. When
Lord Devonport and Mr Neville Chamberlain failed to work
miracles the wand was handed to Lord Rhondda and Sir Auck-
land Geddes. We need not blame these gentlemen, nor deny
that some of them did a little better than others. We need not
pretend that Lord Rothermere, that chief of the Air Service
who wanted to take the British Museum for a comfortable
office, and whose qualification was that he was Lord Northcliffe's brother, would have lasted longer if he had been anyone
else's brother. The point is that just as Henry VIII thought he
could keep the British drama and the British stage in order by
simply handing them over to the uncontrolled government of
his Master of Revels, now called the Lord Chamberlain, so,
precisely, did the British Parliament and the British Press, sup-
ported by the British democracy, believe that it could dispose
of all the emergencies raised by the war by setting up a whole
crowd of Lord Chamberlains to keep everybody else in order
by the exercise of certain fabulous personal virtues entitling
their possessor to be worshipped and obeyed as practical business men, which meant nothing positively, but negatively meant
most emphatically that they were persons who had never read

anything that would have shocked Henry VIII, though Henry, to give him his due, read many things that would greatly have shocked them.

QUEEN VICTORIA'S IDEAS NOW TOO MODERN

And all this occurred because, thanks to the spread of education, Henry VIII is now in undisputed command of the elementary schools, of the secondary schools, of Eton and Harrow, Winchester and Rugby, Oxford and Cambridge, St Paul's and Westminster Abbey, and consequently of the British nursery, the British dinner table, the British bench, the British jury box, the British pulpit, and the British parliament. Even Queen Victoria is now too liberal for us.

But the most significant collapse of all was the sudden abandonment of representative government itself. It is bad enough that our rulers should be so ignorant of the commonplaces of economics that their only idea of war economy seems to be, not the increase of general production and the utilization of wasted or parasitic labor by a vigorous and impartial industrial and financial conscription, but simply the reduction of expenditure and the hindering of communication and travel: in short, by physical starvation and paralysis and a moral return to barbarism. The attempt to shut up the schools and all the cultural institutions of the country as mere luxuries that could not be afforded in war time was only to be expected in a country where schools are prisons in which the prisoners are as carefully cut off from culture as the convicts in Portland. But our representatives, as persons whose schooling had included at least a few historical commonplaces about the growth of British liberty through representative institutions, and some references to Magna Charta and King Charles' Head, might not unreasonably have been expected to think twice before they abolished the whole constitutional structure which alone gave us the smallest ground for claiming that we were fighting the Prussians in the character of democrats fighting autocracy. Yet they never thought once about it. Instead of taking advantage of the fact that a general election is a far easier business when the voters are organized and disciplined in regiments and companies and platoons in which the roll is called and the individuals identified every day, as the Canadians did, they abolished elections altogether. They scrapped the Septennial Act; discarded the Cabinet and replaced it by triumvirates whose members did not even appear in parliament except as occasional visitors; used the House of Lords to take the newspaper proprietors into the Government without popular election; substituted military tribunals sitting *in camera* for British juries; abolished the liberty of the Press, of conscience, and of speech; set up a military Inquisition with all the powers of the Holy Office through the Defence of the Realm Acts; and did all this, not under any real stress of necessity, but simply because they sincerely believed, as practical business men, that constitutional safeguards are either intellectual fads which may be all very well when we are at peace and nothing matters except having a large bank balance, but which sensible men cannot tolerate when we are at war and our skins are in jeopardy, or else dangerous conspiracies between pacifists and pro-Germans to secure immunity for traitorous efforts to drive us into a German peace.[2]

2. The typescript here contains the following canceled paragraph: "During all this we have reviled the Germans for having systematically used their schools and universities to inculcate veneration for feudal institutions and kingship by divine right, and a morality militarist on its executive side and commercial and competitive on its theoretical side. A stranger would conclude that our own schools and universities must be sedulously inculcating the sternest republican principles of government and the noblest ideals of Christian Socialism in industry. The fact is that our schools and universities are teaching exactly the same political and social morality as the German schools and universities, the only difference being that as the Germans are doing it more thoroughly and consciously, and see no reason to be hypocritical about it, the disastrousness and obsolescence of the doctrines are a little more obvious when the search lights are turned on. In practice the Prussian Government seems to be rather more Liberal than its critics. We hear that Dr. Liebknecht, an uncompromising enemy of the German State: that is, what we should call an avowed traitor, is undergoing a sentence of four years imprisonment. From Republican America we hear of clergymen sentenced to sixteen years im-

THE LABOR PARTY'S SHARE OF THE COMMON LOT

Let us now see how all this bears on the Labor Party and its future. The Labor Party was made by Socialists: that is, by men who had broken away completely from the teaching of their schools and universities and the prejudices of their families, and educated themselves by individual study or in voluntary associations. The Fabians, belonging to the professional and official class, were not interfered with by the Government. The poorer Socialists were bludgeoned and imprisoned occasionally, None of them were encouraged. They spread their ideas by speeches and pamphlets. My own case is a typical one. When I became a Socialist I spent twelve years of my life in public speaking, during which time I must have delivered in all parts of the country not much less than 2,000 addresses; and I wrote essays and pamphlets, and helped to organize the propaganda generally. The others did the same. Now we cannot do that all over again. Our old audiences are dying out like ourselves: we are a worn-out generation. And the number we reached was never very large compared to the numbers that the British family and the British schools and the British universities reached.

---

prisonment for refusing to lend their churches for war meetings, and officers sentenced to twentyfive years imprisonment for resigning their commissions as convinced George-Washingtonian non-interventionists. And we are so astonished at the publication in Germany of documents like the Lichnowsky memorandum that we think the German Government must be trying to pave the way towards a reconciliation between the English and German peoples at the expense of its own character. But it would be rash to conclude that if all these instances were carefully scrutinized they would shew any real difference between the belligerents in point of Liberalism. What they do shew is that German children, British children, and American children receive the same dangerous, obsolete, anti-Socialist, violent and vindictive education, so that when it comes to the point, it is safer for the propagandist of modern Socialistic views to live in a feudal country than in a democratic one, just as it is safer to fall into the hands of an imperial police than into the hands of a vigilance committee or a negro lynching mob."—Ed.

We taught our modern doctrine for a couple of hours three times in a fortnight perhaps in a few places. The schools and universities and families taught their doctrines every day and all day to every child and adolescent in the country. There must be already in the Labor Party ten members who have been educated at Church schools for every one who has been educated at Socialist lectures. I am not making this announcement as a disappointed and disillusioned man. I foresaw it and prophesied it twenty years ago. When the Labor Party first rallied round Keir Hardie, Socialists to a man, our enthusiasts said that the party would grow more and more Socialist as it gained in strength. I said it would do just the reverse. I said that all the Socialists would join its first generation, and that it would grow thereafter from recruiting among the Trade Unionists. I said, more specifically, that the triumph we were then looking forward to, of enlisting the half million organized coal miners, would be the end of the Labor Party as a Socialist Party and the beginning of it as a Trade Unionist Party with the ideas of old Radicals like the late Harry Broadhurst, or the old working class Tories like the late Maudsley. The fulfillment of my prophecy is filling you with dismay today. The veteran Thomas Burt, contemptuously described by a younger generation as a Lib-Lab, must stand aghast at the reactionary attitude of certain leaders of the Labor Party who are nevertheless more representative of the average working man than Keir Hardie ever was. When Mr John Burns was made a Cabinet Minister, the end of the old world of class privilege seemed at hand. I could name younger Labor leaders who might be placed on the throne without causing the slightest political uneasiness, though no doubt socially the event would be a nine-days' wonder. If the same cannot be said of Mr Henderson, that will not matter in the long run. Mr Henderson will not live forever; and meanwhile, if he wishes to have his children well started in life, he will have to send them to schools and universities where they will be taught to combine a dutiful affection for his person with a grieved disapproval of his unfortunate opinions.

EXAMPLES OF FUTILE REMEDIES

I need hardly say that I am not the first prophet whose eyes have been opened to this danger. But the remedies proposed have always been hopelessly individualistic. They are indicated by the cry "We must have our own schools and our own Press." But where are we to find teachers and writers to offset the multitude of teachers and writers from the public schools? We must have the nation's schools and the nation's press, or all our advances will be wiped out by the counter-attack. Let me describe to you the two most serious attempts yet made in our movement to found a Socialist college and a Labor newspaper.

It is now nearly quarter of a century since I took some little part in the establishment of a great public school of economics and political science, founded under the will of a Fabian convert who left his property to the Fabian Society to spread the principles of Fabian Socialism. Mr Sidney Webb and Mr Graham Wallas lecture in that school to this day for the good of its soul; and I have once or twice been unofficially invited by the students to open a debate there for a lark. Its governing body was largely dominated by convinced Socialists for a long time; and its present director was once a famous Minister of Labor at the Antipodes. Though it is now a college of London University it has not lost much of its original independence. Yet before it had been many months in existence I walked one day into a class on economics, and found the professor teaching the doctrines Mr Asquith had been taught, and perfectly ready, if any student ventured to put in a claim on behalf of Mr Webb or the pious founder of the institution, to call the porter and have him thrown out of the building. Yet I had to recognize that this was quite unavoidable. It was impossible to staff the school without falling back on the only teachers of economics who were regularly in that business; and they had all been trained in the old universities and colleges.

THE LATE DAILY CITIZEN

Later on, the Labor Party and the Trade Unions determined that Labor must have a newspaper. They spent a colossal sum on founding and running the Daily Citizen. And they began by falling helplessly into the clutches of the practical business man. Lord Northcliffe was supposed to be the practical business man of the newspaper world; and it was from his school that most of the journalists of The Daily Citizen were selected. The result, of course, was a very inferior Daily Mail, with a column of news about strikes instead of a court circular. When a book of advanced views of any kind was published, the Daily Citizen reviewed it exactly as the Harmsworth Press would have reviewed it: in fact, it employed the same reviewers. In every respect The Daily News was a couple of centuries ahead of it. I took it in piously, but found it quite unreadable; and when it perished, nobody, as far as my experience went, had a good word to say for it. It was not, in fact, a Labor paper at all. By a Labor paper I mean a paper that not only reports actual doings in the Labor world, and refrains from denouncing strikes in the manner of The Morning Post, but criticises public affairs, current religious, artistic, and literary movements, and especially the activities of parliament, in the light of a theory of society and a view of the future completely distinct from the commercial theory of Manchester and the feudal theory of the country house. If we cannot find a qualified staff for such a paper, or if, having found such a staff, we find that the workers will not buy the paper because they prefer Lord Northcliffe's way of looking at things, then we must leave the Press, and with it the souls of the people, in the hands of Lord Northcliffe, confessing that we have tried for better things and failed. But not to try at all—to attempt to cut out Lord Northcliffe on his own ground under cover of producing a Labor paper, and then to be beaten by him after spending a huge sum of the workers' money—this was not only failure but disgrace; and it is largely responsible for the utter contempt with which the masters of

the press and their nominees in parliament have since treated
the vanguard of the Labor Movement.

THE DOOM OF SISYPHUS

This example of the paper is far more disquieting than the
example of the school; for the school had really no alternative;
and the selection of the present Director, and the use it made of
Socialists like Mr Sidney Webb and Mr Graham Wallas, shew
that it went ahead as far as it could. But in the case of The
Daily Citizen there was a deliberate choice of reactionary journalism because it was believed to be attractive, and a deliberate
exclusion of Socialism because it was believed to be repulsive.
The atmosphere of the paper was not in the least Socialistic: it
was the ordinary atmosphere of commercial wage labor vitiated
by the special atmosphere of Fleet Street journalism. And it
propagated its atmosphere and disparaged and discredited any
attempt to clear it with a little Socialist sunshine as timidly as
The Daily Telegraph, which was perhaps the next most timid
newspaper in the world. And the root reason for this, and for
its falling so short of the school, was that its final control was
not in the hands of the advanced spirits who founded the Labor
Party but in the hands of the nation's schoolmasters. If you send
every child in the nation into a school in which the ideas of the
anti-Socialist party are sedulously and exclusively inculcated
and propagated, and keep them there until they are old enough
to be flung out into a struggle for life in which all the prizes
are given to the upholders of these ideas, and the upholders of
the Socialist ideas are slandered, cut off from eminent employ-
ments and dismissed from common ones, with penal laws holding over their heads a continual threat of imprisonment, then it
is silly to suppose that Socialism can ever prevail against the
universal environment it allows its opponents to maintain. As
long as we leave the young in the hands of the parson, the
squire, and the merchant, not only shall we not prevail, but it
will be apparent that we do not really know our own minds,
and that with our mouths full of Socialist phrases we still keep

our hearts full of the snobbery that has been rubbed into us from our cradles. Our labors will be the labors of Sisyphus, continually rolling the stone to the top of the hill only to have it descend with a crash on us when we are exhausted. The modern Sisyphus is typified by Mrs Josephine Butler, who was hardly cold in her grave after a lifetime spent in discrediting and destroying the Contagious Diseases Acts when her stone was down at the bottom of the hill again, and the Government benches were re-enacting the repealed Acts and assuming as a matter of course that they would rid the army of disease instead of spreading it by sham guaranties of security. We are like an army that proceeds without establishing lines of communication or fortifying the strongholds it reduces, with the result that it is cut off, surrounded, annihilated, and has all its conquests undone after each of its expeditions. It captures all the citadels by super-human efforts and sacrifice, and then allows the enemy to put in the garrison.

FREE EDUCATION VERSUS MR FISHER'S BILL

The moral of the situation is, as usual, complicated. Should the Labor Party have resisted Mr Fisher's Bill and declared themselves implacably opposed to every extension of secondary education in schools, and even demanded its abolition? Not quite; for the result in most cases under existing circumstances would be that their sons and daughters would get no secondary education at all instead of getting a Henry VIII education, which is at least better than nothing and is a very material class advantage, however mischievous it may be socially. The real remedy lies in the direction of enabling young people to educate themselves very much as the Fabians educated themselves, by giving them money enough and freedom enough to choose their own subjects and organize their own instruction, and employ their own teachers. It may be taken as a sound general rule that it is waste of time to teach secondary subjects to any-one who does not want to learn them. Ninetynine out of a hundred of our university graduates might as well be so many Shakespears in point of having little Latin and less Greek, in spite of the years they have wasted on both languages. On the other hand there is no need to compel secondary students to learn the things they want to learn: they will seek the instruction if they are not prevented by a compulsory curriculum of subjects they dislike, and by what is practically imprisonment with intellectual penal servitude. Give every laborer's family a thousand a year tomorrow, and at the same time close all the secondary schools and hang all the school teachers, and you will soon have more secondary education than you have ever had before, with voluntary colleges and popular teachers rivalling great preachers and politicians in popularity, and a public opinion that will make it as difficult for a young man to do without secondary education as it is now to do without fashionable clothes. A hundred years of Mr Fisher's Act will not do that for us: it will only destroy the little genuine culture the previous Acts have left us. Even in the matter of primary education the path of progress is not on the lines of crude compulsion to make poverty literate: we should proceed by attaching privileges to its acquirement instead of punishments to its neglect.

I have been asked whether I really want private venture schools to spring up again in all directions. I certainly do not want anything like the ordinary private adventure school as we have it today ever to spring up again, except as a consequence of a violent assault on its seat. But I do most emphatically want to see voluntary organizations of all kinds formed for the discussion and propagation of literature, science, art, politics, philosophy, law, medicine, and every conceivable subject of secondary education. Knowing as I do that a man may learn more by attending the meetings of the Fabian Society, the Medico-Legal Society, and the Sociological Society for one season than in a whole lifetime spent in Oxford or Cambridge, I propose that Oxford and Cambridge shall be cleared out, and the buildings let to voluntary self-educational organizations for Summer Schools, which are now Spring and Winter schools

as well. I know of no other way in which education can be
made really free. There can never be any mistake about such
freedom. Free education is always controversial; and the man
who has not learnt his subject controversially does not know
it. Dogmatic education leads to nothing but conceit and
disastrous ignorance, and makes it impossible to dare to teach
anything new, or even to teach what is old as if it meant anything. On the other hand you can allow anything, however
startling, to be taught if you can be sure that the teaching
will be open to immediate contradiction. By all means let the
Socialist State provide the buildings, the lecture theatres, the
laboratories, the libraries, the collections and so forth. By all
means let it provide also a police and elaborate a constitution
for the regulation of such institutions, just as the House of Commons has its police and its regulations. But the constitution must
be a free constitution: the learners must employ the teachers as
the consumers must employ the producers, and be free to
criticize the product, and accept it or reject it as they please. No
teacher who can teach will need to have his class locked in
and forced to listen to him in obedient silence any more than
an actor who can act needs to have his audience secured to him
in the same fashion. But I cannot on this occasion elaborate a
scheme of really free education. My immediate business is to
consider the prospects of the Labor Party in terms of things as
they are. Now there is no getting away from the fact that under
existing circumstances, though the attainment of a Labor majority in Parliament with Mr Henderson as Prime Minister is
just as possible here as it has been for a long time past in
Australasia, yet if Mr Henderson were under such circumstances to introduce a thoroughly modern scheme of Socialism
in industry, and combine it with a revision of the thirtynine
articles of the prayer-book in the light of Creative Evolution,
and a corresponding readjustment of the philosophic, economic
and historical courses at our universities, the Labor Party would
be more scandalized than Lord Lansdowne, and would hurl
Mr Henderson from power with a violence that would hardly
stop short of prosecuting him for sedition and blasphemy.

WHAT A LABOR PARTY CAN DO ON EXISTING IDEAS

Is there then no advantage in having a Labor Party instead of a Capitalist Party in power? To answer in the negative would be to fly too far to the opposite extreme. Consider, for instance, the effect on the famous Reform Act of 1832. This Act, which its supporters thought was the beginning of a new era, really only completed the process of transforming the English governing class from squirocracy to a commercial plutocracy and shopocracy which had begun as long before as the reign of Henry VII. Consequently it produced none of the millennial effects which had been predicted by radical reformers. But it cannot be said that it made no difference, or that the difference was not well worth making. Although the new men sent by Birmingham and the other newly enfranchised cities had the same education, and consequently the same superstitions as those whom they supplanted, yet it is roughly true that whereas before the Reform Act the country had been governed in the interests of the landed classes, it was run afterwards in the interests of the big business man, for the simple reason that the old men were landlords or their nominees, and the new men were men of business elected by men of business.

What does this experience promise as to the future of the Labor Party? Clearly that if you get a House of Commons majority of Trade Unionists elected by Trade Unionists (including the professions if they will come in) the country will be run, on the whole, in the interests of organized Labor and not of organized Capital. It will immediately be objected that this is far too cheap a generalization, because the change from squirocracy to shopocracy involved no change in the established methods of organizing Labor and producing wealth, nor even in the distribution of that part of the wealth which went to the nine tenths of the population whose labor produced it. It was only a matter of the division of the spoils. A transition from Plutocracy to Socialism, involving a redistribution of income, is altogether a different affair from a redistribution of seats in which Birmingham is substituted for Old Sarum. What new element in politics can we count on to effect this transition in a House of Commons which will still have been taught at its mother's knee and in its schools that Socialism is a disreputable abomination, and that God created the world with all its fauna and flora complete as we see them at present, in a single week?

The answer is, Trade Unionism. And the question I propose to deal with is how far Trade Unionism can produce Socialism in the hands of men who are not Socialists, and have even been taught to regard Socialism as wicked. In the year 1914 I addressed myself, in the course of a series of Fabian lectures at the Kingsway Hall, to this very question; and I shewed then that Socialism was the inevitable goal of Trade Unionism, if Trade Unionism were pushed home. There was, however, a point in my argument at which I had to assume a certain action on the part of the State for which there was no convincing precedent, and which was contrary to all the traditions of Manchester economics. Fortunately the war has supplied the missing link. The thing I was told Parliament would not do and even ought not to do has been done again and again; and I can now repeat my demonstration without having at any point to leave the appeal of theory unsupported by the bludgeon of fact.

SOCIALISM THROUGH TRADE UNIONISM

In the main, what the Trade Unionist demands is more money for shorter hours of work. The process of obtaining this began long ago, and has been aided by the State even under Capitalist Governments by Factory Acts limiting the length of the working day, and, of late years, fixing a minimum wage for that day. The reason the first steps in this direction have won the approval even of employers is that their effect has been to enrich most of them. Before it began they were killing the goose that laid the golden eggs by forcing the laborer to work so long for so little that they destroyed half his efficiency as an instrument of production. Instead of producing more in twelve hours than in ten or eight he produced less. Instead of yielding a larger profit at sixpence an hour than at tenpence, he yielded less. These are very mild and cautious statements in view of recent experience. We find the famous Mr Ford, with his scientifically managed motor car factories, coming to the conclusion that a workman who earns less than £20 a week is not worth employing. He refuses to accept employees, even in the humblest capacity, who are not much more respectable in their conversation and dress and habits than a successful employer was expected to be in Manchester or the Potteries, say, fifty years ago (I could give a later date if I dared). Even when the workman was admitted to a small share in the profits, it was found that the privilege stimulated him to produce so much more than his share in addition to his ordinary output that the Trade Unions had to bar this method of meeting their views. In short, the first century of modern Trade Unionism had greatly enriched the employers, and consequently the landlords and capitalists; and some of them are under the cheerful impression that this effect will continue forever.

In this ingenuous expectation they deceive themselves, as the less fortunately circumstanced among them have already found out. If a worker produces £3 by working 12 hours at a stretch, and gives one pound to A and another to B, keeping only one for himself, he may quite easily find that if he works only eight hours, he can produce £5, and give A and B half as much again as before whilst doubling his own share. But if A and B, in their joy at the success of this experiment, conclude that if the workman works only one hour, or, better still, does not work at all, they will be richer than ever, they will find that there is a point below which the workman cannot reduce his hours of labor without diminishing the product, and below which consequently he cannot keep more for himself without leaving less for them.

Now when the worker ceases to be what is called a Henry Dubb, and becomes a Trade Unionist, he will not be stopped in his demands for more by the consideration that others who are not helping him will get less. He will ruthlessly tell them that if they want money they had better go and work for it, as he does. He will squeeze them until he squeezes them out; and he will lighten his work until he finds that he is squeezing himself out by not producing enough for himself.

Why has he not been able to do this under the Manchester system? Simply because if he drove the employer to a point at which, after paying his workmen and living on the business himself meanwhile, he had no money left to pay the landlord, the landlord evicted him and put an end to the business, leaving the workers unemployed in the streets. There was also the capitalist to be paid; but there is a way of getting round that. When an employer finds that he can just manage to pay the landlord and live on the business, provided he has not to pay interest on capital, he turns the concern into a joint stock company by pretending that it is flourishing to such an extent that it needs fresh capital for enlarged operations. By this device he can live on the business as its salaried manager, and avoid paying interest by the simple expedient of not declaring a dividend. Companies sometimes go on for many years on this footing; and if the employer has been careful not to put anything in the prospectus that comes under the legal heading of misrepresentation, the shareholders have no remedy. But though the shareholders can do nothing, the workers can still press for higher wages and shorter hours; so that in the end the employer finds that if he pays the rent there will be nothing left to pay his salary, and if he does not the landlord will sell the concern up and finally evict him. He can then go to the Trade Union, and invite them to send in their own auditors to examine his books and thus convince themselves that they have reached the limit, and that if they insist on a further advance, the business must cease, leaving nothing for anyone.

THE KEY TO THE MANCHESTER DEAD LOCK

Now this, under the Manchester system, is checkmate for the workers. It is useless for them to plead that other businesses in the same trade are making high profits. The reply is that some businesses have the pick of the trade and others only the leavings; that some have to bear much heavier working expenses than others through being less favorably situated; that some have access to much more fertile natural sources than others; and that unless the workers in the less lucky establishments can transfer to themselves some of the profits of the more lucky ones, the less lucky ones cannot afford to pay their employees as much. In other words you can equalize the conditions of labor in an industry in two ways only. One is the way actually practised under the present system. It is to pay all the workers in the industry as little as the workers in the worst situated establishments must be content with if the concern is to be kept going. The other is for the State to step in; pool the product of the entire industry; and average the wages and the hours of labor.

This latter expedient, which marks the change from industries conducted by a host of private ventures, separate and unconnected, to socialized industry, is the *pons asinorum* of the Socialist Euclid; but the war has now driven us all across it by putting on pressure from above instead of from below. Circumstances forced the Government to fix the prices of several commodities at a figure lower than that arrived at by the Manchester system of leaving the price to the play of supply and demand in the market. Immediately the marginal businesses, as the ones which are just able to scrape along are called, said that they must shut up shop; and they were able to prove that they could not sell at the Government's price and carry on, just as I have pictured them proving to their employees that they could not pay the Trade Union rate and carry on. The Government promptly took the necessary jump into Socialism. It said "Sell at our price, and we will make up your loss." It made up the loss, of course, in the only way a government can, by taxing industry in general, and thus pooling the national product to the required extent. Thus the trick which I explained in 1914 is now done, as the irony of fate will have it, not, as I suggested, through the direct pressure of Trade Unionists demanding higher wages and shorter hours, but by direct pressure from a Government faced with a threat of high prices that would have meant famine to the workers at the very moment when it was a matter of life and death to keep them able-bodied. When, just before war, the Thames Iron Works had appealed to the authorities to save it from extinction in this manner, the authorities refused to consider such a course as possible. But the Kaiser succeeded where Mr Arnold Hills had failed.

Thus the old evil power of the commercial system, the power to keep every worker in the country down to the subsistence level of the man barely worth employment in the poorest corner of the industry, the power to keep the condition of the agricultural laborer on our richest soils as miserable as that of the man striving to drag a living from the barrenest patch worth cultivating at all, the power that has so long been accepted helplessly as a necessity imposed on us by Nature and the laws of political economy, has been smashed by the war as completely as the old Russian Tsardom. The Trade Unionist has nothing to do, apparently, but simply refuse to understand either his employers' books or the alleged laws of political economy, and obstinately demand a decent living wage whether his shop can afford it or not, and the effect will be, not to shut the shop, but to compel the government to subsidize his employer at the expense of some luckier shop. And to this process there is no economic limit except the limit set by Nature to the total product of all the industries of the entire nation. All that is needed is a Labor Party in power to do the parliamentary part of the business. It is, after all, only a method of pooling; and industrial Socialism is, in one word, nothing but pooling.

THE NEW LAISSER-FAIRE

To some wise and experienced Socialists this demonstration of the possibility of an automatic development and realization of Socialism will cause the deepest alarm. If there is one abomination of the Manchester School that can be singled out as the tap root of all its evil, it is its pretence that if we are all intellectually lazy and commercially selfish without shame or stint, the millennium will work itself out for us very obligingly free of charge. The Socialist instinctively sets up against it that older and sounder article of faith, "Eternal vigilance is the price of Liberty," and quotes Goethe's lines

"Nur der verdient sich Freiheit wie das Leben
Der täglich sie erobern muss."

I sympathize with this protest. I do not believe in Socialism by Natural Selection, nor in the Shakespearean Providence that shapes our ends, rough hew them how we will. It is quite true that we handle political affairs so unskillfully and ignorantly that both the bad and good intentions of our Governments are often defeated by results of their action that they never foresaw, and would not have worked for if they could have foreseen them. In the present war, for example, the one solid result achieved so far is the destruction of Russian Tsardom, and the setting up of a revolutionary government in its place. There has been a good deal of discussion as to the intentions, good and bad, of the diplomatists; but nobody suggests that any of them intended that. The war of 1870 established the French Republic. That was not the intention either of Napoleon III or of Bismarck. It is a general characteristic of legislation and State action generally that whether it produces the result aimed at or not, it sets such vast powers in motion that it cannot help producing a dozen other results as well, mostly quite unforeseen; and no mortal can tell which of these results may prove the most important. The Fabians have done a good deal by looking out for such unconsidered consequences. Had the Ministers who brought in the County Government Act of 1887 had the faintest notion of the use the Fabian Society was to make of it, they would have abolished local government altogether sooner than have touched it. We are driven again and again to console ourselves for the corruption and blindness of our rulers by the reflection that facts and Fate are too strong for them; that God is not mocked; that the Prime Ministers at their worst are, like Mephistopheles, "*ein Theil von jener Kraft die stets das Böse will und stets das Gute schafft.*" We are tempted at last to fall into an optimistic fatalism worse than that of the Manchester School, because Manchester at least taught an energetic selfishness, whereas Marx has led many a man to sit down idle and wait until the river of Capitalism flowed by. Now no doubt, in the future as in the past, both Socialists and Anti-Socialists will take many steps that will lead them, like St Peter, to destinations they never intended to reach.[3] But we cannot build on the unforeseen. A party assuming that the result of all parliamentary action must be precisely contrary to its intention would be a party of madmen.

BREAKERS AHEAD

Let us then consider whether the course of Trade Unionism which I have sketched is likely to run smoothly into Socialism without knowing it.

To begin with, the workers are not poor enough to be absolutely desperate; but they are poor enough to be very timid and very easily contented. Offer a millionaire £500 and you are only offering him half a week's income: it will not cost him the faintest sensible privation to throw it back in your face, nor, if he accepts it, will it gain him a single gratification that he cannot obtain without it. Offer it to a laborer, and you are offering

3. There follows a canceled paragraph which reads: "The frustrations will not be all on one side, and never have been. Those who hoped to see France and Russia set free by Republicanism have been quite as much out-witted by the event as Bismarck or the Kaiser. I do not believe that Socialism will ever be established except as feudalism and capitalism were established, by men who knew what they wanted and meant to get it, and who listened to and acted on the theories of theologians and philosophers and economists as well as on their own immediate personal interests. Unless some future Prime Minister pays as much attention to the Industrial Democracy of Mr and Mrs Sidney Webb, and reads the third act of Man and Superman as a devotional exercise, as William Pitt read Adam Smith's Wealth of Nations, we may try several Socialistic experiments by accident; but we shall not establish Socialism; and we shall not have any security against the continual attempts that are being made either to repeal the Factory Acts altogether or to go back to the old forms in which they were ineffective. Indeed we have still to see that the war, which has suspended them, will not abolish them and leave all the work to be done over again, and thereby throw us back for a century."—ED.

him six years wages in a lump, and enabling him to procure experiences beyond any that his ordinary life can promise to his most sanguine hopes. Under such circumstances a millionaire with a grievance usually has his grievance redressed, because it would cost more to buy him off than to give him what he wants. But there is hardly any political demand a laborer ventures to make that cannot be avoided by giving him another shilling a day, or another hour's liberty, or sacking an obnoxious foreman. This contentment of the workman is the safety valve which prevents Socialism from steaming ahead to equality. The spring is so weak that it is never possible to get up enough pressure to burst the boiler of Capitalism. There is a danger of a dead point being reached, representing the Servile State so much dreaded by Mr Belloc. The plain truth is that it would pay the proprietary classes of this country to pool their property and raise the wages, shorten the hours, and generally improve the conditions of life for the workers to an extent which would not only satisfy them and thus deprive the Socialist lecturers of their audiences and the Labor Party of its income, but fill them with such a dread of disturbing their contentment and perhaps going back to the bad old times that they would become as conservative as peasant proprietors, and make the propagation of Socialism a dangerous trade. In fact the proprietors are actually doing this through that form of property pooling known as the Trust. Thus we see that though the path of laisserfaire leads to complete national Socialism if the workers go to the end of it, Proprietary Socialism will build a halfway house so comfortable that we shall never get the workers past it until they are born again and born different.

THE PROBLEM OF THE SLACKER

There is another form of the same difficulty which must soon put into the hands of whichever party controls the country the formidable weapon of Industrial Compulsion. The case for it will be as irresistible from the Socialist as from the Capitalist point of view. On a previous occasion I demonstrated from this

platform that Industrial Compulsion is a necessary plank in the
Labor Party platform: no sane party can assert a Right to Work
with one side of its mouth and concede a Right to Idle with the
other. And the logic of that argument is working itself out in
practice in this way.

We are confronted in all directions by the fact that if you
take a worker who has been forced to work like a galley slave
in order to produce for the idle rich more than he is allowed
to keep for himself, and, by means of a Land Purchase Act, or
through the operation of a rise in the market value of Labor
caused by the war, lift that burden from him, he makes no
serious effort to raise his standard of expenditure and is content
to live almost as miserably as before, and to take out the difference in leisure. The most benevolent landlords find that they
must rack rent a farm if it is to be cultivated to the utmost;
and Socialist employers have to cut the piece work rate to compel their men to work six days a week instead of three.

THE VALUE OF LEISURE

Now no thoughtful person will say that the country is altogether the poorer for this tendency. Leisure, though the prop-
ertied classes give its name to their own idleness, is not idleness.
It is not even a luxury: it is a necessity, and a necessity of the
first importance. Some of the most valuable work done in the
world has been done at leisure, and never paid for in cash or
kind. Leisure may be described as free activity, labor as compulsory activity. Leisure does what it likes: labor does what it
must, the compulsion being that of Nature, which in these lat-
itudes leaves men no choice between labor and starvation.

The practical problem which Government must solve is, how
much leisure can the country afford? The individual citizen
asks how much labor he *must* do in order to be able to do what
he likes the rest of the time. And this immediately raises the
question, what sort of life do he and his fellow-citizens desire?
Are they to live what is called the simple life; or are they to live
in a highly-complicated, artificial, expensive way? King Lear's

daughter Regan, a grasping, unimaginative, typical rich middle class Englishwoman, was of opinion that the simple life was good enough for her father, and asked him what more he needed. Lear's reply is very much to the point:

> *"Oh, reason not the need: our basest beggars*
> *Are in the poorest thing superfluous:*
> *Allow not nature more than nature needs,*
> *Man's life is cheap as beast's. Thou art a lady:*
> *If only to go warm were gorgeous,*
> *Why, nature needs not what thou gorgeous wear'st,*
> *Which scarcely keeps thee warm."*

A Labor Government will be continually occupied with this problem of where to draw the line between King Lear and Regan, between the extremes of the simple lifer who is really a beach comber, a gipsy, or a savage, and the artificial voluptuary who envies Sardanapalus. Also, I may say, between the two sorts of ascetics who desire, respectively, as much strenuous work, and as much pious meditation as the human frame can bear: Mr Samuel Smiles in his counting house and St Simeon on his pillar. Leaving this to chance or to taste is all nonsense: a Labor State can no more tolerate idleness or savagery than our present State can tolerate nakedness. The notion that the Labor Party can oppose Industrial Compulsion, or even refrain from making it a fundamental part of its policy, is an illusion produced by reading the conditions of the present into the future, and conceiving Socialism merely as a defence against the dangers it will abolish.

Unfortunately, Trade Unionism is violently opposed to Industrial Conscription. It is not even reconciled to Compulsory Military Service, which is much less important. It has therefore no remedy for the tendency to take out every increase in wages in establishing three Sundays and two Saturdays per week instead of a higher standard of life for the workman and his family. Whether the extra Sundays are spent in playing the piano and reading the poets, or in looking at other people playing football and in standing drinks and consuming them, will make no difference to the shortage that will ensue if the Government allows to the worker the old privilege of the capitalist not to work as long as he has money enough in his pocket to amuse himself.

The employers will be the first to point out this shortage and to demand legislation compelling the worker to put in a certain minimum of work per week. The Socialist will say "Certainly: we will legislate to compel *everybody* to put in that minimum." But the Trade Unionists, if they are Trade Unionists and nothing more, will waste their strength and discredit their party by fiercely opposing Industrial Compulsion; and though the facts must beat them in the long run, yet their resistance may delay the advance towards Socialism; split the party; create the same sort of mistrust of its practical capacity as Europe now feels towards the Bolsheviks; and even finally give the capitalists the victory by enabling them to pass Industrial Compulsion as a class measure applying to the proletariat only: in other words, as the consummation of Proprietary Socialism and Proletarian Slavery. Then indeed Mr Belloc would be able to say "I told you so."

STALEMATE EITHER WAY

It would be far better if the Trade Unionists were victorious, and made Merrie England like Hampstead Heath on Bank Holiday for five days in the week. Anyone who has ever observed how much more miserable sober people look at the end of a holiday than at the end of a hard day's work! how cross the women are! how the children are on the verge of tears and the men sulky to the verge of violence! will hardly doubt that they would be fed up with holidays almost as quickly as a confectioner's shop assistant is fed up with sweets. But would they seek relief in a return to labor? Experience does not promise that they would. Our idle rich at present are bored and miserable enough in all conscience when they have no occupation except the West End variety of the revels at the Bull and Bush. But they do not seek relief by crowding into the factories and mines. They make occupations for themselves, and wear themselves out at them so effectually that they need at least four months' holiday in the year, whereas a factory operative is content with a fortnight, and a laborer regards holidays much as his wife regards pearl necklaces, as not for the likes of him. But these occupations are the occupations of leisure, not of labor. Even when the actual thing done—for example, driving a motor car—happens to be just what a paid chauffeur does as necessary labor, the leisured driver drives where he likes and when he likes, and not where and when he must. Very reluctantly therefore I must abandon the hope that the evil of slacking must cure itself. I cannot deny that there is every reason to believe, and none to doubt, that long before the workers would learn public spirit spontaneously, their reaction against excessive labor into an excessive leisure would produce an industrial crisis, followed by a revolt among that very large section of their own class which would still be dependent on the incomes of the present upper and middle classes, which would either wreck our civilization as so many former civilizations have been wrecked, or else force the Trade Unionists to capitulate hastily and accept Industrial Compulsion on the employers' own terms.

SOCIALISM REQUIRES STATESMEN, NOT MERE OPPORTUNISTS

There is therefore no way out for the blind man: there are too many pits digged in his path. We have all had enough of the practical business men whose practicality consists in being able to smell nothing but money, and grabbing at it whilst decent folk are seeking higher things. And we shall soon be equally tired of the practical Labor man whose practicality consists in smelling another penny an hour and grabbing that to do what he likes with. Socialism will not be the work of so-called practical men, meaning mostly ignorant men: it will be the work of statesmen educated by those metaphysicians and those theorists in economics and sociology who are also So-

bayonet to walk slowly through a lane of many hundreds of soldiers each of whom was compelled, on pain of suffering a similar punishment, to strike him with all his strength with a stick. In the British army the soldier was reduced to a condition of utter abjection by equally savage floggings, inflicted not only for offences against ordinary morality, but for what was called "dumb insolence," which meant simply looking an officer in the face instead of cringing before him. The soldier's orders took no account of his life: it was nominally at the disposal of his country in case of necessity, but really at the disposal of Kings who wished, like Frederick the Great, to set the world talking about them, or Capitalist governments suppressing strikes, or military castes in which war was a kingly sport and a professional opportunity. The soldier had absolutely no political rights at all, not even that of trial by jury; and the attractions which made it possible to procure voluntary recruits under such circumstances, and even to make soldiering popular with men of a certain temperament, were complete security of livelihood; escape from anxiety about meals, clothes, or housing; above all, relief from all moral responsibility. Just as, in The Pilgrim's Progress, Christian, bent under the heavy burden of his conscience, found it drop from his back and leave him free when he reached the foot of the cross, so the soldier found the same burden drop from him when he passed through the barrack gate. Thenceforth what Cowper called "the insupportable fatigue of thought" did not exist for him. The whole duty of man, which never ends and is never quite certain for the anxious civilian, is reduced in the army to the Articles of War, the regulations, and the regimental orders, none of which require any thought or are beyond a very common rustic capacity. That continual thinking what we ought to do, which turns the civilian's hair prematurely grey, is reduced in barracks to such painless decisions as which girl to walk out with, and which sort of liquor to order in the public house. All the rest is decided for the soldier and dictated to him; and if he does it he will not get into trouble in 999 cases out of 1000. It is true that he is not, like Shelley's Titan, "Good, great, and joyous, beautiful and free," nor can he say of his service (though he sometimes does) that "This is alone Life, Joy, Empire, and Victory"; but as these are spiritual luxuries which the average soldier does not crave, he considers that he has made a very good bargain when he has traded them off for freedom from poverty and anxiety.

Now the indispensable material condition of military slavery is nationalization of the means of military production, distribution and exchange. All that was needed five years ago to complete the parallels between the machinery of Militarism and the machinery of Socialism in England was compulsory military service; and that we have now got. Properly speaking therefore, what the war has brought us has not been the Socialization of industry, but its militarization. All the improvements it has effected in the lot of the worker are the military improvements: regular rations, clothes, shelter, and freedom from care and conscience on easy conditions. Every scrap of our work in organizing the workers for material Socialism can be captured by our opponents and made the instrument of a slavery as complete as that of the soldier. This is not a reason for turning back. The converse is equally true. The Collectivist machinery will do the work of a Socialist State as well as of a Servile State if the Labor Party will capture it for the people. I do not say if they *can* capture it, because they can if they choose: the question is, will they choose? If they are Socialists they will. If they are only Trade Unionist Opportunists, I am not so sure.

THE DIAGNOSTIC OF SOCIALISM

What is the crucial difference between the object of Militarist Collectivism and Socialist Collectivism? Simply that the first aims at privilege and the second at equality. And when we are asked privilege in what? equality in what? we must answer, in income. When Arthur Wellesley was made Duke of Wellington on his merits, it was none the less necessary for parliament to give him half a million to keep up the state proper to his title. When Alfred Harmsworth made a million, parliament found it

necessary to make him a baron to supply him with a title proper
to his money: and it may be assumed that he went on making
millions, as they subsequently had to make him a viscount. Thus
whichever way you take it, whether it is the title that needs the
money or the money that needs the title, whether it is the merit
that earns the privilege or the privilege that assumes the merit,
the indispensable condition of privilege is inequality of income.

Now I cannot honestly say that Labor is sounder on the
question of equality of income than the privileged classes are.
A bricklayer is at least as scandalized by the notion that a
bricklayer's laborer should have as much money as himself as a
duke is scandalized by the same proposition applied to himself
and his butler. Men cling very hard to distinctions of any kind;
and the only distinction within the reach of a man of no more
than ordinary ability is a distinction of income. It is a suspicious
circumstance that the most resolute advocates of equality in the
Socialist movement of our time have been men like William
Morris, [who was] perfectly aware that the reputation which
distinguished him from the general mob of mankind was independent of money and titles, and would in fact be much more
conspicuous if there were no other sort of distinction recognized except distinguished personal capacity. Equality of income
has not yet appeared, as far as I know, on the program of any
political party, or even of any Socialist Society; and the occasional use of the word Equality to denote one of our principles does not differentiate us from the French Republic, which
writes up the word *Égalité* on every public building in France.

WAGES HAVE ENTERED INTO OUR VERY BONES

What is worse, our laborers, having lived for generations by
the sale of their labor for wages, cannot get away from the
idea that their income must necessarily consist of wages. However loudly their orators may talk of abolishing the wage system, I find it almost impossible to advocate equality of income,
as I so steadfastly do, without finding that I am supposed to be
talking about equal wages, or equal remuneration, or being

asked, as I was even by so gifted a man as Mr Gilbert Chesterton, whether I seriously meant that a baby should have an income like everyone else. Trade Unionism is a method of dealing with wages; yet Trade Unionism can never advance to Socialism until it rids itself completely of the notion of remuneration, and perceives that the people must be placed in the position of shareholders receiving dividends, and receiving them just like our own joint stock shareholders: that is, without the smallest reference to their moral character, their idleness or industry, their drunkenness or sobriety, their age or sex or color or creed or anything but their bare membership of the community. Who is going to teach our people this fundamental truth? They will all be taught from their childhood that it is a wicked falsehood, and in their adolescence that it is a ridiculous paradox. And it will seem even more absurd to the Trade Unionist than to anyone else.

NATURE OF THE ARGUMENTS FOR EQUALITY OF INCOME

The arguments for equality of income do not lie on the surface of individual interest. They are, as I have formulated them, first, the economic argument that as national needs should be satisfied in the order of their importance, equality of purchasing power is needed to prevent Ritz hotels from being built for idlers whilst workers are paying half a crown a week for half a bed in an overcrowded cottage; second, the political and legal argument that really representative parliaments and juries are impossible in a community broken up into antagonistic classes by differences of income; and last, that the supreme importance to the race of the fullest and widest sexual selection makes it imperative that the whole community should consist of inter-marriageable persons, and not, as at present, of individuals whose choice is limited to the narrow social circle formed by the local people of the same income. All these arguments are essentially comprehensive arguments: they do not occur to politicians who are pursuing merely individual interests for themselves and their constituents. My own habits of thought are as comprehensive as can be expected even from a trained Socialist; but though I saw clearly all through that Equality was the goal of Socialism, and that there was indeed no sense in economic Socialism except as a movement towards that goal, yet I preached Socialism for twenty years before I made out the dry case for equality of income apart from all appeal of sentiment. I am still waiting, however, for the universities to invite me to lecture on the subject or to offer me a chair of sociology.

I must conclude bluntly that Socialism will not take root and grow in the soil cultivated by our present educational system, nor flourish in the artificial climate such cultivation produces. The Labor Party will not assimilate that system automatically through the Labor vote; on the contrary, the system will assimilate it with the greatest ease; and Mr Henderson's successors will take in duchesses to dinner as often as some of his Labor contemporaries do. The most serious task before the Labor Party is not the passing of this or that measure for the immediate relief of the poor and the final benefit of Proprietary Socialism. It is nothing less than the conquest of the established religion and the established education of the country by a Reformation far more radical than Luther's.

Now such a revolution can no more be made catastrophically and instantly than the economic revolution. It must be done by the Fabian method of permeation until the balance of power has shifted to the Labor side, when the finish may be as fast as Lobor pleases. But before you begin permeating, you must have something definite to permeate with. Fabianism did not change the character of the whole Socialist movement in Europe, and force even the British Liberal party to fight a general election on the Newcastle Program, by a combination of negative criticism with pious aspiration. It brought forward a new doctrine and new methods, embodied in new measures. One of the morals of its success is that you cannot overthrow the Church of England or any other Church by simply putting out your tongue at it. If you ask a man to come out of it, he will refuse until he finds another lodging ready for his soul; and if that lodging is either some conventicle ten times more narrow and stifling and ugly than the Church, or some Secularist Hall where nothing of the Church teaching is discarded except faith in miracles, and the Individualism and Materialism which is only the Old Testament half of the Church doctrine is made the whole duty of Man, you will have taken your proselyte farther from Socialism instead of nearer to it. Jesus Christ, having to rebuild a temple which had become a den of thieves, did not call on the thieves to come out of it, but brought honest men into it and drove the thieves out. But he first had to teach the honest men; for they were all alike thieves originally. To drop the metaphor, Jesus, who was a Jew living among Jews, never suggested that any Jew should cease to be a Jew, and never abjured the Jewish faith. He declared emphatically that if you rooted up a man's native form of religion to substitute your own form, you would root up his soul in the process: the wheat, he said, would come up with the tares. His view was that there were certain truths that all men must recognize and act on if they are to find salvation, whether they be Jews or Gentiles. My point here is that he had his truths ready; and that we also must have our truths ready. They are, by the way, essentially the same truths. Negations are useless except to clear the way for affirmations. If we had nothing better to do with the human soul than to create a vacuum, we should fail because Nature abhors a vacuum. We should even do worse than merely fail; for there are many devils looking for a lodging that are blacker than the Church devils. Socialism must have a positive religion, characteristic of and proper to the epoch which it is to inaugurate, with articles of faith and commandments based on it and accepted as the foundations of the Socialist State. And it must be a scientific religion, not only dissociated from, but actively hostile to and openly contradictory of all sorts of nonsense, physical impossibilities, fictions pretending to be facts, and idolatries.

Has such a religion yet formed itself out of the intellectual chaos produced by the break-up of the old religions and the dissolving force of the modern Democratic spirit? By this time we can answer quite confidently in the affirmative. Socialism is being pioneered by men who believe that man has undergone an evolution which has raised him from a speck of protoplasm to the comparatively wonderful thing he is at present, and that the same force that has brought him all that distance can carry him still farther until he attains a power and wisdom which we should now call divine. There is a penalty for failing to attain that divinity; and the penalty is that if man cannot attain it he will most assuredly be scrapped and superseded by some being who can. We know positively that one species after another actually has been evolved and scrapped and superseded in this way. There is really a law of the survival of the fittest: not the survival of the fittest to slay and destroy, but the fittest to evolve and attain. During the last half of the XIX century those false prophets of science, the mere naturalists, persuaded us that we evolve by adapting ourselves to our environment; and presently they tried to drive us into the still more horrible belief that our environment forced the adaptation on us, and that we had no part in the process at all, but must go whither the wind blew us and take such shapes as the avalanche might crush us into. Socialism, preoccupied as it was by the evils of the environment produced by Capitalism, was very far from being unridden by this nightmare: it even welcomed it as an argument for a complete change of environment. Marx's theory of history is Natural Selection applied to economics. The Fabian Society, having to devise the political and bureaucratic environment of Socialism so as to rescue it from Utopia by giving it a practicable political constitution, found itself accused of believing that this environment, once established, would force the human organism to adapt itself to it, and thus become Socialist whether it meant to or not. This ridiculous expectation is described as Socialism by Wirepulling. But we cannot induce men to accept a Socialist environment before they are Socialists. And they cannot become Socialists by Natural Selection without a Socialist environment. Which is to come first, the egg or the chicken? The only egg that Capitalism is likely to lay is Proprietary Socialism: and Mr Belloc smells it prophetically and declares, with reason, that it is a bad egg.

Fortunately all that neo-Darwinian nonsense is now knocked on the head. Evolution is a creative impulse, a living force seeking more life, and having the power to produce it, and to build actual tangible structures of bone and muscle and nerve into the monsters whose skeletons now have to be placed outside our museums because there is not room enough for them within, or into poets and prophets. Men can change themselves into Socialists by willing to be Socialists; and, if the change required eyes in the back of their heads and as many extra pairs of arms as an Indian god has, they could evolve them. Even if they decided to carry the statement that two heads are better than one to its fullest practical application, the power of which they are the instrument could give us an extra head as surely as it has already relieved us of a superfluous tail.

Our work then is to encourage the will to Socialism, to inculcate its ideas, to associate it with honor and success, to saturate the atmosphere of the family and the school with it: in short, to be as much in earnest about it as the German military monarchy is about Hohenzollernism. What can we do in that direction for a beginning? Well, I suggest that we might contrive to make Socialism a little more attractive. What is there in it that repels so many of our young people, and drives them into the various forms of Anarchism that are always appealing to their craving for freedom? Why is it that in the professional classes we meet so many vigorous spirits who tell us that they know all about the horrors of Capitalism, but cannot stomach Bureaucracy as an alternative? Everywhere we meet with the same objection: the fear that our system will destroy freedom. It is easy for us to say, in our superior manner, that law is the mother of liberty, and that the man who can obey a hundred regulations is freer than the savage who cannot understand or obey one. Goldsmith was far nearer the mark when he said that law seldom comes to the poor man's door save in the shape of oppression. There is no necessary connection whatever between law and liberty or between bureaucracy and organized efficiency; and there is a very strong historical connection between law and slavery, and between bureaucracy and robbery and job-

bery, tyranny and insolence. No doubt if you want to make a
man free you must do it by means of law and bureaucracy; but
if you want to enslave him, you must do it by law and bureaucracy also; and that is precisely the use of law and bureaucracy
with which the man in the street is most familiar. Even the Factory Acts present themselves to him not as the instruments of
his own emancipation, but as fetters on his employer. As a child
at school he is a beaten slave; and the first thing he finds us all
agreed on is that he should have several years more school with
the dentist added to the schoolmaster. At the end of that there
is compulsory military service, and then compulsory industrial
service, which is, I repeat, an essential and inevitable part of
Socialism, and even of any considerable rise in the standard of
living for Labor. Even when he is unemployed he is not to be
free: he may not even loaf and starve. The program we present
to him is one of continual compulsion: he is to be a wheel in a
machine endowed with perpetual motion. Gradually the Socialist becomes in his eyes an ogre: there is really no reason to suppose that the absurd descriptions of Mrs Sidney Webb with
which Mr Chesterton enlivens the pages of The New Witness,
and which kept Mr Wells's novels going for several years, are
drawn in intellectual bad faith. I have always thought it a crime
to allow anyone to read Law's Serious Call: but I am not sure
that the vision of life it presents and enjoins on pain of damna-
tion is more depressing than the vision of life presented by the
tracts and reports of the Fabian Society. After all, there was to
be Heaven at the end of Law's Hell on Earth; but at the end of
the Fabian Hell on Earth there is nothing but that last plank in
our platform, free funerals.

The truth is, we have taken too much for granted. I have
already said that Mr Webb and I took for granted when we
started that, as everyone was as familiar with Mill's Essay on
Liberty as we were, all that no longer needed saying. But the
Fabian Society did worse: it absolutely refused to publish anything written from the point of view of the artist aiming at a
rich, free, and joyous life. Some of us pleaded for Oscar Wilde's
Soul of Man under Socialism, for Richard Wagner's Art and

Revolution, for a more sympathetic relation with Morris, for a serious view of Carpenter, for a place for Ruskin in our library. But the Fabian Society would have none of them: it proceeded on the common British assumption that metaphysics are rot, that art is immoral, that painters and musicians are long-haired cranks and free lovers, and, strangest of all, that the less we had to do with people like ourselves, the better. Now it happens that the Fabian Society was quite right at that time. Our special business then was to work out the political and industrial environment of Socialism, and leave others to rhapsodize about the joys that would follow their application. Besides, which of us could seriously believe that the melancholy beauty of such really fine art as our middle class could produce would appeal to the working classes, or be of much use to them? The art of Burne Jones, for instance, which represented the greatest achievement in painting of what may be called the Morris movement, did not exhilarate the English working man. Charles Rowley in Manchester has devoted a life-time to popularizing the finest art of the nineteenth century, and all the centuries, from the twelfth to the fifteenth, on which that art founded itself, with the result that he has barely succeeded in keeping together a small band of enthusiasts called the Ancoats Brotherhood in one of the poorest quarters of Manchester: but nobody can pretend that it is a representative body. Mr Chesterton's gospel of carnal jollity strikes a more attractive note, though it is rather a forced note, and seems to the worker, when he hears it, to involve an intolerable deal of preaching to a halfpennyworth of beer. I really do not think that either the Fabians with their middle class art culture, or the Labor leaders, with their religious and ethical doctrine, or Mr Chesterton with vine leaves in his hair, can put the joy of life into the Labor movement. It cannot be done by a gospel of art or beer or any other gospel of a class or sect.

I suggest that what we have to promise to all classes alike is freedom. Even if we must teach that utter freedom is impossible, and that no man can be free, save at the expense of another, until he has discharged those duties as a citizen which are his real debt to nature, yet the object of organizing those duties in a framework of law so strong that no one will be able to escape them is that everyone will have a far greater share of uncontrolled life than is possible even to the privileged under our system. What is called the tyranny of Socialism is the price of the maximum of freedom; and men will voluntarily set it up and endure it only on that understanding. And in this they are profoundly right according to the characteristic scientific religion of Socialism, and rashly and rebelliously wrong according to the religions they are officially taught.

For just consider for a moment what this characteristic scientific religion of Socialism, this faith in Creative Evolution implies. As opposed to the doctrine that "the heart of man is deceitful above all things and desperately wicked," it implies that wicked as we certainly are, and boundless as our powers of selfdeception seem to be, yet what we are driving at all the time is greater wisdom, and that if only you will let men go their own way they will take the upward path. No other assumption is politically practicable in the long run; for if human nature is radically corrupt, and man essentially a devil, you cannot mend matters by putting some of the devils in command of the others: all your law and order can do under such circumstances is to produce such an improvement in efficiency for mischief as pirates produce when they elect a captain and obey him. The old Whig doctrine that the function of a government is to suppress crime and lunacy and then let people do what they like is sound enough once it is recognized, first, that this cannot be done by excluding idleness from the category of crime and actually making the idlers the government, or by excluding war from the category of lunacy and making the lunatics kings; and, second, that the political constitution of the highly developed modern State includes its economic structure, and that its police duty includes the regulation of its industry and the distribution of its product. With that enlargement it remains as true as ever that the function of the State is finally to keep the ring for the struggles of the soul towards the light.

Until this is known to be our religion, we shall make no headway, because we shall seem the apostles of a great tyranny

instead of a great liberation. How, it will be asked, can a movement which proclaims four cardinal equalities, involving four
great compulsions, take on any aspect of liberty? Let us deal
with the question schematically. The four cardinal equalities are,
1, economic equality, 2, military equality, 3, political equality,
4, sexual equality. The four corresponding compulsions are, 1,
compulsory industrial service, 2, compulsory military service,
3, compulsory political service, and 4, compulsory sexual service. It is at once apparent that the compulsion in the last case
must be the compulsion of public opinion, and it is almost
equally obvious, though less essentially so, that the political
compulsion must be of the same nature. But in truth even military compulsion could not be carried out if public opinion were
opposed to it. In England, it has been savagely enforced; but not
until so large an army had been put into the field by voluntary
recruiting that it is not to this day certain that the unwilling
could not have been dispensed with. In Ireland, where it would
be easier to raise an army to fight against England than for her,
physical compulsion was a desperate expedient, impracticable
as a means of strengthening the army, and advocated really as a
method of war on the Irish people. It is the will to fight of the
majority that makes it possible to torture the unwilling minor-
ity. The same is true of industrial compulsion. Without a
strong general opinion that everyone ought to work, and that
everyone who does not is, as Ruskin pointed out, either a thief
or a beggar, there can be no industrial compulsion. The present
strong public opinion that it is a low thing to work and that the
essence of gentility and nobility is perpetual leisure, inculcated
in England so strenuously that it is second nature in us, is the
sole obstacle to an industrial compulsion by public opinion
alone. If we could get rid of corrupt inculcation, we should in
a single generation reach a condition of public opinion in which
we should accept the four equalities with their obligations with
no more sense of tyranny than we now feel when we dress and
wash ourselves before walking down Piccadilly. Nevertheless
we do make dressing compulsory by law. It may be that there
are hygienic, artistic and moral reasons why we should not do

so, and that the country in summer should be on the footing of a sun bath in the Black Forest. But that is not the point: a law with an overwhelming public opinion behind it is not felt as a restriction of freedom, but as a defence against savagery.

In a reasonable educated community it would be easy to produce such an overwhelming opinion in favor of industrial conscription. An idler inflicts on the community exactly the same injury as a thief; and he will certainly be treated as a thief from the moment when he ceases to control the government, the schools, and the Church, as he has done in Europe ever since the robber barons, who at least fought for their livelihood, evolving into *fainéant* landlords and capitalists. But the case of the Mugwump, or political *fainéant*, is much more difficult. It raises not only the question of making a man work, as to the justice of which there can be no doubt, but the question of depriving him of his choice of what he shall work at, and setting him a task which may be odious to his taste and beyond his powers. It is true that under existing circumstances men have very little choice of occupation, and that even in the most scientifically organized and democratically constituted society the demand of the needs of the community would determine the work to be done, and the individual would have to do his share of it whether he could find a congenial department with a vacancy for him or not. A choice between tinker and tailor, soldier and sailor, is not great consolation to the man who has no vocation for any of them. All that can be done for him is to give him the widest possible choice and make it easy for him to change when he is tired. But the choice between one routine employment and another is a very simple matter compared to the choice between a routine employment and one which consists in making decisions based on mental work. In most instances the problem solves itself: for example, if an individual is mentally qualified to be an astronomer, the work will be so congenial to him, and the work of, say, keeping the observatory instruments clean and efficient so irksome and wasteful of his powers, that he will be glad to work as an astronomer for less than he could, under a system like ours, earn as an attendant.

And as Socialism would offer him the same share of the national income whether he was astronomer or attendant, he would volunteer for the more congenial job without putting the community to the trouble of forcing him. In short, in most departments of human activity, the capacity is itself the inducement to exercise it: indeed this is so true that in some of the highest departments, such as poetry and philosophy, we have had poets and philosophers in spite of every penalty of poverty and scorn and calumny, summed up by one of these as "Toil, envy, want, the patron and the jail" that we could attach to their work without making it positively criminal.

But this natural safeguard is not so trustworthy in the case of high political work. Here the motive we have depended on has been ambition. The deepest remark in the play of Hamlet is the hero's "I lack ambition," the result being that the throne of Denmark is occupied by an ambitious drunkard, libertine, and murderer instead of by Hamlet himself, who has all the qualities of a prince. How are we to banish the demagogue and the climber from our councils and enlist the public spirited Comprehensionist? He, as Plato pointed out, will always be reluctant; for the work is most burdensome and thankless, and the attraction of its intellectual and artistic activity, as exercised in debate and oratory, can be found in a higher degree in other careers. We have the case of Hamlet and Claudius all over the parliaments and chanceries of Europe. The front benches are filled with men of ambition and political hacks whose qualification is the power to work at official routine for sixteen hours a day for thirty years without thought or conscience, whilst the born statesmen are engaged in science and art, never voting and seldom reading the newspapers. Cincinnatus may leave his plough to become an explorer: Goethe may be seduced from literature by science: Shakespear needed no compulsion to give up poaching and take to poetry. But it is impossible to conceive any of them taking spontaneously to the politics of a modern State. They would be more likely to be found using every artifice to escape even being summoned on the jury.

And yet anything like crude coercive compulsion would be

defeated by the fact that you cannot compel a man to do anything until you know exactly what it is you want him to do. It is said that you may take a horse to the water but cant make him drink. This, however, is not true: any trainer of performing horses will testify that it is not more difficult to make an unwilling horse drink than to make him waltz. But the most ruthless or ingenious trainer could not make a horse go to Putney if he did not know the way thither himself. You can make a Prime Minister introduce a bill by threatening to hang him if he refuses but in this case as you already know what you want, your minister might as well be a performing horse as a man: he is not exercising statesmanship: he is obeying an order and the statesmanship rests with those who give him the order. But if you simply take a person whom you believe to be a political genius and make him Prime Minister with an intimation that if he does not govern the country well it will be the worse for him, you cannot carry out your threat because you cannot tell whether he is governing the country well or not: he may be sowing the seeds of a war or a famine or an eclipse of culture or a succession of plagues twenty years ahead for all you know.

You must therefore come humbly to your great man, and appeal to his public spirit. You must not ask him to take up the burden for longer than, say, six years. And you must make him a free man in respect of all involuntary work for the rest of his life in consideration of his having taken on that tremendous stunt.

But it is when we come to the other two compulsions: the military and the sexual, that we are on the most delicate ground. Here the repugnance to the work, if it exists, is of the deepest and most poignant character: it is the repugnance of prostitution. Let no one suppose, because military compulsion has been so easily achieved, whereas sexual compulsion seems to be an almost unthinkable outrage, that the two are not on the same footing. Military service has not been imposed easily: it has been imposed on pain of death, defeat, ruin, slavery, rapine and pillage and all the horrors of war. It is true that, under the terror of these, compulsory military service seems a trifle, just as a danger of damp sheets or the shame of nakedness seem trifles if the house is on fire. But to compel a human person to shoot and stab and blow to pieces his fellow creatures, or even to exhibit him in public practising with a bayonet on bags or straw representing his fellow creatures, is a horrible violation of his moral nature. And it is not surprising that many men endure the extremity of persecution rather than submit to it, or that parliament should flinch from ordering that persecution without some hypocritical and ineffectual pretence that it is to be applied only to slackers and cowards.

Notes on the British Museum Manuscripts

The condition of the manuscripts of the lectures and essays in this collection varies from good to what might be described candidly as chaotic. Since they present very different problems from the editorial point of view it has seemed best to describe them separately.

1. Shaw's "MS of Lecture That the Socialist Movement is Only the Assertion of Our Lost Honesty" is in longhand in black ink. The pages are numbered from one to twenty-six, with three extra pages inserted between pages one and two. There are a moderate number of words, phrases, and sentences crossed out and rewritten, but generally the revisions, like the text itself, are clearly readable.

2. "The New Radicalism" is also handwritten in ink, with rather more corrections than the first lecture, the first page, in particular being completely interlined. Again, these are all readily decipherable even when the hand is small. The pages are numbered from one to twenty.

3. "Freedom and the State" also fills twenty handwritten pages. In a few places Shaw indicated that he intended to write notes but did not include them.

4. "The New Politics" presents many more difficulties than the preceding lectures. The text, which is untitled in the manuscript, is written in two sewn lined notebooks. Somewhat confusingly, the pages of the first are numbered 325 to 374 and the second 271 to 324 in Shaw's hand. The lecture is written on every other line on every other page. The name "Schultze-Delitzsch" is misspelt "Schultze-Delitzch" throughout. There are several dozen blank spaces where Shaw has neglected to fill in dates, statistics, names, et

cetera, and, in one place, a long quotation. In this edition, some of these have been filled in from reference works; others have required extensive research. Fortunately, the British Museum collection contains some of the notes Shaw made for his lecture, and many statistical details in his account of the International have been transcribed from these, as has the passage from Bakunin's manifesto. Details that remain conjectural have been so marked in the text. The most puzzling section is that on the Commune hostages, for which no notes appear to exist.

5. "Socialism and Human Nature" is the first of the lectures to be typed instead of handwritten. The typing is accurate, but there are a fair number of revisions in longhand. The pages are numbered one to twenty-four, with two inserts marked A and B after eighteen.

6. "Bureaucracy and Jobbery" consists of thirty-one typed pages. Revisions have been added in ink. The essay is probably incomplete since the last sentence fills the page and is not finished.

7. This essay, which I have titled "Capital and Wages," presents problems totally different from any of the other chapters of this book. It is very unskillfully typed, obviously by Shaw himself. For once, Shaw seems to have had difficulty finding words for his thought. In nearly every other sentence he has typed a word or phrase or clause and then typed an alternative expression. The difficulty is that he did not cross out rejected words or indicate his final choice. Sometimes the alternative word will be typed above the first one, but more often it simply follows it without any indication that it is meant to replace what goes before. Most of the time I have simply transcribed what was Shaw's second choice but sometimes neither phrase makes quite complete sense and I have had to combine them somewhat arbitrarily. In other places the second phrase does not fit into the rest of the sentence and it is necessary to return to the first. Occasionally, this will make construing a sentence a kind of elaborate jigsaw puzzle. In addition there are a great many

typing errors or omissions. Except in the really uncertain cases these have been silently corrected.

8. "The Simple Truth about Socialism" is typed by an accurate typist, but many pages have handwritten changes by Shaw. In a few cases these run to half a page in length, but nearly all are clear and legible. The first fourteen pages are numbered in type, the rest, up to the last page, forty-nine, by hand.

9. The long essay published here as "Redistribution of Income" is based on twelve short separate manuscript sections, varying in length from three to twenty-four pages, brought together under one general heading in the British Museum collection. Each fragment bears the subtitle which appears in the present text, and is numbered separately, except for "The Law of Minimum," which appears as a subtitle within the section headed "How the Change to Equality of Income is Actually Happening." If we label each of the sections in the present text, including "The Law of Minimum," with a letter from *a* to *m*, the order in which the sections are arranged in the British Museum (1968) comes out *ahlcedfimgjk.* It will be seen that, apart from starting with the same section, the order of the sections finally adopted in this edition bears no relation to the British Museum ordering at all.

The main clue to my reordering has been the internal logic of Shaw's argument. While this may seem to be a somewhat subjective criterion, it has nevertheless been possible to establish the relative position of many sections by the references Shaw makes back to what has gone before. Apart from a few relatively self-contained sections, such as *c* ("The Discourse of a Traffic Manager and a Railway Porter"), which might have been introduced at some other point, the order the editor has arrived at seems as good an order as it is possible to get, considering that (1) the fragments do not make a complete whole, and (2) Shaw may have dashed off some (like *c*) independently without a clear idea himself as to where he wanted to fit them in.

Despite these difficulties, however, it has been possible to verify my proposed "best order" by an independent test. Shaw's series of lectures on the "Redistribution of Income" was reported in *The Christian Commonwealth* under the following titles: 1. "Income, Equality, and Idolatry" (Nov. 4); 2. "An Examination of Idolatry" (Nov. 11); 3. "Equality and Incentives" (Nov. 18); 4. "Incentives, Prostitution, and the Middle Classes" (Nov. 25); 5. "The Fate of the Capitalist" (Dec. 2); 6. "The Case Against Inequality" (Dec. 9 and 16). These detailed accounts of each lecture indicate (1) that Shaw's general pattern of thought throughout the series followed roughly the general pattern of this edition; (2) that he did not speak from a manuscript but from brief notes; and that (3) he frequently introduced other topics, used different illustrations, and made spur-of-the-moment digressions. The first two lectures covered many of the ideas on equality and idolatry included in sections *a* ("Redistribution of Income") and *b* ("The Passing of the Idols") but apparently omitted even more. In the third lecture, Shaw, in reply to questions and letters about his first two speeches, takes up the problem of incentives, which he claims he had not originally intended to deal with, and covers many of the points in section *d* ("Incentive") and the short section *h* ("The Incentive to Irksome Work"), but is not recorded as using the ideas in *e* ("The Incentive to Think"), *f* ("The Incentive to Bodily Labor"), *g* ("The Appetite for Distinction as an Incentive to Production") or *i* ("Money as an Incentive"), though, as some of these sections are short, he may have used them without being reported. The opening section of lecture four, on "Prostitution," does not correspond to anything in the British Museum manuscripts, but halfway through this, and throughout lecture five, Shaw pursues the argument that the rise of wages and taxes may eventually freeze out the capitalist and landlord which appears in *j* ("How the Change to Equality of Income is Actually Happening") and *k* ("The Law of Minimum"). The reports make no reference to the ideas of *l* ("The Incentive to Use Money as Capital") or *m* ("Why State Morality and State Economics are Unique"). Instead, the series ended with a recapitulation, not contained in the British Museum fragments, of the economic, political, and biological arguments for equality Shaw put forth in his 1910 lecture above.

10. The manuscript of "Socialism and Culture" consists of fifty-seven typed pages, with a moderate number of revisions in ink in Shaw's hand. There are very few subheadings in the original typescript; the vast majority were added by Shaw in longhand. The last fourteen pages, however, have no subheadings at all. Though the final paragraph concludes before the end of the last page, Shaw's argument is apparently incomplete.

No reference to published versions of any of these manuscripts has as yet appeared in any Shaw bibliography, and the assumption is that none of them has seen the light of day, barring some very obscure appearance indeed. It is, of course, possible that newspaper reports of some of the lectures may yet turn up. However, for various reasons, even very full newspaper accounts of speeches by Shaw often differ widely from manuscript material with the same title, as the "Redistribution of Income" series demonstrates.

liquid hanging above. We were all silent while she did her job.

"I have a million questions," I said.

"I'm sure you do," she whispered. "I wish I had a million answers."

And then she started to talk, for maybe the first time in our lives together. And I started to listen, maybe for the first time.

"I wasn't born with a lot of motherly instincts. To be honest, I really didn't have the slightest idea what to do with you."

I remembered what I'd read about none of us having a single cell left in our bodies from the day we were born. The person who came out of her was literally someone else.

"Your father knew," she said. "He knew from the first minute they put you in his arms. With him around, I could count on someone knowing what to do, how to raise a baby. When he died, eleven years with no practice, I was just as lost as the day you were born.

"I can't really apologize. God made me who I am. God and my own mother. The eternal victim. She died before you were born. I promised myself when I was a little girl never to be like her. She went from one crisis to the next, almost each self-created, and blamed everyone around her. She lived off sympathy and guilt, and killed herself on her thirtieth birthday. I was nine years old."

"How?" I asked.

My mother looked at me, aggravated by the interruption.

"Pills," she finally said.

It was quiet again. Unbelievably quiet.

"Maybe that answers some of your million questions," she said. "Maybe not. You know, we like to believe we get better every day. We like to believe we wake up every morning a little better than the day before. I'm not sure it's true. Maybe we peak long before we get old."

The quiet seemed to settle around us, and my mother's eyes closed slowly. She whispered, "Why don't you come back tomorrow and we'll talk some more."

I sat in the hospital room for at least another hour and watched my mother sleep, and then I watched her die. There was no shouting or convulsing. No struggle to hold on for one last word. She just died, and left me very, very alone in the big world, with a dry soul, a family history of suicide, a guilty conscience, and tears rolling down my cheeks.

She also left me a letter, folded neatly in an envelope:

James Early Winwood,

From the day you were born you were taught to be strong. As tiny men, even learning to walk on your little legs, you are all told not to cry. Crying is weak, and men are never to be weak.

Men stand tall, they wear uniforms, they fight on battlefields, real and created, and they provide for their families.

At some point, some critical point, in order to truly know God and yourself, you must separate what you have been ingrained to become from what you must do. We must be weak to truly know anything. This weakness will let you say, "I love you," to those you love, to cry for no real reason, to reach those places inside your heart I was never able to reach until the end. You see, it isn't really weakness at all, is it?

The greatest debate inside every human in the history of civilization is the debate over the proof of the existence of God. But there is no debate. No need to argue or require. There is a God, because there must be, and that is all to be said.

I thank God for you and your father. Without you two I would have never known love, spoken or unspoken, never known the reason for this life. God will bless us both, now and forever. I know this to be true. He has told me many times when I have been tired and needed to hear His whisper.

I love you,
Your Mother

As you might imagine, she left her affairs in perfect order. The house was packed up, everything in boxes, with notes where each box should go. I never found the letters from Bruce, but she left me a box of things about my father, and it was like getting to know him for the first time.

Inside the box I found his little league baseball trophies, pictures of me as a baby in his arms. The three of us on the beach. The same snow-white sands, building a castle at the edge of the surf. My mother was smiling in the picture, the same smile I'd seen with Bruce's arm around her shoulders.

There were poems my father had written, and letters to my mother, and little, odd things like an old bullet, three baby teeth in a small, black, cloth bag, a firecracker, and a picture of a dog that I'd never seen before, and all those other things that reminded me how little we know our parents. And now there was no one left to ask the million questions. Those people who created me, those with the closest connection, were both dead. And Allen Jr. held me so tight, and watched me like a grown man watches a child.

He stood next to me at the funeral and put his hand on my shoulder when I couldn't hold myself together. Gretchen sat two rows behind with her mother and Russell Enslow. She looked at me with misunderstanding, perhaps the same way I had always looked at my mother.

Samantha was lost in the role of providing comfort to a crying man, but I will never forget Allen coming home from college and sitting up late at night with me. Calling the office every day for months, pretending he needed this or that, when it was me who needed. The very boy whose father I murdered. The very boy who turned to me after his own daddy's funeral and asked if I would be the one to throw the ball with him in the front yard from now on. And with this very boy, who had become a man, I would forge the strongest bond I would ever have with another person in my lifetime. Perhaps even stronger than the bond that I held with my long-dead father.

How the current of life flows as we struggle in the waters to get to one side or the other, to control our own destinies, when all along the current will decide. The current will take us, willing or not.

five

If my first marriage was like the lighting of a match, quick and bright, burning out as soon as it began, then my second marriage was the opposite, a slow rot. After Allen moved out and my mother died, there was an unforgivable onset of loneliness. At least it seemed Samantha was unable to forgive me, for anything, but particularly my hints of insecurity. She had hated Allen Kilborn Sr., but at least she respected the man.

I couldn't figure out how to fix things between us, or if I wanted them fixed at all. I couldn't even figure out how to get laid in my own house, with my own wife, in the bed I paid for. It was more complicated than sex with a complete stranger, and my mind began to drift to the idea of other women. Kate, or the lady across the street getting her mail from the box on a Saturday morning, short pants and gardening gloves. I had a particular fantasy where I walked over to her garage, we didn't say a word to each other, and she simply positioned herself bent over the hood of her black BMW, and then pulled down her shorts to her ankles and watched me over her right shoulder.

I felt guilty about it. The Bible says the sin is committed with the first thought of lust, but my mind wouldn't leave it alone. It was easy to shift the blame to Samantha. She was cold, unproviding. She'd rejected me so many times, how could I expect anything different? But still, I struggled with the immorality of it all. I knew if I took the first step toward making it real, more than just a fantasy, it might actually happen. If not with the woman across the street bent over the BMW, another woman, somewhere else, bent over something else. It wasn't the fear of getting caught. It was the fear of not getting caught, and becoming like those men who cheat on their wives every time they go out of town, like it's just something men do, they can't help themselves, regardless of vows, or promises. I think if you do it once, it becomes easier the next time, and the next.

The letters from Kate kept coming. All full of innuendo and code. She was unhappy, I was unhappy, so I wrote back, in the same code and innuendo, imagining her husband would see the letter one night when Kate drank too much red wine and got caught taking the box down from the top shelf to peek inside.

Early,

I keep remembering those days locked up in your apartment.

It was a long time ago, but not so long. I also remember the first time I ever saw you out by the cemetery where we used to go back in high school to see Onionhead. You kept staring at me, and now it's me doing the staring. Maybe you could explain why I need to send you letters. I have several theories, but I'd like to hear yours. Maybe you could explain why you wrote me back after all those years, especially when I did all I did to you.

It's hard to even figure out why anymore.

Kate

I would lie awake on the couch and imagine sending a letter saying, "Meet me in Kansas City, next Saturday, in the lobby of the airport Sheraton Hotel, and stop asking why." I'd buy a plane ticket, invent a reason to go to Kansas City on business, and spend a weekend of naked bliss in a hotel room. Would she show up in the lobby, or was she only willing to dance around the words of handwritten letters? If I actually sent the letter, and got on the plane, and sat in the lobby pretending to read the paper, and Kate actually got on the plane and showed up through the front door with a red dress, how would our lives change? It was like the fantasy with the lady across the street, or suicide, or the murder of Allen Kilborn. Once it became more than just an idea. Once it began to happen, it was like the current, out of control, deciding for itself.

Besides, I would tell myself, "It was a mirage." One of us needed to be smart enough to remember how bad it was and how bad it probably would have gotten. I was a kid. I fell in love with my own imagination. A girl that didn't exist. How long can such a thing last? Not long, apparently. So how could anyone expect it to work itself out twenty years later? But still, the Kansas City hotel weekend was worth all the hours thinking about it.

As my mind drifted and my marriage crumbled, Samantha scheduled counseling. We sat in the office of Dr. Paulette Long. She kept us at a safe distance across her antique cherrywood desk. The woman was entirely pointy. Thin, her face coming quickly inward to the sharp nose. I didn't like her the moment I saw her, and I don't think she liked me either.

"So, why don't we start with you, Mr. Winwood. Tell me a little bit about your marriage."

"I think it would be better if Samantha starts."

"Why?"

"I just do."

There was an awkward silence. She reminded me of a big pencil.

"Okay, Samantha, would you start?"

It seemed to me they'd met in the office before, without me, and discussed their strategy for proving I was to blame for everything wrong in all of our lives.

Samantha said, nervously but rehearsed, "There's a distance between us. I don't feel the closeness we had before."

It got quiet again. Apparently, it was my turn to say something.

"There's no closeness because she sleeps as far away from me in the bed as she can get without rolling off on the floor. My wife hasn't touched me in three months, and before the occasion three months ago when she nearly fell asleep in the middle of intercourse, it was about four months before that."

Dr. Paulette Long stared at me with her dark, beady eyes.

"I think, Mr. Winwood, Samantha was speaking of emotional distance, emotional closeness. Not physical."

"No shit?" I said.

It came out wrong. Sarcastic, impatient, like a man in the room with two conspiratorial women and seven months of locked-up sexual tension.

Samantha said, "Are you having an affair, Early?"

I thought to myself, if imagining the lady across the street bent over the hood of her black BMW with her white panties around her ankles constitutes an affair, then I'm guilty. But it doesn't. It might be a sin, but it's not an affair.

"No," I said.

Dr. Long asked, "Why would you ask that, Samantha?"

It sounded like they were actors in a bad movie. They each knew exactly what to say.

"Well," Samantha spoke, "it may sound silly, but I read about certain clues when your husband is having an affair. There are just things I've noticed on the list."

"Like what?" the doctor asked.

"Well," Samantha spoke again, "he stays late at the office for one. He recently got a haircut and new shoes. He doesn't try to kiss me or touch me anymore. Those things are on the list."

I couldn't listen to much more. "You know what? This is stupid. Maybe eating is a clue also. Or scratching my ass. That could be a clue."

The doctor looked down her runway nose. I didn't wait for her to ask another question.

"I stay at work late so I can afford our oversized house in a rich neighborhood that my wife can't live without. I haven't tried to kiss or touch her because after you've been turned down fifty times in a row with stupid excuses like falling asleep at eight o'clock, or having PMS two weeks before her period, you'd stop trying, too. Who likes being rejected over and over?

"And the haircut. I get about four or five haircuts a year, every year, since I've been a grown man. I had no idea the timing of the haircut and new shoes had such significance. Maybe I should grow my hair down to my asscrack and wear these shoes until my toes stick out the holes."

Samantha was crying. The doctor hated my guts.

"Mr. Winwood, you have a great deal of anger. We need to find the source of that anger."

"Let me just ask you this," I said, "are we searching for the source of my anger for my benefit, or for the benefit of this marriage? Because honestly, Samantha, do you want to stay married to me?"

We were all struck with the possibility that she might say no, but after only the tiniest of hesitations, Samantha said, "Yes. I wouldn't be here if I didn't. Allen loves you.

We're a family. If you're going through some mid-life crisis, get a motorcycle, write a book, whatever."

For ten weeks we met once a week with Dr. Paulette Long and explained every facet of our relationship at two hundred dollars per hour. I learned a lot about people, myself, women, and other worldly pursuits. At the end of ten weeks Dr. Long announced our marriage would have a better chance of surviving if I moved out of the house and continued to pay all the bills. So that's what I did.

In the back of the newspaper there's a section for dead people. A section with photographs, sometimes old photographs above obituaries of people who have recently died. I've always stopped in those sections and looked at the people's faces, read about their lives.

On a winter morning, sitting at my desk, I saw the picture of Eddie Miller above his obituary. It was an old picture, maybe from high school, with his eyes full of light and hope. It didn't say how he died. I hadn't talked to Eddie since he was arrested. They only held him in jail a few weeks, probably like I said, to see if they could put the pressure on him or me, break open the case.

People told me how Eddie went downhill after that. He got a divorce. The wife took the kids. He drank a lot, spent time sitting in barrooms. And now he was dead. A picture on a page full of pictures of dead people.

The Catholics believe the only unforgivable sin is suicide. It seemed impossible to me that God would turn his back on the very children who needed Him most, until I figured it out. It's a good rule, but it's not for the people who actually kill themselves. The rule is for the people who just think about it. Religion is the ultimate slippery slope. We're told to believe in the comfort of a God who loves and provides, but we're told not to completely embrace the idea of Heaven, because if we did, everyone would be killing themselves to get there. Why not? It's wonderful. No worries. Surrounded by the warmth of God's love. It's Heaven.

So they made a rule. A bump on the slippery slope to stop us from going all the way to the bottom. Believe, but don't believe too much. Doubt, but don't doubt too much. Float around in the middle until you die of natural causes and get your picture in the paper.

The letter went like this:

Kate,

Saturday. January 20. Kansas City airport Sheraton hotel lobby at two o'clock in the afternoon.

Two days. Room service. Hot baths. Never leave the apartment.

Wear a red dress.

Early

I even put it in the envelope, a stamp in the corner, and drove through the post office parking lot. I sat in my car, the window down, in front of the big blue mailbox with the envelope in my hand. And then, believe it or not, I dropped the damn thing in the box. It was like my hand, and then my arm, just decided for themselves.

There was immediate regret. Immediate. I sat in my little ugly rental house and drank a half bottle of Jack Daniel's before I came up with the brilliant idea to go back to the post office at two o'clock in the morning to retrieve the letter. As are most decisions made at two o'clock in the morning after a half bottle of Jack Daniel's, it was a mistake.

There was no one around. The parking lot was empty under the glowing lights. My hand couldn't get down the hole. The same hand, and the same arm, that earlier decided to send the letter, now couldn't get it back. I decided to steal the entire mailbox. It was huge. Too big to fit in the car, and as an added problem, it was bolted into the cement.

That's when the police car arrived. I tried to explain. "There's a letter in here I need to get."

"Have you been drinking, sir?"

With a noticeable slur I said, "How is that relevant?"

At the police station, under arrest for public intoxication, I sat in the holding cell with my face in my hands, already feeling the beginning of a hangover. When I lifted my head, Investigator Frank Rush was sitting across from me on the metal bench. I hadn't heard him come in. At first I thought he was a hallucination, like a story by Edgar Allan Poe or something.

"Did you read about Eddie in the newspaper?" he asked.

I took a long, deep breath, trying to gather my wits before I spoke.

"Yeah."

We were quiet. He watched me breathe.

"How'd he die?" I asked.

Frank Rush seemed to think a moment.

"Some people just die, Early. They don't really die, it's more like they just stop living. Other people, like Allen Kilborn, don't get to decide. Someone decides for them, like you did."

"You're wrong," I said. "Allen Kilborn made his decisions, not me."

He felt the weakness.

"It's time Early. It's time to get this off your chest. It's time to tell me how it happened. We both know he was a son-of-a-bitch. I never said he didn't deserve it."

It was like the whiskey evaporated from my bloodstream in a split second. It was like my mind rose up from the fog at the exact right moment. I leaned back against the cold cinder-block wall and waited. From his face I could see that Frank Rush was watching the moment of weakness pass. His chance for a confession disappearing before his eyes. I remembered the letter in the box. I thought of Allen Jr. with his arm around me at my mother's funeral.

"Eddie was a good kid," I said. "We grew up together."

"I know," Frank Rush answered.

And that was it. I closed my eyes and let the exhaustion carry me under. I woke up alone.

six

A few days before January 20th, Little Allen called. His voice was the voice of a man. He had something he wanted to tell me, but not over the phone. At first I was worried, but his laugh gave away the goodness of whatever it was he wanted to talk about. We decided to meet at my little rental house the next day.

Allen was living and working two hundred miles away. We talked on the phone often, but he came home less and less. Not out of anger or anything negative, but simply his life pulling him in the direction it was meant to go. I missed him being around. He had taken the news of me and Samantha's separation better than I would have. He seemed to already know it was coming and prepared himself.

When we talked, we mostly talked about baseball, and

work, and things like that, gently veering away from the subject of his mother. I found the conversations comforting, stabilizing, and I wondered if he could see our roles changing ever so slightly, almost unnoticeable, like a child growing from one day to the next.

I watched around the curtains through the front window as he pulled into the driveway. There was a woman in the passenger seat, young and pretty. I watched them walk together toward my front door. They were a couple. Comfortable with each other. The comfort that only comes from being in love. She held his arm, and he smiled at the touch. Allen was bringing a girl home to meet me, and not just any girl. I remembered bringing Kate home to meet my mother. Now it was my turn to learn how my mother felt that day. Happy, concerned, maybe a little jealous.

I opened the front door and acted surprised to see the young woman. Her smile was absolute and genuine, like she hadn't figured out yet how fucked up the world really is. A smile you could look at and believe everything would be okay. I immediately envied Allen, and immediately wondered if my mother had felt the same about Kate, or whether it was obvious to everyone except me that Kate's smile hid things we were all afraid to see.

Standing at the door, Allen said, "Dad, this is Emily. Emily, this is my dad."

Since the beginning, we had mostly stayed away from words like "dad" or "son." I would overhear him call me his "stepdad" on the phone with his friends. After all, he had a real father, and our last names were different, and I didn't show up in the boy's life until he was half-grown.

But now, standing at the door, he introduced me as his father, and I shook Emily's small hand. It made me wonder if Gretchen, on the other side of the world, might be introducing her boyfriend to Russell Enslow and calling the man her father like I didn't exist. I suddenly remembered I was leaving on a plane early the next morning bound for Kansas City. Maybe I wouldn't show up. Maybe I'd just go to work like a regular day.

Allen wasn't the kind of man who would bring just any girl to meet the family. I could see they were way beyond the awkward stage. Sitting in the living room, every now and then she would glance at Allen, probably wanting the same comfort he provided to me in our telephone conversations. She would grow old and the beauty would fade like a painting, but there was something strong about her. She didn't need saving. Neither of them did.

"We're getting married," Allen said. She watched my face carefully, looking for the reinforcement of an instant smile, and that's what she got. I didn't need to fake it. There was a light around them, and I hoped it would never go away.

Before I could catch myself I said, "I hope you have children."

Emily and Allen looked at each other. I had the feeling she knew my story, or at least the parts Allen knew to tell her.

"We hope so, too," she said.

I could feel the tears fill up my eyes, and I continued, "Because children are the best thing this world has to offer."

It occurred to me I was getting old. She saw me as an old man, lonely, exiled to a stranger's house, looking across the couch at the embodiment of youth. And then it happened again. I came outside of myself. There we were, in the living room of my little rental house, me in the chair, Allen and Emily sitting on the sand-colored couch across the coffee table, except I was seeing me from Emily's eyes and feeling Allen's hand on mine. I was afraid and calm at the same time. Wanting it to stop and continue together.

One second became two and then three, and I wondered if Emily was inside of my body, or if it was just me, and then I wondered if it would never go back to normal, stuck. But then in a blink I was back in the chair and there was no hint of awareness in Emily's eyes. Certainly, if she'd suddenly floated into someone else's body, there would be some reaction, some recognition of the odyssey.

When they left I felt a little shaken. I sat down in the same chair and searched around inside my mind for a foothold. My second marriage was collapsed. The hollowness of my career was beginning to reveal itself. My daughter was distant, and now I was planning a weekend of debauchery with my first wife, who was married to another man, and I'd just gotten a close-up look at myself through the big, brown eyes of my stepson's fiancée. The stepson whose father I killed, and who now introduced me as his dad, and who was getting married, starting a family of his own, and drifting further away.

I went to bed. It was three o'clock in the afternoon. I was exhausted, but couldn't sleep. I got up and packed, and then went back to bed. I got up and ate, and then crawled in bed again. I went over in my mind everything we could possibly do in a hotel room over two days and nights. I got up and made a list: champagne, chocolates, a red rose. I tore up the list and took a shower, colder than usual.

It was after midnight before I finally fell asleep. The alarm went berserk at three-fifty in the morning. I was in a whirlpool of doubt on the drive to the airport. Turn around. Don't turn around. Are you stupid? What are you doing? It might be fantastic. Maybe we were always right for each other, we just needed to grow up. Maybe these years with Russell and Samantha made us appreciate each other. Maybe I have a chemical imbalance that allows me to drift into the bodies of other people from time to time, but doesn't allow me to stop doing stupid shit. Like killing people and meeting my ex-wife in Kansas City.

When the door slammed shut on the airplane, I felt the way I felt weeks earlier when my hand dropped the letter in the big blue mailbox. Panic and exhilaration. Much like I imagine it would be shooting up methamphetamines for the first time. Waiting for the feeling to start.

I checked in the hotel at 11 A.M.

"One bed or two?" the man said.

"One. King-size."

"Will you need a key to the minibar?"

"Yes."

I put my bags in the closet and inspected the room. The bed was big and soft, covered in pillows. Six big pillows, I counted. The tub was large enough for the two of us. Little bottles of shampoo and bubble bath, sky blue.

I opened the curtains to see the airport in the distance, planes landing. Maybe Kate's plane. Maybe it was touching down. I ran downstairs to the lobby. It was big. Lots of couches and chairs. I found a couch with a view of the front door and the check-in area. It was perfect.

There was a newspaper on the table. I began to read, holding the paper up to cover my face. What if someone from home spotted me, started up a conversation, just before Kate arrived? What if Samantha's cousins wandered into the lobby and saw me reading the paper, looking suspicious? I would probably stand up and scream, "I'm a fornicator. I'm a sinner."

It was eleven thirty-three. I could still go home. I could run upstairs, grab my bags, and be back at the airport. Fly home and make it to the office before it closed. I could sit in my favorite chair across from the couch at night and drink the rest of the bottle of Jack Daniel's. Lock myself in the house. Sift though the mail every day to get the letter from Kate. The letter that says she went to Kansas City to see me, and I wasn't there.

Out of all the people I didn't expect to see, my childhood friend, Jake Crane, was probably on the top of the list. But there he was, standing in the line to check in. He looked out of place. I lifted the paper to cover my face, peeking around the edge of the sports page. He was looking around like he'd been sent there to find me. Sent by Frank Rush. I closed my eyes and suppressed the pure paranoia. It was just a coincidence. A weird coincidence. Surely he would leave before Kate arrived.

It was eleven-fifty. Any minute the red dress would walk through the big glass doors. We would act like we didn't know each other, accidentally end up in the same elevator. Exit separately on the same floor, and then run giggling down the hall to the wonderful room waiting for us.

Out of all the people in the world who knew Kate, and all the people in the world who knew me, Jake Crane was unfortunately one of the few who knew us both. One of the few people on the entire planet who would know it was no accident we were in the same elevator together. His presence was a dirty omen. What were the chances? I began to feel the paranoia press down, but I held my position. Regulated my breathing. Finally, Jake finished checking in and walked past me to the elevators. I carefully maneuvered the paper to cover my face as he passed and turned to the left. It was five after twelve. Thank God she was a few minutes late, I thought. The omen was no longer nasty, but humorous instead. A good story to tell someone later, I'm not sure who.

I think it was twelve-fifteen when the possibility fully occurred to me Kate might not come. Maybe she made it as far as the airport. Maybe she actually got on the plane and ran out before the door slammed shut. It's possible she got as far as Kansas City and just got on another plane back home. Maybe she ran into Jake at the airport coffee shop, panicked, and went back to California.

Then it occurred to me there were two Kansas Cities. Kansas City, Missouri, and Kansas City, Kansas. Maybe there were two Kansas City airport Sheratons. Maybe she was waiting in another lobby for me, her legs crossed, the edge of the red dress at her knees.

I asked the lady, "Excuse me, are there two Kansas City airport Sheratons?"

"No, sir. This is it."

"What time is it?"

"Twelve thirty-four."

The lady patiently waited for me to speak again.

"Have you seen a woman with a red dress? A pretty woman with a red dress? Mid-forties, brown hair?"

She smiled like she knew everything about me and why I was there.

"No, sir. Sorry."

I sat back down on the couch in my spot with the perfect view, and then went back to see the lady again.

"Do you have any messages for Early Winwood, room 833?"

She tapped around on the computer keyboard. Shaking her head, she said politely, "No, sir. No messages."

The elevator ride to the eighth floor was long. No one was accidentally in the elevator with me. No one ran down the hall giggling. The bathtub and the bed were big and empty. I ordered room service and ate alone, falling asleep in the middle of a repetitive pornographic movie. It's a sure sign you're getting old when you can fall asleep to the grunts of a pornographic film, but that's what I did, and to tell the truth, I slept like a baby. It was one of the best night's sleep I'd had in my life. I woke up the next day at noon to a knock on the door.

Noon. A knock on my hotel door. The Kansas City

airport Sheraton. Had I gotten the wrong day? Had she gotten the wrong day? And I realized my first feeling was fear. Fear that Kate Shepherd would be at the door, and make me feel the way she always made me feel. Sky-high, on top of the world, and then waiting for the fall. And waiting. And waiting.

A voice came from the door. "House cleaning," the voice said, and on top of the fear, above all else, I was disappointed.

seven

The letters stopped, mine and hers. From time to time, late in the evening, I'd sit at my desk, in front of an empty piece of paper, and imagine, far out in California, Kate doing the same. But neither of us had the courage or weakness to send anything.

There was nothing left of my marriage to Samantha, and both of us seemed beyond blaming. I can't remember who called who, but we met over dinner to negotiate the end. I remember seeing her sitting alone at the restaurant when I arrived. She was staring out the window holding a glass of white wine. Her face was very still, resigned. I just watched her for a moment, wondering what I would eventually feel, and then feeling nothing.

She turned to look at me, and we stayed that way, both of us sure now, until I tried to smile. It was a childish smile.

The fake kind, but openly fake, purely to bring an end to the moment before. A transition to the next moment.

On the walk to the table, escorted by a waitress, I thought to myself, "It's not my job to make everyone happy. It can't be done. Where did I ever get an idea it was possible anyway?"

"What do you think of Allen's girl?" was the first thing I said.

It was our common ground. It was the only thing we liked about each other. I watched her chew a piece of bread slathered in butter and wondered what it was that I ever liked about Samantha Kilborn. She watched me take a sip of water, and I knew from her eyes she felt the same way about me. I was conscious of my lips on the edge of the glass. Too much, not enough. We had moved beyond love, beyond hate, to the land of annoyance. We didn't even care to purposefully annoy each other anymore, it just happened, and I swear I wouldn't have touched her naked body if we stood alone in the Garden of Eden, which is saying something.

"Do you want your tools out of the garage?" she asked.

"Yeah. I guess so."

"I like Allen's girlfriend. She's different than I expected."

"How?" I asked.

"It's hard to explain. Just different, that's all. Not like I expected."

It was at least her second glass of wine. She kept staring out the window at nothing in particular.

"You can have the house," I said. It was the same house she had when we met. Every year was a new renovation project. Guest room. Island in the kitchen. Always something new and expensive, but I didn't care. I never wanted to go back there. I never wanted to set eyes on the island again.

After the first sip of her third glass of wine, Samantha said, "Let's make this the last true conversation we ever have. After this, let's just be cordial when we run into each other at the grocery store, or end up in the same place with grandchildren, but let's not talk about anything important."

She was distant and serious.

"Okay," I said. "Can I get some copies of the pictures in our photo album?"

And then she looked at me and said, "Early, did you kill my husband?"

I wasn't ready for the question. If I'd been ready, the answer would've flowed. But I wasn't ready, and maybe she planned it that way. Other than Frank Rush, no one had ever asked me point blank.

She wasn't staring out the window anymore. She was staring directly across the table at me. Maybe it was over-due.

Then I grasped the wording of the question. "Did you kill my husband?" Allen Kilborn Sr. wasn't her husband when I shot him in the head at the top of the stairway. They were long since divorced.

"No," I finally said, the word coming out a little too quickly.

She held the stem of the wine glass between her index finger and thumb, twisting it slowly as the base rested on the white tablecloth. I looked down at the golden liquid, and then back up to Samantha's face.

"Did you cheat on me?" she asked.

It was amazing the woman would consider the questions equal in her mind. Executing a man in his own home and bending the neighbor lady over the hood of the BMW. It was amazing I was capable of a moral transgression at the level of murder and then concerned with finding a loophole in the wording of a question in order to tell a lie.

"No," I said, less quickly than before.

Her eyes drifted back out the window.

"Do you want your golf clubs?" she asked, her words flat.

My answer was yes. I really did want my golf clubs. I hadn't played in five years, but I wanted them anyway.

That night, when I was alone in bed at my rental house, I thought of something I'd completely forgotten. It came back to me like a brand-new memory, alive and sharp, as if it happened the morning before.

Gretchen was about six years old. I looked forward to our time together like a man in prison looks forward to seeing the sun. Not just pleasant, but life-giving, like water.

We went to the ice cream parlor. It was next to the movie theater and we had tickets to the matinee. Gretchen was shy, whispering in my ear the flavor of ice cream she wanted instead of telling the lady herself.

It was early spring, cool but not cold, and we sat outside on a glassy blue day at a table under a big white umbrella. Gretchen had birthday cake ice cream in a cup made of white chocolate with colorful sprinkles covering the top of the ice cream.

She took her first bite and a smile came across her little face. A real smile, the opposite of the one I gave Samantha from the other side of the restaurant. Gretchen's smile was so genuine, so pure, I remember I started to cry. I don't believe I've ever seen anything as important.

I sat there and started to cry. I had to look away from her. Put the napkin to my eyes. Pretend to cough. The girl was so perfect and so happy, and so far out of my life. That little smile over something so small as colored sprinkles left me unbearably alone, like the day my mother died.

She looked up from her ice cream.

"Daddy," she said, "how much does the sky weigh?"

"I don't know, baby," I said.

She took another bite of ice cream covered in tiny bits of color.

Gretchen said, "I think it weighs a million miles."

I wanted to hold it forever. The ice cream, the smile, the sky, the day. All of it. Just hold it close to me. The weight of a million miles.

I sat in the church at my daughter's wedding. Two hours earlier I met the man she'd marry for the first time, and I didn't like him much. He was plain and hard, a face like stone. He'd never know the Gretchen who sat with me outside the ice cream parlor, and I'd never know the woman he was about to marry. All I had was snapshots of her life. Little pieces that didn't fit together.

Russell Enslow gave her away. I guess she was his to give, but it left me sad anyway. Kate was aloof. I watched her at the reception. She never looked my way. Never smiled to acknowledge Kansas City, or the letters we once wrote to each other, or the night we'd conceived the child who just walked down the aisle and exchanged vows with the stone-faced man with big hands.

I wasn't sure what I expected. Maybe I hoped something miraculous would happen, or maybe I just hoped the sight of Kate would change everything. For the most part, that's what happened. Seeing her made her real again, if just for a few hours, and there's nothing quite like reality to douse the fire of fantasy. She was looking older. I didn't like her hair. It was too short. And she was skinnier than I remembered.

It was deflating. I wanted to feel that feeling again, if only for a few minutes. The way she always made me feel in her presence. Just to know such a thing still existed. But she wouldn't look at me, at least not while I was watching, and I stood alone by the big plate of shrimp, not knowing a single soul at the wedding reception for my only daughter. Not able to muster the energy to cause a scene, or maneuver Kate into a conversation, or do much of anything. I felt listless and average.

Less than a year later, I stood at the window of the nursery at the local hospital with Allen. His wife had just given birth to a fat, healthy boy, and the nurse held up the baby for us to see.

"Jesus, Allen, he's beautiful."

Allen touched his hand to the glass, fingers outstretched, finding himself in the middle of a miracle.

"He is, isn't he. Guess what we named him?"

"What?" I asked.

"Early James Kilborn."

I couldn't really say anything back to him. The boy named his son after me. It was even better than a white chocolate bowl of ice cream covered with sprinkles, and I smiled like Gretchen smiled, like all was good with the world, and might be forever, but I knew better.

eight

I slid gently into the disillusionment of my career. My job simply was not capable of providing any permanent identity. It helped temporarily, sometimes for stretches of years, but ultimately it was only a job, even when I loved it. Just a means to survive, refined and diluted by civilization. The cavemen may have loved the hunt and loved the meat from the hunt, but the purpose was much higher. The purpose was to feed the children, keep the mate, survive another day. Those purposes really no longer existed for me. Going to work every morning was just part of the routine. A diversion from imagining strange ways to kill myself or obsessing over my lack of sexual opportunities.

Nearly a year and a half since I'd seen Kate at the wedding, she called one night out of the blue. I knew immediately from her voice it wouldn't be good. There was no lazy, sexy cadence of too much wine on a lonely night, no nervous introduction before strolling down memory lane. It was business. Something was the matter.

"It's Gretchen," she said. "He beat her up. It's the second time, and this time it's bad, Early. Real bad."

It was the first time I'd heard her speak my name in many, many years, but the feeling was overshadowed.

"What are you talking about?" I said.

"Mike, her husband, the asshole, hit her in the face. Her eye is black. He's a drunk. He stays drunk."

"Jesus Christ, Kate. Why haven't you called me before?"

"For what? What could you do halfway across the country? We put him in jail, and he got out. We got a restraining order, but she went back to the asshole. She's here now with me, but he knows where to find her. A piece of paper won't stop him."

"What can I do?" I asked. "Do you want me to come out there?"

"No," she said quickly. "I want Gretchen to come stay with you. At least for a little while. She'll be safe there. Talk to her. Tell her to leave him. Tell her it'll never end. He won't change. Nobody changes, Early. We all know that."

I thought of Kate's father, the man in the chair with the rotten foot propped up. Sitting in the dark. A bottle of vodka in his hand. I remembered the smell. Old cigarette smoke, the odor of dog. Gretchen had probably never met the old man, but somehow, deep inside her, she carried the pain of her mother, and probably the pain of her mother's mother. It would never end.

"I think that's a good idea," I said, and as the words

came out of my mouth I felt an old familiar feeling. My mind began to form the beginnings of a plan. Just a seed. A seed of redemption, freedom, and just a little bit of revenge.

Maybe that's what Kate wanted. Maybe she knew, she always knew I was capable of such a thing, and now, after so many years of not needing me for anything, raising Gretchen with Russell Enslow, now she needed me for something. And maybe it was my purpose on this earth to kill people like Mike Stockton, and Allen Kilborn Sr., in order to set other people free.

I lay in bed almost the entire night thinking. It was more complicated than the time before. Mike Stockton lived far away in California. Unfamiliar territory, both geographically and otherwise. No built-in murder weapon or alibi witness. No hazy motive. If I was anywhere in the vicinity I'd be the first suspect.

When I fell asleep, the dream of the black circle came back. It was there on the floor between my bed and the door. Bigger than before. Even blacker somehow, with a gray ring around the edge.

In the dream I heard a noise and sat up in bed. The only light in the room came from the streetlight out the window. I could barely see the doorknob turn slowly, and the door began to open. In the crack I saw something. At first it was just a form, near the knob between the crack. Then I could see Gretchen's face. She was a little girl again, around five or six.

The door opened wide and we could see each other. She was wearing the same little shirt and pants she wore the day at the ice cream parlor. And then she smiled. The same smile I remembered.

"Daddy?" she whispered.

I couldn't speak. I opened my mouth, but I couldn't speak. I saw her lean forward. I saw her take the first step running toward me, but I couldn't yell. I couldn't tell her about the black circle on the floor between us. And then it was too late.

I woke up angry. What kind of man hits a woman? What kind of man chooses alcohol over his family again and again? Such a man deserves no respect. In my mind I could see the back of his hand come down against my little girl's face. I could hear her crying, balled up on the floor, wondering what existed inside of her to create such a situation, to deserve such a choice.

The dream led me to the next step, a blank piece of paper, a pen, a plan written out, a first draft. Written on the hard desk instead of a pad of paper, to be sure the sentences didn't bleed through to the pages below. Written left-handed, and mostly in words that reminded me of other words, so the plan only really existed inside my head.

Gretchen arrived at the airport. She was skinny, like her mother. Her bones seemed to be held together by only her clothes. Underneath the makeup I could see the blueness around her right eye down to the edge of her nose.

I took a deep breath and smiled. We were mostly strangers, but maybe we wouldn't be anymore. Maybe there was an opportunity to find out about each other, without judges, or Kate, or even Samantha, in the way.

I cooked supper. When she was a kid her favorite was

spaghetti and meat sauce. No meatballs. They were gross. And the meat sauce couldn't have onions, or peppers, or anything weird.

At the dinner table she asked, "Who's the child in the picture on the bookshelf?"

"It's Allen's little boy."

"He's cute," she said quietly.

"I made you spaghetti and meat sauce. No meatballs. No onions. Just the way you like it."

She started to say something and changed her mind. Maybe she started to say "I'm not a little girl anymore. I have other favorite foods now. Adult foods. And I've smoked cocaine, and given blow jobs, and lied intentionally to hurt people, and married a man who treats me like a possession. All because you were a shitty father."

But she didn't say anything like that, and I was glad. We talked about good things we remembered about each other. We talked about the weather, and her mother, and then ran out of things to say in a short period of time. I locked the doors, checked the windows, and pulled the curtains closed.

I took a vacation from work. Gretchen slept the first night in the guest room. The next morning, when she was in the shower, I went to make her bed. Under the pillow I found a gun. It was small and loaded. I put it back under the pillow and left the bed unmade.

Gretchen and I spent the next three days together. We found things to talk and laugh about. We ate lunch in restaurants and visited Allen and his family. There wasn't much left of the child I'd once known, my little girl, but I liked the person she'd become. She was smart and fragile like her mother, but without as much outward defense. There were shimmers of vulnerability and silence, but I chose just to watch and learn for awhile.

After our third day together, I decided to start a conversation about her predicament. "Why don't you move here? You can stay with me until you get on your feet."

She seemed displeased I would talk about anything unpleasant.

"I can't," she said.

"Yes, you can. It doesn't have to be forever. The guest room is yours. You can stay as long as you want. I'll help you find a job. Maybe you could even work at my office."

Gretchen looked down at her hands. She was still wearing a wedding ring. She wanted all the badness to just go away magically. She wanted everything to fix itself without confrontation.

She said, "There's a picture of a man next to the picture of Allen's little boy. Who is that?"

She didn't even know what my father looked like. She didn't know anything about him, or what he meant to me.

"Stay here," I said, and I went to my bedroom closet for the box my mother had left me.

Sitting down across from Gretchen at the table, I said, "It's my father. He died when I was eleven. I still miss him every day. I still think about things we did together, places we went. I remember words he used."

I handed her the photographs of me with my parents at the beach. I had no actual memory of the day, but the pictures were like their own memory. Gretchen looked through the pictures slowly, smiling back at the smiles. She loved my mother. They were important to each other. But just like my mother, Gretchen seemed to hold some resentment over my interruptions in their relationship, warranted or not.

"Is this your dog?" she asked.

It was the picture of the unidentified dog.

"No, I don't think so."

"Whose dog was it?"

"I don't know."

Gretchen looked at me for an explanation.

"I'm not gonna throw it away," I said. "It's in the box. It needs to stay in the box."

I handed her a picture of my father holding me in his arms. I wasn't more than a few months old. She looked at the photograph a long time before she said, "I like his face. He's got a good face."

That night, Gretchen went to bed early. I stayed up late at my desk thinking about Mike Stockton. Almost anybody is easy to kill if you don't mind getting caught. It's the loose ends. Gretchen couldn't know. Kate couldn't know. I had to pinpoint a location. A time. A way to be two places at once. What else could I do? Sit back and watch my girl crawl home to the man who'd eventually beat her down like a dog? The man who'd find a way to keep her from leaving him again, through babies, guilt, sympathy, promises. Lots and lots of broken promises.

"I'll never do it again."

"I swear there won't be any more drinking."

"I love you."

"Just this one last time."

"I'll be home at five o'clock."

A sea of broken promises and days strung together by lies. What kind of a father can wait around and watch it happen?

I closed my eyes and thought about what had to be done. In the silence, the very clear silence, came a pounding on my front door. BAM, BAM, BAM. Hard, strong, crazy, and purposeful.

I looked at the clock. It was two-thirty in the morning. There was only one person it could be. Mike Stockton. He found her. He came a very long way and found the right house.

I ran to the guest room. In the dark I whispered, "Gretchen, Gretchen."

No answer.

My eyes adjusted. The bed was empty. The pounding on the door came again.

"Bam, Bam, Bam." Three times. Even harder than before.

I heard a noise in the room with me. A low sound. On the other side of the bed, crouched in the corner between the bed and the wall, Gretchen held the gun.

"It's him," she said. Her voice cracked in fear. It was hard to see her face in the darkness, but she was crying, the gun held tight in both hands near her cheek.

A figure passed the window outside, a shadow from the streetlight across the white curtain of the bedroom.

I ran through the house, turning off the lights in the office and then the living room. I grabbed the phone and brought it back to the guest room.

Gretchen was where I left her. I got down beside her, our faces only inches apart.

"Listen to me," I said. "Do exactly what I tell you to do. Exactly. Do you understand?"

She didn't answer.

Without raising the volume of my voice, I hardened the tone to get her attention.

"Do you understand?" I repeated.

She looked at my mouth, the place where words had come from, and then moved her eyes to my eyes.

"Yes," she whispered. "I understand."

"Give me the gun."

I took the gun from her hand and replaced it with the telephone.

"Is it loaded?" I asked.

"Yes, it's loaded."

Slowly I said, "Now listen, call 9-1-1. Tell them what's happening. Mike's trying to get in the house. Tell them what he did to you before, and how you had him arrested, and how you got a restraining order. Tell them you came here to get away from him and now he's tracked you down, trying to break in the house."

She waited a second and said, "Okay."

"It's very important, Gretchen, you tell them everything so they'll understand the seriousness of the situation. So they'll send someone immediately."

I stood up with the gun in my right hand. It was smaller than Allen Kilborn's gun. It felt like a toy in my palm.

"Stay here," I said. "Don't leave this room until I tell you to come out, or the police tell you to come out."

She seemed very much like a child huddled against the wall, small and afraid, waiting for me to fix it all.

I walked cautiously down the hallway to the living room, listening for any sound, trying to determine if he'd found a way in the house yet. There was nothing.

The living room was dark. Very gently I turned the knob on the padlock to unlock the front door. Very gently I turned the little button on the doorknob to unlock everything.

I stepped back from the door about ten feet, careful to negotiate the coffee table, and stood in the small space between the coffee table and the couch, the same couch where Allen and his girlfriend sat when they gave me the news of their wedding, when Allen called me "Dad." It seemed like a long time ago.

I could hear Gretchen's voice on the phone in the bedroom. It was low and muffled, but every few words came clear. She was doing as she was told, and I imagined the dispatcher relaying the information to a police officer on night shift, bored, patrolling the quiet neighborhoods, and now with an emergency call. A home invasion. Blocks away. It was just a matter of minutes, and I waited, the way I've always waited, listening to the clock in the kitchen tick and tick. Listening to my little girl's voice on the phone down the hall. Taking deep breaths to keep my hands from shaking.

It happened amazingly fast. No warning. No small noise followed by bigger noises. The door just swung open and slammed hard against the wall.

Mike Stockton stepped into the doorway. He seemed huge, the light behind his back illuminating his frame. Large arms hanging at his sides. Far off in the distance there was a siren. The bored officer, adrenaline now pumping through his veins, on the way. Only seconds now. Only seconds away.

I raised the gun and fired. The sound was loud, but not like before. Not like the explosion at the top of the stairs that blew Allen Kilborn's head into small pieces.

Mike Stockton didn't move. I fired again immediately, and then a third time after that. Three shots, ten feet away, into the man's chest.

I heard Gretchen scream. I saw the body fall to the floor. The flashing colored lights of the police car appeared. Through the open front door I could see the officer exit his vehicle, gun in hand, assessing the situation, wide-eyed.

I reached over to the wall and flicked on the living room light. Gretchen was standing by the kitchen, the phone still in her hand. I set the gun down on the coffee table.

It was done, I thought. It was all done. There was no choice. What choice could there be? All those years of failing my daughter were brought to an end in a few seconds.

It would be a new beginning. A clean slate, as they say.

But then I watched Gretchen run to the man on the floor. I watched her wrap her arms around him in a way I've never seen, like she could pull him back from death, hold on so tight he wouldn't slip away to wherever he was going.

She turned and looked at me with a hatred I couldn't understand. A black disdain, total and complete, for me and what I had done to the man in her arms bleeding out on my carpet.

"What did you do?" she yelled. "What did you do?"

She waited for an answer. Just looked at me and waited for an answer.

"I shot him," I finally said.

The walls of the room seemed to close from all sides. It was just Gretchen looking at me for an explanation, her arms around the dead man on the floor.

I remember closing my eyes and concentrating on breathing, slowly in, and then slowly back out again. Trying with every piece of my brain to reconstruct the memory of Gretchen outside the ice cream parlor, remove myself back to that certain day, outside of my living room, away from the demand to explain to my broken daughter why a father might kill the man who beat her senseless and tracked her down thousands of miles away, until it dawned on me.

I opened my eyes and asked her, "You told him where I lived, didn't you?"

PART IV
the golden years

I found myself alone in a room at the police station. Mike Stockton was dead, three small caliber bullets to the chest and a pond of thick red blood at my threshold. It was done, and I couldn't say I was sorry, no matter what happened to me.

Frank Rush came through the door into the cold room. I think I almost saw a smile on his face. He sat down across from me at the table, two files in his hands, one thick and one thin. He placed the files next to each other between us, carefully lining up the edges. I could see the labels. The fat one was the file on Allen Kilborn Sr., and the thin one had "Mike Stockton" written across the top.

I waited for him to speak.

"Well, James Early Winwood," he said, "here we go again."

As before, I tried to concentrate on my breathing, in and out, slowly and as deeply as possible without sound or movement. It made me wonder how we are able to breathe at all. What force exists inside us to suck air inward and then push it out again? To regulate the speed and pressure?

"Usually, Mr. Winwood, I'd let the suspect talk first, tell me what happened, but this time, I think I'll go first."

I chose not to say anything and waited.

"This is how it looks to me," he said, "people around you end up shot. Not just random people, but now we have a pattern. Do you see the pattern?"

I think he just wanted to hear me speak. He wanted to hear my voice in the cold room.

"No," I said.

"Well, I do. Bullies. Specifically men who bully women."

He waited for me to say something, but I let the air go a little deeper in my lungs than before. Let it fill a pocket usually left unfilled, vacant.

"Allen Kilborn bullied your wife—your ex-wife, Samantha. And Mike Stockton bullied your daughter, Gretchen. You found a way to bring it to an end each time. A permanent end."

He continued, "Now granted, you picked two very different methods, but still there's common ground. Each was a shooting. Both times you used someone else's gun. And each time you succeeded."

I said, "The man came all the way from California to hunt her down. He beat on the door, came in my house. Gretchen is still black and blue from the last time he beat her up. You would have done the same, Mr. Rush. You would have done what needed to be done in order to protect your child and yourself."

We were quiet for a time. I was exhausted, almost a chemical exhaustion. The results of a pill I didn't take.

"Maybe," he said. "Maybe, but there's a few unanswered questions I have."

He leaned back slightly in his chair, an older man now. A little heavier, less hair, more lines around his eyes.

"Why was the door unlocked?" he asked.

"I guess I forgot to lock it. I was still awake, sitting in my office, when he started banging on the door."

"It's just hard for me to believe, Early, that a man like you, a cautious man, a smart man, knowing what Mr. Stockton did to your daughter, would leave the front door unlocked at two-thirty in the morning. I checked. All the other doors were locked tight. The windows were all locked. But somehow you forgot the front door."

"I guess so," I said. "I guess I forgot to lock the front door."

Frank Rush raised his arms and put his hands behind his head.

"I'm curious how he found the house. You're not in the phone book."

"I don't know," I said.

"Gretchen says she didn't talk to him. She says the only people who knew where she was were you, her mother, and her stepfather. If we take a look at your home phone records, will it show any calls to Mike Stockton's phone?"

"Not from me," I said.

"You didn't call the man and tell him where she was, did you, Early? You didn't lure him down, leave the door unlocked on purpose, make sure the gun was loaded, tell Gretchen what to say when she called 9-1-1, did you?"

I listened to his words. We knew each other better this time around.

"No, Mr. Rush, I didn't."

"Because Gretchen says you were very calm. She says you brought her the phone and told her exactly what to say. You calmly turned off the inside lights, told her to stay in the bedroom, and went to the living room alone to wait. All while a crazy man was beating on your door and circling your house."

I wondered how he knew Mike Stockton circled the house, leaving the front door for awhile. I didn't have to ask the question.

"Gretchen wasn't the only person to call 9-1-1. One of the neighbors heard the banging, watched out their window, saw Mike try the doorknob, walk around the back of the house, and then come back to the front door. Only this time, the door was unlocked. He was able to step inside. Into the dark room. Where you waited for him."

I asked in a monotone voice, "Am I under arrest?"

Frank Rush stared at me, and I stared back. I think he wanted to rip my head off and look inside, like the answer would be floating around in there, easy to see.

"No, you're not under arrest. Right now, you're free to leave any time you want."

"Is Gretchen here?" I asked.

"No."

"Where is she?"

He said, "She gave a written statement and asked if she could go back home. I told her yes. She packed up her things and left in a taxi."

I suppose it was unrealistic to believe Gretchen would stay with me in the house where I killed her husband, but I hadn't imagined her leaving, either. The sun was probably rising outside. A new day beginning.

"It must be difficult," he said.

He wanted me to respond, but I didn't. I also didn't get up to leave.

"It must be difficult," he repeated, "doing something to help someone else and having them not appreciate you. I mean, you kill the man who abuses your daughter, and she hates your guts for it. You kill the man who makes Samantha's life hell, and she divorces you anyway. Kicks you out of the house where you paid the bills."

Sometimes you can't see how much open space there is down below until you get up in an airplane. I started to rise above myself and look down on my situation. The balance is delicate between who we are and who others believe us to be. It is the greatest struggle a man faces between birth and death, the endless process of separating the threads of your individual identity from the expectations, needs, demands, and imaginations of all other humans. Who would I be if I was the only person in the world? Who would I have killed, and who would I have protected? Would the open spaces be so much easier to see?

304 FRANK TURNER HOLLON

There was the possibility I'd been used, by Gretchen, or more likely Kate and Russell Enslow, purposefully or subconsciously, but used nonetheless, to accomplish a purpose. After all, it was my fault. Everything was my fault. Gretchen's father issues. Kate's lifeless marriage. Samantha's intolerance. They were my problems to fix, and so I fixed one, at least temporarily, but then again, everything is temporary, isn't it? Sticking band-aids on the cracks in leaking dams, each leak proof of the impossibility of permanence in this life, a reminder that everything we care about goes away, as well as everything we don't care about.

I started to get up from the chair to leave the ice-cold room, but my legs were hollow, the physical weakness beyond anything I'd ever experienced. It was like I was Mike Stockton, all the liquid from my body drained dry. I kept my hand on the table to steady myself.

Frank Rush pulled a piece of paper from the file. It was my written plan, left on the desk in my house, found by Frank Rush, and a now a part of the permanent file. As permanent as a file can be.

With his stubby hand the investigator pushed the piece of paper across the table in front of where I stood. He turned it around so I could see my words right-side up. They were written left-handed. Words used in place of other words. A code.

"I found this," he said, "in your house, at the desk, the ink pen still on top."

I worked very hard at not letting my knees buckle. I leaned over, pretending to look at the piece of paper, transferring part of my weight onto my hands, braced against the tabletop. The weakness had nothing to do with what he showed me or the conversation. It was an independent weakness.

Frank Rush looked up into my face. "Does M.S. stand for Mike Stockton?"

The code was no code at all. I had written the words expecting them to burn long before any other eyes would search the page. But they were the words of a different plan, a plan never to be executed, in a faraway place.

He began to read, "M.S., CAL., Kate, miles, time, ice cream, R.E., Kate again, weapon?"

I needed something to drink. Maybe orange juice would replenish the blood.

"What do the numbers mean, Early?"

I looked from the paper to his face and said slowly, "They don't mean anything, Mr. Rush. Nothing does. Just scribbles. Can I go now?"

Allen was waiting in the lobby. He stood when I came to the door, and I wanted to collapse in his arms like a child. Like I was sick, and he was my father, strong and sure, and I could fold into his arms and sleep it all away.

He led me to the car, and we started the drive back to my house. I wondered if it would be surrounded by yellow police tape. I wondered how I would step across the stain of blood into my home, if I had a home at all.

"Who called you?" I asked.

"The lady across the street. She said you shot somebody. By the time I got there, they'd already taken you to the station. The investigator told me it looked like self-defense. He just wanted to ask you a few questions."

There was still no strength in my legs. The weakness was an actual feeling, its own separate, dull ache centered in the knees.

Allen said, "What happened?"

Looking out the window at a girl riding a red bicycle, I said, "I killed a man. Gretchen's husband. He beat her up. She came to stay with me. He found her, and I killed him."

The girl on the bicycle was pedaling like mad. She was late for school. Maybe fourth grade, or fifth. Her hair was very black, tied in a loose ponytail up top near the crown of the head. She wore dirty tennis shoes. The girl saw me look at her and looked away in the direction she was going, down the sidewalk.

"I didn't even know you had a gun," Allen said.

I looked at him and said, "I don't. It was Gretchen's."

We rode along. I didn't pay any attention to our direction.

"Where is Gretchen?" he asked.

"She's gone. She went back to California."

We rode along in silence. It was a beautiful morning. I noticed things I never noticed before. It seemed like I'd been gone a long time, and while I was gone they planted new trees and built new houses in empty lots.

We pulled up in front of Samantha's house. The house I'd lived in for years, helped raise Allen in, paid to update, then renovate, in order to keep up with people I'd never met.

"What are we doing here?" I asked.

"Mom's out of town. You don't need to go back to the

rental house right now. I'll go there this afternoon, clean up, get some clothes. You can stay here a few days."

"Where's your mother?" I asked.

There was hesitation. He didn't want to say. She was probably with another man. On a trip with another man to some Caribbean island covered with palm trees and surrounded by water the color of emeralds. In fact, as we sat out in front of the house, she was probably down on her knees in the bathroom of a beach bungalow giving the man great pleasure. I smiled. After all, she was no longer my wife. I was a man without a wife.

"Nevermind," I said.

It was strange being in the house again, especially without Samantha's permission. After Allen left, I crept around like a burglar. On the screened-in back porch, behind the potted plant above the door, I found my stale cigarettes. The matches were damp. I had to light the cigarette off the stove and run outside to make sure the smoke didn't seep into the flowered wallpaper and raise Samantha's suspicions.

I sat on the wooden chair. The same mystical force allowing me to breathe oxygen pulled the cigarette smoke deep into my chest, releasing the whiteness ever so slowly until I could feel the nicotine reach the center of my mass. It had been a while since I'd smoked, and during the first three drags I remembered how much I loved it. Toward the end of the cigarette I realized how it always left me unfulfilled. The expectations too high and the results too average.

But I lit another one right after the first anyway and

sat alone thinking for hours about what I had done. Trying to figure out what part of me was responsible, and what part of me wasn't.

two

Most of my suicide scenarios included a common theme. Apparently, subconsciously, I was concerned about offending the person who might find my body washed up on the beach, or bloated and smelly three days in the bed, or even lying peacefully in the backseat of my car in the garage. I'm not sure exactly what this means.

I kept thinking about digging a hole. Finding a secluded place down on the beach about ten yards up from the water's edge. Around noon I'd go out with a shovel, ice chest, and a few books. I'd begin digging a deep, deep hole, piling up the sand on the side of the hole facing the water. Between digging, I'd have a cold drink, lay out on the towel reading my favorite books, watch the seagulls and pelicans frolic along the shoreline.

If anyone passed, walking along the beach, I'd keep my face in the book and pretend I didn't speak English. I would intentionally select the day of the month with the highest tide, a full moon, I suppose.

After the sun went down the water would begin to rise, creeping up the sand a little further with every breaking wave. When the waves began to touch the pile of sand in front of the six foot hole, I would remove the gun from the plastic bag inside the ice chest. The metal would be cold on my hands, and I'd be careful not to set the gun down in the sand.

I'd throw the shovel, ice chest, and my favorite books down into the hole. Then I would position myself at the far end of the hole, standing upright, leaning slightly forward. The gun would be in my right hand. I would look one way and then the other down the beach, to make sure there were no flashlights. No families walking the beach, or young lovers, or people unprepared for the horrors of finding a dead body late at night.

At that point, I'd be ready. Standing stiff, I would lean forward until my body, a victim of gravity, would begin to fall. In midair, the gun pointed at the side of my head, I'd pull the trigger, ending my life and allowing my body to end up in the very bottom of the hole next to the shovel, ice chest, my favorite books, and the gun.

The moon would exert its strange force upon the water, pulling it upwards, opposite from the gravitational force plunging my body into the deep hole, and eventually the waves would push the pile of sand down into the hole on top of me, burying my dead body far below the surface of the pristine beach. I would be allowed to rot in peace, going back to the earth the way God intended.

Maybe I'm not really concerned about those people who could find my lifeless body. Maybe it's a control issue. I don't like the idea of my body being flipped around, drained of fluid, dressed up and locked down in a dark, sealed casket.

I spent so much time thinking about dying, I never considered the possibility of slowly falling apart. The doctor said the tingling sensation down my right arm was caused by the impingement of a nerve in my neck. The impingement was caused by the herniation of a disk, probably the result of the constant pounding of jogging, or maybe my insides were rotting for no reason.

"You're getting older," he said. "You can put up with the pain, or we can replace the disk."

I tried to put up with the pain, but it just got worse. One morning I woke up with my head cocked to the side. Something had shifted inside my neck during the night and fire shot down my arm if I tried to straighten my head. It made me wonder how people in chronic pain coped before modern medicine. Did they pray every day for their chance to die? Did they spend hours thinking about killing themselves and ending the pain?

Waiting for surgery, nearly naked with my head still cocked to the side, I felt the same loss of control a dead body might feel. The same lost feeling I had the day they told me my father died. The medicine began to drip and the warmth slowly rose through my pitiful limbs. For some reason, I started to tell a story that wasn't true.

"I hated my wife's Yorkie. It was a pain in the ass. Bark, bark, bark. We lived out in the country on fifty acres, mostly woods. One night I was eating dinner and the damned dog just wouldn't shut up. So you know what I did?"

The overweight nurse said, "What?"

The warmth had invaded my head. I don't remember anything else. I woke up in a hospital room with Allen and Emily standing by the bed. The overweight nurse was busy in the room. I was convinced death was upon me. From the outside, I was sure I looked the way my mother looked the day she died.

"That was a horrible story you told," the nurse said.

I didn't know what she was talking about. Maybe I'd recounted the excruciating details of the murder of Allen Kilborn, or my trip to Kansas City, or the time I thought I had herpes and it turned out to be a spider bite.

"I love dogs," she mumbled, her face tight like a ball of rubber bands.

"What story did you tell?" Allen asked me.

My mouth was dry. "I don't know," I managed to say.

The nurse couldn't leave it alone. "He told a story about his wife's Yorkie, and how he hated it, and how one night at the dinner table, after his wife left the room, he rubbed gravy on the dog and put the poor thing outside in the woods so the coyotes would eat him alive."

Allen laughed. "I never heard that before."

I noticed Early, my grandson, my namesake, sitting off to the side. He was around five years old at the time, and he was listening to the story. His eyes were red.

I gathered the energy to say, "It isn't true. My wife never had a Yorkie. I've never even seen a coyote in my life."

The doctor entered the room.

"Everything went well, Mr. Winwood. We ended up removing two disks. Just like we talked about, I scraped out the leftover material and replaced the disks with cadaver bone. We didn't have any problems with the titanium brackets. I think the screws are secure."

After the doctor left, and the dog-lovin' nurse closed the door, Early came over to give me a hug. He smelled all fresh and wonderful, and held me tight.

"Grandpa," he said, "what's a cadaver bone?"

Allen answered for me. "It's the bone of a dead person. Sometimes the doctors use cadaver bones to help fix people who are hurt."

Early seemed to think about it for awhile. There was much to consider.

"What dead person?" he asked.

It was an interesting question. I hadn't thought about it much.

Allen said, "Well, we don't know."

That night, with the morphine rolling steadily through my veins, I dreamed I was a black man named John Evans. The people in my dream knew who I was. They hugged me, and called me by name, but I didn't recognize their faces.

One woman in particular, an older woman, black as coal with a big smile, kept saying, "John, where'd you leave the key? I told you ten times not to take the key. Now where is it?"

I looked down at my hands. They were the hands of a working man, like my grandfather's, the hands of a carpenter. But I didn't recognize them as my own. I'd never seen them before.

I woke up several times in the hospital room, and each time slid gently back into the same dream, with the same people who recognized me, but I didn't recognize them.

I remember saying, "Why do you call me John?"

And the woman in the dream raised her voice, "Don't be a fool. Now give me the key, John Evans."

She was mad, but not really. The way old women sometimes act mad at their husbands, but it's all just part of the relationship. The anger is for show.

The dreams continued for months. I started to wonder if maybe the dead man's dreams were somehow trapped in his bones. I liked the idea of having a carpenter's bones in my neck. It made me think about my grandfather, the same grandfather who saved me at the lake that day.

Paw-Paw had a basement. In the basement he had a workshop full of tools, and saws, and pieces of wood. I can still smell it. The fresh-cut cedar. He built things like birdhouses and little cabinets, and everything in the basement was in a particular place. The place it belonged. I never saw the hammer anywhere except in my grandfather's hand or on the wall hanging on the hammer hook.

I loved the order. I loved the feeling of being in the basement, just me and my grandfather, making something no one else was making. No one else in the whole world.

He would say, "Early, mark this spot right here with the pencil. This is exactly fourteen inches."

And I would mark the spot, watching his hands drift across the surface of the wood, imagining my grandfather could build just about anything in the world.

Lying in the hospital bed, in my mind I began to draw a diagram of my grandparents' house. Beginning at the front door, down the hallway, each of the bedrooms, and back to the kitchen. I was able to close my eyes and see the house exactly as it was so many years ago. A house now lived in by strangers, my grandparents long since buried in the ground. It occurred to me, with my death there would be no one with any true memories that my grandparents had ever lived at all, ever existed, and my mortality, lying alone in the hospital room, became unbelievably certain. I would die also, and be remembered, and then forgotten, like every person who ever lived.

It was a turning point of sorts. Difficult to explain. Certain things became enormously important while others lost all value. I turned my attention to my grandson. Maybe it was for his sake, and maybe it was for mine. What difference does it make?

Behind my rental house was an old building. At one time it may have been a garage. It was a perfect size for a woodworking shop, and I dedicated myself to the idea of creating a place like my grandfather's basement. A place of simplicity, and order, with no telephones or televisions. A place filled with the smell of cut cedar.

I took my grandson with me to the hardware store to buy all the tools, and saws, and pieces of wood. We picked out hammers and nails, screwdrivers and wire, a tape measure and a set of wrenches. We loaded up a cart, and then another cart, asking questions and settling on a plan to build a doghouse for a dog we didn't have. It was Early's idea, maybe as a way to equalize the imaginary murder of a certain Yorkie.

The man at the cash register said, "You two sure did find a lot of stuff."

Early stood behind my legs, peeking around the edge of my pants at the man. He found the courage to move forward enough to see the items being scanned, one by one.

"That your grandson?" the man asked.

"It is," I said.

"I can see the resemblance."

I smiled and paid the man.

We spent the whole weekend building the workshop. On the wall above the wooden table I hung a piece of plywood just like the piece of plywood above my grandfather's wooden table. I made hooks for all the tools and tried to place them in the same order I remembered, the hammer on the far left, the hacksaw on the far right, a row of paintbrushes. Over the table hung a light, a single bulb with a switch at the base of the bulb. On the left edge of the table we secured a metal clamp designed to hold things tight so the piece of wood wouldn't slip as the saw pulled back and forth.

"Mark this with your pencil," I told Early, and he did, exactly where I told him to make a mark, and we cut the wood at the line, the first board for the doghouse.

There was one moment, one I remember, when Early

looked at me the way I looked at my grandfather so many years earlier in the basement. His eyes seemed to understand and focus, etching the grooves of a memory to last his entire life. I reached out and touched my hand to his face, holding my fingers to his cheek, and he let me do it, without pulling away, like he knew how important it was for me. Like he was me, and I was him, and we were together in my grandfather's basement, making something new.

On Sunday, after Early went home, I laid on my couch. I wished I was Mike Stockton. I wished I could go outside and then come through the door and have someone waiting for me in the dark. I didn't want to, but I started thinking about buying a small fishing boat. Taking the fishing boat up to the lake on a Monday morning. Bringing along fishing equipment, a cooler full of cold drinks, my favorite books, a cement block, a rope, and a pistol.

I'd fish in the cool morning, watching the fog burn away in the rising sun. Catch a fish, maybe two or three. Nothing big. Little fish, bream, hold 'em in my hands, let 'em swim away back to wherever they lived. I'd have a drink, take off my shirt in the midday heat, maybe read a little if I wanted. And after the sun set beneath the tall pines to the west, I'd start making preparations.

I'd sit on the side of the boat, careful to balance myself, the cooler and the tackle box placed on the far side of the boat to offset the weight. I'd tie one end of the rope to the cement cinder block and the other end around my waist, pulling the knots tight and tying double-knots.

Then I'd lift the cinder block to my lap and let it rest across my upper thighs. It would be dark. I wouldn't have a single light on the boat. My eyes would search the horizon to make sure no other boats were near. Then I'd cock the pistol, stick the barrel in my mouth, lean back slightly to the edge of tipping over, and pull the trigger.

The force of the bullet would help the inertia of my body falling backward into the water, the cement block rushing to the bottom of the lake, and the rope pulling tight, carrying me down. The boat would drift through the night coming to rest the next morning on the muddy bank. The fish would eat my flesh and gnaw my rotten bones over the summer months until nothing remained except a cement block with a rope weaving in the current.

three

I knew it was a clean killing, if there's such a thing. The man had a history of violence, a history of threats, and entered my home illegally. The neighbor corroborated my story. She heard Mike Stockton beat on my door. She saw him stalk around the house at two-thirty in the morning. There was no evidence I purchased a weapon in anticipation of killing. There was no witness to testify I'd bragged of my intentions to kill the man who beat my daughter. It was self-defense, and defense of Gretchen. A man's house is still his castle, and no jury would convict me. I knew that, and so did Frank Rush, but it didn't change our history. It didn't change what we knew.

My fiftieth birthday came and went without much fanfare. I was twice divorced, estranged, and living alone at the scene of a crime, more or less. I fell silently into a routine, occasionally interrupted.

Keith Perkins worked in my office. He was a few years younger than me, and for the most part we didn't pay much attention to each other. He was pleasant and bland, a forgettable combination. The man seemed to smile a lot for no identifiable reason, and sometimes I detected the slightest smell of alcohol around his person. Like maybe he kept a little silver flask in his desk drawer, and when nobody was looking, took tiny refreshing sips of warm vodka.

One evening, out of sheer loneliness, we ended up together at a downtown bar after work. Over the course of several hours we both drank too much, and the conversation went from stilted to strange.

"I don't ask for much," he said. "I really don't. I work hard. I provide my wife and kids a nice house in a nice neighborhood. She's got a closet full of shoes. How could anybody need seventy pairs of shoes?"

"I don't know," I said.

We were quiet for a long time. Keith Perkins seemed to be wrestling with something. I really didn't give a shit what it was, and truthfully I had no intention of listening to him unburden himself. I hoped he would wrestle with his problem and then decide to talk about the baseball game on the television behind the bar.

"I love baseball," I said out loud to myself.

"You know what?" he said. "I don't need to feel guilty about anything. Why should I? Do you know how many hours I work every week? I don't care about clothes or a fancy car. I don't smoke pot or gamble."

Whatever it was he wanted to talk about was only a sip or two from sneaking out into the open. He turned and looked at me.

"You're a single man, right?"

"Yes."

"You've been married before, right?"

"Twice."

"Well, then I'm sure you understand. Kids?"

"Yeah," I said, and finished my bourbon and water.

"Let me get you another one," he demanded, and I let him do it.

Keith leaned toward me and said in a drunken whisper, "I've got this girl. A call girl, I guess. Whatever you want to call her."

He stopped talking. It was a little test to see how I'd react. I didn't react at all, just stared at the baseball game.

Keith moved his body back straight on his stool. I looked at the side of his face and saw something sad about him. I was nearly a stranger, and yet he needed to tell me something. Something he probably hadn't told anyone else. Not his brother, or his parents, or his wife—nobody except me.

"She's beautiful," I heard him say in a low voice, looking over the drink he held in both hands. "And she does things for me."

I was curious. "What kind of things?" I asked.

He turned back to me like a puppy excited at the sound of my voice. "Anything you want. And she smiles while she does it. Smiles the whole time."

We were quiet again. The barroom around us was

loud, glasses clinking together, the sound of pool balls slamming against each other. I wanted a cigarette.

"It's not like having an affair or something. I work hard. Last year I was only sick two days. Only two days. Did you know that?"

He was nearly begging for my approval. Something, anything from me to ease the guilt.

"Seventy pairs of shoes," he said. "That's a hundred and forty shoes."

So I gave him what he wanted. "You deserve it," I said.

I could tell he loved the word, "deserve." He loved it. It spoke volumes. It was the word he was afraid to use. The word that somehow didn't sound right.

"I tell you what," he said, "I'm gonna give you her number."

"That's okay."

"No, I'm gonna give you her number. You don't have to call her if you don't want to, but you'll have it."

Keith scribbled the number on a napkin, folded the napkin, and slipped it to me like a drug dealer.

"Tell her you know me," he said. "It's worth it. You deserve it, too. I've got to go home. I'll see you tomorrow."

I stayed at the bar for an extra drink. I unfolded the napkin. Her name was Gina, or at least that's the name he wrote on the napkin.

I was drunk. Certainly too drunk to drive home, but I did it anyway, concentrating like a madman on the road ahead, radio off, seatbelt firmly fastened, thinking the entire time about Gina and all the things she could do with a smile on her face. I wondered the price, and whether it was too late to call.

"Hello," she said.

"Hello."

I froze. I froze like a boy in high school confronted with a girl's voice.

"Hello," she said again, and then I was unfrozen.

I managed to talk. "May I speak to Gina?"

"This is Gina," she said, and her voice was exceptionally soft and smooth. It ran my imagination into a frenzy.

"I'm a friend of Keith Perkins."

She hesitated, and then said, "Okay."

"Is it too late?" I asked.

It sounded like she was eating something. Maybe a grape, or a tangerine wedge. Something juicy.

"No," she said.

I fumbled around with a plan. A standard motel. I'd call her with the room number. And the next thing I knew I was back in the car concentrating on the road again, making my way to the motel across town.

I felt like a fugitive at the front desk, started to give a wrong name, and then panicked at the prospect of being asked for my driver's license. I paid cash, yawned, talked about being on the road all day and looking forward to a good night's sleep, and then called Gina with the room number.

I sat on the edge of the bed in the motel room, waiting. The idea a beautiful woman would knock on the door, take off her clothes, and do anything I asked, was dynamic. The thought of unconnected sex was foreign to me. No hidden agenda. No undercurrents of guilt, or love, hatred or compromise. Just two people in a small motel room fornicating, shaking hands, and walking out the door afterward.

I took off my jacket and then put it back on. I removed a shoe, smelled my sock, and then took a quick shower, dressing again. It was all very odd. Several times I stood to leave and then sat back down.

The knock on the door was light. Keith Perkins was correct. She was beautiful. She reminded me immediately of the sixteen-year-old girl at the beach so many years ago. The girl who took me by the hand to the pool. The similarity was something in her eyes and cheekbones.

"How old are you?" I blurted out.

"Twenty-two. How old are you?" she asked, with a genuine smile, looking around the room.

My drunkenness had given way to a slight headache and a numb feeling around my face. I sat down in the chair, and she stood in front of the television. Gina wore a short dress, not too revealing, but perfectly formed around her hips. She was extremely aware of her body, but she didn't overdo it. Her hair was brown, medium length. She could have been a college student.

"Aren't you afraid?" I asked.

"Afraid of what?" she answered.

"Afraid somebody might kill you or something. I mean, it's the middle of the night and you're in a strange man's motel room."

She smiled again and put her hands on her hips. "You're not a strange man," she said.

I leaned forward in the chair and rubbed my tired face

in my hands, pressing small circles at each temple in uni-
son. The pressure relieved the pain momentarily. When I
opened my eyes she was still standing there.

I said, "When you're finished, I mean when you're finished having sex with a man for money in a room like
this, a man like me, how do you feel?"

She made an expression of disappointment. Not disgust. Not anger. Like it wasn't the first time she'd been
asked the question.

"You're one of those guys," she said, looking down at
me.

"What guys?" I asked.

She took a few steps forward and pulled my face
against her stomach. Her hand felt small and light on the
back of my head. We stayed that way, and I could feel her
heartbeat, gentle and rhythmic. My right hand reached
and touched the inside of her thigh. Slowly, I moved it
upwards, aware of the short distance between the tips of
my fingers and the magical place nestled between her legs.
My hand moved so slowly upwards I could barely detect it
was moving at all. The skin was smooth and accepting,
sure of itself, and I moved again, now only a whisper from
the warm place. She waited patiently, waited for me to do
as I wished. And for a moment I thought I could do it. I
thought I could be a man who could enjoy the bodily
pleasures of a strange and gorgeous woman. But I was
wrong. A wave of nausea rose from my stomach, and I
leaned back in the chair, looking up at the girl above me.

I was old enough to be her father. Who was she to
trade intimacy for money? Who was she to mock the

myth of love? The strongest, most organized and essential myth in the history of mankind, and for a few hundred dollars she'd let a man touch her and pretend she loved him.

It was me who was disgusted, and without a word I stood up and laid face-down on the bed. I never heard another sound from her. I must have fallen asleep in only a few minutes. She could have killed me, or hit me with a baseball bat, or anything else she wanted. Instead, I suppose she decided to leave my kind alone in my own misery, untangling the reasons for being unable to move my hand the final inch.

I woke the next morning and didn't know where I was. I arrived at work two hours late and people stared at me like I was covered in blood. Keith Perkins winked when I passed his office door, and I was glad to close the door of my own office and sit in silence.

On the desk was a stack of mail, and on top of the stack was a handwritten envelope from Kate. It was the first letter since the Kansas City proposal. The letters had stopped, and after a while, I stopped looking forward to the daily mail. Stopped rifling through the business envelopes searching for her handwriting.

But there it was, the envelope in front of me. I held it in my hands and wondered if it was a coincidence, Kate's letter arriving the morning after my night in the motel room alone. The mistakes in this life are all patiently waiting to be made, but I opened the letter anyway.

Early,

Whether it is true or not, I've come to believe you are the only person who has ever really known me. I was a daughter to my screwed-up parents, a wife to Russell, a mother to Gretchen. With you, I was simply me. It was raw, and right, and scary, which is probably why I ran away. It was like running away from myself.

Meet me Saturday, June 10, at the Kansas City airport Sheraton hotel lobby at 2 o'clock. Two days. Room service. Hot baths. Never leave the apartment like before. I'll wear a red dress.

Love, Kate

God help me, but I felt like a teenage boy. Just a few words on a piece of paper written by her hand held the power to bring me back to the way she made me feel. A lightness. Clear-headed. Ready to face the day, and June 10th was only two weeks away. The world was good again.

four

The definition of success doesn't always include longevity. I mean, we think a restaurant in business twenty years is successful based solely on the period of time, or a fifty-year marriage, or a man who spends his life employed at the same place. I looked back at my own life and realized many of the most pleasurable experiences were short-lived. Most people would think my marriage with Kate was a failure, but that's not true. My feelings for her, good or bad, were as intense and concentrated as any feelings I have ever experienced. I learned more about myself through Kate in a short period of time than maybe any other span of my life. And despite my best efforts, I still loved her, or at least I loved the thought of her. The idea of Kate Shepherd still existed as a separate entity, like a painting on a wall in a museum.

If I'd been thirty years younger, pride would have kept me from going to Kansas City. I would have left her sitting on the couch in her red dress watching the glass door the same way she left me years earlier. But I wasn't thirty years younger, and I never would be again. I was becoming an old man, and one of the benefits of being an old man, besides watching your body fall apart and thinking of suicide constantly, is recognizing why pride is included in the list of deadly sins.

I had two weeks and a plane ride to think. I suppose I should have waited to marry Kate, at least until we got to know each other, but youth isn't for waiting. It's for doing. Blindly doing. What else could it be for? Would we prefer to spend youth rationalizing and contemplating, preparing for retirement and eating low-cholesterol bran muffins? Such a small percentage of my time on this earth was spent in Kate's presence, but so much time was spent thinking of her.

I hadn't made a reservation at the hotel. Since Kate was the one who invited me, I left it to her. I wouldn't have the opportunity to prepare the room, set up champagne and strawberries. I'd just arrive, and let things happen. No written format. No forcing one planned moment to follow the next planned moment, drowning in the anxiety of possibilities. Like the possibility Kate wouldn't show up again, or if she did, we'd quickly learn we'd both become very different people. Too much in between to overcome in a few short days. Maybe we'd even hate each other, one person leaving the other in the middle of a bitter lunch, storming out, packing a bag, no strawberries.

It was a long flight. I had a drink to calm my nerves. My thoughts flowed from fear to pure and divine lust. In my mind, Kate's body was the same as it had been before. The same as it existed so clearly in my memory, naked and brilliant, her breasts firm and round, but it dawned on me they may no longer be firm and round, but instead elongated and elastic, attacked by gravity. Maybe her face would show wrinkles, and her hair would be peppered gray. And how would she see me? Would I look like an old man in the bedroom, a walking skeleton, my testicles distended?

So I had a second drink and thought about the prostitute. She was young and beautiful. What stopped me from touching her, but allowed me to kill people? Who is responsible for the moral minefield inside me? Jesus was allowed to save the world. The ultimate Savior Complex. Did God make some people unsavable, even for Jesus? And if so, why? Why would He create such a person to live a life without hope? And is it true that people who live their lives to save others, like myself, are truly the people who need saving the most?

I stared out of the taxi window on the way to the airport Sheraton Hotel. It was only 1:40. I was twenty minutes early. I considered asking the driver to ride around for the next half hour, but I didn't. It was raining. Clear strands of water spread like long fingers across my window from front to back, witch's hands shaking in the breeze. I became lost in thoughts I can no longer recall, and the driver had to speak before I realized we were in front of the hotel, on the other side of the glass door.

I paid the man and stood on the sidewalk in the rain,

my bag over my shoulder. Through the glass I could see the lobby and the couch where I sat before. The couch was empty. Nothing red inside. I entered the door, looking left and then right on the way to the couch, and sat down with my bag at my feet.

At five minutes until two I felt the way I'd felt before. Was I an idiot? Sitting in a hotel in Kansas City, waiting for no one again? The same clock on the same wall. It seemed the same people, besides Jake Crane, were milling around the lobby on the marble floors. How long would I wait this time, and would I spend the night alone or fly home?

For some reason I looked to the right at the golden elevators fifty feet away. The elevator door opened and Kate stood alone inside. We were looking at each other, me on the couch in the lobby, Kate in the red dress, standing alone. No one around us could know we were together. We'd always been together, no matter how far apart, and no one needed to understand, not in high school and not now.

She held up four fingers. The elevator door closed slowly. I smiled to myself. She'd come all the way from California. Our room was on the fourth floor. Now it was just a matter of controlling expectations. Navigating the great abyss. Reconnecting without consequence.

I stood casually and walked to the elevator. On the fourth floor I turned the corner to look left, and then right, down the long empty hallway. There was no one. I must admit, for a minute I questioned myself. Had I seen her at all? Had I wanted so badly for Kate to show up I'd created her in the elevator, a mirror image of the woman inside my mind, a delusion? Was I standing in the hallway once again, waiting for no one?

I heard a door open. I saw a flash of red. Kate's head peeked out. I walked her way. The door was cracked, and I went inside. She was standing in front of the television. We smiled at each other. A knowing smile, and she opened her arms. I dropped my bag, and we held each other. It was just a matter of who would let go first. Tears came to my eyes behind her back, and I didn't want her to see them. There was still the part of me that needed to be seen strong. The part my mother's letter told me to leave behind. But it's not so easy. I was a man, after all. If not for our strength, who are we?

I started to speak.

"Shhhh," she said quietly.

On the table I could see a bottle of champagne resting in a silver bucket of ice, two crystal glasses next to the bucket, and a single red rose in a long slender vase. I'd brought nothing.

Kate pulled away. She closed the curtains on the window and turned off the only light in the room. The bathroom light allowed me to see her.

I started to speak again.

"Shhhh," she said quietly. My silence was necessary for her somehow.

Kate was barefoot. In the near-darkness she unbuttoned my shirt. I touched her face with my fingers, and she smiled like she remembered something good.

My body below reacted even before Kate removed my

pants. It took every molecule of control not to touch her, but just like my silence, it seemed important to wait. Necessary.

Kate's red dress dropped to the floor around her feet. She stepped out, and we stood naked in silence, thirty-five years after the last time we'd been naked together in my college apartment, when days passed wrapped up in each other's bodies. The darkness, the silence, the patience, were all necessary now when they hadn't been before, but it felt so much the same. The same out-of-control desire I'd always felt in her presence. The need to harness and explode at the same time. Touch and deny myself simultaneously.

She took me by the hand and led me to the bed. The sheets felt clean and cold. Side by side, we kissed gently. I wanted to lick every single inch of her body, but I waited, and eventually, she touched me. It seemed the entire purpose of my desire my whole life was Kate Shepherd. At the moment of my conception, that crazy moment with Bobby Winters watching outside the bedroom window, my DNA was programed with Kate Shepherd in mind. It seemed she was the reason for my existence, the intention of my pleasure, and now she let me, wanted me, to kiss every part of her skin. So that's exactly what I did. I started at the top of her painted toe and moved upwards. There was no hesitation. The silence solidified the simplicity. Kate made low noises when I stopped at certain places, her hand light on the back of my head.

There was nowhere else to go. We were exactly where we wanted to be, and neither of us spoke for hours until it was like going back in time. The covered window could be any covered window, anywhere. The light from the bathroom could be any light, anywhere in the world, like the light in my college apartment bathroom, and with no words or sights to provide context, we were twenty years old again.

Afterwards, we found ourselves lying next to each other in the bed. One of us, at some point, would speak. Lights would be turned on, our flaws revealed, but I didn't want it to end. I could hear a television in the next room. Someone walked down the hall rubbing the bottoms of their shoes against the short carpet. The thin line of light between the curtains was yellow.

"Do you remember," Kate said, "the list you made of everything I needed to do to change my life?"

I remembered the list. Education. Finances. Spirituality. Baby names. I remembered it was all in my handwriting, not Kate's. They were all my ideas, not Kate's.

"I remember," I said.

Just the words, the words spoken in the air, changed everything. The context had been established. The borders of time had framed the moment. We were forced to remember.

I reached out and turned on the lamp. Kate was on her back. The sheet was pulled up to her neck. On the outside of the sheet, Kate's hands were folded together. I noticed her fingernails were chewed down to the quick, and I was just as surprised as I'd been in high school when I'd first noticed.

I looked at the side of her face. It wasn't the same. We weren't the same. I thought of the burnt doll in the yellow house. The shirtless man on the mattress who had touched Kate before me. Jeff Temple, the baseball player who told the story of Kate Shepherd on her knees behind the concession stand, his dick in her mouth. And that day at the courthouse, my baby in the arms of Russell Enslow, my baby in another man's arms.

Without speaking, or looking at Kate, I got out of bed and went to the bathroom to take a shower. Under the warm water something occurred to me. Something I'd never acknowledged before. My life, my entire life, had been more affected and directed by unrequited love, by the people who couldn't or wouldn't love me as much as I loved them, than by those who loved me the most. Kate, my mother, Gretchen. My life was a reaction to their rejection, and I prayed to God Kate would be gone when my shower ended.

I turned up the hot water and felt it cascade down my back. The rain was probably still falling outside. Kate would need time to gather her things. Maybe she only wanted to stir up her life a little. Keep it from settling in the bottom of the glass. Maybe her reasons for coming to Kansas City on June 10th were very different than my reasons. Maybe it had always been that way, and I was too stupid to know the difference.

In that shower, praying to walk into an empty room, I was more alone than I'd ever been before. I dried my ugly body and listened for a sound outside the bathroom. Any sound. A door closing. The zipper of a suitcase. I wrapped the towel around my waist, took a deep breath, and walked out of the bathroom.

She was gone. Her clothes were gone. I was alone in the room, and again, immediately, I regretted my prayer. Wished I could take it back. Unpray.

The champagne was open. She drank a glass before she left. Next to the rose, at the bottom of the slender vase, was a ring. I picked it up and held it to my eyes. It was my grandmother's ring. The ring I'd given Kate so long ago. She left it for me. She returned it.

five

Nothing compares to the present. Nothing. How could it? Yesterday, how could we possibly possess the imagination necessary to paint the tiny details of today? And tomorrow, how could we possibly possess the memory to resurrect every point of light, every sound, from the exact moments of the day before? Knowing this, I tried anyway, but losing the idea of Kate left me floating out into the universe. Allen was the only person who knew me well enough to notice.

"Is everything okay with you these days?" he asked.

My house smelled funny. Like men, we talked around the issues.

"Yeah. Everything is fine. Just workin' too hard."

"Early wants you to come to his baseball game tonight."

Sitting there in my living room, I started thinking about Allen's father. I started thinking about those last few seconds before I pulled the trigger, standing behind him at the top of the stairs, when his fingers stopped on the computer keyboard. He sensed something in his house, someone behind him, and then the gun went off.

Maybe there was no justification. Maybe it wasn't my decision to make, just like it wasn't my decision to kill Mike Stockton.

"How's your mother?" I asked Allen, trying desperately to change the track of my thoughts.

"She's doing pretty good," he answered. "I took her out to the grave…" And then he stopped himself.

They'd been out to the man's grave together. They probably brought flowers and talked about things they could never talk about in front of me. I wondered if Early was with them. If they told him it was his grandpa's grave, and he'd been murdered, and they never caught the person who did it. Murdered in his own house, with his own gun, by a coward.

When other people complain about being depressed it sounds like horseshit, but something was the matter with me. Nothing seemed good. Ice cream. The beach. A cigarette. Even building something with Early in the workshop. My mind floated from Kate to Allen Kilborn Sr. and back around again in an endless cloudy circle of doubt and regret.

I think there are still active volcanos somewhere in Hawaii. I imagined planning a trip, flying to Hawaii, staying a week in expensive hotel rooms, eating roast pig and drinking pineapple juice. I could spend every last dime on whatever I wanted to, maybe leaving a small trust fund for Little Early.

On the last day of the trip I could rent a car to drive out to the volcano. I'm sure there must be tour guides and hiking trails. I could make plans in advance and act nice and normal, like nothing was up.

Later, people would say, "He acted nice and normal, like nothing was up."

But when I'd finally reach the crest of the volcano, and the tour guide would turn his back, I'd jump down into the red molten lava. My body would disintegrate instantly into the intense heat, disappearing for eternity. No bones to find later. No cakes of dried blood. Just a bewildered tour guide standing at the edge wearing a backpack wondering if I'd fallen accidentally or purpose-fully incinerated myself. There would be no need for explanation. I'd be dead.

So I asked the question. "Did you and your mother go out to your father's grave?"

Allen looked down at his hands. Maybe he thought it was disrespectful to talk about the man in front of me, or maybe he'd just gotten used to the idea of keeping us sep-arate inside himself.

"Yeah," he said.

I wanted to know more. I wanted to know all the details.

"Do you go there a lot?"

He looked up from his hands. It wasn't my business. Allen's relationship with his father, and now with his mother, wasn't my business anymore, and maybe never was.

It was that moment I decided I needed to tell Frank Rush the truth somehow. At least Frank Rush, if not everyone in the world. I didn't want to spend the rest of my life locked in a prison cell, but what was the difference. I had to get it off me somehow, and Frank Rush was a man who might just understand why I did what I did. Maybe he could even help me see things I didn't see before.

So when I was alone, I got out my pen and paper again. This time to plan something good. I started a fire in the little fireplace, a tiny volcano, and sat in front in a wooden chair. In longhand I began to write the words I would use to tell Frank Rush the truth. Not just the words, but where we would be for the conversation, and when, and how it would all be arranged.

If possible, I wanted to confess my sins without reper-cussion, an unrealistic goal, but a goal nonetheless. I didn't want to lose Allen or Emily. I didn't want to die in jail. I didn't want Gretchen sitting in the back of a court-room staring at me like I was Charles Manson. I didn't want to see Kate's envelope in a stack of prison mail. I did-n't want Early standing over his grandpa's grave hating me, his namesake, for killing the man he never got to know. A man, so many years later, remembered as some-one he wasn't.

The planning went on for weeks and then spread into the next month. I decided to learn Frank Rush's routine. I'd pick the right date to accidentally find myself sitting next to him on a park bench or at a movie theater, away from his office, away from his little tape recorder. He'd know why I was there. He'd know it wasn't an accident.

The words would come to me, a combination of all the best parts of each written confession I'd tossed into the fire. And then we'd talk about it. Man to man. Father to father. He'd tell me what he knew, and I'd fill in the blanks, holding back any information that might lead to physical evidence. After that, I was unsure what would happen.

I'd tell him, "I won't plead guilty, Frank. I'll deny we had this conversation. I'll never tell you where to find the other buried things, or the spare key."

On a Tuesday morning I picked up the newspaper at the end of the driveway, like usual. I sat in my office with the door closed, reading. In the obituaries I saw a picture of Frank Rush. It was right there, in color, amongst the other faces. He was smiling. He was dead. Died of a heart attack. The article under his picture said lots of good things about him. Frank Rush was retired. He'd served in the United States Navy, had eight grandchildren, and loved model airplanes. It didn't say anything about me.

I suppose, if you wait long enough, everybody dies. It's just the way it is. Like when I was a boy and asked my mother about my father dying. She told me we never really figure it out. We just become more comfortable with the mystery somehow. I wasn't comfortable with the mystery at all. I'd never planned for Frank Rush to die. He was like a mountain. He died never knowing. I wondered if he thought about me, and Allen Kilborn, and Mike Stockton, the day before he died. Probably not. He was probably thinking about his grandchildren, or model air-planes, or whether it would rain, leaving me with visions of volcanos and no one to talk to.

I went to work like normal the next day. Since the night in the bar with Keith Perkins, every time I passed his office he winked at me. We were co-conspirators, forever linked by Gina, the woman he enjoyed, and I couldn't.

This time I stopped at his office door. "Keith," I said.

His eyes grew wide like he feared I would reveal our secret. Scream across the office, "Keith loves whores," in my loudest, angriest, stock market voice.

"Yes," he said meekly.

"Don't wink at me anymore."

He seemed relieved and confused. I didn't wait for him to answer.

I stopped by the grocery store on the way home after work. I always loved the grocery store. I kept finding myself roaming around up and down the aisles instead of going home to my empty house. The store was so well-lit, and colorful, with the smell of baked bread, and I didn't have to talk to anybody if I didn't want to.

I stood in front of the cheese in the dairy section. My attention was drawn toward a figure to my right. Ten feet away, in front of the milk, stood Samantha. The scene was exactly as we'd stood years ago when I'd orchestrated our meeting. When I went to the grocery store every day for a week at the same time until I saw her, and stood in front of the cheese, and waited for her to turn around and look at me, and then forgot the lines I'd rehearsed. Dumbfounded like a school boy.

This time I hoped she wouldn't look at me, but I couldn't seem to move. I couldn't seem to stop watching her as she squinted over her reading glasses to read the labels on the milk jugs. I'd seen her from time to time at Early's games or other events, but not so close. Her hair was shorter. She'd gained a few pounds around the middle.

So long ago the sight of Samantha had left me speechless. The thought of her nakedness cleansed my mind of everything. But now it was like we'd never known each other. Like we'd never shared anything at all. Just two people in the grocery store, struggling to read labels on dairy products.

She turned to see me and for a moment seemed not to recognize my face.

I spoke first, automatically, without expression. "Hi," I said.

She smiled politely, like she promised she would do. "Hi," she said, and then turned and walked away with a milk jug in her hand. I watched her go.

I left the store, buying nothing, and drove to the little league baseball park. Early played shortstop and was one of the best kids on the team. He was more aggressive and competitive than his father had been, watching the scoreboard over his shoulder, nervous.

I waved, and he saw me take my place in the aluminum bleachers next to Allen. Emily was home, pregnant with their second child. A girl. A baby girl on the way into the world. A world that seemed too angry and confusing for a little girl, but who was I to say?

A ball was hit hard to Early. He dove and missed, out of reach, and then banged his glove on the red dirt, mad at himself.

"Good try," a man yelled below me.

I smiled. It was really a very pleasant place to be, the baseball park. It was well-lit like the grocery store, with kids, and peanuts, and the smell of hot dogs. They smell much better than they taste, the red texture always disappointing.

I wished my father could be there. He'd be an old man. I did the math in my head, eighty-one years old. If it wasn't for the train, or any other tragedy between the train and the ballpark, my father would be sitting next to me in the bleachers, probably wearing a jacket, maybe a hat to cover his gray hair, eating peanuts. He would have liked Little Early, the competitive spirit, slamming his glove down in the red dirt.

He would have said, "Good try, boy," and patted me on the leg, choosing not to acknowledge the horrible things I'd done after I'd sat down next to him on the park bench and confessed my sins to him. The plan to kill Early's grandfather. The squeak on the seventh step. The man's head exploding like a balloon, blood and bones sprayed across the computer screen. Mike Stockton's black figure in the doorway, the light from the streetlight behind him, maybe just waiting to talk to his wife, straighten things out, apologize.

But my father would have understood why I did what I did. And in the last inning, when Early hit the ball to the fence and scored the winning run, my father would have stood up and yelled for his grandson, dropping his peanuts, and putting his arm around my shoulder.